Praise for *Someday, Som*

"Warm and funny, charming and smart."

—DIANE KEATON, *New York Times* bestselling
author of *Then Again*

"Graham deftly captures what it's like to be young, ambitious, and hopeful in New York City."

—CANDACE BUSHNELL, *New York Times* bestselling
author of *Sex and the City* and *The Carrie Diaries*

"Well-written and charming . . . *Someday* is a light, fast-paced and snappy read that pays homage to a pre-Facebook era that consisted of answering machines and face-to-face conversations."

—*The Free Lance-Star*

"Fresh and funny and full of zingers, Lauren Graham's charming writing style instantly drew me in, but it was her relatable characters (complete with doodled datebook entries!), irresistible romantic twists, and delicious plot that kept me turning pages until well past my bedtime."

—MEG CABOT, bestselling author of the Princess
Diaries and Heather Wells Mystery series

"Graham has fashioned a lively and engaging read with warmth, reflective wisdom, originality and wit. Franny's authentic and relatable tale is gratifying and, at times, even laugh-out-loud funny."

—*Shelf Awareness*

"A blithe, behind-the-scenes take on aspiring actors and their world."

—*Booklist*

Someday, Someday, Maybe

Someday, Someday, Maybe

A NOVEL

Lauren Graham

Ballantine Books Trade Paperbacks

New York

2014 Ballantine Books Trade Paperback Edition

Copyright © 2013 by Lauren Graham
Reading group guide copyright © 2014 by Random House LLC

Published in the United States by Ballantine Books, an imprint of Random House, a division of Random House LLC, a Penguin Random House Company, New York.

BALLANTINE and the HOUSE colophon are registered trademarks of Random House LLC.
RANDOM HOUSE READER'S CIRCLE & Design is a registered trademark of Random House LLC.

Originally published in hardcover in the United States by Ballantine Books, an imprint of Random House, a division of Random House LLC, in 2013.

Grateful acknowledgment is made to Hal Leonard Corporation for permission to reprint an excerpt from "The Miller's Son" from *A Little Night Music,* words and music by Stephen Sondheim, copyright © 1973 (renewed) by Rilting Music, Inc. All rights administered by WB Music Corp. All rights reserved.

Reprinted by permission of Hal Leonard Corporation.

Library of Congress Cataloging-in-Publication Data
Graham, Lauren.
Someday, someday, maybe : a novel / Lauren Graham.
pages   cm
ISBN 978-0-345-53276-3 (trade paperback : acid-free paper)—
eBook ISBN 978-0-345-53275-6
1. Actresses—New York (State)—New York—Fiction.
2. Self-realization in women—Fiction.   I. Title.
PS3608.R373S66 2013
813'.6—dc23   2013000558

Printed in the United States of America on acid-free paper

www.randomhousereaderscircle.com

2 4 6 8 9 7 5 3 1

Book design by Caroline Cunningham

I think your self emerges more clearly over time.

—*Meryl Streep*

Acting is happy agony.

—*Jean-Paul Sartre*

Someday, Someday, Maybe

2 Monday

③ Tuesday

6 MONTHS UNTIL DEADLINE!

(GAAACK).

4 Wednesday

Thursday **5**

Friday **6**

Saturday **7**

Sunday **8**

1

....

"Begin whenever you're ready," comes the voice from the back of the house.

Oh, I'm ready.

After all, I've prepared for this day for years: The Day of the Most Important Audition of a Lifetime Day. Now that it's finally here, I'm going to make a good impression, I'm sure of it. I might even book the job. The thought makes me smile, and I take a deep breath, head high, body alert, but relaxed. I'm ready, alright. I'm ready to speak my first line.

"Eeessssaaheeehaaa." The sound that comes out of me is thin and high, a shrill wheezing whine, like a slowly draining balloon or a drowning cat with asthma.

Shake it off. Don't get rattled. Try again.

I clear my throat.

"Haaaaaawwrrrblerp." Now my tone is low and gravelly, the coarse horn of a barge coming into shore, with a weird burping sound at the end. "Hawrblerp?" That can't be my line. I don't think it's even a word. Oh, God, I hope they don't think I *actually* burped. It was really more of a gargle, I tell myself—although I don't know which is worse. I can just picture the scene, post-audition: *That* actress? We brought her in and she positively *belched* all over the dialogue. Is she any good? Well, I suppose you could use her, if the part calls for lots of *gargling*. Sounds of cruel laughter, phones slamming into receivers, 8 × 10 glossies being folded into paper airplanes and aimed into wastepaper baskets. Career over, the end.

"Franny?" I can't see who's speaking because the spotlight is so bright, but they're getting impatient, I can tell. My heart is pounding and my palms are starting to sweat. I've got to find my voice, or they'll ask me to leave. Or worse—they'll drag me off stage with one of those giant hooks you see in old movies. In Elizabethan times the audience would throw rotten eggs at the actors if they didn't like a performance. They don't still do that, do they? This is Broadway, or at least, I think it is. They wouldn't just *throw*—

The tomato bounces off my leg and onto the bare wood floor of the stage.

Splat.

"Franny? Franny?"

I open my eyes halfway. I can see from the window above my bed that it's another gray and drizzly January day. I can see that because I took the curtains down right after Christmas in order to achieve one of my New Year's resolutions, of becoming an earlier riser. Successful actresses are disciplined people who wake up early to focus on their craft, I told myself—even ones who still make their living as waitresses—like me. I started leaving the alarm clock on the landing between Jane's room and mine so I'd have to actually get out of bed in order to turn it off, instead of hitting snooze over and over like I normally do. I also resolved to quit smoking again, to stop losing purses, wallets, and umbrellas, and to not eat any more cheese puffs, not even on special occasions. But I already had two cigarettes yesterday, and although the sun is obscured by the cloudy sky, I'm fairly certain it is far from my new self-appointed rising time of eight A.M. My three-day abstinence from cheese puffs and the umbrella still downstairs by the front door are my only accomplishments of the year so far.

"Franny?"

Only half-awake, I roll over and squint down at the pitted wood floor by my bed, where I notice one black leather Reebok high-top lying on its side. That's strange. It's mine—one of my waitressing shoes—but I thought I'd left them outside the—*thwack!*—a second Reebok whizzes by, hitting the dust ruffle and disappearing underneath.

"Franny? Sorry, you didn't respond to me knocking." Dan's voice is muffled and anxious from behind my bedroom door. "I didn't hit you with the shoe, did I?"

Ahhh, it was my *shoe* that hit me on the leg, not a tomato. What a relief.

"I dreamed it was a tomato!" I yell at the half-open door.

"You want me to come back later?" Dan calls back anxiously.

"Come in!" I should probably get out of bed and put Dan out of his misery, but it's so cold. I just want one more minute in bed.

"What? Sorry, Franny, I can't quite hear you. You asked me to make sure you were up, remember?"

I suppose I did, but I'm still too groggy to focus on the details. Normally I would've asked our other roommate, my best friend, Jane, but she's been working nights as a P.A. on that new Russell Blakely movie. Since Dan moved into the bedroom downstairs a few months ago, I haven't noticed much about him except how unnecessarily tall he is, how many hours he spends writing at the computer, and the intense fear he seems to have about coming upon either of us when we're not *decent.*

"Dan! Come in!"

"You're decent?"

In fact, I went to sleep in an outfit that far *exceeds* decent, even by Dan's prudish standards: heavy sweatpants and a down vest I grabbed last night after the radiator in my room sputtered and spat hot water on the floor, then completely died with a pathetic *hiss*. But that's what you get in Park Slope, Brooklyn for $500 a month each.

Jane and I had shared the top two floors of this crumbling brownstone with Bridget, our friend from college, until the day Bridget climbed on top of her desk at the investment banking firm where she worked and announced that she no longer cared about becoming a millionaire by the time she turned thirty. "Everyone here is dead inside!" she screamed. Then she fainted and they called an ambulance, and her mother flew in from Missoula to take her home.

"New York City," Bridget's mother clucked as she packed up the last of her daughter's things. "It's no place for young girls."

Jane's brother was friends with Dan at Princeton, and assured us that Dan was harmless: quiet and responsible and engaged to be married to his college girlfriend, Everett. "He was pre-med, but now he's trying to be some sort of screenwriter," Jane's brother told us. And then, the ultimate roommate recommendation: "He comes from money."

Neither Jane nor I had ever had a male roommate. "I think it would be very modern of us," I told her.

"Modern?" she said, rolling her eyes. "Come one, it's 1995. It's *retro* of us. We'd be *Three's Company* all over again."

"But with two Janets," I pointed out. Jane and I are different in many ways, but we worked hard in school together, we're both brunettes, and we've both read *The House of Mirth* more than once, just for fun.

"How true," she sighed.

"Franny?" Dan calls out, his voice still muffled. "You didn't go back to sleep did you? You told me you'd try if I let you. I promised I'd make sure—"

I take a deep breath and I bellow, in my most diaphragmatically supported Shakespearean tone: "Daaaaaaan. Come iiiiiinnnnnnnn."

Miraculously, the left side of Dan's face appears through the crack in the door, but it's not until he's confirmed my fully covered status and stepped all the way into the room, leaning his oversized frame awkwardly against the corner bookshelf, that I suddenly remember:

My hair.

I have no romantic feelings toward Dan, but I do have very strong feelings about my unruly, impossibly curly hair, which I piled into a green velvet scrunchie on top of my head last night while it was still wet from the shower, a technique that experience tells me has probably transformed it from regular hair into more of a scary, frizzy hair-tower while I slept. In an attempt to assess just how bad it is, I pretend to yawn while simultaneously stretching one hand over my head, in the hopes of appearing nonchalant while also adjusting the matted pile of damage. For some reason this combination of moves causes me to choke on absolutely nothing.

"Is it . . . (*cough, cough*) . . . is it really late?" I sputter.

"Well, I went to the deli, so I don't know exactly how long your alarm's been going off," Dan says. "But Frank's been up for at least two hours already."

Shit. I am late. Frank is the neighbor whose apartment we can see into from the windows in the back of our brownstone. Frank leads a mysterious, solitary life, but one you can set a clock by. He rises at eight, sits in front of a computer from nine to one, goes out and gets a sandwich, is back at the computer from two until six thirty, is gone from six thirty to eight, and then watches TV from eight until eleven P.M., after which he goes promptly to sleep. The schedule never changes. No one ever comes over. We worry about Frank in the way New Yorkers worry about strangers whose apartments they can see into. Which is to say, we made up a name for him and have theories about his life, and we'd call 911 if we saw something frightening happen while spying on him, but if I ran into him on the subway, I'd look the other way.

"It's kind of cold in here, you know," Dan announces, scrutinizing the room from beneath his long brown bangs. Dan always needs a haircut.

"Dan," I say, sitting up, pulling the covers to my ears, "I have to tell you—this flair for the obvious? Combined with your shoe-throwing accuracy? You should submit yourself to the front desk at The Plaza Hotel or something, and start a personal wake-up service. New Yorkers *need* you. I'm not kidding."

Dan knits his brow for a moment, as if concerned he might actually be called upon to present his qualifications for the job, but then a little light comes into his eyes. "Aha," he says, pointing his forefinger and thumb at me, play-pistol style. "You're joking."

"Um, yes," I say, pulling an arm out of my blanket cocoon to play-pistol him back. "I'm joking."

"Did you know, Franny," Dan begins, in a bland professorial tone, and I steel myself in anticipation of the inevitable boring lecture to come, "the statue in front of The Plaza is of Pomona, the Roman goddess of the orchards? 'Abundance,' I believe it's called." Pleased with his unsolicited art history lesson, Dan squints a little and rocks back on his heels.

I stifle a yawn. "You don't say, Dan. 'Abundance'? That's the name of the bronze topless lady sculpture on top of the fountain?"

"Yes. 'Abundance.' I'm sure of it now. Everett did a comprehensive study on the historically relevant figurative nude sculptures of Manhattan while we were at Princeton. Actually," he says, lowering his voice conspiratorially, "the paper was considered rather *provocative.*" He pumps his eyebrows up and down in a way that makes me fear his next words might be "hubba-hubba."

Dan and Everett, engaged to be married. Dan and Everett, and their mutual interest in the historically relevant figurative nudes of Manhattan. Apparently, that's the kind of shared passion that tells two people they should spend the rest of their lives together, but you wouldn't know it to see them in person. To me, they seem more like lab colleagues who respect each other's research than two people in love.

"That *is* fascinating, Dan. I'll make a note of it in my diary. Say, if it's not too much trouble, would you mind checking the clock on the landing and telling me the actual time?"

"Certainly," he says, with a formal little half-bow, as if he's some sort of manservant from ye olden times. He ducks out of the room for a moment, then sticks his head back in. "It is ten thirty-three, exactly."

Something about the time causes my heart to jump, and I have to swallow a sense of foreboding, a feeling that I'm late for something. But my shift at the comedy club where I waitress doesn't start until three thirty. I had intended to get up earlier, but there's nothing I'm actually late for, nothing I'm missing. Nothing I can think of, anyway.

"You know, Franny—just a thought," Dan says solemnly. "In the future, if you put the alarm clock right by your bed, you might be able to hear it better."

"Thanks, Dan," I say, stifling a giggle. "Maybe tomorrow I'll give that a try."

He starts to leave, but then turns back, again hesitating in the doorway.

"Yes, Dan?"

"It's six months from today, right?" he says, then smiles. "I'd like to be the first to wish you luck. I have no doubt you'll be a great success." And then he does his little half-bow again, and plods away in his size-fourteen Adidas flip-flops.

I flop back on my pillow, and for a blissful moment, my head is full of nothing at all.

But then it comes rushing back to me.

What day it is.

The reason I asked Dan to make sure I was up.

Why I'm having audition anxiety dreams.

A wave of dread crashes over me as I remember: when I looked at the year-at-a-glance calendar in my brown leather Filofax last night, I realized that, as of today, there are exactly six months left on the deal I made with myself when I first came to New York—that I'd see what I could accomplish in three years, but if I wasn't well on my way to having a real career as an actor by then, I absolutely, positively wouldn't keep at it after that. Just last night I'd promised myself that I'd get up early, memorize a sonnet, take in a matinee of an edgy foreign film. I'd do something, *anything*, to better myself, to try as hard as I could to *not fail*.

I throw off my covers, now welcoming the shock of the cold. I have to wake up, have to get up, get dressed, for . . . well, I don't know for what exactly yet. I could go running . . . running—yes!—I have time before work, and I'm already in sweatpants, so I don't even have to change. I trade the fuzzy pull-on slipper-socks I slept in for a pair of athletic socks I find in the back of my top drawer, and I tug on the one Reebok that's lying on the floor. I'm going to run every day from now on, I think to myself as I wriggle on my stomach, one arm swallowed beneath the bed, fishing blindly for the second shoe. I realize there's no direct line between running this morning and reaching any of my goals in the next six months—I don't think I've ever heard Meryl Streep attribute her success as an actor to her stellar cardiovascular health—but since no one's likely to give me an acting job today, and there probably won't be one tomorrow either, I have to do something besides sit around and wait.

And I'm not going to break my deadline the way I've seen some people do. You start out with a three-year goal, which then becomes a five-year goal, and before you know it you're still calling yourself an actor, but most days you're being assigned a locker outside the cafeteria of the General Electric building so you can change into a borrowed pink polyester lunch-lady uniform and serve lukewarm lasagna to a bunch of businessmen who call you "Excuse me."

I've made some progress, but not enough to tell me for sure that I'm doing the right thing with my life. It took most of the first year just to get the coveted waitressing job at the comedy club, The Very Funny, where I finally started making enough in tips to pay my own rent without any help from my father. Last year, after sending head shots month after month to everyone in the *Ross Reports*, I got signed by the Brill Agency. But they only handle commercials, and it's erratic—sometimes I have no auditions for weeks at a time. This year, I got accepted into John Stavros's acting class, which is considered one of the best in the city. But when I moved to New York, I envisioned myself starting out in experimental theaters, maybe even working Off Broadway, not rubbing my temples pretending I need pain relief from the tension headache caused by my stressful office job. And one accomplishment a year wasn't exactly what I had in mind.

Still wedged halfway beneath the bed, it takes all my strength to push a barely used Rollerblade out of the way. At this point, I'm just sweeping my arm back and forth, making the same movement under my bed as I would if making a snow angel, only the accumulated junk is a lot harder to move. I give up for a moment, resting my cheek against the cool wooden floor with a sigh.

"Do you have any idea how few actors make it?" people always say. "You need a backup plan." I don't like to think about it—the only thing I've ever wanted to be is an actor—but I do have one, just in case: to become a teacher like my dad, and to marry my college boyfriend, Clark. It's not a terrible scenario on either count—my dad makes teaching high school English look at least vaguely appealing, and if I can't achieve my dream here, well, I guess I can picture myself having a happy normal life with Clark, living in the suburbs, where he's a lawyer and I do, well, something all day.

I played the lead in lots of plays in high school and college, but I can't exactly walk around New York saying: "I know there's nothing on my résumé, but you should've seen me in *Hello, Dolly!*" I suppose I could ask one of the few working actors in class, like James Franklin, if he has any advice for me—he's shooting a movie with Arturo DeNucci, and has another part lined up in a Hugh McOliver film, but then I'd have to summon the courage to speak to him. Just picturing it makes me sweat: "Excuse me, James? I'm new in class, and (*gasps for air*), and . . . whew, is it hot in here? I'm just wondering . . . (*hysterical giggle/gulp*) . . . um . . . how can anyone so talented, also be *so gorgeous?* Ahahahahaha excuse me (*Laughs maniacally, runs away in shame*)."

I just need a break—and for that I need a real talent agent. Not one who just sends me out on commercials, but a legit agent who can send me out on auditions for something substantial. I need a speaking part at least, or a steady job at best, something to justify these years of effort that might then somehow, eventually, lead to *An Evening with Frances Banks* at the 92nd Street Y. Most people probably picture receiving an award at the Tonys, or giving their Oscar acceptance speech, but the 92nd Street Y is the place my father loves best, the place he always took me growing up, so it's easier for me to imagine succeeding there, even though I've only ever sat in the audience.

Six months from today, I think again, and my stomach does a little flip.

Trying to imagine all the steps that come between lying on the chilly floor of my bedroom in Brooklyn and my eventual appearance at the 92nd Street Y, I'm sort of stumped. I don't know what happens in between today and the night of my career retrospective. But on the bright side, I can picture those two things at least, can imagine the events like bookends, even if the actual books on the shelves between them aren't yet written.

Finally, my fingertips graze the puffy ridge on the top of my sneaker, and I wedge my shoulder even more tightly under the bed, straining and stretching to grab hold of it. The shoe emerges along with a box of old cassette tapes from high school, my Paddington Bear with a missing yellow Wellington, and a straw hat with artificial flowers sewn onto the brim, which Jane begged me to throw out last summer.

I push these shabby tokens of the past back under the bed, put on my shoe, and get ready to run.

January 1995 HAP
PEE
NEW
2 Monday YEE CALL DAD MORE
GET IN BETTER SHAPE
BECOME EMPLOYED

LUCKY NEW YEAR CLOVER

3 Tuesday RAN 3 ML. MAIL RENT
CHECK

6 MONTHS UNTIL DEADLINE!

(GAAACK).

DON'T FORGET
EARLY SHIFT 3M. CORKSCREW,
CRUMBER

4 Wednesday

REHEARSE W THAD
12 30
MEET 19TH/5TH

EARLY SHIFT 3M

Thursday **5**

RENT DUE
$500

STAVROS CLASS   SCENE FROM:
                 DREAMER EXAMINES
                 HIS PILLOW
RAN 3 MILES   Friday **6**

BUY
PENS
SELTZER
T.P.

LATE SHIFT   43° — CLOSING

Saturday **7**

LATE SHIFT 430 —

Sunday **8**

MOVIES W JANE.

PRET 'A PORTER
5:45 ANGELIKA

ONE WEEK + NO CHEESE PUFFS =

2

....

You have two messages.

BEEEP

Hello, this message is for Frances Banks. I'm calling from the office of Dr. Leslie Miles, nutritionist. We're happy to inform you that your space on the wait list for the wait list to see Dr. Miles has finally been upgraded. You are now on the actual wait list to see the doctor. Congratulations. We'll call you in one to sixteen months.

BEEEP

Hello, Franny, it's Heather from the agency. You're confirmed for Niagara today, right? Where's the ... Sorry, all these papers! Here it is. Also, just wondering if—do you have a problem with cigarettes? I'm working on a submission for a cigarette campaign to air in France, I think, or someplace Europe-y. Anyway, you wouldn't have to actually smoke the cigarette, I don't think—Jenny, does she have to put it in her mouth? No? Okay, so you'd just have to hold the lit cigarette while smoke comes out of it. You'd get extra for hazard pay. Let us know!

BEEEP

Today, I have an actual audition, which helped me to arise promptly at—well, only a few minutes past—my ideal rising time of eight. But that victory is behind me, and now I stand in front of the bathroom mirror and glare at my reflection in an attempt to look menacing. I'm a matador facing the angriest bull, but I won't be defeated. Armed with the diffuser attachment by my side, I dip my fingertips deep into the jar of piney-smelling, jiggly Dep gel and pull out a giant dollop of green goo. Today, I'll get you with *quantity*—you didn't see that coming! Take that, hair!

I finally tear myself away from drying and scrunching to face my very small, very packed closet. Over time I've realized that commercial characters tend to fall into one of three types, so I've gotten it down to three audition uniforms: Upscale Casual (person who works in an office—black blazer with padded shoulders, collared shirt), Mom Casual (person who works at home—denim shirt or plain sweater, khakis), and Slutty (person who dresses slutty). I'm so used to choosing an outfit to play someone else that on my days off, I struggle to get dressed as myself. I keep trying different looks, but I'm not sure what "me" wears yet. A few weeks ago I thought I'd found it: *I'm bohemian*, that's it. I wear hippie skirts and hand-embroidered cloth shirts. I'm colorful but laid back. I combined the best of my flow-y pieces and proudly modeled them for Jane.

"Was there a clearance sale at Putumayo?" she said, after a moment of silence.

"It's my new look," I told her.

"For the Stevie Nicks Fan Club?"

"Jane, seriously. Say something helpful."

She tilted her head, studying me carefully. "Honestly, Franny, all I can think of to say is—you look like you work at a really great bakery in Maine."

I have class tonight after my audition, so today I go for young mom meets acting class: black sweater, black tights, short black wool skirt, and my Doc Martens oxford lace-up shoes—not super momish, but practical for walking. I've worn this combination so many times before that today my all-black outfit feels a little boring, a little blah. *What would Jane do*, I think to myself, and pull a chunky brown leather belt from the top shelf of the closet, slinging it low around my hips. Finally, taking weather and product into consideration, I take the top part of my hair and tie it into a small black velvet scrunchie on top of my head.

The phone begins to ring from its place on the landing between my room and Jane's.

"Hi, Dad."

"Hello?"

"Yes. 'Hi, Dad,' I said."

"Franny? This is your father."

"Dad. I know."

"How did you know it was me?"

"I told you. We have caller ID now."

"Is it curable?"

"Dad. It's that thing where your number comes up when you call."

"What a horrible invention. Why would anyone want that?"

"So you know who's calling before you pick up."

"Why don't you just say, 'Hello, who's calling'?"

"Dad. What's up? I have an audition."

"To the point, then. Your Aunt Mary Ellen wanted me to remind you to book a room for Katie's wedding."

"*Shit*—er, shoot. I keep forgetting."

"Of course the wedding's not until June, but if you want to stay at The Sands by the shore, she said to book early."

"Okay, thanks."

"Franny, I'm worried about you."

"Why?"

"Well, from my initial calculations, this new telephone identification system could save you upwards of twenty to twenty-five seconds per day. I'm concerned about how you'll adjust to all the new free time."

"Har har."

"Also, one of my students says there's a show called *Friends*? Apparently it's a popular one. Maybe you should try to apply for that."

"Dad, it doesn't work that way. Besides, I'm not skinny enough for television."

"Who wants to be skinny like those girls? Those girls look sick. You're healthy."

"I don't want to look healthy."

"Who doesn't want to be healthy?"

"I want to *be* healthy. I just want to *look* sick."

"And for this, you studied the classics," he says with a sigh.

My father cares about literature and poetry, the symphony and the opera. He owns just a small black-and-white television with tinfoil attached to the antenna, which he uses mainly to watch the news. He doesn't understand what I'm doing exactly, but he tries to be supportive. The year I moved to New York, he gave me my brown leather Filofax. "To keep a record of your appointments," he said. "You'll have no shortage of them, I'm sure."

My father and I have always been close, especially since the day he pulled me out of school in the middle of making clay ashtrays in Mrs. Peterson's sixth-grade art class and told me, while sitting in his beat-up Volvo in the parking lot, that Mom had died. He explained that her car had been hit when she accidentally turned the wrong way down a one-way street, and I thought:

He's wrong.

But in my heart I knew he was telling the truth.

For some reason, instead of imagining my mother's face, or trying to think of the last thing she said to me, all I could picture was the worn burgundy paperback cover of J. D. Salinger's *Franny and*

Zooey, the book she named me after. I think I was in shock, since accidentally turning the wrong way down a one-way street just didn't seem like something that could possibly have happened to my intelligent, observant mother, who noticed even the smallest details. "Look at this beautiful thing, Franny," she'd say of a chipped porcelain cup she picked up for pennies at a flea market. "Look at the tiny dot of yellow on the pink petals. See?"

So I pretended it wasn't happening to me. I imagined it was happening to someone else. I'm not sure if that had anything to do with me becoming an actor, but that's the first time I remember realizing that it was easier to think about what I'd do in someone else's shoes than mine, and that pretending was a way to feel better.

Almost.

After hanging up with my dad, I think I hear Jane downstairs, home from the set which means I might actually get something to eat before I get on the train.

"I made it onto the actual wait list!" I call while coming down the stairs.

"To see the famous nutritionist person?"

"Yes. Also, do I have a problem with cigarettes?"

"You seem to be doing just fine with them," Jane says, dumping a large brown bag onto the top of our never-used oven with a thud. She's wearing a trench coat we found at the Goodwill in Prospect Heights, and her signature giant red vintage sunglasses. Jane grew up in Greenwich Village in Manhattan, and has style. Where I struggle to match a black shirt with black pants, she throws on jeans and a T-shirt and nine chunky cuffs on one wrist with an air that says, "So? I dare you to not find this cool." She shops at Century 21 and Bolton's and secondhand stores, and somehow makes it all look expensive.

"Wait—Jane Levine, you're not *just* getting home, are you?" I ask, peeking into one of the brown bags. "Can they do that to you?"

"They can do anything to me. I'm not union." Jane leans dramatically on the door frame between the kitchen and Dan's room, and puts the back of her hand to her forehead, the way they do in black-and-white films when they're about to faint. "This movie," she sighs. "They're trying to kill me. Russell sent me out for a McD.L.T. at four A.M. The McDonald's in Times Square was closed because of a shooting. But I found another open one in Midtown, and Russell now wants to have ten thousand of my babies. A bunch of us were hanging out in his trailer after wrap this morning. We had mimosas!" She grins crazily. "I'm sort of drunk!"

Jane is trying to become a producer, which is perfect because she's very smart, and one of those people who inspires confidence in others by appearing to have all the answers even when she has no real factual information. In the meantime, she's a production assistant on the new Russell Blakely movie, *Kill Time*. The job seems to entail mostly food retrieval, occasional paperwork delivery, and attending to the whims of the movie's star. Whenever Jane talks about Russell Blakely, all I can picture is that line everybody was quoting from his last movie, *Steel Entrapment*, where he calls out to Cordelia Biscayne, "Honey, I'm home," while hanging by one hand from the landing gear of a helicopter, bare-chested.

"Today's specials from the set of *Kill Time*: an assortment of bagels that were only out on the craft service table for about three hours, but are not, sadly, accompanied by cream cheese, and that Chinese rice thing that Dan likes, which I don't think was too aggressively sneezed upon."

"Bagel, please. And outfit approval, if you can see anything through those shades."

"Please. I'm a professional." Jane dips her glasses slightly, but only slightly, down her nose, and studies me carefully.

"Now, of course, I've seen this outfit before. But today, it's *really* speaking to me, positively singing to me with personality. Today it says: happy housewife who loves staying at home, who's devoted to her family and possesses an enthusiasm for floor wax seldom seen in the Western world."

"Close. Passionate love of clean clothes."

"Ahh. Laundry detergent! You're perfect. So wholesome, I want to run to the laundromat immediately. That face! Familiar, yet a breath of fresh air, *and* your hair seems positively subdued."

"Thanks, Janey."

"I would, however, lose the belt."

I hang my wayward attempt at fashion on the banister, and for no particular reason decide to make a dramatic entrance out of the kitchen/alcove into the living room where Dan is working, and pose, *Price Is Right* style, like I might be illuminating the features of a NEW CAR!

"Hey, Dan," I say. "Do I look like someone with really clean clothes?"

"Hmmph?" he says, not looking up.

My first pose having gone unappreciated, I decide to change it up and attempt an even more dramatic attitude, a sort of King Tut, Egyptian-tomb look.

"Dan," I say, standing mummy style, hands bent in an L-shape at the wrists. "Jane's home. She brought food."

"Garphmm," he mumbles, scribbling furiously in his notebook.

Finally, I clap my hands at him. "Dan, emergency! Your fly is open!"

"What?" he asks, finally looking up, blowing his bangs out of his face. "Sorry, Franny, I'm really struggling with the Photar creatures." Dan is trying to write a science-fiction movie for some sort of competition. I'm sure he'll win. He was apparently a straight-A student at Princeton, and no one is more passionate about aliens than Dan. When he tries to describe the story to me, I find myself counting the planks in our floor, weighing the merits of vegetable versus scallion cream cheese, but I'm sure it's better than it sounds.

"How's my hair? I'm taking an apartment-wide poll." For some reason, this time my question is accompanied by a weird sort of tap-step flourish, in order to "sell it."

I hate myself. I must be stopped.

"Um, big?" he says, hopefully.

"Huh?"

"Well, that's what you're going for, right? Big, with a sort of curly fountain thing on top?"

From the kitchen/alcove I can hear Jane snort, as though orange juice just came out of her nose. Worse, I realize that while waiting for Dan's answer, I've stayed sort of frozen, still holding my Bob Hope–movie, high school dance recital jazz-hands pose. Dan just stares at me.

Defeated, I let my hands drop to my sides.

"Yes, 'curly fountain' is definitely what I was after. Thanks, Dan."

As I start out on the six-block walk to the Seventh Avenue subway station, I decide this: I must work harder to achieve my goal of not seeking approval from those whose approval I'm not even sure is important to me. This includes, but is not limited to, people I grew up with who I see when I go home for Thanksgiving; people with real jobs of any kind, especially those requiring suits or high heels; people in my acting class; people who work at Barney's New York; people on the subway; taxi drivers who question my choice of route; people who work at the deli on Eighth Avenue where I sometimes ask for extra mayo; other people's mothers; dance teachers, aerobic instructors, or those who habitually wear or have seen me in spandex, and gargantuan freak boys who write about Photar creatures.

I must not seek approval from absolutely everyone, or anyone really. Actresses should be poised and confident, like Meryl Streep and Diane Keaton. I should be more original and unique, like they are. I'll take to wearing men's ties!

The woman behind the glass who sells the subway tokens eyes me warily. I've been known to pay my $1.25 in small change, sometimes in the very smallest. It's not a proud moment when I'm holding up the line while she counts my pennies, but some days it's come to that. Today, though, I have actual paper money. We share a nod, like things might be looking up for both of us.

I put my token in the slot, and as I wait for my train, I decide to use my time on the platform to think only positive thoughts, in the hopes that I might create a more positive outcome at my audition today. I read somewhere that positive thinking is very powerful and you should train your mind to think about happy things more often, instead of letting it wander to why your jeans feel tight or whether you have enough in the bank to take out twenty dollars, or if there will ever come a day where your life isn't measured in twenty-dollar cash withdrawal increments.

Positive thoughts. Positive thoughts.

It's not always easy to think positive thoughts.

Um.

Just start somewhere.

Accomplishments.

Positive things in my life right now.

Um.

I'm alive.

The obvious. Always a good place to start.

I had a good time with Clark over the holidays.

Not an accomplishment, exactly, but still, a fun thing to think about.

Clark and I met at freshman orientation and were inseparable from that day on. Everyone who knew us assumed we'd get married. We never talked about it exactly, but I'm pretty sure we both thought the same thing.

Then Clark only got into law school in Chicago—not in New York at Columbia, like we'd planned. He asked me to come with him, he wanted us to move in together: "They have great theater in Chicago, too," he'd said, but I couldn't give up on New York, not before I'd given it a try. So we made one of those "agreements" to sort of take a break and see where we were after he finished school in three years. That's where my deadline came from—I figured if he could get a law degree in that amount of time, it was long enough for me to make some measurable progress, too. I've had a few dates since then and he probably has, too, but nothing serious. And when we see each other it's still like no time has passed. He tells me every time he knows we're going to end up together.

"Are you sure you won't come back with me *now*?" he asked last time, as I waited with him at his gate at the airport.

"I just—not yet."

"Okay," he said. And then, with a wink: "Call me when you change your mind."

Sometimes, when the tips are bad and my feet ache, I wonder why I'm putting off the inevitable. I wonder why I don't just pick up the phone and move to Chicago rather than continuing to attempt something that has a less than five percent success rate.

But for some reason, I don't.

As much fun as I have with Clark, it can also be confusing when I see him. I miss him, a lot sometimes . . .

Shit.

Do you see why focusing on the positive is such tricky business? You've got the slippery guy for a minute, and then he turns all negative on you. I'll be more specific—I'll just think positive *work* thoughts. Thinking about my personal life is not helping me. I came to New York to be an actress, not a girlfriend or a happy person.

Positive thoughts about work.

Well.

I did book that one job.

Before Thanksgiving, right after Dan moved in, I got a small regional commercial, my first, for a local discount clothing store called Sally's Wear House. It was a holiday promotional to run for just a few weeks, featuring really bulky sweaters, made out of acrylic and ramie, whatever that is. Mine had a gray and white argyle pattern and padded shoulders with white fur trim around the neck and cuffs, and I had to wrap my arms around myself in a hug, and say, "Yummy, Yummy." In another shot, I had to jump up in the air and yell, "I'm dreaming of a white Christmas!" Then, I had to look up at absolutely nothing and say, "Ohhh, snowflakes."

The three of us went out to the upstairs Chinese place, whose name we can never remember, to celebrate. Then the commercial happened to come on a few weeks later, while we were all together watching *Law and Order*, and first we all screamed, then Jane practically fell down laughing. Not in a mean way, but she just couldn't believe I'd managed to appear happy while wearing such an ugly sweater. It was shocking to see myself on television. No one had thought to set the VCR, and it was gone in what felt like a few seconds. All I could remember after it was over was thinking that my face seemed round, and I looked much taller than the other girl I was with.

"I'm a giant!" I said, covering my face and peering out between my fingers.

"You're not a giant," Jane said, still laughing/coughing/hicupping. "You're a fucking great actress is what you are. I totally believed you loved that sweater that came from where angora goes to die."

"Those snowflakes they added looked so fake," I said, still in shock.

"But *you* looked great," Jane said. "Really pretty."

Finally, Dan spoke up.

"So, it's an ad for Christmas sweaters?" Once again, nailing the obvious.

"Um, yes, Dan," Jane said, rolling her eyes at me. "I think we can all agree that what we learned in those thirty seconds is that the commercial was for Christmas sweaters."

Dan nodded slowly, as if he were making a very important decision about something, then he smiled at me.

"Well, Franny, I felt that," he said. "It was very Christmas-y. You looked like Christmas, Fran."

What does that even mean, to say someone "looks like" Christmas? Jane and I shared a look, and I immediately began to formulate my snappy comeback, the way I do whenever I'm complimented. But something about his sincerity stopped me, and for some reason, for once in my life, I nodded at Dan and blushed a little, and just kept my mouth shut.

I made seven hundred dollars on the sweater job, the biggest amount by far I've ever seen on a single check. But I haven't booked anything else since. It was probably a fluke. I'll probably never work again.

Positive thoughts.

Well.

I got that one job.

And today I have a chance to get one more.

There. I did it.

When the subway arrives, I find a seat and take a deep breath. The D train between Brooklyn and Manhattan is one of my favorite lines, because at one point the train emerges from underground and goes high over the river along the Manhattan Bridge. Sometimes I put on my headphones and listen to music, sometimes I do the *New York Times* crossword, and sometimes I read, but no matter what else I'm doing, I consider it very bad luck if I forget to look up as the train crosses over the East River, even just for a second, before it goes back underground. It's just a superstition, but looking at the river, the boats, the sign leaving Brooklyn that says "Watchtower" in big red letters, is a ritual that reminds me I am small, I am one of thousands— no—one of *millions* of people who looked at this river before me, from a boat or a car or the window of the D train, who came to New York with a dream, who achieved it or didn't, but nonetheless made the same effort I'm making now. It keeps things in perspective, and strangely, it gives me hope.

January 1995

16 Monday

CALL DAD
BACK.

NEED.
  MILK
  COFFEE
  PAY JANE FOR GAS BILL

Franny Banks

17 Tuesday

RAN | 3.2 MILES | ALONNY PARK.

CASH CHECK

½ BAGEL / TUNA
B.BERRY YOGURT.
SUSHI DELUXE IS TOO EXPENSIVE FOR YOU STOP
                    ORDERING IT REGULAR IS
| SHIFT 3am | JUST FINE YOU DON'T NEED EXTRA

18 Wednesday

                    PIECES BLURB
                           BLAH
                           BLARP

| CLUB |
CLOSING | SHFT 43 → | filofax

Franny Banks ♀ ♀

DOC MARTENS
‑ PICK UP FROM SHOE REPAIR

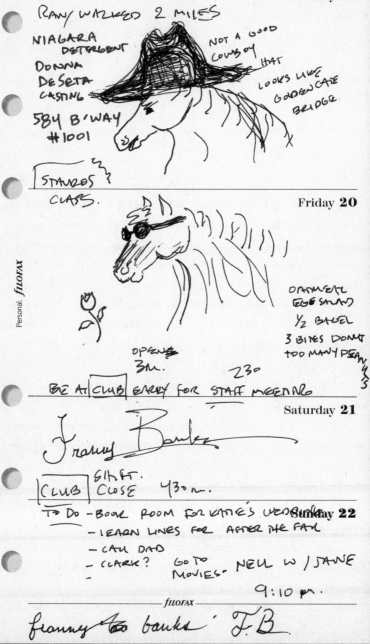

RANY WALKED 2 MILES

NIAGARA
    DETERGENT
DONNA
DESETA
CASTING

584 B'WAY
#1001

NOT A GOOD
COWBOY
HAT
LOOKS LIKE
GOLDEN GATE
BRIDGE

STAVROS?
CLASS.

OATMEAL
EGG SALAD
½ BAGEL
3 BITES DONUT
TOO MANY PEANUTS

OPENS
3M.

230

BE AT CLUB EARLY FOR STAFF MEETING

Franny Banks

CLUB 6½ FT.
CLOSE 430 M.

TO DO ‑ BOOK ROOM FOR KATIE'S WEDDING
      ‑ LEARN LINES FOR AFTER THE FALL
      ‑ CALL DAD
      ‑ CLARK? GO TO
                MOVIES- NELL W/ JANE
                    9:10 PM.

Personal *FILOFAX*

franny ~~too~~ banks · F.B.

3

The casting place that's holding the session for Niagara dishwashing detergent has one of those bathroom-stall-sized ancient New York elevators that move so slowly you think it might be stuck, and I'm crammed in with what appear to be two child actors and their mom. They're twins, I think, a boy and a girl, with reddish hair and freckles. The little girl flashes me a big smile that looks like it's been perfected by hours of practice in the mirror. She twirls a fat, shiny curl around and around her finger.

"Pretty hair," I tell her.

"I sleep on a special silk pillow so the curls don't smoosh," she replies, beaming.

"Fancy," I say, smiling back at her but achieving nowhere near her wattage. "You guys want to push the button for me? I'm going to four."

"I'll push it!" the little boy offers.

"No! *I'll* push it," his sister says, giving him a little shove. "It's *my* callback."

The little boy shrinks back from the elevator buttons and I smile sympathetically at their mom, but she seems mesmerized by a spot somewhere north of the top of my head, so I decide to take a sudden interest in the laces of my shoes and endure the rest of the long, creaky ride in silence. Even in the best of elevators, I think, there's no place where time passes so slowly.

Upstairs, the waiting room is crowded, which means there must be a few different casting calls. There are boys and girls near the age of the elevator twins; a couple of men in their fifties, both in suit and tie; and several girls who remind me of me, but a better, more put-together me. The me who would play me in the TV movie of the fictional life of the real me.

I sign in.

Name
Time arrived
Time scheduled
Agency
Soc Sec #

While writing my information in the tiny spaces allotted by the sign-in sheet, I try to subtly scan and analyze the list of those who've auditioned before me. I'm a sign-in sheet sleuth looking for clues. I'm trying to figure out how many people they've seen already today, and if I know any of them, and if they're from my agency, and if they were on time, and if they have neater handwriting than mine. Anything at all to indicate what a person who books a job does differently from what I do. If my appointment were five minutes earlier, would I book the job? If I made a smiley face out of the "o" in Penelope, like the person who signed in a few people in front of me did, would I work more? If I were the first person they saw today instead of the tenth, would I—

"Franny? Is that you? It's Franny, right?"

My cheeks go hot. I've been caught. I drop the pen more quickly than a truly innocent person would, and look up.

"Franny Banks, right? From Stavros's class? Or have I gone totally koo-koo bananas?" The girl standing before me laughs, doubles over with laughter in fact, like someone who might truly be koo-koo bananas, and continues laughing at a volume that says she doesn't care that the other twenty or so people in the waiting room are all staring at her.

I've never seen this person before, and I don't know how she knows me or my acting teacher, John Stavros, but the first thing I'm struck by is her incredibly long, shiny blond hair. Also, she's tiny, like a doll who became a person, or a person pretending to be a doll, with her hands elegantly angled, fingers outstretched and ready to hold a variety of objects, and her toes forever slightly pointed, waiting for their interchangeable plastic high-heeled shoes. She's wearing a thick stack of jangly gold bracelets, and her tiny wrist looks like it could snap under their weight. Even though it's a bleak day in January, she's wearing white jeans, perfectly fitted and to the ankle, as if she's Mary Tyler Moore on a special Hawaiian-vacation episode of *The Dick Van Dyke Show*.

"Um, yeah, that's me. I'm Franny." I feel like I'm towering over her. I suddenly feel awkward, like they gave me an extra arm by accident and I can't figure out how to use it.

"I knew it! Oh, God, you must think I'm so rude. Hello! I'm Penelope Schlotzsky. I *know*, terrible name, right? They're probably going to make me change it." She laughs again and swings her blanket of hair so that it all cascades over one shoulder. You can almost feel a breeze, it's so thick.

I'm sort of at a loss for what to say, which rarely happens. All I want to know is who "they" are and if they have any advice for things I should change about myself.

"I'm new in class with you!" she squeals, before I can pull myself together. "I had my first class last week but I was sitting way in the back, like, petrified, so that's why I wasn't sure if you were *you*, or just someone who looks like *you*, but I *just had* to risk it and say hello because I swear to *God*, you were, like, the *best actress*. So *funny*. You like, really *go* for it. You're going to do great in *the Showcase*."

Stavros doesn't encourage this kind of talk among his students. "Who's better, Pacino or DeNiro?" he'll say to us. "Don't waste time comparing. Keep your eyes on your own paper." And while I'm secretly thrilled by her compliments, I'm shaken by her (very loud) mention of the Showcase: the Showcase that's looming in exactly two weeks, the Showcase we've been working toward for months, the Showcase that is the one opportunity we get all year to be seen by agents and directors and casting people, who come because they respect Stavros and his taste in actors. It's a night where anything—or at least *something*—could happen. Last year, Mary Grace got cast in the chorus of a Broadway musical from the Showcase, and two other people got agents, and that's how James Franklin got the screen test that eventually led to that Arturo DeNucci movie. He's the best example of what could happen. But he's an amazing actor—I could never hope for something that big. All I want is to get an agent, or even a meeting with an agent. That's all I'll let myself hope for.

"Wow, thanks!" I say. "And welcome to class. You're going to *love* Stavros."

I mean what I'm saying, but something in my voice sounds strangely insincere. I'm trying to match her enthusiasm, but with less volume, and the combination makes me sound fake, like one of those ladies who sell stretchy flowered pants on that new home shopping channel. The elastic waistband is *so comfortable*. You'll *live in them*.

"Oh, Stavros is the best!" Penelope gushes. "So *sexy*, right?"

The truth is that our acting teacher is very attractive, but it embarrasses me to hear her talk about him like he's one of us. It doesn't seem respectful. "Well, he certainly does talk very fast," is as close as I can come to agreeing with her.

"*Right?* So passionate! I'm still totally shocked I got in, especially since he doesn't usually take people right before the Showcase. But I guess he was like, she already *has* an agent at Absolute, and she's got two movies in the can, so like, you know, fine—just one more beanpole to deal with!"

This is the kind of confidence you're supposed to have as an actress, I think. I mean, I would personally never announce that I had an agent at Absolute Artists, the best agency in town, or talk about movies I'd done, or refer to myself as a "beanpole," especially loudly and in a room full of people. But then again, in my case, none of those things are true.

"So are you going to class from this torture session?" she says, flicking an incredibly shiny strand of blond hair back from her face. "Want to go with me to that diner on Eighth and get a salad in between?"

Salad. Oh yeah. I'm supposed to eat more salad. It just never seems appealing. In fact, I was already planning to go to "that diner" on Eighth for my usual pre-class dinner: grilled cheese, french fries, and the *New York Times* crossword puzzle. But for some reason I find myself making an excuse.

"I, ah, can't. I have another, you know, torture session after this one."

The lie comes out before I can even consider stopping it. I'm totally unprepared if she asks what my other audition is for, or where it is. Maybe I can recycle one from a few weeks ago, but what if it's one she had, too?

Luckily, she doesn't seem to care. "Good for you," she says, punching me lightly on the shoulder. "You're PERFECT for commercials. I suck at them. I totally TANKED in there."

Somehow I doubt that Penelope "tanked" in there. I bet she seldom "tanks" anywhere. And something about the way she said I'm "perfect for commercials" makes me bristle. That's the only explanation for what comes out of my mouth next.

"Yeah, and actually, after that, I have, um, a rehearsal, too." I roll my eyes like, Rehearsals, pah, I have them every day.

One summer at camp, they tried to teach us to water-ski. I stood up for approximately two seconds before I fell. Forgetting everything I'd been told, I held onto the rope and was dragged, bumping across the lake, until the driver finally noticed and brought the boat to a stop. That's the feeling I have right now, telling lie after lie to Penelope—I'm powerless to stop myself.

"Auditions *and* rehearsals!" Penelope exclaims, as though she's just seen her two best friends in the whole world. "Isn't it all so *mad*?"

"It *is* mad," I tell her. "Mad."

"Well, next time then. Nice to meet you, officially," she says and shakes my hand, gold bracelets clattering and clinking. "See you on the boards!" She giggles and waves over her shoulder, a general wave that is for me, but also seems to generously include the entire room. *Charisma*, I think to myself. That's what someone with charisma does to a room full of strangers. Together we watch as Penelope and her tiny white pants disappear down the hall.

I feel sort of depressed after she leaves, but I don't know why. The spectators in the room seem similarly unsettled. They stare after her longingly, like they miss her already and wish she would come back. Gradually, they seem to realize their entertainment won't be returning, and one by one they go back to reading, looking at their newspapers or their commercial copy—something I should have been doing this whole time.

I must never lie again, I think. Why did I say no to Penelope and her offer of salad, besides my ambivalence regarding salad? Because she's the type of person who uses the word "mad," as if she thinks she's British? Now I'll have to go to the worse diner on Sixth Avenue, two long blocks farther away from class and much more expensive.

Keep your eyes on your own paper, I hear Stavros say, and right then, I resolve to become friends with Penelope. I imagine how wonderfully supportive I'll be from now on, clapping loudly after every scene she does in class. I'll be gracious, I'll be kind, I'll eat more salad.

"Frances Banks, you're next," a monotone voice says. A bored-looking girl in vintage '50s glasses, a baby-doll dress with a suspender clip in the back, and a pair of lace-up combat boots reads my name from the sign-in sheet.

Crap. I thought I had more time. I haven't even looked at what I'm supposed to say, not one word of it. I should have gotten here earlier, shouldn't have spent time chatting. I was basking in the glow of compliments and having envious thoughts about hair when I should have been preparing. I can't afford to mess up an opportunity. My heart is pounding hard and fast now.

"Ready?" she asks, with a listless half-sneer that she might intend to be a smile.

"Um, yes. Totally. Totally ready."

I would be great in a car crash, or at giving CPR. I'd be the one you'd ask to perform the Heimlich maneuver if someone started choking in a restaurant. Because in a crisis, I get very, very calm. I'm calmer in a crisis than I am in actually calm situations. So while she puts film in the Polaroid camera, I quickly scan the copy, remaining calm, focusing on my lines, ignoring the stage directions. They won't be helpful for this kind of commercial anyway. They're usually descriptions like "she inhales the intoxicating scent of the fluffy towel." There's never anything real: "She sits at laundromat breathing through her mouth due to sweaty guy hogging dryer nearby."

The lines, learn the lines: " . . . smelling like a fresh spring day . . . waterfall take me away . . . Niagara—honeymoon in a bottle." I don't quite have them down, but I'll be fine. The material doesn't seem particularly original, thank God. For once, I'm relieved to have just the same generic mom commercial I've had a dozen times before.

I take a deep breath as Vintage Glasses snaps a Polaroid of me against the stark white wall, stapling it to my eight-by-ten head shot and résumé so the casting people can see what I actually look like today, in contrast to how my face looks when I've had a chance to have it enhanced and retouched.

I follow her into the audition room, which is carpeted and windowless and bare, except for two chairs where the casting people are sitting, and a rolling cart with a TV and VCR on it. A video camera is set up on a tripod, which is pointed at a T-shaped mark made of masking tape on the floor where I'm supposed to stand. Facing me from about fifteen feet away are two women, both in their thirties, with matching parted-down-the-middle stick-straight hair. Vintage Glasses pops a tape in the camera and a red light near the giant black lens comes to life. The lens feels like another person in the room, a person who never speaks or smiles, who only stares without blinking, never looking away.

"Hi, Franny, how are you, great? Great. Really great to see you," one of the stick-straights singsongs without looking up from her clipboard. "If you don't have any questions about the material, then state your name and agency and go ahead whenever you're ready thankssomuch."

I try to swallow, but my throat is too dry. This is the kind of room that's hard to do well in. If they're in the mood to talk, I can crack a few jokes, make a small connection, and give myself a moment to settle down. But these girls are all business.

I look down at the paper. I'm not going to panic or ask for more time or tell them I didn't really have a chance to go over it yet. I'm going to remain calm, as if I'm a professional. *What does your character want more than anything?* Stavros always asks us. *Clean laundry*, I say to myself. *More than anything, I wish I could get my laundry cleaner.* I try to breathe, I can only manage to suck in a tiny bit of air. It will have to do.

"You know what's hard about being a mom? Nothing." *Clean laundry.* I smile, as if I'm sure I've got this whole mom/laundry thing under control. *There's nothing I want more than whiter whites.*

"I always have time for my kids. They're my number-one priority." I relax a little, picturing a kid named George I used to babysit in high school. He liked to be tickled, and he couldn't say his "F"s, so he called me "Whanny."

"I always have time for my friends. It's all about balance, ya know?"

The stick-straights are giggling, I think, or is that my imagination? I can't hear that well due to the volume of blood pounding in my ears. I resolve to speak the lines even more emphatically so they know I'm taking laundry more seriously than anyone ever has.

"*I always* make time for myself. Smelling like a fresh spring day makes it all a breeze."

The stick-straights are really laughing now; there's no denying it. I must be doing a really bad job. I try to finish extra strong, so as not to let them see how disappointed I am. *I have the cleanest laundry!*

"When my husband asks me how I do it, I tell him, 'It's easy!' Every day I think of our honeymoon in Niagara, and let the waterfall take me away. Niagara. It's like a honeymoon in a bottle."

I lower the paper and look up, defeated, only to see that the stick-straights are smiling, beaming, actually. They look at each other and share a nod.

I'm totally confused.

"Awesome!" one of them gushes. "SO funny."

"Really cute."

"Quirky!"

I have no idea why they liked what I did, but I know I should play along.

"Thanks!" I say, and then for no reason, "Any adjustments?" *Stupid. Stupid. Don't ask to do it again when you don't know what you did in the first place.*

"Ummmm . . ." They both cock their heads at the same angle, like two puppies in a pet store window. Then they nod to each other again.

"Sure, yeah, let's do one more, just for kicks!"

"Yeah! I mean, that was great! But let's, in this one, like, really have fun with it!"

"But also, take it seriously, like you did."

"Yeah! Serious, but fun, like you're talking to your best friend."

"Yeah! Like you're sharing a secret with your best friend."

"Yeah! It's a big secret, but also it's really casual. Like, it's a secret, but also it's no big deal."

"Yeah! Just throw it away."

"Yeah! But it's important, too."

"Yeah! And could you, maybe, put your hair in a ponytail?"

"Yeah!"

I'm even less sure of what I did the second time, but the stick-straights laugh again anyway.

"I think her hair is funnier down, don't you?" one of them says to the other, who nods vigorously back.

As I leave the room, I stuff the paper with the copy on it in my bag, even though you're not supposed to take it with you, and bolt for the elevator.

I walk a few blocks in I'm not sure what direction. I'm so excited that they seemed to like me that I'm dizzy and disoriented. Finally, I slow down a bit and, finding myself near Union Square Park, decide I'll stop and sit down and try to analyze what just happened. It's important to figure out why they thought it went well. A cigarette. I really want a cigarette. I think there might be one left in a crumpled pack in the bottom of my bag. I know there is, in fact, because I pretended to myself that I forgot about it but secretly know it exists.

I retrieve the pack I fake-forgot about, but I can't find a light. I keep digging in my bag, hoping something will appear. No matches, no lighter, nothing. I'm the worst smoker. I never have the two things you're supposed to have at the same time. I hold the unlit cigarette in my hand anyway, for support, and uncrumple the paper from the audition. For the first time, I read the whole thing.

I had assumed from the dialogue what the action would be: generic shots of someone being a great mom, playing with generic perfect kids, drinking generic perfect tea with generic perfect girlfriends, and other predictably generic-perfect-mom activities.

That's not at all what the description says.

My stomach lurches.

The action between each line is the exact opposite of what the line is. After "Kids are my number-one priority," it says, "Rushing mom gets daughter to school just as the bell is ringing." After the thing about always having time for friends, it's "looks at answering machine guiltily and decides to screen the call." At the end, the harried housewife stuffs an impossible amount of dirty clothes in the washer, which miraculously come out clean, and she gets a huge hug from her approving husband.

The commercial was supposed to be funny.

They thought I was taking myself seriously as a choice, when I was honestly trying to sell myself to them as a perfect person with a perfect life. If I'd understood it properly, I would have played it differently. I would have played it more obviously sarcastic or something. I would have tried to let them know that I realized it was comedic, to show them I understand funny. But I played it trying to be serious, and they laughed anyway. Which either means I don't understand funny at all, or I understand it better than I think I do.

They thought I was funny; isn't that all that matters? Does being accidentally funny count as being funny? I'm not sure what happened in there. Today was either a great success or a terrible failure. I wish there were someone I could call and ask, some sort of all-seeing audition judge in the sky, the omnipotent God of Funny, who could help me decipher this endless parade of baffling incidents. But all I have today is myself on a bench, with a crumpled piece of paper and an unlit cigarette, hoping for some clarity, or maybe just a light.

4

....

Most of the streets in Manhattan go in just one direction. Some of the larger crosstown streets and some of the major north–south avenues have two-way traffic, but in general, the odd-numbered streets go west, toward the Hudson River, and the "evens go east," as Jane, the native New Yorker, taught me. Even our neighborhood in Brooklyn has mostly one-way streets, so I must see the sign with the familiar white arrow and bold black letters a hundred times a week, but I never take it for granted. For most people it's an indication to look for the traffic coming from one direction, but I always take care to look both ways, in case someone missed the sign and is accidentally going the wrong way. It's been this way for most of my life. I check not once, not twice, but three times before I cross a one-way street. And that's how, one Tuesday afternoon before class, I see James Franklin.

I'm sure he wasn't there the first two times I checked the traffic headed west on 45th Street, but when I check for the third time, there he is. James Franklin, the working actor who's still in class, the one who got the part in the Arturo DeNucci movie. He's wearing a green army surplus–type jacket and faded jeans and has a long blue and red striped scarf looped around his neck. His hair is dark and a little wavy. He's so handsome that it almost hurts my eyes. Even from across the street he stands out like the sun is shining just a little more brightly on him, giving him the slightest bit more attention and warmth than everyone else.

He's across Sixth Avenue heading west, and I'm about to head north. If I can cross 45th before the light changes, and stall convincingly for a moment, there's a chance we'll accidentally run into each other. Maybe he'll recognize me, maybe even remember my name, although he's been back in class only a month or so after being on location and I'd just started with Stavros when he left. But if he does recognize me, maybe I'll ask him for a light, and we'll stand on the corner having a smoke and talking about class, or maybe he'll ask if I want a cup of coffee, and we'll go to a diner and sit down and talk about . . . *Shit.* What will we talk about? I'll think of something. I'll think of something funny to say and he'll say, "You're funny. I never realized how funny you are. I'm so glad I ran into you." And maybe we'll go out sometime, and maybe we'll fall in love. And someday we'll happen to be walking down this very street and he'll say, "Remember that day when we accidentally ran into each other here?" But none of that can happen if he walks by me on the street today.

I make my way across 45th Street and hover near a trash can, digging in my bag as if I'm looking for something I need to throw out, waiting for his light to change. Finally, I can see him start to walk across the street. I look away so he doesn't see me staring at him, and when I glance up again, I've lost him in the crowd. My heart starts to pound in panic but then he emerges again, and my face flushes with embarrassment. *Calm down.* He has a tan canvas messenger bag slung across his chest and a pager on his belt. The bag looks pretty full and I wonder what's inside it. Maybe he had to pick up a script to prepare for an audition. Or maybe he gets his scripts delivered to him by messenger—I've heard they do that when you start to do really well. Maybe he's carrying around books by John Osborne or Charles Bukowski because he's trying to make sense of his darkly romantic view of the world. I'll bet he brings a notebook with him everywhere in case he has a deep thought about something, which I'm fairly sure he does on a regular basis.

As he nears my side of the street I focus intently on my bag while facing the trash can, sighing in exasperation and shaking the bag dramatically up and down in an effort to "find what it is I'm looking for." "Where *is* it?" I say too loudly for the audience of no one. Finally I retrieve the only believable trash I can find, a thin foil piece of gum wrapper, so light that—even with the force of my melodramatic aim—it flutters, missing the container entirely, and when I look up, James Franklin has disappeared.

My mouth falls open in dismay, and my bag slides a few inches down my shoulder as it slumps in defeat. Seconds later, some pedestrian slams into me, and my open bag is knocked off my shoulder and onto the ground. It's what I deserve, of course, for my appallingly hammy bag acting, and for moving the bag from a stable cross-body position to the more vulnerable single shoulder in order to capture the attention of James Franklin—who is suddenly standing right in front of me.

James Franklin is standing right in front of me.

His canvas book bag hit my canvas book bag just as he passed. It's like our shoulder bags kissed.

The thought of our shoulder bags kissing and eventually falling in love and moving in together makes me smile a little, which is bad, because finding myself amusing is taking up the space I need in my brain to conjure a way to be charming. I've got to think of something to say. Something devastatingly witty. I'm running out of time. He's just staring at me. I pick my bag up off the ground and stare blankly back at him, frozen like those lottery winners on TV who scream without forming actual words, or one of those actors accepting an award who you know will regret not having written a speech later as the clock ticks by and they completely blank on who they were supposed to thank. "Your wife!" you yell to them through the television, but the orchestra swells and their chance is gone.

"Whoops—sorry about—"

"I'm in class with you!" I announce, too squeakily.

"Oh, yeah?"

"Yes! Stavros's class? I've only been there for a few months and you've been gone . . . you . . . working actor, you . . . ." I trail off, smiling at him idiotically.

"Oh, yeah. Yeah. I think I recognize you . . . ." He nods, slowly, and smiles in a slightly lopsided way. "Yes."

He has some sort of accent, almost a drawl. He's from the South somewhere. Maybe he grew up on a farm in Texas, or Georgia. Maybe he had chores in the barn every day, and helped his father harvest corn.

He still hasn't looked away from me. He stands perfectly still, not shifting at all. I can feel myself rocking back and forth on my feet. I try to stay steady, like he does, but it's impossible for me to do.

"I really like your work in class," I say, ducking my head.

"Oh yeah?" He looks embarrassed, glancing down at his feet. *He's shy*, I think. The city must be so loud for him after all that wide-open quiet space he's used to.

"Yes! I mean, we've all seen guys who yell 'Stella! Stella!' Like Brando? But you made Stanley really, uh, *you*. I think."

I've got to get a grip. I hope I don't sound pretentious. Anytime a person uses "Brando" in a sentence, the odds of sounding pretentious are high. I take what might be my first breath in the whole conversation. "Anyway." I smile and try to hold his gaze the way he held mine, then hold out my hand. "Franny."

"Franny. From class." His eyes narrow a little, probably to avoid the smoke as he takes a drag off of his cigarette, but I feel like he's sizing me up. "You said you're new?"

"Who, me? Well, sort of, yes. I'm new to class, but I've lived in New York for a little while—two years. Over two years. I worked for my dad at his school, and then I was in a theater company for a long time before that. Touring. Also, I've done one commercial. And uh, that's it!"

Ugh. I'm babbling. At least I didn't tell him the company was called GO! KIDS! and we played stupid fairy-tale characters and the only places we "toured" were elementary schools in the tri-state area. Oh God, what if he asks what company I was in? I wish I hadn't mentioned the commercial, either. He would probably never do commercials.

"That's cool, that's cool," he drawls, giving me a smile. "Work is work, right?"

"Right. Yes! Work *is* work, isn't it? How true!" I'm relieved. I must stop repeating him, though.

There's an odd buzzing sound and James reaches down to check the pager on his belt. "Sorry about that. That's my agent," he says, casually. "I'm supposed to meet him somewhere."

"So you aren't going to class?" I say, with way too much panic in my voice.

"No," he says. Then he pushes his bottom lip out a little. "Not tonight, sweetheart."

He looks almost sorry for me, as if he's canceling some sort of prearranged date, or I'm five years old and he just told me we can't go to the zoo. I resent his assumption that I'm even slightly disappointed that he won't be in class tonight, although the truth is I'm inexplicably crushed.

"Me neither. I'm not going to class either, because ah, it's funny, but I have to pick up some scripts, too, actually." *Shit. Lying. Stop lying.*

"Oh yeah?"

"Yeah. And then, I have . . . ah . . . stuff, you know . . . with all my uh, agents, also," I say, hands flapping vaguely in the air.

"Very cool. Who are you with?"

I realize I'm too exhausted to continue. "I'm with It's All in My Head, Inc.?"

"You're, wha? Oh, I get it. You're kidding. Ha."

"Yes, I'm kidding. I'm currently between agents. Currently and formerly between them."

"Ah, well . . ." James trails off. He looks embarrassed. I've blown it. We'll never speak to each other again. I'll wave to him across the theater once in a while, but mainly I'll pretend this whole thing never happened. My face is burning as I try to think of a quirky exit line, something Diane Keaton said in *Annie Hall*, when James lowers his cigarette and smiles a slow, Southern smile.

"Can I get your number?" he asks.

I was definitely not expecting that. It seems to have come out of nowhere. It occurs to me that perhaps this is his way of compensating for my not having an agent. I decide I don't care.

"My number? Yes. Sure. For representation?"

He looks confused. "No, for—oh. Kidding again. Ha."

It's a little weird how he says the word "ha" instead of actually laughing. He must be one of those cool people who appreciate humor subtly from the inside, who never giggle uncontrollably, streaming tears and spitting milkshake down their shirt.

I tear a scrap of paper from my Filofax and write my number down. When James says goodbye, he gives me a little kiss on the cheek, brushing my face with his so that I can feel the stubble on his chin. "I'm glad I ran into you," he says in his raspy voice, and my knees almost buckle.

"Literally," I say coolly, and this time he laughs for real.

Success!

I'll have to hurry now to make it to class on time, but I don't mind. Navigating the crowd on the sidewalk is a challenge I like. I'm running without touching anyone else on the street. I'm a character in a human video game, keeping my bubble of space from being invaded, eyeing an open slot on the sidewalk, speeding up to grab it before someone else does, slowing down until I see another space, working together with the strangers on the street as though we're all performing an elaborate dance perfectly choreographed for thousands of people.

I'm happy. A guy I like got my number. Everything will be okay.

But I'm so excited that I run a little too fast, and I manage to get to class at exactly the wrong time. Stavros opens the doors to the theater at precisely five fifty-five and closes them at precisely six. If you get there too early, practically the whole class is clustered around the door, and there's a nervous tension in the air and no way to avoid overhearing almost every conversation.

CONSEQUENCES OF GETTING TO CLASS AT EXACTLY THE WRONG TIME

Characters overlap, all are talking the whole time

CASEY. *(20s, beautiful, can be weepy, talking to Franny)* Franny! Thank God! Did you hear? About what? Franny, I left a message on your tape, how can you go even an hour without checking your machine? Okay, listen. Remember that diet I told you about that all the girls in L.A. were doing? Where you eat a banana and then wait until you are totally starving and then you eat a hard-boiled egg and wait until you are about to pass out, and then you eat another banana? Well . . .

CHARLIE. *(20s, brooding, talking to another brooding guy)* Why would you see that horrible show, man, why? It's the biggest piece of commercial bullshit in town right now . . . They are? Oh, really? They're replacing the guy in that part? How did you hear that? Really? You're going in on it? Do you think they would see me for it? I mean, not to, but, would you mind? Can I tell my agent? I mean, we're so different, man, it's not like we're competing in any way, we're both so totally different. No, well, I said that, but, I didn't mean it was the worst thing I EVER saw. I've definitely seen worse, and anyway I snuck in at intermission, so I only second-acted it. Maybe if I'd seen Act One the whole thing would have made more sense . . .

DON.   *(20s, male, bubbly, talking to another classmate)* You don't know it? You're kidding. Yes, you do. From "A Little Night Music"? I'll just do a little of it. Sorry, I can barely . . . I have a slight sinus infection: *(sings into friend's face)*

> OR I WILL MARRY THE MILLER'S SON
>
> PIN MY HAT ON A NICE PIECE OF PROPERTY
>
> FRIDAY NIGHTS FOR A BIT OF FUN
>
> WE'LL GO DANCING
>
> MEANWHILE . . .

(cough, cough) Sorry. No, that's okay, I'm fine. I want to do this for you. Let me start again . . .

CASEY.   Obviously you haven't tried it yet, no offense, but thank God I caught you, because they just found out a banana has like SO much sugar in it, or too many enzymes or something, I forget exactly what the medical word is, but it's some new discovery they just made and they're telling everyone in Los Angeles first, but it turns out bananas are like so sugary or dense or something that I guess your body gets all confused and treats the banana like it's a piece of cake . . .

CHARLIE.   Well, I wouldn't say I would be amazing in it, although thanks for saying so. I think I'd just be okay in it. I mean it *is* sort of right in my wheelhouse, but I think you'd actually be great in it, I'm serious. I mean I could do it, I guess, and I probably would do it if they asked, but, I think my problem with it isn't the play itself, but the guy who's in it now, what's his name? Anyway it doesn't matter, I just think he's not really acting so much as just smoldering or something up there, and I'm like, Buddy, you can't just play every scene sexy, I mean, that's not an active choice—the guy has to have some layers or something . . . No, I know, I know, they're saying he might get *nominated* or something, that's probably why he's leaving, now that he thinks he'll get an award he's probably going off to do a film or something . . .

DON.   *(sings)*

> IT'S A PINCH AND A WIGGLE
>
> AND A GIGGLE IN THE GRASS
>
> AND I'LL PITCH THE LIGHTS FANDANGO

CASEY.   . . . and seriously, you might as well eat a whole cake as far as your body is concerned. Isn't that so scary?

CHARLIE.   You know who he reminds me of? And this is not sour grapes, they just really remind me of each other. Come closer. James. Yeah, right? Fucking James in this class, man.

Upstage, we see Franny (late 20s, bad hair) turn her head toward Charlie.

CHARLIE (CONT'D).   Like the girls all like him, but is he really gifted? Chill out, I *am* whispering. But there's something a little phony about him, don't you think? No one is listening, dude, relax. Why is everyone, like, so in love with the guy? It's just an opinion. Anyway . . . whatever. I'm probably just bitter. I heard he just started seeing Penelope Schlotzsky, man. I'm pissed. I kind of had a thing for her. James and Penelope, man. Why do the beautiful, shallow people get all the breaks?

DON.   *(sings)*

> OR I
>
> SHALL MARRY
>
> THE MILLER'S
>
> SON

(cough, cough) Really? You don't know it? *Uch.* How is that even possible? It's Sondheim!

The doors open, and the class files in. Franny is the last to enter, and as she closes the classroom doors, slowly, sadly, we:
> *BLACKOUT*

January–February 1995

30 Monday

RAN 2 MILES

BUY
BEER
TOMATOES
BREAD

W JANE
BEFORE SUNRISE 1230 m
ANGELIKA

TAKE·OUT FROM·
UPSTAIRS CHINESE PLACE 8.50 NO NO $
NO NO

31 Tuesday

BAD
HAIR
DAY.

SUB·
CLUB 435 — CLOSE FOR RICKY

1 Wednesday

RAN 3 MILES

CLUB 3M·

FILOFAX

RAN 3 MILES

TO BRING:

JANE'S BATHROBE
BLAZER
BLACK PUMPS
FAKE GLASSES FOR LAWYER SCENE
(BORROW DAN BRIEFCASE)

RUNNING LINES
W CASEY 4PM.

STAVROS' CLASS

SHOWCASE

- MAIL RENT
  CHECK.
- BOOK ROOM FOR
  KATIE'S
  WEDDING
- RENT CAR
  FOR WEDDING

CLASS 430

"I LOVE ACTING. IT IS SO MUCH MORE
REAL THAN LIFE"

- OSCAR
  WILDE

CLASS 3PM.

I

RENT
DUE
MUST MAIL
BY FRIDAY

5

....

You have four messages.

BEEEP

*Frances, it's me, your father. I believe your Showcase appearance
event is tonight. If we ever actually spoke, I would be able to wish
you luck personally, but in these days of advancing technology I suppose I will have to settle for wishing you recorded, taped, good fortune. We're starting* Heart of Darkness *next week. Please call me by*
Lord of the Flies *at the very least. Also, about Katie's wedding—oh
well, not to nag—just give me a call.*

BEEEP

*Franny, it's Casey. I'll meet you at the theater at five, okay? Can we
run lines? I keep messing up that one speech where I confess to the
murder. I'm totally freaking out, are you? See you tonight!*

BEEEP

Hi, Franny, it's Clark. Just, uh, seeing how you are. Call me.

BEEEP

Dude, it's cousin Katie. Your dad says you can only come to the wedding and not the rehearsal dinner 'cause you need to keep your shift on Fridays? Please don't sweat it—I'm just glad you can come at all. I can't wait for you to meet him. See you in June.

BEEEP

The applause is dying down, but the blood is still pounding in my ears so loudly I can't tell whether it was the really appreciative kind of applause or the "we feel sorry for you" kind. My face is burning as I hurry offstage, still trying to make sense of what just happened—on this of all nights.

Before this, the thing worrying me the most was how miffed Herb seemed that I had to take a night off from the club, and the confusing fact that James Franklin asked for my phone number when he's clearly dating Penelope. But in light of what happened tonight, everything I've worried about in the last two weeks—or ever, really—seems totally insignificant.

The scene with Casey went pretty well. I played a lawyer who interrogated her until she broke down and confessed to being the killer and wept, of course. While the stagehands whisked the table and chairs away, I had just a brief moment to change into my costume for the monologue in the tiny curtained area backstage. I don't know what I was thinking.

Well, I *do* know what I was thinking. I was thinking that my character is supposed to have just had sex with her boss, so she'd be wearing a bathrobe, and she'd be naked underneath. I mean, I had underwear on, but no leotard or slip or anything, so that I'd have the extra feeling of, what? Vulnerability or something? *No one will know*, I thought. It would just be my secret, a secret between me and myself that I hoped would give me some special edge over the competition.

But then it happened.

Who falls onstage wearing nothing but a bathrobe?

Why? Why? Why? Why?

The monologue was going so well, too, or at least I think it was. I'm not sure of anything now. The audience seemed to be laughing in all the right places. That's actually what threw me, I think. Their laughter threw my whole rhythm off—having to wait until it died down before I could continue. But still, it was all okay until I tried to sit down. The stage was just so dark. And the lights were in my eyes. It was like that dream I always have where I'm frozen onstage, confused about what play I'm supposed to be doing, so nervous I lose the ability to speak.

But it shouldn't have been complicated to find the *one piece* of furniture on an otherwise bare set. A chair—just *sit* in a chair, how hard can that be? I should never have planned to sit; that was my first mistake. My character wouldn't sit anyway—she's too agitated about having just slept with her boss. Why did I ever decide she should sit? If only—*no, don't think about it.*

And then I *just* missed the chair. Just by the tiniest bit. I could tell when I started to sit down that the chair wasn't where I thought it was, wasn't totally beneath me, but I thought I had it, I really did.

It's just that Jane's silk bathrobe is so slippery—much more slippery than the terry-cloth one I used in rehearsals. I was excited when she loaned it to me because it's exactly the sort of sexy thing you'd wear if you thought you might sleep with your boss, and I thought the bold blue and white flowers would help me stand out. I should never have borrowed that robe. If only I'd stuck with the terry-cloth rehearsal one, none of this would have happened.

To my horror, the robe flew open as I slipped. I mean positively billowed open, as if I'd passed over a subway grate.

There's no way at least some of the audience didn't see at least some . . .

Oh God, don't think about it.

And then what happened? Did I say something? I think I said something, after I thudded to the floor and scrambled to cover myself with the loose ends of the robe. There was a moment of awkward silence, and I didn't know what to do, and it felt like everyone in the audience was holding their breath, waiting for me to say something.

What was it I said?

Oh yeah.

"WHO PUT THAT THERE?"

Oh no, is that what I said?

Yes, that was it. I have no idea why. It doesn't even make sense.

"Who put that there?"

How stupid! I just couldn't think of anything else.

They laughed though. I think they laughed. Maybe they gasped in horror. No, they definitely laughed when I said that. They gasped when I fell, that's what it was. Was it a gasp of disgust, or were they merely expressing concern for my safety? I can't remember. It doesn't matter anyway. Either way, I blew it.

Maybe it wasn't that bad, I try to convince myself as I emerge from the dark theater into the hallway where the dressing rooms are. Maybe no one saw anything too revealing. Maybe I caught the left half of the robe in time.

"Hey, Franny, nice ass."

Oh Great. Charlie saw the whole thing. Everyone already knows. Everyone knows I fell. They saw everything. I'm humiliated.

"What's that?" I say, trying to buy myself some time to figure out how to respond with dignity.

" 'Nice class,' I said."

"Huh?"

"Right? Everyone seems to be doing well tonight."

"Oh, right. Yes, they do. Did you, by any chance, see my monologue?"

"No, sorry. But I heard part of it on the monitor. Sounded like you really went for it."

"Oh, thanks. Yes, I do think I went for it, part of it at least."

"Cool. Well, good luck with the callbacks."

The callbacks. I forgot about the callbacks. There's probably no hope of one now. But maybe it wasn't as bad as I thought. Maybe there's still hope if only, I can't help thinking—if only I stayed standing, if only I hadn't missed the chair, if only I made better undergarment choices.

I want to ask someone how bad it was exactly, but the backstage area is so small that all the students here now are waiting for their turn and too nervous to talk. Anyone who could have been watching from the wings is probably downstairs now in the green room, smoking cigarettes and talking about themselves. As much as I want feedback, I don't feel like going down there. I can face one person trying in vain to convince me it wasn't so bad, but not a sea of pitying faces.

Instead, I duck out into the alley behind the theater. I figure I'll just have a smoke and be by myself and maybe figure out what actually happened.

But of course, I'm not the only one who thought of the alley, either; five or six classmates are already out there smoking and talking in hushed tones.

"Hey, how'd you feel?" Don asks, looking genuinely interested.

Don can be catty and competitive, but he's also a walking theater encyclopedia. He has a huge collection of Playbills he inherited from his father, who was a Broadway director, and he's memorized them to the point where he might actually believe he not only saw every one of the productions, but was in them, too.

"I'm not sure. I think there was something weird in the monologue, but I'm not sure what."

"I didn't see it," Don says with a shrug.

What a relief! News hasn't spread. At least, not yet.

"But I heard some of it on the monitor. You dropped a section," he says, his eyes narrowing.

"I did?"

"Yeah. You dropped the stuff about how your mother knows where you go on Monday nights, and how she has a crush on your boss, too. But it was just a couple of lines. I'm sure no one noticed."

Don turns back to his conversation, and my head starts spinning. I dropped a section. I fell, exposing a yet-to-be-determined portion of my naked body, *and* I dropped a section. That information destroys the last bit of hope I had that, despite the obvious blunder, it might have gone better than I thought.

I picture the audience, the agents and casting people I'll probably never get to meet now, and I'm suddenly and overwhelmingly tired. I wish I could go home. I wish I could go back to Brooklyn and get in bed and hide, but I have to wait until everyone is done and help clean up the theater and then get feedback from Stavros, as if there could be anything to say to me except "don't fall next time."

I don't feel like running into anyone else, but there are no other places to hide. I could wait in the lobby, but the audience will be letting out soon. Maybe I'll just stand outside and then slip back in when people start leaving. At least I can be alone outside.

Avoiding the greenroom means avoiding my coat, and after only a few minutes of loitering in front of the theater, I'm already shivering. But it feels good, too. I want to feel something that is actually something. A feeling that is identifiable and real.

A sense of gloom creeps over me. The cold is helping me think more clearly and I can almost put into words this ominous thought I haven't yet named.

Then, all at once, it comes to me: *What's the point?*

If I left show business tomorrow, no one would know and no one would care. And what kind of person wants to work in a business that's completely indifferent to her efforts? If I stayed, no one would thank me for my presence, either. I'm not exactly Alexander Fleming, who discovered penicillin, something people are still thankful to have. If I'd never come to New York, someone else would have taken my place: in class, on the train, as a waitress at the club. No one would be sitting at home saying there's something missing from this Sally's Wear House commercial. No one's thankful that *I* did it. No one would say, "If only Frances Banks had done more. What a contribution she could have made! Think of all the lives she could have saved by wearing that fuzzy acrylic sweater."

I feel a tap on my shoulder.

"Aren't you cold?"

It's James Franklin. The last person I want to see right now. Nothing could make me feel worse after what happened tonight than to be reminded that a guy I gushed all over got my phone number but never called me. Even after I learned that he and Penelope were some sort of couple, I held my breath every day for the last two weeks while waiting for the machine to rewind, hoping he'd left a message. But he never did.

James smiles at me and stamps his feet, rubbing his hands together and blowing on them. He's wearing his green army jacket and his blue and red striped scarf. Standing this close to him for the second time, it occurs to me that his scarf is homemade, and I feel a pang of jealousy, wondering who knit it for him.

"I like to be cold," I say, in what I hope is an appealing yet mysterious way that will make him regret not calling me, while trying not to shiver. "Did you—were you just in there?" I ask, eyeing him carefully. Please, God, say no.

"In the audience? Yeah. I was standing in the back. It's over. They just had curtain call. Stavros is giving his little speech about how to fill in the callback sheets. They'll be coming out in a minute."

I missed the curtain call, forgot there even was one. I missed the chance to bow with everyone and to be seen one last time actually upright on two feet. And the callbacks. Stavros will be collecting the response sheets right now, where the agents and directors and casting directors will put a check next to the names of people they want to see again. Suddenly I'm deeply, freezing cold. I hug my arms around myself, trying to warm up, and stare down at my feet, attempting to look tough.

"You sure you're warm enough? Want my coat?"

"No, thanks, I'm fine."

"Well, take this at least." James unwraps the long striped scarf from around his neck and drapes it over my head, winding the ends round and round. I want to protest, but my knees are shaking from the cold, and I'm afraid I'll cry if I speak. Besides, it does make me feel better to think he wouldn't be offering his scarf to me if it were some precious item an old girlfriend had made for him. This small bright spot in my otherwise miserable evening emboldens me.

"So, you saw me fall?" I might as well just get it over with. I want to know how bad it seemed from someone who saw it.

"Yeah, but that was nothing. You'll laugh about it someday. You really held it together well."

That's not what I wanted to hear. People who are admired for "holding it together" are not people who are about to get agents; they're people who are recovering from cancer, or undergoing a murder trial.

"And I dropped a section," I add, hoping he'll say he didn't notice.

"Yeah, I know. But I only know because I'm obsessed with that guy's work. No one will dock you for that."

It's not exactly a glowing review, but he doesn't seem totally horrified. Still, he's avoiding the thing I most want to know.

"But when I fell—I mean, how bad was it? Was it really—"

"Can I tell you the truth?" James looks very serious. He's going to tell me it's even worse than I thought; I can tell by his face. Why does he have to be the person to deliver this information? I'll never be able to look at him ever again.

"Sure." I pull myself up a little taller, steeling myself for what's to come.

"Usually you . . . I hope you take this the right way . . . you're usually kind of, covered up, I guess? In the way you dress? But tonight, and I hope you won't be offended by this, but what I saw tonight told me, well, you've got a very pretty little body under there. You should show it off more often. Not just by accident."

James turns red and stuffs his hands in his pockets, and holds my eyes with his. I don't even care if he's lying to make me feel better, because I do; I feel better. I want to say thank you, maybe even give him a hug, but then the heavy theater door bursts open, and Penelope appears in a short, blinding white fur jacket. She smiles when she sees James, but then her gaze shifts back and forth between us and her eyes dart down to his scarf around my neck, and her smile seems to crack, her eyes narrowing a bit. She recovers in an instant, though, and cocks her head at me, making a sad face and pushing out her lower lip in a little pout.

"You poooor thing," she says, coming toward me with her arms outstretched. "C'mere, sweetie. I bet someone needs a *hug*." She encircles me with a surprisingly strong grip and lays her head on my chest, rocking us both back and forth like we're an eighth-grade couple slow-dancing to "Freebird." "Awwww," she whispers into my clavicle.

Arms welded to my sides, I look helplessly over Penelope's head to James.

"Uh, Pen?" he says gently. "I was just telling Franny how the chair thing wasn't really a big deal . . ."

"Well, of course not!" she exclaims at full volume, releasing me with such force that I have to take a step back. "Not a big deal *at all*!"

"I was telling her the performance was still there," he adds.

"Absolutely!"

"And that she'll laugh about it someday."

"Of course she will!" Penelope nods, turning away from me and beaming at James. She slides over to him and slips her arm casually through his.

"Yeah, I'm almost ready to laugh about it now, in fact. Ha, ha, ha," I singsong.

James nods sympathetically at me, and slaps his knee in faux enthusiasm. Penelope smiles and then tries to stifle a giggle, but she doesn't seem to be able to control it, and it erupts and grows into a full-blown laugh that eventually spills out into a sort of snort. "Well, *that's* a relief," she cackles. "I mean, it *is* pretty funny." She's laughing so hard now that she's having trouble breathing. I smile like a good sport and chuckle a bit, trying to play along. I did say I was ready to laugh about it, after all, but Penelope is curiously on the verge of some sort of hysteria. She holds her stomach and bends over a bit, gasping for air. "The funniest part ... (*giggle, giggle*) ... is that ... (*gasp, cough*) ... *it isn't even Monday*." And she lets out a whoop that pierces the cold night air, then punches me on the arm in a way that's meant to be playful but is just hard enough that something in me snaps. She has an agent, she has a boyfriend, she didn't fall onstage tonight revealing her inaccurate choice of days-of-the-week underwear, and I'm inexplicably mad at her for no reason.

"Is that real?"

"Huh?" Penelope asks, still panting a bit.

"Your jacket. Is that made of real fur?"

This is mean. But my arm hurts where she punched it and I'm upset. I don't think I really care if her jacket is made of real fur. I guess if I thought about it, I would say I'd have to come down against fur jackets made of formerly frolicking bunnies, but it's not something I've spent a lot of time thinking about. And even if I give it more thought, and someday decide I'm very definitely against wearing the same animal that brings Easter baskets to little children, it's not really like me to judge someone else for her rabbit-related choices.

Penelope's face falls and she looks down at her jacket.

"You know," she says, "it *is* real. I wasn't sure about it myself. But it was my mother's, and so I figured, it's vintage . . ."

She trails off and absently runs her fingers over the silky white collar. When she looks up at James, he puts his arm around her and gives her a little squeeze.

I feel terrible now. I wish I had something my mother had left me, besides the baffling legacy of being named after a character in a J. D. Salinger story who does nothing more remarkable than pick at a chicken salad sandwich and a glass of milk and then faint on a bad date with a pretentious college boy. I wish I had something of hers that made more sense, something I could wear or look at and remember her by. But my mother accidentally went the wrong way down a one-way street, and after that, the sight of her books and blue jeans and white cotton shirts was too much for my father, and he gave them all away. How could he have known I'd be standing across from Penelope Schlotzsky fifteen years later, feeling jealous of her mother's vintage fur jacket?

Penelope is wearing her dead mother's jacket, and I'm trying to make a political statement about something I only decided I cared about five minutes ago.

"No—I didn't mean—I wasn't saying—is your mom—? That's so sweet. She passed it down to you, after she . . . ?"

Penelope scrunches up her usually unfurrowed brow, but then her eyes light up, and she throws her head back and laughs.

"Oh, you thought she's—? Oh hell no, my mother's not *dead*. She's alive and well and probably sitting by the pool at her condo complex. She just gave it to me to wear 'cause she thought it had a little Hollywood glamour in it!"

After I give James back his scarf, I duck back into the theater and run downstairs to get my coat and bag. The greenroom has almost emptied out now, but I have to face Stavros, and the results, and I'm dreading it. I'm fairly certain I've blown the one real chance I've had in over two years to achieve something. There will be another Showcase next year, but my deadline expires way before then and I refuse to break it. I refuse to become one of those people who can't accept the truth that it just isn't going to happen for them.

Something cold grabs my heart and my mouth falls open.

Maybe I've already become one of them while I wasn't looking.

Maybe I can't accept the truth that it just isn't going to happen for me.

Maybe I already know, but I can't admit it. How many more days of waiting do I really need before I have to face facts?

Maybe there's enough evidence already—I don't need to wait for the results of the Showcase to decide. Maybe I have to accept that time's up.

This revelation makes my hands start to sweat.

I've been in New York for over two and a half years. It took me that long just to get a semilucrative waitressing job and a commercial agent who sends me out sporadically. What acting job could I possibly get in the next few months that would tell me that this is absolutely without a doubt what I'm meant to do?

The theater is nearly empty. It's my turn to see Stavros. I can't keep him waiting. I'll tell him right away that I'm thinking of leaving, to make it easier for him to admit he thinks that's the right thing to do. Maybe he'll say he was planning on telling me he didn't see a future for me, and anyway he'll be relieved that I figured it out on my own.

Then I'll call my dad and tell him I'm leaving New York. "You're doing the right thing, honey," he'll say. "Now you can get your teaching certificate."

I imagine what a relief it will be to have a real job. I'll have a regular paycheck, and a desk and a phone and a fax machine. I'll have a computer, which hopefully will come with someone to teach me how to use it, and I'll have people to go out with sometimes after work for a drink at Bennigan's, who'll tell me about their boyfriend or their kid or a project they're working on in their garage. Maybe my work friends and I will talk about what we watched on TV the night before and I'll say, "You know, I tried to be an actress for a while."

No one will blame me for giving up. Everyone says it's impossible anyway. I'll be normal and maybe that's fine. Maybe my life story is to be a person with a normal job and a normal life. That's what most people have. I was wrong to believe I was any different. I'll call Clark. I'll explain to him that I'm finally ready to get married like everyone always thought we would. In fact, I kind of want to call him right now. Maybe I'll book a flight to go see him in Chicago after my shift tomorrow. My backup plan is looking pretty appealing right now.

I think of all the goodbyes I'll have to say. I'll miss my dad, and big, clumpy Dan, in a weird way. It will be hard to be without Jane, but Chicago isn't too far away.

It's the right decision. I know that now.

Slowly, I take the last few steps down the hallway toward the closed door of Stavros's windowless office in the back corner of the theater. I take a deep breath, then knock three times.

(Goodbye, New York.)

6

································

You know, Frances, you did really well tonight. You have two callbacks
and they're both with respected agencies but if I had my way you'd just
study for another year and not start auditioning yet. It's such a differ-
ent skill than the work we do here and you can develop some bad
habits so please whatever happens don't stop training. The business will
take your energy and class will be more necessary than ever; you have
to keep filling up the well. You're so young and God this business can be
so draining. I wish it wasn't the way but try to work in the theater. Don't
forget the goals you had for yourself. It's so easy to give in to a paycheck
but if you aren't doing work that feeds you and feeds the audience
you're only contributing to the worst in us as a society. We need to see
the human condition reflected by artists—that's what this calling
is—and don't forget that you have real ability and you're a gifted
comedienne, and that can have the worst traps of all. It's such a talent to
be able to make people laugh but God forbid you end up on something
joyless and soul-crushing like that show with all the nurses.

(Hello, New York!)

The first person I spot outside the theater is Deena, smoking with a
few other classmates. Deena is one of the older members of our class,

in her forties maybe, and is still sort of famous from a show she did in the '80s called *There's Pierre*, which I remember watching all the time growing up. But she never mentions it, so I don't either. She's one of my best friends in class, but I wonder sometimes how she feels about having gone from the lead of a hit TV show to commercials, which is mainly what she does now. And not the kind where she's playing Deena Shannon, formerly of the hit show *There's Pierre*, but just a regular actor pretending to like one brand of orange juice over another.

"Anything?" she asks, flicking an ash on the ground.

"Um, yeah, actually. I got two callbacks, with agencies."

"Yeah!" she says. "You only need one."

"I almost quit show business tonight," I say, a little breathless, still astonished to have gone from complete despair to something like euphoria in such a short time.

"Again? You just quit two weeks ago."

"I did?"

"You're a sensitive kid," she says, laughing. "That's okay. You'll get tougher. Let's have non-farewell-to-show-business drinks instead. I'm meeting Leighton at Joe Allen. Want to join?"

Deena and I sit at the glossy wood bar at Joe Allen, crowded with actors whose shows have just let out and patrons who've come from the theater. I almost feel as though I belong in this crowd tonight, or that it's possible I could someday.

"Absolute Agency! You're kidding me! Look at you." Deena hugs me hard when I tell her the news, her perfectly polished red nails squeezing my arms. "Rock star!"

"And another agency called Sparks."

"Sparks! That's Barney Sparks. It's just him. He's the whole of-fice. He's great—he's been around a long time." Deena holds her wineglass up, already half empty, and smiles. "Another toast. I'm really happy for you. It's a real sign of encouragement. I think you may make that deadline yet."

Later, Deena's boyfriend Leighton Lavelle walks in. He's tall, with a long nose and curly light brown hair that makes him look like a guitar player in a '70s rock band. Deena waves, and he slips easily through the crowd and kisses her on the lips. "Hello, Angel," he says and orders a drink from Patrick, the bartender, before claiming a space among the crowd between our bar stools, where his lanky frame just barely fits. I've met him a few times but I've never been this physically close to him. He won a Tony last year for *Shining Country*, and it's silly, but it takes my breath away to be this close to an award-winning actor. Some of his show makeup is still visible around his collar. I try to imagine what it might be like to have just come from a show on Broadway. The thought makes my heart pound, but to them, it seems to be no big deal.

"How was it tonight, babe?" Deena asks him.

"Not great. Shitty house. It's this stupid weather. They over-cranked the heat and it made them really sleepy." He glances down, shuffling his feet, then looks up and breaks into a grin. "Jesus. Listen to me. Blaming them. That's what we all say, right? It couldn't possibly be *us*, could it?" Deena laughs and so do I. He rolls his eyes at me, including me even though he hardly knows me. I allow myself to imagine I've just come from a show, too, and have my own theory on the temperature of the house and its effect on the mood of the audience.

"What about you, Franny?" Leighton says. "When will we see you out there?"

"I don't know," I say, and even the idea makes my head go light. "Someday, I hope."

Leighton's hand rests on Deena's shoulder as he plays with her dark, glossy hair. "And you, my love?"

"Probably never," says Deena, happily.

"But why not? It's every actor's dream to perform on Broadway," I protest, and she gives me an indulgent smile.

"I don't mean to shit on your dream, sweetie. But I'm mainly out of show business these days. This is as close as I want to be to that life," she says putting her arm around Leighton's waist. "I just lost what the point of it all was—and anyway, no one is exactly breaking down my door."

"You never know, sweetheart," says Leighton, "*The New York Time*s said some very nice things about her, Franny."

"Ancient history," Deena says, but she's smiling.

"And what about . . . ?" Ever since I saw Deena in class, I've wanted to ask about the series she did, and tonight, with a drink in my hand and the giddy flush of the day behind me, I'm finally feeling bold enough to bring it up.

"The show?" she says, sharing a look with Leighton, who smiles sympathetically.

"Sorry—I don't mean to . . ."

"It's fine," Deena says, shaking her head. "You, I don't mind telling." She takes a deep breath, and exhales with a sigh. "Well, it goes something like this: I did this play when I was just starting out—"

"The one *The Times* liked," adds Leighton.

"Yes, but I hadn't worked much after that, and, while it got nice notices, it was only a little thing, downtown, no money. I had, in general, no money at all. But my agent called—"

"Your *then* agent," says Leighton.

"Yes, a fellow who is no longer with us—"

"He's *with* us, generally speaking," says Leighton.

"But he's not my agent anymore—"

"A scumbag," Leighton says, winking at me.

"He would later reveal himself to be a scumbag, yes, but at this point I was still thrilled to have him, and he said—"

" 'I've got an audition for you, sweetheart,' " Leighton says, in his best sleazeball Hollywood agent voice. " 'It's something kinda special.' "

"He said 'the elements' were there," Deena continues. "I didn't know what that meant, but he made it sound important. It was a high-concept half-hour pilot, he said—'cutting edge' was the exact phrase he used, I believe. He said it had taken some convincing to get me an audition since I had no television experience, but they'd agreed to see me. So I read the script, and it doesn't seem like a TV show to me, but I'm used to reading plays where anything can happen, in the world of someone's memory, or whatever—"

"You were used to reading things that were abstract," Leighton says.

"Or imaginative, not totally set in reality, yes—so I'm picturing what it could be, if done correctly. Plus, it was very political—"

"It *was?*" I say, surprised.

"Oh yeah. Before they changed it and tested it and ended up putting it on Friday night? It was supposed to be the next *All in the Family*. So I call my agent—"

"The scumbag," Leighton says.

"I call the scumbag, and I say—what is this? Is this for real? And he says—" Deena pauses, as if the next part of the story is particularly hard to tell. "And he says, 'Only two things will happen with this: one—it's a giant hit and you're thanking me every year at the Emmys, or two—they'll make the pilot, it won't work, it'll never air. There's no scenario in between. If, for some reason, they put this on the air and it isn't a hundred percent fantastic?' he said . . ."

" '*It'll never last,*' " Deena and Leighton say together, then Deena slaps her palm to her forehead, as if she still can't believe it. "But he was wrong—it lasted for a long time."

"Right," Leighton says. "They fired the show runner, took all the politics out of it, replaced that with fart jokes, added that obnoxious kid to the cast—"

"York the Dork?"

"Him," Deena says. "And moved it to Friday night at eight, where it lay there, winning neither awards nor merciful cancellation, for seven years. Seven years of my career, of my youth! The guy who played the boss was a drunk, never showed up on time, York the Dork banged extras in his trailer, the head writer thought himself some sort of genius, and it was all a thoroughly miserable experience. And that, my friends, is the story of how I came to spend seven years on the very-definitely-not-cutting-edge series, *There's Pierre*."

"The talking cat from France!" Leighton says triumphantly. "All together now!"

"*Sacre bleu!*" we all say.

"Also why I'm mainly out of the business of show," Deena says.

"So why even keep doing it, then?" Leighton asks, a smile playing over his face, and I can tell he already knows the answer, but I lean forward, because I don't, and I've often wondered the same thing.

"Because, Leighton, as you well know, there's one thing I have left to do, one thing only that I actually care about, one last dream that hasn't been beaten out of me, and I won't leave this horrible business without it."

"Tell her, Dee," Leighton says with a grin. "Tell Franny what it is."

Deena turns, eyeing me from beneath her long eyelashes.

"Just about every actor in this city who's worth a shit has something on their résumé that I don't have. And I'm not stopping until I get it."

"What's that?"

"A part on a show that I can one hundred percent say I'm right for." She takes a deep breath and narrows her eyes and says, slowly and deliberately, "I won't quit until I get something on my favorite show: *Law and Order*."

"*You've* never been on *Law and Order*?" I say, surprised. "But you're perfect for it . . ."

"I know. I'm even Irish *and* Italian. Who knows cops and criminals better?"

"So, why? You haven't auditioned for them, or . . . ?"

"People known for being on the most ridiculed talking animal show of the last decade sometimes have a hard time being taken seriously."

"But that was eight years ago!" I say, indignant.

"Funny thing about this business," she says a little sadly. "It's hard to tell ahead of time what they'll forget and what they'll remember."

Eventually, the three of us stagger out of the bar, among the last to leave. We form a triangle on 46th Street, just like the one we had in the bar: Deena and me across from each other with Leighton in the middle. I realize I'm swaying slightly. The air is cold but gentler now, and I'm feeling giddy.

"I love you guys," I say, fighting back tears, and Deena gives me a big hug.

"Wow. You really can't hold your booze, can you?" she says, still hugging me.

"Well, I love you guys, too, so there," Leighton says. "Deena, my one true, let us to home."

"It's late, honey," Deena says to me. "You're taking a cab, right?"

It can be dangerous to take the subway all the way to Brooklyn this late. I should take a cab, she's right, but I'm too embarrassed to tell her I have only about eight dollars in cash on me, and probably less than twenty dollars in my bank account, so I can't even go to a cash machine. I'll get tips and a tiny paycheck at my shift at the club tomorrow night, which I'll take directly to the check-cashing place on the skeevy part of Fifth Avenue in Brooklyn, which will charge me almost a quarter of the check to turn it into immediate cash, but I can't wait the five to seven days for the bank to clear it or the electric bill will bounce. Jane is the best friend ever, but a bounced utility check sends her into a very dark place.

Without waiting for me to reply, Deena smoothly stuffs a twenty in my hand and hails a cab.

"You'll get me back next time. Keep in touch this week, okay? Let me know how it all goes."

As I fold myself into the backseat of the cab and wave goodbye out the window, Leighton and Deena wave back. "Sorry in advance about your hangover!" he yells, and Deena blows me a kiss.

I give the driver my address and though he grumbles about the distance to Brooklyn, he finally agrees to take me, and we race down Ninth Avenue. The neon signs that sometimes glare too loud and lonely seem warm and friendly now. Tonight, they blink cheerfully at me, almost in unison, as if in celebration, letting me know they're glad I decided to stay.

7

· · · · · · · · · · · · · · · · · ·

Back at home, I creep up our creaky stairs, letting myself in as quietly as I can so I don't disturb everybody, but then I remember that it's just me and Dan in the house since Jane is at work tonight. I take my shoes off in the living room anyway so I don't disturb the neighbors downstairs, and pad through the kitchen, hovering at Dan's door for a minute. I put my ear against it, curious to see if he's still up. I hope he is. I'm not ready to go to sleep yet. I want to share my news.

As if he can hear my thoughts, the door swings open, and I jump back just in time to avoid being smacked in the face.

But it isn't Dan. There, in a tortoiseshell headband and the pink terry-cloth robe with the green ribbon trim that's always hanging on the back of Dan's bathroom door, is Everett.

She lets out a gasp.

"Oh, my gosh!" she says, putting her hand over her heart, and for a moment I think she might actually faint.

"Sorry, it's just me," I say, trying not to look like someone whose ear was just touching her bedroom door.

I'm smiling at Everett, but my heart sinks. I must have missed her Chanel bag in its usual place on the dining room table. It's made of navy-blue quilted leather and has a gold chain instead of a strap, and she told me once it was a college graduation gift from her parents. She usually leaves it out on the table, and she always lays one of our cloth napkins underneath it. I'm fascinated by the bag, because to my knowledge it's the single most expensive item I've ever seen up close, but the napkin thing always bothers me, as if she's implying our housekeeping isn't quite up to her standards.

Still, Everett's perfectly nice, and I want her to feel welcome here. She has an apartment in Manhattan, and she almost never stays here in Brooklyn since she has to be at work in the city so early every day.

"Sorry," I say again. "Did I wake you guys up?"

"Heavens, no," Everett says. "Dan sleeps like the dead, but I have an important meeting tomorrow, and I've barely shut my eyes. Will you have some tea with me?"

I don't really drink tea, and didn't realize we had any in our mostly empty cupboard. Everett was clearly the one who bought the foreign-looking red tin canister, which she brings down from one of the upper kitchen shelves. It's fascinating to watch her scoop out the loose tea and pour the hot water out of the kettle. I'm mesmerized by her easy way with the awkward-looking spoon-shaped strainer that holds the tiny leaves, and by the diamond engagement ring that glitters on her hand. I wonder if she ever takes it off, and if it has a napkin it rests on at night, too.

"Milk or lemon?" she asks.

"Um, milk, I guess?"

Everett and I are the same age, but something about the formal way she does everything makes me sit up straighter on the sofa, as if I'm at the house of an older relative instead of in my own living room in Brooklyn.

"So, Franny." She dips her headband down over her eyes and flips it back to its home behind her ears, smoothing a nonexistent stray hair off of her forehead. "How is the whole acting thing going?"

I'm not sure how to explain it to Everett in a way I think she'll understand. What do I say? *"Oh, fine, thanks, today was great, but it doesn't take away my general fear that I'm not now nor will I ever be good enough."*

"Oh, fine, thanks."

There's a silence as we both sip our tea.

"My whole family just went to see *The Phantom of the Opera*," Everett says. "Have you seen it?"

"No, I haven't."

"Oh, it's wonderful. So magical! There's a giant chandelier that appears right out of the sky. We just loved it."

I imagine being in the cast of that show and having to listen to people talk about the chandelier as their favorite part. I don't know how to respond. Then I remember that Everett said she had a meeting the next day.

"I, ah, just found out tonight actually, that I'm going to have some meetings with agents," I say, trying to bridge the gap.

"Oh, meetings!" she says, like some people might say, "Oh, ice cream!" Or, "Oh, free diamonds!"

"Yep. I'm going to have two of them, actually. Two meetings."

"Ahhh. *Two* meetings? For your work? Is that . . . that's positive, right?"

"Yes, I—I just got the callbacks, the ah, meetings, tonight. They still have to be set up, though."

Everett nods but looks concerned, as if she's suspicious of having meetings with no date attached.

"It's *so hard*, isn't it?" she says, sighing and shaking her head sadly.

"It *is* hard, I guess. Well, I mean, which part do you mean is hard?"

Everett looks up at the ceiling as if she just noticed it existed, and blinks her large brown eyes at it a few times. Her profile is sharp, her whole body a series of angles that have somehow, improbably, folded themselves on their hinges into the soft chair. There's something so regal and linear about her. I can't imagine her ever collapsing into giggles or crying hysterically. She's taking her time to consider what to say next, in a way that suggests she's used to people waiting for her.

I wonder what that's like, to never worry about filling the silence. Her eyes eventually float back to me.

"Well, it's this. Between us girls, when I listen to you, I think about Dan, too, and frankly, I worry. I know he works hard, as hard as if he had a *real* job, but, how do you know? How can you tell if anything will ever come of it? How can you endure the waiting for someone else to, well, recognize you? How can you stand the *not knowing?*"

"I don't know, actually. You just do it, I guess. There isn't another choice but to wait and see, as long as you can take it."

"But how do you know when it's time to give up? I mean, in Dan's case, no one is telling him no, exactly, and like I said, I know he works hard, but no one's saying yes either. It's all sort of a, *a vacuum*, isn't it?"

"Yes. It can be, I guess." Everett isn't saying anything I haven't thought before, but there's something so depressing in her description, something less than comforting in her attempt to be understanding.

"In my work," Everett says, "in mergers and amalgamations, we're seeing a real boom. LBOs are still the cornerstone of the business, obviously, but the increase in global capital flows is translating to even more revenue. It's an exciting time. And there's real security there. We work hard, and there's a measurable gain, or, yes, occasionally, a loss, but at the end of the day, win or lose, we can all look at the same numbers and acknowledge we've accomplished something. It's *real*, you know what I mean?"

I nod vigorously, to show her I agree, but honestly, Everett's world doesn't sound like a more measurable one than mine at all, and the closest I can come to picturing what she's talking about is imagining numbers dancing around gaily on a computer screen while giant piles of cartoon cash rain down from the ceiling at the end of each day. My mind began to wander somewhere around "LBOs."

Everett is leaning forward now, cheeks flushed, and I'm trying to focus on the point she's making, yet I'm distracted by her diamond ring and how it catches the light, and her freshly manicured nails. They're so perfectly even, shiny and buffed. Or is that a gloss? Does nail polish come in the color of natural nail, or is that a clear color, and the skin under her nails just happens to be exceptionally pink? Is hers a style where you're supposed to look like you're wearing nail polish, or like you aren't? Does she use the same color on her toes, or does she go with something bolder? Is it classier in her world to match your fingernail color to your toe color, or would that be considered tacky?

"He really does, you know?" Everett is saying.

Shit. I've completely lost the thread of the conversation. I have no idea what she's asking me. "Sorry, who does what now?"

"Dan. He thinks you're really talented."

"He does?"

"Yes. I guess you did a, some kind of television commercial? And he saw you in something on Theatre Row, I think it was, just after he moved in. Is that Off Broadway, or, sorry, is that Broadway? You played two parts: a psychiatrist and something else, a French housekeeper?"

"A cockney maid. It was just a two-night thing. Not really even off Broadway. Very Off Broadway, I guess."

"Yes! That's it. He always talks about how he didn't recognize you as the maid character at first, because the two were so different. He was impressed. So there you go. One fan and counting!"

Everett seems pleased with herself, as though she's given me the gift of my very first fan, as if I have a jar somewhere to put them all in, and when it's full I'll be a legitimate object of the public's affection.

"Well. Thanks for keeping me company," she says, setting down her teacup with a delicate little clink. "This was a hoot. I've been dying to get to know you girls better. You're such good friends to my Dan. I'll leave you my number at the office. Maybe if you're in the neighborhood sometime we could schedule a lunch."

I smile in agreement, although I'm distracted by her use of "a" in association with "lunch." Is "a" lunch what corporate people have, leaving the rest of us stuck with regular old "lunch"?

"It's so funny," Everett sighs, as she unfolds herself out of the chair. "When Dan and I met at Princeton, he was pre-med. He was on a real path. But then he gave it all up, for this. I suppose we have to get these things out of our system, right? Like cutting one's hair too short on a whim, or backpacking through Europe?"

The lights have been out in Frank's apartment for hours. I should have fallen asleep by now, but I'm wide-awake. I've played the details of the Showcase over and over but for some reason, my thoughts have now wandered to trying to picture Dan and Everett in bed together. It's something I can't really imagine for some reason, no matter how hard I try. It's the headband—I'm having trouble picturing Everett without her tortoiseshell headband. I keep seeing her, still wearing it, getting into bed with him, snuggling up to him, whispering "I love you" in the dark. And maybe Dan wakes up a little and turns over and whispers "I love you" back to me.

An ambulance passes by outside, siren blaring, and my eyes fly open.

To *her*, I mean. He whispers "I love you" back to *her*.

Even though no one knows what I've been thinking, my face burns. I don't know why I'm having a silly twisted fantasy of wearing someone else's headband and being told I'm loved by a person I don't even think of that way, who's totally wrong for me. I think maybe I'm missing Clark.

Maybe I'll finally call him back tomorrow to tell him the good news. He left that message awhile ago but I keep putting off calling him, for some reason. Maybe I should wait just a little longer. Maybe he'd feel worse to hear the story of my little triumph—to hear that in some measurable way I might be inching closer to my goal here, which might mean moving farther away from him.

I'll wait, I think to myself, and for once, instead of the ever-present worry about my deadline bearing down on me, hurtling toward me, ever shrinking, I allow myself a luxurious thought:

I've still got time.

8

·················

You have two messages.

BEEEP

Frances, it is I, your father. The one from Connecticut. I say this in the event that your mail, which you've undoubtedly been sending me, has been rerouted to another father in another state. I've sent your check. Don't worry about the money. You don't have to pay me back. Just call me before we start Ring Lardner on Tuesday, okay?

BEEEP

Franny, uh, hi. (rustling, crumpled paper sound) *It's James. Franklin?* (sound that could be cigarette exhale, or just loud breathing) *Um, yeah. I was just thinking we could—uh, we should all have a drink sometime. So, uh, yeah.*

BEEEP

Things are really looking up. I actually got that Niagara laundry detergent commercial, and I've scheduled the two meetings with those agents, and James Franklin called, even though his message was sort of vague. But there it was anyway, his raspy, sexy voice on my machine, a voice I can't quite bring myself to erase. I played it over and over, until finally deciding I needed Jane's help to decipher it.

"He's asking me out, right?" I say, after replaying the tape for her a third time.

Jane shakes her head. "He said 'we all.' 'We all' is not asking you out."

"But why leave a message just to 'we all' me? I think he's asking me out, in his own way."

" 'We all' means: I asked for your number because I think you're cute, but I'm seeing someone so I'm trying to pretend to myself that I just asked for your number to be friends with you, and I'm asking if you want to have a drink sometime with me *and my girlfriend*, which will never happen, but it helps me feel like less of a shithead for asking for your number in the first place. You've been 'we-alled,' my friend. Now can we erase the tape? Remember what happened last time."

The Brill Agency had a hard time reaching me about the Niagara job, because neither Jane nor I noticed our answering-machine tape was full. So I decided to get a service, where they give you your very own phone number and an actual person who answers, as if you have a real office and he's your assistant. At first, it was thrilling to call in to see if I had any messages. But after a few days and no messages, I thought I detected a note of pity in the voice of the answering-service guy, so I had Dan call, just so I'd have a message to check.

"But what do I say?" he asked, looking baffled at the prospect.

"Anything," I told him. "Just give me a callback for something. Something believable, but a little impressive."

"I'd feel better if I more clearly understood the parameters of this assignment," Dan said, furrowing his brow.

"Dan, I'm late for work. Just pick a play and make up a theater. No one's grading you, okay? I just need the guy to think I have something going on." Even though he seemed flustered, I trusted Dan to treat the whole thing like the perfect student he is, so I was feeling pretty confident when I called in the next morning.

"Frances Banks's line," the voice said.

"Hello, this is she," I said primly. "Any messages?"

"Yes, Ms. Banks. You have received a callback for a play."

"Oh, great," I said with the kind of breezy confidence that told him I get callbacks a lot. "Can you give me the details?"

"It's for the role of Martha in *Who's Afraid of Virginia Woolf.*"

I'm about twenty years too young for that part, but at least Dan gave me the lead in something. "Oh, wonderful. Good old Martha," I said fondly. Maybe he'd think I'd played the part dozens of times. That would teach the anonymous voice to respect me.

"At the Old Horse Theater in Princeton, New Jersey," he said. Did I detect a hint of sarcasm in his voice?

"Okay, thanks." There was a silence on the other end. "Any other details?"

"Well, it's none of my business, but I'd never heard of it, so I looked it up, and that theater doesn't seem to exist."

He looked it up? How? In what? Does he just spend the day traveling around to towns in New Jersey trying to uncover fraudulent theatrical claims? "It's a small theater," I said, somewhat indignantly. "Small, but very well respected."

"Well, if you say so. We have the booklet of all the LORT theaters, A through D, and I didn't see it anywhere."

Ugh. There's a *booklet* of all the regional theaters? There are *categories*, from A to D? I didn't know any of that.

"Yes, well, it's new. They've added, recently, an 'E' category. E, for ah, experimental," I added lamely, and abruptly hung up.

The next day, I canceled the service, and Jane and I have pledged to be better message-erasers.

Only I won't erase James's message. Not just yet.

— — — — —

I had to join my first union, the Screen Actors Guild, which cost over a thousand dollars. I didn't have to join on my last commercial because they let you work once non-union, but on the second job you're required to join. Due to the fact that I have eighty dollars in my bank account, I called my dad to ask him to send me the money Western Union, which he said he would, although it took me awhile to explain why my getting a job was costing him a thousand dollars.

"Why can't you pay the union after you get paid for the job?"

"I can't do the job unless I'm in the union."

"But they let you audition for the job even though you aren't in the union?"

"Yes."

"And they know you're going to get paid because it's a union job they let you audition for. And now they know you have to join the union because they know you got a job."

"Yes."

"They know you're going to get paid, because they know you're going to get paid by them, but they won't wait for you to get paid by them before you have to pay them?"

"Dad. Yes."

"And I thought Marx was confusing."

Then I had to take a shift off from work. Herb said it was my second warning, and I'd better be careful not to miss another shift for at least a month, or he would think I didn't take my work seriously.

That afternoon, the call sheet that tells me what time and where I'm supposed to go comes through the fax machine, and my heart leaps to see my name is very first on the list under "cast." Under "character" it says "Wife." On the other commercial, I was listed as "Sweater Girl #3." I can only dream of the day I play someone with an actual name.

My alarm goes off at four thirty A.M., and for a minute I think I'm being robbed.

"Hello?" I say into the darkness. Then I remember.

I'm ready in record time, and I hurry to catch the train. The other riders are similarly bleary-eyed and the car is quieter than normal. At 72nd and Broadway, I get off the subway and walk a block toward the park before I realize I'm heading in the wrong direction. I walk quickly back west, not waiting for lights to change, weaving through the cars. The traffic isn't too bad yet, and the sun is still low in the sky. I pass a few trucks parked on 72nd, flanked by orange cones and signs stapled to the electrical poles that say "No Parking Allowed—Permit to Film."

This must be the shoot, *my* shoot. A stocky girl is standing on the corner by the trucks, wearing a giant fur hat with earflaps and speaking into a walkie-talkie.

"Hi, excuse me," I say. "Uh, what is this, uh, for?"

"Mayonnaise commercial," she says gruffly.

I'm in the wrong place. How can I be in the wrong place? How can there be two commercials shooting in the exact same location?

"It's a commercial," I say, just to be sure, "for mayonnaise?"

"Yes," she says, as if I'm thick. "Excuse me." And she turns her back to me.

I circle the block, jogging a little, looking left and right, starting to sweat. There's nothing else that looks like it could be my location. No one will be at the agency yet to help me. I don't have a watch on, but I'm sure I'm late now.

Finally, I circle back to the mayonnaise commercial, where massive trucks are being emptied by burly guys carrying loops of electrical cord on their shoulders and sandbags with a sort of nylon handle in their hands.

The earflap-hat girl is still on the corner, now smoking a cigarette and talking to a guy who's wearing a heavy-looking leather belt with a walkie-talkie hanging from its holster. She sees me coming and her eyes narrow.

"Uh-oh," she says out of the corner of her mouth.

I almost keep walking. I don't want to talk to her again. She obviously thinks I'm some sort of mayonnaise fanatic. But I need help.

"Hi, sorry, me again. I know you told me this is a mayonnaise commercial, but I'm an actress, and I'm supposed to be shooting a commercial for Niagara detergent? And it's supposed to be near here somewhere, and I didn't know if maybe you guys all know each other or something—"

Her face totally changes and she drops her cigarette. "They're looking for you," says the guy with the walkie-talkie belt.

"Oh shit," says the girl. "I'm sorry. I thought you were—hi. I'm Mavis. I'm the second-second. Let me show you where your trailer is. Can I take your bag for you?"

Mavis walks heavily in front of me, babbling all the way.

"I'm so sorry, I usually work on features with like, you know, famous actors, not that you're not . . . shit, anyway, and that's what they always tell us to say when people ask what you're shooting, you say 'mayonnaise commercial,' because no one wants to know who's starring in a mayonnaise commercial, so it keeps people moving and not hanging around asking questions and trying to catch a glimpse of Russell Blakely, or whoever, but I should have—the character is just listed as 'Wife' on the call sheet, and no offense but you don't look old enough to—I mean I'm sure you'll play a great wife, but . . ."

As she prattles on, I realize I'm experiencing a feeling I've never had before, something I can't quite put my finger on. I was completely intimidated by Mavis and her hat and her walkie-talkie, but now everything has changed and she's apologizing to me, trying to make me feel good. She's treating me as if I'm important, as if she works for me. I've never even had an employee, and I don't want Mavis to feel the way I felt ten minutes ago.

"Well, here's your trailer. Hair and Makeup are in the next one, see that big trailer with the pop-out? Someone from Wardrobe will be here in a second with your changes, and I will tell them I made you late, it's a hundred percent my fault and I will tell the director—"

"Mavis," I say, stopping in front of the door to the trailer.

"Yeah?" she says, her eyes squinting into the sun, almost hidden by the furry front of her hat.

"This is my first real shoot. I don't know anything. For instance, I have no idea what a second-second is."

Mavis smiles and seems to relax. "Second assistant to the second assistant director. I basically tell you where to go when, and am in charge of the general awesomeness of your day. Want some coffee?"

"Um, sure. Where is it?"

"I can get it for you."

"No, no, that's okay, I'll get it." I don't want to get on Mavis's bad side again.

"Okaaaay. It's just that they need you in Hair and Makeup right away, and it's sort of complicated to explain where crafty is. I can get it for you. Unless you need . . . do you like it a particular way or something, in a way that you think is too complicated for me to make?"

I'm trying to be polite, because of course I wouldn't dream of asking someone I've never met to fetch me coffee, but somehow it seems as though Mavis thinks I'm being rude by not allowing her to get it for me. I don't know where I'm going wrong. This world seems to have different rules from the other world I've been living in all of my life. I wonder if I'll ever learn them.

"No. Nothing special. I guess, okay, um, just milk and sugar, if it's no trouble."

"No trouble," Mavis says, in the way people say "no worries" when they have lots, or "no biggie" when something is a colossal headache.

From the minute I walk into the wardrobe fitting, in a trailer near mine, I'm confused. There are two giant rolling racks, one full of tan trousers, one stuffed with thirty or forty identical blue shirts.

"Oh, are there . . . are there more people coming?" I ask a harried-looking woman nearby. She looks at me as though I've said something strange.

"What? Oh, the racks? Noooooo. These are all for you."

"But, aren't these all the same pants?" I say, laughing a little.

"Well, no, there's actually quite a variety," she says gravely, indicating that, to her, pants and their similarity to one another are not a laughing matter. "I'm Alicia, by the way, the costume designer."

I wonder how Alicia feels to have the title "costume designer" when it refers, in this case, to the choosing of one blue shirt and a pair of khaki pants.

"Sorry if it looks like a lot, but they aren't sure if they want a twill or a gabardine, and don't get me started on their limited comprehension of the stirrup pant. God forbid they allow for a little *fashion*. Anyway, we'll have to try them all on. The client is very specific about what they want. I fought for jeans as an option, but the client didn't want to make too urban a statement."

I don't know who "the client" is, but already I'm worried about their opinion of me and their strong conviction regarding khakis versus jeans. So I obligingly try on endless pairs of pants, which all look the same to me, and pretend to agree with Alicia, who finds them all very different.

Finally, Alicia finds a pair she likes, except they're a little snug in the waist.

"These are perfect. Let's Polaroid these, too. We might have to cut them in the back, though," she says. "You guys really shouldn't fudge your sizes, you know?" She attempts a smile, but I can tell she's irritated.

"I didn't fudge my sizes," I say, as nicely as I can. "At least, I don't think I did."

"Well, what jean size did you give them?"

"Um. Eight maybe?"

"In inches, I mean."

"I'm not sure. I didn't know they made pants in sizes like that."

"Well, that's how they size jeans now. It's probably where we got the signals crossed. Don't worry. You're sitting most of the time, thank God, so we can improvise. Like I said, we can cut them if we have to."

I can't believe she's going to cut a brand-new pair of khakis just so I can sit down in them for a few hours. And I feel guilty that I'm not the right jeans size.

"What's a *good* size to be? In inches, I mean."

Alicia looks thoughtful, then seems to decide I'm worthy of being educated. She takes a deep breath.

"Well, I usually do features." She pauses, somewhat dramatically.

"Uh-huh," I say, confused as to whether that's my answer.

"So like, on this last feature I did, I worked with Cordelia Biscayne?" She raises her eyebrows.

"Oh, wow." I'm trying to look as impressed as I can tell Alicia wants me to be.

"Yes, I know. I was one of the assistants to the designer, but still. Cordelia's a *doll*, by the way. And anyway, her jean size is twenty-six, twenty-seven. Yours is probably, twenty-nine or thirty? So," Alicia says, sympathetically. "Not that you should feel bad—I mean, you look fine, and not everyone can be Cordelia Biscayne, right? But, something to aspire to."

Of all the lists I've made of goals, and all the visions I've had, it never before occurred to me that I could be this specific, that I could aspire to a goal actually measurable in inches. I wonder if this is how successful people do it. I wonder if the difference between success and failure could more accurately be described in the waist sizes for jeans. "Well, I'm doing all right, I guess," I imagine myself saying, "but I'm about three inches from where I really want to be." I think of how much effort it has taken me to even be a 29. I can't imagine what else I could do to be a 26. But it makes sense, too, that the Cordelia Biscaynes of the world are literally measurably different from the rest of us.

Three inches might as well be three hundred to me today.

"Hi, I'm Carol, I'll be doing your makeup. Any allergies or preferences I should know about?"

I'm looking into a giant mirror on a wall of mirrors, each framed by dozens of fluorescent lightbulbs. In the blinding light, my face looks nothing like the face I have in Brooklyn. I wonder if this is my real face, or if the face I have in Brooklyn is the real one, and what my Queens face might look like.

"Um, no, not that I can think of," I tell her. I wonder if I will, over time, develop preferences, and what they might be in regard to my face being made up. I hope I do this long enough to have time to acquire some, so I don't feel so unprepared for these types of questions.

She snaps a switch by her station and what seem like a hundred more round bulbs spring to life.

"Wow, do I really have all those freckles?" I just can't get over how different my face looks in this mirror.

"Mmm, let me see." Carol puts on the glasses that hang on a chain around her neck and brings her face just inches from mine. I hold very still, as if I'm being examined in a doctor's office. "Well. You have some freckles, it's true. I don't think they're distracting, though. I don't see them as a problem, but I can even out your skin tone if that's what concerns you." Carol sighs. I don't think she likes me.

"Okay, great. Whatever you think. Thanks."

"Want a magazine?" she asks.

"Um, yes, sure. Thanks. Again."

I'm not sure whether Carol is generally grumpy or if I made her that way. I thumb through the copy of *The National Enquirer*. MICHAEL GOES AFTER ELVIS' $200 MILLION! CORDELIA BISCAYNE SHOPPING SPREE! CANDICE BERGEN DEATHBED DRAMA! I wish I'd brought something else to read. This magazine makes my stomach hurt.

So many people on a set to get to know, I think, while skimming PRINCESS DI'S LOVE LETTERS! So many names. How can I remember all the names of all the people I'm meeting in just one day? But isn't it rude to not at least try? *Mavis, Alicia, Carol*, I say to myself. *Mavis, Alicia, Carol.*

"Do you like to do this yourself?" I look up from my magazine to find Carol waving a strange metal object in front of my face. I have no idea what it is or what it might be used for.

"I'm sorry—what is that?"

Carol peers over her glasses at me in surprise. "You've never seen one of these before?"

"No."

"But of course you have. It's an eyelash curler! I'm sure your mother has one."

My mother could have had one, it's true, but I didn't have my mother during the time I might have been interested in what it was, something I don't feel like explaining to Carol.

"Oh yeah, probably," is all I say.

Carol brings the menacing instrument to my face, clamping my lashes between the narrow opening and then squeezing hard. I feel as if my whole eyelid is being stretched up and over the top of my head, and my eyes start to water.

"Feel okay?" she asks.

"Fine," I say through gritted teeth. I want to ask Carol if I can do the second eye myself, but I'm afraid I'm already on her bad side, so I endure the discomfort once again. When she's done, my lashes look like the ones on a doll I had when I was little whose eyes never closed, even when you laid her down.

Finally, I'm done in Makeup and shuttled two chairs down to Hair. "Hi, I'm Debra, I'll be doing your hair." (*Mavis, Alicia, Carol, Debra.*) Debra is a black woman with dimples who appears to be about fifty, and not grumpy at all. "Look at those curls! You sure you don't have one of my people mixed up in your family?" She laughs, squeezing my shoulder. "Don't you worry. I know just what to do with this mess."

Miraculously, she does know what to do. Instead of trying to flatten my hair, she curls it with a curling iron, which is the last thing I would ever have thought of. It makes all the curls look neat and shiny instead of the irregularly frizzy, uneven way they usually look.

Debra tilts her head and regards me in the mirror. "There we go," she says, wrapping a curl around her finger, smoothing it down. "They'll drop a little more, too, by the time we're on set. Pretty girl." She pats me on the head and starts unplugging her irons.

I smile at Debra, and the person in the mirror with the Manhattan face and hair smiles back. I look so little like me, the Brooklyn me, that I can actually enjoy looking at myself without most of the usual dissection. Maybe the trick is for me to always be in some sort of disguise, to always be dressed to play someone else. Only then can I really appreciate myself.

"The client," as it turns out, isn't one person but a group of seven people, five men and two women, all with suits and shiny hair, whose names I barely catch, so I don't even try to add them to my list. One by one they shake my hand and introduce themselves, and then I don't see them for the rest of the shoot. I do periodically get reports as to their levels of enthusiasm delivered from behind the video monitor where they're watching.

"The client loved that take," Bobby the director (*Mavis, Alicia, Carol, Debra, Bobby*) occasionally says, or, "The client is wondering if you could smile more?" I sit in a chair and do the monologue into the camera lens, my too-tight khakis split open in the back, my too-loose shirt gathered with an industrial-looking clamp sticking out from the middle of my back. From the front I look put together, but every other angle would reveal how false the front of me is, how much effort has gone into presenting a one-sided image of perfection.

Bobby is an easygoing guy in his thirties, with very curly brown hair spilling out from underneath his New York Mets baseball cap. He seems to have a lot of confidence and shakes my hand with a strong grip. He's wearing jeans and a blazer with running shoes. He tells me he usually does features, so this shoot should be a snap.

"I lit this very softly, too, so the freckles will sort of fade. I heard you were concerned." He looks at me directly and with gravity, the way I imagine a doctor might say, "You have leukemia."

"Oh, that's, no, I wasn't saying . . ." I want to tell him it's all a misunderstanding, but I can't figure out how to explain without sounding like I'm complaining about Carol the makeup artist. I decide it's too complicated.

"Okay, yeah, thanks."

I say the exact same lines over and over again until they lose all meaning. Someone with a stopwatch times me, and for about four hours I'm either speeding up or slowing down by increments of one second, two at most. Takes that are twenty-eight seconds strangely feel longer than ones that are twenty-six. Smile more, smile less, tilt my head, talk to the camera like it's my best friend, raise inflection on the name of the product, but don't sell it, not too much, not too little, have fun with it, now really have fun with it. Finally, some combination of speed, inflection, enthusiasm, or just exhaustion makes them say, "That's it! That's the one!"

I'm confused, because I know they have done lots of different shots: close-ups of my hands and suds and the laundry coming out of the dryer. I know they will use all the different pieces and somehow assemble them into one coherent piece, so I don't know why it was so important to get that one perfect take, but I'm too shy to ask, as if revealing myself now as the novice I really am might make them doubt their satisfaction with me.

I shake the hands of the client, one by one, and say thank you, goodbye, I had a great time, which is sort of true, and a brunette in a blue suit says, "You were adorable! You remind me a little of myself at your age." Then, she leans closer and whispers in my ear, "Don't worry, I hated *my* freckles, too."

9

....

Barney Sparks, of the Sparks Agency, answered his own phone when I called. He must have been having phone trouble on his end, because he practically yelled the address at me and told me to come by the next day around noon. His office was far across town in the West 40s near Ninth Avenue. I figured the safest way to get there was to walk across on 42nd Street, which is not my favorite route because it's full of hookers and places advertising live peep shows of various kinds, and drug dealers who walk back and forth trying to sell what sounds like "sense sense, sensamelia." I know that's some sort of drug but I'm not sure what kind exactly, or even if I'm hearing it correctly. It's a harrowing walk but at least there are lots of people, whose presence, although somewhat freaky, makes it less likely there will be no witnesses when I'm abducted and forced into prostitution.

It's four flights up to Barney's office. I'm puffing by the time I make it to the top. There's no secretary sitting at the desk in the little front room.

"Hello?" I say to the emptiness.

"Back here, dear!" comes a loud and raspy voice.

There's a desk with a window behind it and bookshelves on either side, which are stacked to the ceiling with scripts and old Playbills. The titles are written in Sharpie on the edge of the pages so they can be read when stacked face-to-face, and the block print is bold but shaky. Barney wears a light blue sport coat and has thick white hair cropped very close to his head. The whole place smells like cigar smoke and dust, but there's something comforting about it. I'm afraid my nervousness is obvious, especially when I discover that the only way to sit in the one huge armchair opposite his desk is to sink into it and be swallowed. I fight the chair for a minute, trying to perch daintily on the edge, and then give up and sit back, which at least might make me look relaxed.

"Frances Banks!" Barney bellows.

Even with his hearing aid turned all the way up, he tells me, he doesn't have the greatest sense of his own volume. He never raises his voice to people intentionally, but he's always loud. He says volume is his trademark, and the community respects him for it.

"Frances Banks," he says again. "Great name! A classic! You can BANK on BANKS! I can see the headline in *The Hollywood Reporter*." He takes a deep, rattle-y breath, which he seems to have to do anytime he strings more than two sentences together. His breathing is labored and, like his voice, astonishingly loud. "A classy name for a classy gal! Look at YOU! You're a throwback! A girl next door, with looks like Ava Gardner. Unfortunately you didn't get her chest—but HEY! I saw your little show thing the other night. My favorite part was when you FELL."

I'm smiling, but I'm not sure whether he's teasing me or not. "You're kidding?"

"No, dear. I'm a sucker for a klutz. It's where you see what some-one is made of. My father, the great Broadway director Irving Sparks, always said: 'Anyone can smile on their best day. I like to meet a man who can smile on his WORST.' I was his assistant, as a younger man, just nineteen years old, sitting in the very last row in the audience of *Best Foot Forward*, when a red-headed chorus girl took a terrible spill. She got right back up and never stopped smiling. I waited by the stage door to see if I might hail a cab for her, and that's how Mrs. Sparks and I began our fifty-two years together. But HEY. Did I ever tell you about Ruth Buzzi?!"

I wonder if Barney remembers it's our very first meeting ever.

"Um, no?"

"Wonderful actress, a DOLL, a real cut-up." Wheeze, rattle, gasp, then: "They called me from the Coast one time, looking for a 'Ruth Buzzi TYPE' for a new variety show, and I told them, I can do better than that, I've got the real thing! I represent RUTH BUZZI. They said they'd call back. They never called. She didn't get the job. TRUE STORY. Someday, dear, I predict they'll be asking me for a type like Frances Banks. Now tell me, what is it you picture for yourself in this terrible business?"

It's been a long time since anyone asked me that, and I feel suddenly shy. I'm embarrassed to tell a stranger, even a kind one, all that I've been hoping for.

"What a dumb question I'm asking! It's torture telling someone what you want when you don't have it yet, isn't it?" Barney says. "How are you supposed to know yet, am I RIGHT?"

That makes me laugh. "Yes!"

"As my father, the great Broadway director Irving Sparks, always used to say: 'We all have to start somewhere.' So start somewhere, anywhere, and give me an idea of what it is you'd like to do. Tell me EVERYTHING. What is your DREAM?"

"My dream? I guess, honestly, I just want . . . to . . . to work. I really want to work. Here, mostly, in New York. In the theater. That's what I've pictured."

"Theater is wonderful, I agree, although I think you have a face for film, too," he says, slapping himself on the chest to help a few coughs escape. "Theater WAS wonderful, IF you were Ethel Merman back in the day. Now SHE had a paycheck. Theater is NOT wonderful today, IF you want to eat, or have a grand apartment, but HEY! Who am I to argue? I'm here to help YOU."

I feel a surge of pride at Barney's compliment. "I have a face for film" is the kind of thing I could imagine Penelope saying easily about herself, but I'd never dare.

"Now listen, my dear, I have a good feeling about what I saw onstage that night, and I would like to help you get started. SO." He claps his hands together once, for emphasis, as if he's just pulled a rabbit out of his hat and wants to make sure the audience sees it.

I'm stunned.

He just said he wants to work with me. I thought it would be so much harder to get anyone in the professional world to say that, ever. An actual real live agent wants to represent me.

I don't have to do this alone.

I'm shocked.

"What? Is that . . . but . . . really?"

"Yes, dear, really. My father, the great Broadway director Irving Sparks, always said: 'Cream rises to the top.' You, my dear, will rise. AT SOME POINT. Who can say when? THAT is a matter of timing, and luck, and how badly you get in your own way, BUT. There you have it. I know CREAM when I see it."

More than anything, I want to say yes. I have a gut feeling about Barney Sparks that tells me he's the one for me. But something is holding me back. It would be so easy to say yes and leave this room with an agent. Almost too easy. I look around the room, and the walls of old scripts and Playbills that seemed warm and friendly when I first came in now look cluttered and shabby. The leather on the arms of this giant lumpy chair is worn thin, the stuffing is peeking through one of the seams, and the sunlight streaming through the window is cloudy with dust.

I stammer a bit.

"You know, thank you so much, but this is my first, that is, it's all so new, and—"

"You want to think about it. You have other meetings. That's wonderful, dear. You just give me a call whenever you're ready."

I lurch up from the depths of the giant armchair and clumsily gather my stuff. The meeting is clearly over, but I don't want to leave yet. Something is holding me back, and I pause for a beat in the doorway.

"You all right, dear?" Barney booms. "You have other questions you'd like to ask?"

"Oh no, thank you. I just wanted to say thank you again. Also, I guess I was wondering if you have any advice for me?"

"Wonderful question. I've been around a long time. I'm full of advice. A few things I always tell my actors, should you become one of my actors."

"Yes?"

"My father, the great Broadway director Irving Sparks, always said: 'Don't tell stories of a job you almost got. Learn from a loss and don't dwell on it. Move on."

"Okay. Makes sense."

"Also, I've found, when you're starting out, it helps to keep a written record somewhere of your auditions. Write down who you met and how you felt about it. Write down what went wrong or right. Get yourself one of those, what are they called? Mrs. Sparks has one. A fax."

"A Filofax?"

"That."

"I've already got one!"

"Well, look at YOU," he says, beaming. "And dear, if you should someday become famous, don't write a cookbook."

"Um. Okay."

"Not a deal-breaker, if you're some sort of Julia Child–type person. Just a pet peeve of mine. Actors should ACT. Not sell perfume, or write cookbooks."

I don't know what to do with this information.

"Okay!" I say brightly. "Then I'll keep my baked ziti to myself."

I've never made baked ziti in my life, and with more time I probably could have thought of a more innately funny food, but for some reason it makes Barney Sparks laugh anyway. "Baked ziti! Sounds HORRIBLE!"

His wheezing guffaw follows me down the stairs.

When I get home from the club that night around two A.M., Dan is on the sofa with a beer balanced between his knees and a black-and-white movie playing on the TV.

"Let me guess—Fellini's *8½*?" I say, letting my messenger bag slide off my shoulder onto the floor by the front door. I'm happy someone's up, happy not to come home to a darkened house after the long day I've had.

"Very good!" he says, looking impressed.

"It's not that hard to recognize—you must've rented it five times already this month."

"I know," he says, smiling sheepishly. "I hope I'm not driving you guys crazy. Jane was watching it for a while but gave up and went to sleep. She said the last time she sat through the whole thing she dreamt she was eaten by her pillow. It's almost over—want to watch the end with me?"

I plop down beside Dan on the couch, and take off my shoes to give my aching feet some relief. "It's about a director making a sci-fi movie, right? Is that why you like it so much?"

"Well, it's about a director who's in crisis: he's blocked artistically, he's lost all interest in the movie he's making, and his personal life is a shambles. The fact that he's making a science-fiction movie is supposed to show that he's lost all creativity. He's looking for meaning in his life and his art."

"Oh, is that all?"

"Yup. Just the plain old, everyday quest for the meaning of life."

A beautiful actress wearing glasses says something to the director, played by Marcello Mastroianni. Her mouth keeps moving even after her voice has stopped.

"The sync seems off."

"It was the style of Italian filmmakers of the day to dub all the dialogue in later," Dan explains, eyes still pinned to the screen. "And since they weren't concerned about recording the sound live, Fellini famously played loud music for the actors during the scenes to inspire them, and had the actors speak generic lines that he replaced later when he decided what the real ones should be. That's why their mouths don't match what they're saying, but also why the movement is so fluid. They are actually, at times, dancing to music."

"How beautiful!"

On a white sand beach, a procession of the characters from the film mixed in with people dressed as circus performers and clowns, all wearing white, parade by. Then the scene shifts abruptly to a circus ring, empty except for the child who played the young Marcello Mastroianni, who plays the flute as the spotlight on him fades to black. The End.

"Huh," I say, baffled.

"The end is supposed to show that he's come to terms with who he is—it's supposed to show he's been healed."

"Huh," I say again.

"I know. Fellini can be abstract," Dan says, eyes gleaming. "Watch it with me from the beginning sometime."

"I will." I smile back at him, noticing for the first time the flecks of green in his brown eyes. The room seems too dark and quiet suddenly, and we're sitting too close together on the sofa without the glow of the screen and the sound of the movie in the background to keep us company. I stand up quickly and pick up my shoes from the floor. "I should get to sleep."

"Sure. Me too," Dan says, rising and clicking off the TV and the VCR. "Wait—you had that meeting today, right?"

"Yep."

"How did it go?"

"It was good, really good, actually. But I have nothing to compare it to yet, and I think I should go through the process, you know? So I'm going to take a beat, and, you know, keep my options open."

I sound odd to myself, as if I'm playing the part of a professional actress who has meetings all the time and is sort of blasé about them. I loved Barney Sparks, I want to tell Dan, but I'm suspicious of anything that seems too easy. I'm not sure why I can't say that now, and not sure why I didn't jump at the chance to say yes in Barney's office.

It feels like I'm an actor in an Italian movie from the '60s, saying the placeholder lines into the camera, waiting for the real ones that come later.

10

·················

Joe Melville, senior agent at Absolute Artists, has only one opening, at three thirty on Friday. Then he goes to London to visit a client on location, and his next appointment isn't for at least another two weeks. At least that's what the girl with the British accent and clipped tone told me over the phone. I don't want to wait. Everything could change by then. Joe Melville might forget all about me by then.

But I'm supposed to be at the club at four thirty on Friday. I need my Friday shift—I need the money—but if you're even one minute late for a shift, Herb sends you home and calls one of the servers he keeps on call for the night. It's a brutal setup, but it ensures that we're always on time and Herb is never understaffed.

Still, I figure I have a shot with Herb if I tell him the situation up front.

"Herb, there's a slight—and I mean very slight—chance that I will be a few, a very few, minutes late on Friday, because I have a big meeting with a really big agency." I don't usually brag like that, but sometimes Herb is impressed by that sort of stuff. He likes taking credit for all the people who've come through the club, people he treated like shit but then gets sentimental about after they've become successful.

"If you already know you're going to be late, I have to take your shift, Franny," he says sternly.

"No, no, I don't know for sure that I'm going to be late. That's what I'm saying. I probably won't be, Herb—it's only a chance."

"That's a chance I can't take."

Herb watches a lot of cop shows.

"Forget it," I sigh. "I shouldn't have even said anything. I'll be on time."

"Ricky!" Herb yells to my waiter buddy Ricky, who's busy filling up salt and pepper shakers, "Take Franny's shift on Friday."

"Herb!" I'm panicking now. I really need the shift. "No. Forget it, I said. Never mind. I'll be here, I swear. I'll leave in plenty of time."

The comics at the bar—the ones who still drink—overheard the whole thing and they chime in, calling Herb an asshole to his face and buying me a shot of tequila, which they insist I do in front of him. The only people Herb lets boss him around are the comics who still drink, because they're the funniest and he doesn't want them to turn sober. Herb tries to scare them, puffing up his chest and announcing, "I'm the boss around here," but his voice comes out high and squeaky and that only makes them laugh, so finally he gives up, retreating to his office in the basement.

The offices of Absolute Artists are on the thirty-second floor of a sleek glass high-rise building on 56th Street near Fifth Avenue, in the middle of countless stores and apartments I could never afford. I come to this part of town only once in a while to go to Central Park, although I like our park in Brooklyn just as much. The streets are wider here and the buildings are much taller than downtown, and lots of people are wearing suits and carrying briefcases and crossing the street dangerously in the middle of the block. It takes me a minute to figure out west from east, but I finally manage to find the building, where I have to sign in with a guard and write down the time and the name of the agency in a huge book in the lobby.

The guard calls up and says my name to someone on the other end. I'm nervous while I wait to be approved, as if I'm sneaking in instead of going to an appointment. It reminds me of when I was sixteen and trying to get into a bar in East Norwalk with a fake ID. I'd spent the whole ride in the car memorizing Joyce Antonio's older sister's birthday, but when instead of asking my birthday, the bouncer asked me, "What's your sign?" I was caught.

But this guard doesn't throw me out. He hands me a paper badge with my name printed on it and says yes, it's okay for me to go up.

The elevator empties out around the twentieth floor, so I quickly try to use the smoked mirror walls to check my face and hair and outfit. I'm wearing my black stretchy turtleneck with my black wool miniskirt, black tights, and Doc Martens lace-up boots, and now I can see in the reflection in the elevator mirror that the skirt is too short. I try to pull it down, but then my sweater isn't long enough, and if I pull the skirt down to where it looks better, an inch of my stomach shows.

We need a better mirror in Brooklyn, I realize, a proper full-length one that doesn't require me to stand on the toilet to see my lower half.

Maybe this explains why I haven't gotten more jobs. I've only seen either my upper or my lower self; I haven't seen the whole thing all at once in a long time. Maybe my upper-lower unity is not what I thought it was. Regardless, I should have bought a new outfit for this meeting. In a store with a full-length mirror.

I need a full-length mirror. I need new clothes. I need a longer skirt. I should go back to Brooklyn and change.

The elevator doors open.

The reception area is a soothing soft gray. Everything is plush and velvet. The carpet looks like shiny gray silk, and the sofa is a silvery suede that appears freshly brushed, as though no one has ever sat on it. There is a long reception desk, behind which sit two of the most beautiful people I have ever seen, also swathed in gray. The perfect-specimen male is reading a script, and the perfect-specimen female is on a headset talking to someone in a British accent—maybe she's the one I spoke to. Since they both seem busy, I don't know which one to address, and for a minute I stare dumbly back and forth at both of them. I worry that maybe the guy should be taking a call because the phones keep ringing, although phones here in Gray Land don't really ring, rather they ding politely and at a very low volume.

"Hi, uh, hiya, I'm uh, I have a . . ."

"Hello, Ms. Banks, welcome to Absolute Artists." The guy smiles and stands up, emerging from behind the desk to shake my hand. To my relief, his smile seems genuine and he actually seems friendly. "My name is Richard; I'm Joe's number two. I was just sitting on the front while Pamela ran down for lunch. I'll let Joe know you're here, but in the meantime would you like a glass of water, or a coffee, or an herbal tea perhaps?"

I'm so momentarily confused by what a number two is, how someone can be sitting on the front of anything, and why it's three thirty and Pamela's just getting lunch, that suddenly I can't remember what I like to drink or if I like to drink, or even if I'm thirsty. So rather than answer Richard, I find myself pondering—*do* I like herbal tea? It always seems like something that I should like more than I do, though some flavors taste like dirty bathwater. Or maybe I don't like it on principle, because I know it's supposed to be healthy. If it was filled with calories and fat, would I like it more, and why oh why am I thinking about this right now? This is hardly the time to make a ruling on such a difficult subject.

"What, no scotch?" I say, and I can immediately feel my face flush red. I put my hand on my hip in what I hope is a jaunty manner in an attempt to cover for the fact that I'm trying too hard.

Thankfully, Richard smiles. "I wish." Then he gestures for me to follow him down the hall, leading me back to a conference room with a large oval table and about ten chairs positioned around it.

"Joe will be right with you," he says. "You're going to do great.

I'm actually the one he sent to the Showcase, and I told him you were fabulous." He smiles as he closes the heavy door behind him with a click.

The mention of the Showcase still makes my face burn. I'm hoping he didn't tell Joe Melville about *that* part of it. I wonder if people will be tapping me on the shoulder in the subway for years to come. "Excuse me, can you tell me what day of the week it is?" they'll say, and laugh.

I'm leaning awkwardly against the wall near the door, not sure what to do while I wait. Maybe I should sit. Plenty of people use sitting as a way to pass the time. I look at the giant table and multitude of chairs. Unless a bunch of people are going to join us, this seems a strange room to choose for a meeting of two.

Yes, I think, *I'll sit*. But I'm not sure which spot to choose. I'm not totally sure I even want to sit yet, but if I do, it's hard to tell what the right chair to sit in would be. There are so many to choose from.

I wonder if this is part of the audition, and the chairs are a test. I wonder if I'm being watched on a hidden camera. I wonder if I should be worried about the alarming frequency that the concept of being watched on a hidden camera occurs to me. But if I *were* being watched, what chair would the people sitting behind the monitor in the hidden control room consider the right one? Does Absolute Artists work only with people who'd choose to sit at the head of the table? Does that say "I'm a star"? Is that the kind of boldness they're looking for, or does it send the wrong message? Does that chair say "I think I'm so special and important that I'm deserving of the best seat in the house," and therefore does that tell them I'm going to be very demanding to work with?

But, on the other hand, why would they want to work with anyone who would choose a chair in the middle? Isn't that a choice that says "I'm totally mediocre"? Isn't that like choosing a supporting part when you could have had the lead? If I make that choice, I might as well announce to everyone that I have terrible insecurities and can't imagine myself ever being the star of anything, not even of this conference table.

This is silly. I'm way overthinking this. I'll just pick a random chair.

I'm in mid-sit when the door behind me opens, nearly hitting the one I've chosen.

"Franny Banks. Hello. I'm Joe Melville. Please, have a seat on the end."

Shit. I picked the wrong one. I awkwardly reverse my halfway-lowered position to stand back up so I can shake his hand. He directs me to a seat at the head of the long table. Then he sits a few chairs away, in one of the side chairs, which throws me. I sort of expected him to sit in the power seat at the head of the other end of the table so that we'd face each other from across the long distance, the way they do in movies about kings and queens, or couples who don't like each other very much.

Joe Melville looks like he works in a law firm or a bank, not like someone who works with creative types. His dark blue suit fits perfectly, and his skin is taut and smooth and pink and almost shiny, as if he just got a facial and a steam before entering this room. His glow makes me feel sloppy and underdressed. Because he sent Richard, who's obviously a junior person from the office, I've been informed that I have to do my Showcase monologue again for him.

Once we're seated, Joe stares at me for a moment, and I'm not sure if I should just start my monologue or make small talk by asking him a question, or if I should wait for him to ask me a question or tell me to start. I already feel nervous, since it seems odd to try to do in someone's office what I did in the theater, which had the energy of the audience and the other actors from my class. We were lit with bright lights, so you couldn't see the audience very well. But here in this bright office, Joe Melville seems so close to me that I could see every expression on his face, if he were to make any.

"Why don't we get started," he says. "Please go ahead and begin your monologue whenever you're ready. We can chat afterwards. Take your time."

His words are encouraging, but his face is neutral at best. And when there are two people in a room and one of them is there purely to see the other person do something, the notion that that person could actually "take her time" seems ridiculous.

But I try. I try to take a deep breath, but the air gets sort of stuck and doesn't go down all the way to my lungs. I need a minute to calm down, but I can't possibly take it. Are there any actors out there who would go bow their head in the corner or step out in the hall and hum or meditate or jump up and down, or do whatever they liked to do to warm up, to "take their time," making Joe Melville just sit by himself and wait for them? Maybe somebody could do that, but not me. I'm going to start right away, to show him I'm ready, that I'm always ready to go.

I start my monologue, the same one I did in the Showcase. Over and over in the play my character says, "I'm thirty-two years old," as if that should explain everything that's wrong in her life. I don't know what it's like to be thirty-two, but I can imagine. I imagine that she means she's stuck in an in-between time, she's at an age that isn't a milestone but more of a no-man's-land, an age where she's feeling like her hopes are fading.

That I understand.

When we performed the Showcase in the theater, I was standing up at first, but in this room the table makes that awkward, so I decide to stay seated the whole time. The chair I'm using is a cushiony office chair with wheels, and I become aware about halfway through the monologue that I've been sort of sliding back and forth in it, the chair-with-wheels equivalent of pacing. I steady my feet on the floor and command myself to stop moving, which causes me to forget my next line.

Shit.

I've totally lost my place.

I pause, trying to stay in character. I look out the window as though I'm (she's) having an important thought. If I relax it will come to me; if I panic it will not. That's what I've learned in class. If I relax it will come to me.

If I panic it will not.

Relax.

Relax.

Finally, after what seems like a long time, too long, the line comes to me. I finish, then smile awkwardly at Joe to let him know, in case he isn't sure, that I'm done.

"Delightful," he purrs. "Very funny." His voice sounds warm, but his face still doesn't move very much. I can't tell if he actually liked it or not.

After a moment, he clasps his hands in front of his face, pointer fingers up, resting on his pursed lips church-steeple-style. Then he taps his lips with his fingers a few times.

"So tell me, Ms. Banks," he finally says, "about yourself."

"My, uh, self?"

"Yes. I'd like to know what brought you here. Why you came to New York. What kind of work interests you?"

"Um. Well. Theater, mostly. I want to work in the theater and be a real actor, not the kind with a perfume."

"A . . . ? I'm sorry, what about perfume?"

"You know, I want to act, rather than have my own perfume."

"I see. Although one of our clients, Cordelia Biscayne, is having wonderful success with her new perfume, Helvetica."

"Helvetica? That's a perfume?"

"Yes. Surely you've seen the ads: 'Wear the font that fits'? She's really got her finger on the pulse of the recent boom in computers."

"Oh. That sounds great. I mean, I can't wait to, uh, smell it."

"Now tell me, what was it that drew you to acting?"

He waits for my answer, but instead of coming up with a response, I find myself imagining what Joe Melville would be like if he were ever nervous or jumpy or at home wearing a bathrobe. I try to picture him vulnerable in any way, but I can't imagine him anything but calm and self-assured and glowing and pink. I'm not sure if I like that about him. I'm not sure if I like anything about him.

But mostly, I'm not sure if he likes me, and that means that I have to win him over.

"Why do I want to be an actress?" I say, repeating the question idiotically, trying to buy myself some time.

I hate that question, I want to tell him. I don't really have an answer.

It's just the way my brain works, I want to say. It's as if I don't have a choice. I read something about someone and I start to imagine being that person. I see someone on the street or onstage or on TV or anywhere—it doesn't even matter whether it's a real person or an actor playing a character—and if the person or character is interesting in some way, I put myself in his or her shoes, imagine what it would feel like, what I would say or do if I were that person.

I don't remember deciding to do this as a career, I want to tell him. There wasn't any one day where it came to me. My mother died and I started pretending it didn't happen to me, started imagining what it would be like to have someone else's life story, and pretending became a relief. It wasn't a conscious decision. Moving to New York was a decision, but wanting to be an actor was always more of a given. I feel like it chose me. I can't say that, though:

"It chose me." That sounds completely pretentious.

"I feel I have something to say as an artist," I hear myself say. This is an even more insane response, because it isn't true; I've never even thought that before, and it's a much more pretentious thing to say than the thing I thought was too pretentious to say but that was at least closer to the truth. There's something about Joe Melville that makes me act like someone I'm not sure I like.

He doesn't say anything, so I feel obligated to keep going. It's as if I'm not driving this train anymore. I'm just holding on, trying not to crash completely.

"I've always loved the theater," I say. *Thank God*. It isn't original, but it's true at least. "My dad would take me when I was a kid to whatever little show was playing in our town in Connecticut, and we'd also see most of what was in New Haven, and sometimes we'd come into the city, and it wasn't just theater—it was ballet and music and modern dance, too." I pause. "He teaches English," I add, nonsensically, as if that explains his interest in modern dance.

Joe Melville nods blankly, as though what I've said isn't totally uninteresting, but also as if he might be thinking of something else entirely, like the stock market, or peas. I was determined to win him over, but now I'm feeling jittery and light-headed, and it occurs to me that I uncharacteristically forgot to eat anything this morning. I'm suddenly dying to get out of here. I just want this meeting to be over.

"You realize, I'm sure, how competitive this business can be. Are you ready for the competition?"

He arches one eyebrow, ever so slightly, like an evil character in a children's story.

Of course I know how competitive it is to be a working actor, because all anyone tells you is how competitive it is and how only 5 percent of any of the union members make enough money to live on, and out of those 5 percent only 2 percent make a lot of money, which Jane says must mean that Bruce Willis pays for everyone's dental insurance. Of course I'm worried about how competitive it is.

"Oh, I'm not worried. I'm very competitive. I'm from a very competitive family."

"Sports?"

"God no. No. That's hilarious to think about." I laugh, picturing me and my dad—who have been known to spend an entire weekend sitting in the living room reading books one after the other, stopping only to eat a frozen pizza or make popcorn—playing tennis or skiing or kayaking down some rapids.

"Competitive, like, I always made everything a game when I was a kid. I have a good memory and so does my dad, so we'd try to stump each other, like try to start reciting 'Jabberwocky' from the middle. Or I would test myself, like, a song would come on the radio and I would pretend I was in the final round of a million-dollar *Name That Tune* tournament, and I had to guess the title before the chorus started or I'd lose everything. And I was always imagining how to make a tough situation work. Like when the L.L.Bean catalogue would come in the mail, I would pretend I had to get all my clothes for the rest of my life just out of that one catalogue, which might seem easy because they have a lot of variety at L.L.Bean, but not if you think about what you would wear to your wedding."

I'm a little out of breath. I think I've been talking for too long.

Joe Melville is silent for a moment, then asks, "Your wedding?"

"Yes. Or prom. There's nothing in L.L.Bean for that kind of stuff. Unless you were one of those kids who was really alternative and weird and you could pull off wearing madras pants and duck boots."

I think I should really leave it at that.

"And a hunting cap," I add.

Joe Melville is staring at me.

"With a monogrammed tote bag," I blurt out. "As your purse."

I laugh a little, trying to cover for the fact that I know I've strayed too far from the question, but it comes out more like a witchy cackle.

"Also, I should mention, I just booked a national commercial."

"Mm-hmm," Joe says, not looking very impressed. "Those can be a wonderful source of income."

I've lost him entirely, I can tell, but I'm going to try one last time to save myself. I take a deep breath.

"My point is, about the competitive thing? I've always naturally made everything a competition in a way, so I already know I'm tough, and it actually comes sort of easily to me, and I'm not afraid to be hurt or rejected because I have naturally low self-esteem anyway, so I always expect the worst, which is weird because I also have a vision for myself where I can totally picture succeeding—well, almost totally, on a good day. And I'm quick and I'm sure that whatever I don't know yet I can learn quickly, because I'm quick, which I know I just said, because I'm quick—ha ha, get it?—but seriously, for example, today I've quickly learned that if I don't eat anything all day except a giant coffee, I'm bound to crack and start talking about the L.L.Bean catalogue."

I try to smile confidently, but then I hold the smile for a moment too long, as if I'm posing for the family Christmas card, and after a beat I have to drop my eyes and let them rest at the tops of my shoes. I have no more energy for pretending, but I need to pull myself together because I feel like I could start crying. This has all gone totally wrong, not at all the way I'd pictured it. My life story today was supposed to be me exuding composure, and having far less of a gap between the bottom of my top and the top of my skirt. Once again, I've been thwarted by the massive difference between my vision of the successful me and the me I'm currently stuck with.

I force myself to look back up at Joe Melville, expecting him to be frowning, to be horrified, to be speed-dialing security.

But Joe Melville is smiling. Really smiling. It's the first undeniable human emotion I've seen on his face. And then he starts to laugh. I think. Yes, I'm sure of it. He's laughing, and although it's not exactly audible, it's as close as I suspect he comes to having a laughter-like response. He's nodding his head and smiling and sort of rocking back and forth.

"Franny Banks, you're a funny girl," he says. Then he tilts his head to one side and gently shakes it a bit. He's either having a thought or he's got water in his ear from a recent dip in the pool.

"I have a thought," he says.

Well, at least I got that one right.

"Tell me—are you . . . have you taken other meetings?"

"Other . . . you mean . . . other agency meetings?"

"Yes."

"No, well, yes. I met with Barney Sparks. The Sparks Agency?"

Joe gives me a look as though I've said the right thing. "Aww, yes, I remember old Barney. Wonderful agent, in his prime. But you've signed no papers?"

"Papers? No." I think of Barney in his office, with his shabby blazer. I was sure he was the one for me, but I had nothing to compare it to. Thank goodness I didn't sign anything, thank goodness I waited, because I suddenly very much want to be wanted here, the place with the silky gray carpet and the phones that chime in an elegant way.

"There's a casting session going on right now, just down the street. They're seeing a few of our clients for a large recurring role, but there's another part they mentioned—very small, you understand, smaller than I'd normally send a client of ours to. But I'd love for them to meet you, and see how things go. I know it's last minute, but are you free?"

I'm supposed to be at work in something less than thirty minutes. If I leave now, as I'd planned, and get a cab, which isn't a sure thing during rush hour, I might make it there on time. If I go to a casting call, even one just down the street, I'll definitely be late to work, which I swore to Herb I wouldn't be, which could mean he'll take my shift away tonight and maybe take my next shift away, too, and maybe even get mad enough to take away my job entirely.

"Sure," I say to Joe Melville. "I'm free."

11

·················

I've hatched a plan, but it all hinges on Ricky, the waiter who almost got my shift that day. And so far, all I'm getting is his machine from the pay phone outside Absolute Artists. Ricky has a very long outgoing message, in which he performs a combination song from *Evita*/Cher impersonation, and it seems to take forever for the beep to finally happen.

"Ricky. Ricky. Ricky. Ricky. It's Franny. Ricky, pick up. Please pick up. Please oh please oh please—"

"Franny! You're so sweet to call! Wow, everyone must really be talking. I'm thankful, really, for all the support."

"Ricky, thank God you're there. I have a favor—I'm wondering— well, the thing is, I just got an audition for *Kevin and Kathy*. I'm supposed to be there right now."

"Oh." Ricky sounds disappointed. "So you're not calling about my . . . Is *Kevin and Kathy* even still on?"

"I know. That's what I said, too, to the uh, the agent. But yes. It's in its ninth year or something, and it isn't on right now, it's on break or—hiatus, I think he called it, waiting for a time slot, but it's going to air again soon and—"

"Wait. So, did you get an *agent*? From that Showcase thing?"

"Um, I'm not sure, I think so. Maybe."

"Already?"

"Uh, like I said, it's not, totally . . . but maybe, yeah."

"Huh. What's the part you're up for?"

"It's just called 'Girl Number One.' "

"Huh. So you're not calling because you heard about my show?"

"No, I'm sorry, I was calling to see if you could take my shift tonight."

"Oh. Your shift. Hmmm. I don't know, Franny. Why don't you just let Herb call one of the understudies?" he asks, a little too innocently.

"Ricky, please, you know how crazy that makes him. I thought maybe if you showed up, he'd get confused, since he was trying to get you to take the shift the other day, and maybe that's what he'd think had happened, that we did what he originally asked and maybe he'd, uh, get confused, like I said, and I wouldn't get in trouble."

I sort of trail off at the end, because saying it out loud makes my shaky plan sound even flimsier.

Ricky takes an excruciatingly long, deep breath.

"Fine."

"Fine? Yes? Oh Ricky, thank you so much—really, I owe you one, big time."

There's a pause on the other end. Maybe I haven't gushed enough.

"Thank you, really. Thanks again. I should go, ah—"

"Frances."

"Yes?"

"Aren't you going to ask me about my show?"

"What? Yes! I'm sorry. Tell me."

"Well. I'm pretty excited, actually. I just got booked to do my one-man show, *Insights*, in the basement of Hooligan's."

"Hooligan's? That's great! That's—where is that again?"

"You know. The Irish bar on Second Avenue. It has the basement where Claudia did her poetry reading."

"Oh yeah! *That* Hooligan's, yeah, such a great space. Congratulations."

"I was supposed to have a rehearsal for it tonight, in fact."

"You were? Shit. I'm sorry. Thank you again. At least, you know, you won't have to call too many people. To reschedule your rehearsal. Since it's a one-man show. And you're the one man, right?"

I chuckle nervously into his silence, but eventually manage to get off the phone with more apologetic thanking and promises to be the first in line for his one-man show.

Riding up in the elevator to my audition, I think about the basement of Hooligan's. I've performed in an evening of one-acts there, and in far worse spaces, but I allow myself to imagine those days are behind me. Maybe this is the elevator ride where I go from amateur to professional, in just twenty-five floors.

"Excuse me," I say to the receptionist, whose metal desk has a paper sign taped to it with "Kyle and Carson Casting" written hastily in black Magic Marker. "I'm supposed to pick up the script for the 'Girl Number One' character?" I can see she has a very small television hidden behind her desk. She seems disappointed that she has to look away from it to deal with me.

"What?"

"Sorry. I'm looking for the Girl Number One sides?"

She eyes me dubiously.

"Joe Melville sent me?"

At the mention of Joe's name, half of the dozen or so heads in the waiting room snap to attention. I feel a combination of embarrassment and pride. I shouldn't have said it so loudly, but I like the way it sounds.

"You're here for the Laughing Girl?"

"I guess so, if that's the same thing, uh, yes."

"Laughing Girl has no lines. She just laughs."

"She just—so there's no, uh, scene?"

"Nope. She's a girl. She laughs. They want a funny laugher. That's it. Take a seat. They'll be with you in a minute."

I squeeze onto the lumpy sofa next to a skinny brunette wearing high-heeled black boots and funky glasses. I should wear high-heeled boots instead of Doc Martens, I think to myself, as I break into a nervous sweat. I should get some funky glasses. I should have a funny laugh.

Funny laugh. Funny laugh. Why can't I think of a funny laugh? I should make a list of things I might have to do at a moment's notice. There are the things we all know we're supposed to have: monologue—comedic and dramatic; song—up-tempo and ballad. But there's a serious lack of information beyond that. Today I need a funny laugh, but what else should I know how to do? Roller-skating, maybe—that seems to come up a lot lately. Jokes. I should know more jokes, in case I ever get asked if I've heard any good jokes lately, but I'm not a good joke-teller; I always mess up the endings. Maybe I should try to memorize a knock-knock joke at least, just in case.

Focus. Focus. Funny laugh. *Shit.*

I'm not naturally a particularly funny laugher, and I'm at a loss to think of anyone who is. Wait—Barney Sparks had a funny laugh, but that's one I don't think I can duplicate. There's too much naturally occurring lung blockage in his laugh for me to attempt to reproduce it, and trying could possibly cause me to faint. Who else laughs funny? It seems all I can think of are people who have completely normal ways of laughing, or Fran Drescher from *The Nanny*. But that's *her* laugh. It's only funny the way she does it. Or is that what they want? Someone who can copy someone else's already funny laugh, rather than try to invent a better one? Now all I can think of is the laugh from *The Nanny*. Maybe that's what I'll do, then. I can't think of anything else. I'll just try to do a really good version of the laugh from *The Nanny*.

The girls are coming and going out of the audition room with incredible speed. It seems like they're only going in and laughing, then leaving immediately afterward—no discussion, no chitchat. I realize I can hear some of the laughs through the thin wall, and can therefore tell which actresses they're responding to and which ones they aren't. I try not to hear, try to keep my mind set on what I've decided to do and not get distracted by someone else's funny laugh. But I can't help it—I hear a girl do a kind of honking thing that gets a big reaction—maybe that's what I should do. Honking's funny. I'll do a honking, nasal laugh, like I have a cold or—

"Frances Banks, you're next."

Shit. I'm not ready and I'm the last one left in the room. I'd ask for more time, but there's no one to go in front of me.

And suddenly I'm facing four people who are looking back at me, and I still have no idea what I'm going to do. A man with glasses sits in the closest chair.

"Hello there, Ms., uh—Banks, there we are. As you've probably figured out, we're looking for your funniest laugh. You can begin whenever you're ready."

"Okay, great!" I say, too forcefully. "So should I do it into the camera, or . . ." I'm looking around vacantly, not sure where to focus, somehow not finding where the lens is.

"Ah, there's no camera here today, since there's no scene, exactly. Tell you what. Why don't you just do it for Arthur here," he says, pointing to a painfully thin man with red hair and freckles to his left, who looks not exactly happy to have been chosen as my target.

"Okay, great. Can I just, sorry . . . I have a question?"

I think I catch an eye-roll from the other man in the back.

"Sure."

"What is she—what am I—laughing at?"

There's a moment of silence in the room, as if no one's sure how to answer my question. Or maybe they're shocked at the stupidity of it.

"Well, it's just mainly a gag, you know?" says the man in glasses.

"A gag," I repeat.

"Yes. A running gag. Like how she laughs on *The Nanny*?"

"But we don't want it to sound anything like her laugh," the man in the back of the room says emphatically.

"Yes, of course, it's a laugh that's all her own—just a girl who laughs funny. For no particular reason," the man with glasses says.

"Okay, thanks. And, sorry, but, what do I do?"

"Do?"

"For a living. What's my job?"

I can definitely see the man in the back roll his eyes this time, so broadly that the woman next to him swats him lightly with the script she's holding.

"Well. We don't know yet. Probably she's Kevin's secretary. You know our show? How Kevin keeps getting bad secretaries? Sort of like on *Murphy Brown*?"

"Yes."

"So maybe she works for Kevin. But mainly, she laughs this hilarious laugh that will make our audience plotz."

"Two scenes. No lines," says the guy in the back. "Don't overthink it."

"Shush," says the script-holding woman.

"Okay. Thanks. I think I'm ready."

I look at Arthur, who shifts uncomfortably in his seat. I think of Kevin on the show, and in my mind, red-haired Arthur sort of becomes Kevin. The actor who plays Kevin is probably in his late forties by now, and still very handsome, but for some reason I think about the heartthrob he was when the show started ten years ago, and I was still in high school. He'd enter almost every scene with the line "Hello, ladies!" which became a popular phrase people used to copy. What if I'd been his secretary, just for one day, back then, when I was in high school and the show was number one. If I'd gotten that chance, especially then, I'd hang on his every word and try to do my very best, so he'd like me. But maybe I'd be so smitten and nervous in his presence that all I could do was laugh adoringly at everything he did.

My laugh is soft and light when it first comes out, and I'm me, but also the nervous teenage me I was remembering. Arthur's face blushes a deep red, and I can see he's not used to being the center of attention, and he's liking it a little bit, and that makes me love him even more, and I pretend he's just said the funniest thing I ever heard, not just to me but to a roomful of people, and I'm proud to be with him, proud to be the girl on his arm, and I'm so exhilarated by it all that the laugh gets even bigger, and turns into more of a gasp, and I'm almost panting now, in a weirdly inappropriate, almost sexual way that I can't believe is coming out of my mouth, because it's a sound I'd never be bold enough to make even in my own bedroom, but for some reason here I'll do anything to let Arthur/Kevin/actor-who-plays-Kevin know how amazing and special and sexy and magnificent I think he is/they are, and my appreciation reaches its peak, and I'm almost totally out of breath, so I let it soften back down to the small giggle, and finally, exhausted but happy, I let out a little sigh that's interrupted by an almost involuntary hiccup, like I gulped down too much champagne all at once.

It's a blur from that point on, a series of snapshots that flash before me: the woman in the back mouthing "See?" to the disgruntled man, who nods and shrugs at her in a way that says "Who knew?" and the man in glasses asking me to wait in the waiting room, but then almost immediately coming back out to say I got the part, and the dreamlike experience of going back to Absolute and signing papers in Joe Melville's office that say I'm a client of theirs now, and people smiling and shaking my hand, and then walking back out on the street at the most beautiful time, just as the sun is fading, knowing I don't have to go to work as a waitress tonight, that I booked my second paying job in two weeks, and I can walk at a leisurely pace down Fifth Avenue and imagine that someday, maybe, I'll go into one of these stores instead of just walking past them looking hungrily into their windows, that someday, maybe, I'll be carrying a real purse and wearing heels like a grown-up lady instead of walking down Fifth Avenue in Doc Marten combat boots with an apron and a corkscrew and a crumb scraper in my canvas book bag.

Someday, someday, maybe.

Kevin and Kathy, LLC.
Silvercup Studios
42 22nd Street
Long Island City, NY, 11101

Exec. Producer / Director: Margaret Cleary
Exec. Producers: Jessica Blanche, Jennifer Goldyn
Producers: Sinclair Grant Cecil O'Neal
Co-Producer: Joseph Samuels
Line Producer: Emmet Fitzgerald

KEVIN and KATHY
Season 9

8:00AM
CREW CALL
See Individual Call Times on Back

DATE: Friday, February 17, 1995
DAY # 5 of 5
BREAKFAST: 7:30-8am
PRE - SHOOTING CALL: 9:00am
Weather: Partly Cloudy w/ a 20% Chance of Light Rain

	High: 70	Low: 49

Sunrise: 6:45am Sunset: 4:44pm
SCRIPT: GREEN   SCHEDULE: BLUE

1st AD: Christopher Lawrence
2nd AD: Elise Mullen

SCENE	SETS	CAST	D/N	PAGES	LOCATIONS / NOTES
14	INT - MANHATTAN GAZETTE - KEVIN'S OFFICE Kevin and Kathy discuss with the others - he needs a new secretary	1, 2, 7, 8, 16, 27	D1	6/8	Location: Backstage Studios Stage 6
17	INT- KEVIN & KATHY'S APARTMENT - LIVING ROOM Party in full swing - Kathy has already had a little too much to drink.	1, 2, 7, 8, 16, 18, 19	N2	3 6/8	PARKING
20	INT- KEVIN & KATHY'S APARTMENT - LIVING ROOM / KITCHEN Kevin tells Kathy to take it easy - she knocks over table	1, 2, 7, 8, 16, 18, 19	N2	2 4/8	CREW PARKING: North Side Parking Structure (Enter Gate 3)
23	INT- MANHATTAN GAZETTE - KEVIN'S OFFICE Kevin is distracted by giggling secretary and hungover Kathy.	1, 2, 7, 8, 16, 27	D3	1 7/8	
					BASECAMP/TRUCKS
			Total:	8 7/8	Basecamp & Work Trucks Are Located in The Production Lot on The South Wall of Stage 6

#	CAST	CHARACTER	SWF	REPORT	MAKEUP	SET	REMARKS
1	Robert Smith	KEVIN	W	7:30AM	7:30AM	8:00AM	Report to Stage - Rehearsal at Call
2	Allison Castillo	KATHY	W	6:30AM	6:30AM	8:00AM	Report to Stage - Rehearsal at Call
7	Roman Christopher	JAMES	WF	7:00AM	7:00AM	8:00AM	Report to Stage - Rehearsal at Call
8	Clare Platt	MARCIE	W	6:30AM	6:30AM	8:00AM	Report to Stage - Rehearsal at Call
16	Clyde Crooks	DOWNSTAIRS NEIGHBOR	SWF	7:00AM	7:00AM	8:00AM	Report to Stage - Rehearsal at Call
18	Neil Patel	PARTY HUSBAND	SWF	7:00AM	7:00AM	8:00AM	Report to Stage - Rehearsal at Call
19	Ellie Hannibal	PARTY WIFE	SWF	6:30AM	6:30AM	8:00AM	Report to Stage - Rehearsal at Call
27	Franny Banks	LAUGHING GIRL	SWF	6:30AM	6:30AM	8:00AM	Report to Stage - Rehearsal at Call

#	ATMOSPHERE & STANDINS			SPECIAL INSTRUCTIONS
	DESCRIPTION	ARRIVE	SET	
1	Kevin Stand In	8:00AM	8:00AM	Props: On the Day: Food Setup (Multiples for Sc. 23), Food Trays, Wine, Beer, Cocktails, Sc. 14- Cocktail Napkin, Kevin's Phone, Sc. 17- Empty Bottles, Husband & Wife's Baby Pictures in Wallet, Sc. 20- Glass of Water, Dish Towel, Sc. 23- Kathy's Wineglass
1	Kathy Stand In	8:00AM	8:00AM	
1	James Stand In	8:00AM	8:00AM	
1	Marcie Stand In	8:00AM	8:00AM	Art / Set Dressing: Party Decorations, Twinkle Lights on Balcony
				Makeup/Hair: Sc. 23- Kathy Gets Messy
15	Party Guests	7:30AM	8:30AM	Wardrobe: Doubles for Kathy's Wardrobe
1	Bartender / Server	7:30AM	8:30AM	Camera: Shoot Sc. 23 at Varying Speeds
	NOTES			Sound: Music Playback to Get Party Started
Kevin and Kathy is a CLOSED Set. No Visitors Unless Arrroved in Advance by Producers. Thanks for Cooperating!				Grip/Elec: On the Day: Jib Arm w/ Hot Head
				Add'l Labor: Hot Head Tech

Day 1 Monday, February 20, 1995

SCENE	SETS	CAST	D/N	PAGES	LOCATIONS / NOTES
24	INT- KEVIN & KATHY'S APARTMENT - LIVING ROOM Morning after the party. Kathy starts to remember last night.	1, 2	D4	2 6/8	Backstage Studios Stage 6
	MOVE TO STAGE 8				
12	INT- HANK'S BAR The gang talks about how fun the next party's going to be.	1, 2, 7, 8	D2	4	Backstage Studios Stage 8
			Total:	6 6/8	

Line Producer: Emmet Fitzgerald	1ST AD: Christopher Lawrence	2ND AD: Elise Mullen

12

....

"But I thought you liked the other guy better, the older guy with the asthma," Jane says to me over steaming plates of food at the upstairs Chinese place on Seventh Avenue. She's taking me out to celebrate my shoot last night on *Kevin and Kathy*, and we've recklessly decided to order all our favorites. Dan wanted to come to dinner, too, but Everett's parents had gotten them all tickets to see *Cavalleria Rusticana* and *Pagliacci* at the Metropolitan Opera.

"The opera," I said. "How glamorous!"

"I've seen *Cav/Pag* before," he said, glumly. "I'd rather come celebrate with you."

I keep picturing how miserable Dan looked as we said good night, and the big warm hug he gave me before I left, which seemed somehow different than the one he gave Jane, and I think about how happy he is whenever we come here and the way we always tease him for stabbing at his dumplings the way he does, his giant hands useless with the chopsticks.

"We'll bring you leftovers," I reassured him, but he still seemed miserable.

"Franny? Hello? Where'd you go?" Jane says, stabbing a chopstick in my direction.

"Sorry. Yes. You're right. I did like Barney Sparks better."

"Then why did you sign with the Joe Melville shiny-face guy?"

"Because. Absolute Artists represent famous people, and they only take the best people from class. That guy James Franklin is there, and Joe represents Penelope Schlotzsky, too. I'm lucky they wanted me at all. And anyway, I booked the job they sent me on, so it wasn't really a discussion. It was already their commission."

I'm saying all the right things, but for some reason Jane doesn't seem convinced. "Hmmph," is all she says.

"It seemed like it was meant to be," I say sagely, waving my arms in what I hope is a mystical fashion.

"But you said that Melville guy made you nervous, and kind of gave you the creeps. Is your agent supposed to give you the creeps?"

"It doesn't matter. This is a professional relationship. It's not show *friends*, it's show *business*."

"I think that's only what people in show business who have no friends say."

"He got me an actual job. On my first real audition."

"Well, I can't argue with that. So. Tell me."

I take a gulp of wine from my glass and try to remember exactly how it felt last night to be standing on a stage, with bright lights and four giant cameras on wheels gliding smoothly by. "It's like a dream. I was nervous, but some of it actually felt familiar. There was an audience. Sitting in a theater. In a way, it wasn't that different from doing my high school plays. There aren't as many people in the audience as you'd think from all the laughing you hear on television. The sets are much smaller than they look. And darker. The weirdest things made the biggest impression."

"Like?"

"Well. They tailored everything. They knew how many inches my skirt should be from my knee. They measured it. Everything was tailored just for me, and they did it overnight. They tailored my T-shirt. My *T-shirt*. Now all my non-tailored clothes look sloppy to me, or too loose or something." I tug at the front of my sweater and make it flap back and forth. "I mean, look, I'm positively swimming in this."

"Looks fine to me," says Jane, now having moved on to her dish of lemon chicken.

"Also, do you own an eyelash curler?"

"Yes. I never use it, though."

"Well, I didn't even know what it was. It's a barbaric tool. Using it feels like when I'd turn my eyelids inside out on the playground in elementary school to try and impress the boys. But to have someone do it *for* you?" I say with a frown, and Jane shakes her head in sympathy. "They fixed my hair and my makeup after every take—I'd hardly moved at all but they'd fix it again anyway. They kept powdering me even if I didn't feel sweaty—I had to scrape the foundation off when I got home. The director would set the blocking, but then Kevin, or Robert, the actor who plays Kevin, kept forgetting it, so I'd have to change mine, too, and then remember to do it the same way every time, so all the takes would match, only then he'd forget again and I'd get thrown. I was so busy trying to remember if I picked up the phone with my right hand or my left hand that I could barely focus on anything else."

"But did it go well? Do you feel good about it?"

"I'm not sure. I think so. The audience laughed, and lots of people said I did well, but I have no idea who any of them were or if they were the ones I needed to impress. But the laughing thing was getting such a positive reaction from the audience, the writer decided to give me a line."

Jane's eyes go wide. "No way!"

"I know. I got really excited, too, which is so dumb when you think about it. I've done whole plays in summer stock and all those scenes in class, and here I was so excited about one line." I pause and take a gulp of wine. "I got to say, 'You're so cute.' So I'd do the laughing thing and sort of look at Kevin dumbly and sigh, and say 'You're so cute.' "

"Hilarious!"

"People kept telling me it was unusual for them to give a guest star more to do, sort of on the fly like that. Jimmy said Kevin doesn't like last-minute changes, so if they think of something to try, they usually give it to Kathy."

"What's she like?"

"She said I was funny, and she thought it was refreshing that I wasn't a waif like most actresses my age."

"Sounds like someone got a little threatened."

"That occurred to me, too," I say, lowering my chopsticks and my voice. "But that's crazy, don't you think? What would she care about me for? I'm just there for one night. She's the star of the show. Anyway, I guess I don't know how I did. The director did everything so quickly. I was confused because I kept waiting for him to tell me things about my character's motivation and subtext, like Stavros does in class, but he didn't mention any of that. There was only one time when he really gave me any direction."

"What'd he say?"

Cindy, our regular waitress, passes by and Jane gestures for another round of drinks.

"He said," and I pause dramatically, "'Don't do the laugh before you hand Kevin the cup of coffee. Hand him the coffee, *then* do the laugh.'"

Jane and I are silent for a moment, pondering this wisdom.

"Huh."

"And you know what? It worked. I got a better laugh."

"Wow," she says, shaking her head.

"I know. And I have no idea why."

"So, when will it be on TV?"

"I don't know. They don't have a time slot yet. They have to wait for, like, *Murder She Wrote* to get canceled or something."

"Well, *that'll* never happen."

"I know," I say, and sigh.

Jane uses her chopsticks to take another scoop off the top of the still steaming pile of chicken fried rice. "It's all so mysterious, isn't it?" she says, and I bob my head furiously.

"Yes! I mean, wait—what do you mean?"

"Well, I keep expecting to understand show business better, but it's still so confusing to me. Like, Russell Blakely is this huge star, right? And at first I thought everything he did was so interesting and special, and I laughed so hard at everything he said because he honestly seemed like the funniest person I'd ever met, and everything about him was better somehow, like he was more than regular, like he was a person, but from another planet or something. But the longer I work for him, the more I see he's just this guy, this very unusually gorgeous, extremely muscle-y guy, who's sort of funny, and sort of smart, but who's a regular person who married the girl he dated in high school and doesn't seem to know how he got here. He seems totally baffled by his success, and he's always asking my opinion about things, like his wardrobe or whatever, and I'm wondering if he's forgotten I'm just the P.A. on my very first movie ever. He hasn't been in a grocery store in three years, he told me. Someone goes for him. Someone does everything for him. And he seems miserable. He reads everything they write about him in the magazines and he gets so upset. When work is over and his wife is back in L.A. he doesn't seem to know what to do with himself, and he goes out with guys from the crew who aren't even really his friends and they get drunk and it ends up on Page Six. I keep thinking someone should be helping him in a different way, or there should be some sort of manual for him. Because he just doesn't seem to be enjoying any of it." Jane shakes her head sadly.

"I would enjoy it," I say. "I think."

"Yeah, I think I would, too," says Jane. "But who knows?"

"Who knows," I agree, draining the last sip from my glass. "Oh! One more thing, from last night?"

"Yeah?"

"Apparently, we're not supposed to wash our jeans anymore. The wardrobe lady told me. We're only supposed to dry-clean them."

"What? That's insane."

"Yep. We're supposed to buy jeans really tight, as tight as we can squeeze into, so all the fat gets compressed into as little space as possible. Then we want the fat compression level to stay that way for as long as it can, right? Well, washing jeans makes them softer and baggier, and lessens the fat-compression quotient. Therefore, dry-cleaning is the only answer. Isn't that terrible news?"

Jane shrugs. "It sounds expensive, but I don't think it's necessarily ruining my outlook on civilization."

"But c'mon. Don't you agree, dry-cleaning is so unfair?"

"Why?"

"It's like, the clothes charge you for wearing them."

Jane stares at me blankly. "How are the clothes charging you?"

"Clothes that have to be dry-cleaned are already the most expensive clothes. Then it's like they're charging you another three dollars every time you wear them."

"Regular clothes charge money to clean them, if we're looking at it that way. Regular laundry costs money, too."

"But not as much. And you can do regular laundry yourself. Dry-cleaning is like this secret society you're not allowed into. No matter what, you're at their mercy. You can have a Ph.D. in anything, but you still can't dry-clean your own clothes. They'll never tell you how. No one's ever even seen what the machine looks like. Think about it. There's a reason they keep the actual dry-cleaning apparatus hidden behind all those racks of hanging clothes. They don't want you to crack their code. They won't let anybody in. Not anybody. Even rich people. You know any rich people with dry-cleaning machines in their house? Exactly. Even they still have to pick it up and drop it off like everyone else."

"I'm pretty sure they have people who do that for them. Also, in New York they deliver."

"But still. The dry cleaners own you. You're at their mercy. Clothes that have to be dry-cleaned look down on you."

"Is it the clothes who are to blame, or the dry-cleaning professionals themselves?"

"Chicken or the egg, my friend."

"This new dry-cleaning conspiracy theory reminds me of your fear of ironing."

"This is nothing like my fear of ironing, although ironing is another secret society that doesn't want you to know what's up. Do you know anyone who can tell you why the ironing board is shaped that way? How does it help me that it's the size of a surfboard? Why is an ironing board so hard to fold? Does it want me to leave it standing up in my room for days? How am I supposed to do sleeves on that thing? Never mind collars."

"You know what you should do with that shirt you're struggling to iron?"

"I know, I know. Send it to the dry cleaners. But I'm afraid to go to our cleaners now that Mr. Wu has seen my commercial. He keeps asking if he can put my head shot up on the wall. You know how that back wall is covered with head shots?"

"Of course. I think it's cute. Why not just give him one? He's proud of his customers in the neighborhood."

"But haven't you ever noticed, out of all those head shots, there's no one famous, no one even vaguely recognizable?"

"That's not true—there's—"

"Besides him, I mean. Besides that one very famous person, who I doubt has ever actually been to Mr. Wu's."

"You think Mr. Wu forged a famous customer? You think Mr. Wu autographed a picture of someone famous himself? Where would he have gotten the picture?"

"You see them on the street sometimes. I don't know, I'm just saying it's occurred to me. Because other than him, that one very famous person, do you recognize anyone else on that wall?"

"Well, there's that cast photo from *Cats* with all the people in their cat costumes . . . I don't recognize them individually, but as a group they seem authentic."

"But besides the somewhat believable cats."

"Wait—yes—there's that actress—my mother loved her—she was on that detective show in the sixties, what was it called . . . ?"

"*The Uniforms*?"

"Yes! That! Paula somebody."

"Paulette Anderson."

"Yes! So that's one more actually famous person."

"Jane. Paulette Anderson has been dead for at least ten years. This is what I'm saying. I'm afraid being on that wall is some sort of bad luck. Like, if I give Mr. Wu my head shot, I'm doomed to obscurity."

"Better obscurity than death. Better obscurity than *Cats*, for that matter. And what if that picture he has isn't a fake?"

"Well then, I guess I'll either end up dead, unknown, a cat, or Bill Cosby."

February–March 1995

27 Monday

PICK UP SIDES FOR

11AM   A THOUSAND CLOWNS

GENERAL MEETING   BUY PLAY AT

CBS   SAMUEL FRENCH

12³⁰

GENERAL w/ CASTING DIRECTOR

JAY BINDER

321 W 44th #606

GENERAL   311 W 43 8th Fl

4PM MANHATTAN THEATRE CLUB   MONOLOGUE

28 Tuesday

RAN 2.5 MILES

NEW.

HEADSHOTS   PHOTO SHOOT

BRING BLACK BLAZER

DENIM SHIRT

9AM.   BROWN BELT

JEWELRY CHOICES

GET NAILS DONE

ABSOLUTE

PICK·UP SIDES FROM AGENCY

FOR BONNIE FINNEGAN

LATE SHIFT   4³⁰ PM. → CLOSING MTG.

1 Wednesday

A THOUSAND CLOWNS

10AM   PAT McCORKLE CASTING

575 8th AVE 18th FL

12³⁰ HOME BREW ICED TEA

UPSCALE CASUAL

DONNA DESETA CASTING

584 BROADWAY # 1001

X STREET HOUSTON

2PM AMY KAUFMAN GENERAL MTG

180 VARICK ST

EARLY SHIFT 3PM. —

FILOFAX

(SWAP w/ RICKY FOR LATE SHIFT OR NOT

ENOUGH TIME TO GET UPTOWN)

11 AM TODO THANES2 — 130 W 57TH ST #
PICK UP SIDES FOR RAN/WALKER   10A
CAGNEY & LACEY TV MOVIE   2 MILES
    "GWEN"   ↗

Thursday 2

2PM GENERAL W/   LAME
   DANIEL SWEE   ONE CLASSICAL MONOL
   150 W 65TH ST.   ⁵ONE CONTEMPORA
      (GAVE ME SIDES FOR
            KRAMER IN SUNSHINE)
                    △

     · BONJOUR LA BONSOUR
STAVROS   MEMORIZED FOR CLASS

10⁴⁵ JIM CARNAHAN   Friday 3
      A MONTH IN THE COUNTRY
ROUNDABOUT 231 W 39TH ST   MAIL RENT
              #1200   CHECK

CALL GENERAL   BONNIE FINNEGAN
DAD   CASTING
BUT   2M.   12 W 27TH 11TH FL
   REALLY   READ FOR
               CENTRAL PARK WEST
                  "ABBY"
                     WEALTHY, OUT
LATE SHIFT   4³⁰ —   BOHEMIAN
                        STUDENT AT NYU

Saturday 4

    MOVIE W/   BOYS ON THE SIDE
  JANE AND DAN   8¹⁰PM. ANGELIKA
                 ATE AT VESELKA
LATE SHIFT 4³⁰ —
                 TOOK NIGHT OFF ˢᵒTIRED
                 RICKY SUBBED   Sunday 5

SAW JOHN TURTURRO AT OZZIE'S!
  STOOD BEHIND HIM IN LINE · SO AWESOMELY TALL.
  HE GOT COFFEE AND A BAGEL.   ²UT
  JUST LIKE ME · SIGH OF   DUR
                      HAPPINESS
EARLY SHIFT 3 —

March 1995

SEND CHECK TODAY $50 LATE FEE KENT WITH !!

6 Monday

CALL BACK
CENTRAL. PARK. WEST
BONNIE FINNEGAN
12 W 27TH 11TH FL
12M.
READING FOR DIRECTOR AND
PRODUCER
NEED
FAX PAPER   PICK·UP SIDES AT ABSOLUTE
MILK
YOGURT   BUY READ KRAMER IN
PEANUT BUTTER   SUNSHINE AT
4M.   OFFICE
            BERNIE TELSEY 311 W
                           43RD
                           10TH
                           FL

7 Tuesday

                I READ FOR
GENERAL MEETING ALL MY CHILDREN
(9 15)   ABC CASTING
              157 COLUMBUS 2NDFL.
LANZOS (11:40)
TOMATO SAUCE BETH MELSKY
         (2:10)   928 B'WAY # 300
            KERRY BARDEN GENERAL MTG.
                150 W 28TH ST #402
FAX PAPER
    3:30 CLMB —

8 Wednesday

           WORK ON KRAMER IN
RUN LINES   SUNSHINE
         PICK UP SCRIPT
     DONNA DESETA
        BEL-MOR
          INDUSTRIAL [VIDEO

        EARLY SHIFT 3PM ———→

FAX ∘ PAPER ∘ BUY ∘ FAX ∘ PA

BROADWAY RAN 2 MILES
PLAY !! CALL BACK FOR KRAMER IN
MEET W ~~MIKE~~ STANLEY DIRECTOR SUNSHINE
4.30 DANIEL SWEE, CASTING
PM 150 W 65TH ST

BAD
BAD
SO BAD
Booooo

STAVROS
4:30 /LD/CL/SE ~~TOOK~~ ~~NIGHT~~ OFF ~~FROM~~ ~~CLASS~~

SLEPT UNTIL 1PM.

B oooooooooooooooooooooooooooo

LATE SHIFT 430

DRANK 4,582,659 MARGARITAS W
JANE AT SANTA FE GRILL

PERBUYFAXPAPERBUYFAX

March 1995

13 Monday

---

14 Tuesday

2 M. BABY WELL DIAPERS
YOUNG MOM
NOT HIP
DONNA   DESETA CASTING
584 B'WAY #1001

---

15 Wednesday

Thursday 16

Friday 17

LATE SHIFT 43. —

Saturday 18

Sunday 19

Personal. *FILOFAX*

March 1995

20 Monday

RAN 3MI

NEED
COFFEE
DETERGENT
SELTZER
~~CHEESE~~
~~BEEF~~

21 Tuesday

WORK 3Mi

22 Wednesday

RAN 3MILES

EARLY
SHIFT 3MI.

filofax

NEED T.P.
 CHEESE PUFFS

STAVROS CLASS

RAN ONE MILE BECAUSE
WHAT'S THE POINT ????

LATE SHIFT 4:30

MURIEL'S WEDDING
 LINCOLN CENTER CIN.
       5:50
   JANE & DAN

March 1995

27 Monday

HEY
FOLKS
IT'S
NATIONAL
CHEESE PUFF WEEK

28 Tuesday

EARLY SHIFT 3AM.

29 Wednesday ★

★ SAW JOHN TURTURRO AT OZZIE'S

filofax

Thursday 30

CLASS

Friday 31

Personal. *FILOFAX*

LATE SHIFT 430

Saturday 1

CHEESE
PUFFS ARE
CRUNCHY CRUNCHY

MAKING
DOODLE GRASS
MORE
EXCITING THAN
CAREER

Sunday 2

13

....

You have no messages.

BEEEP.

I've had no auditions in the last two weeks and I'm starting to get nervous.

Joe called the Monday after the *Kevin and Kathy* shoot to congratulate me again, and say that he wanted me to come into the agency at some point and meet the other agents, because "they were all very excited" about me. But the first two weeks after *Kevin and Kathy* were so full of auditions and meetings with casting people, there wasn't time to schedule an appointment. And in the last three weeks, no one called to set one up.

I tried my best to be prepared for every audition, but I'd never had such full days before. It was all a blur of papers coming off the roll from the fax machine and time spent rushing from one building in Manhattan to another. But then we ran out of fax paper and I kept forgetting to get a new roll, so I had to cold read a few times, and I'll admit, there were a few days when I showed up at an audition not really prepared. And then there was the big audition I *had* prepared for, a small part in a Broadway play directed by Mike Stanley, but I was so nervous to meet him that I left out an entire page of the scene and he didn't ask me to read it again, and when he asked me if I studied with anyone in town I went blank and couldn't think of Stavros's name, and I went home and cried.

"The feedback was that you seemed a little green," Richard explained, delicately.

Those first few weeks, Joe would come to the phone when I called, but now Richard, Joe's assistant, is the only person I get. I thought that was fine at first since he was the one who actually saw me at the Showcase, but now I worry that I've been demoted. It was Richard who sent me to the photographer that "Joe loves" to get new head shots, even though I'd had new ones done just a few months ago that cost over a hundred dollars. Richard said that Joe thought mine were too smiley and commercial, and I needed some that looked like I could be a dramatic actress, not just a comedienne. I thought my new one looked more angry and stiff than dramatic, but he assured me the photo would transform after it was retouched, a painstaking process using a tiny paintbrush to take out imperfections on the blown-up negative before the photos can be copied. The retouching took two weeks, and the eight-by-ten glossy copies cost three hundred dollars. Now I have no freckles, and the half-moon area under my eyes looks oddly whiter than the rest of my face, but I still look angry.

I thought it made sense that I'd had no auditions while the agency was waiting for the new pictures. But there were no auditions the week after I dropped them off, either.

I'm worried that those first three weeks were my chance to prove that getting the *Kevin and Kathy* job wasn't some sort of fluke, but I blew it and they've forgotten about me now. I read an article in *Backstage* that said it's important to remind your agent that you are available and interested in working, so I finally braced myself and called Absolute at the beginning of the third silent week. The problem was that because I didn't really have a reason to call, I sort of choked on the phone. I asked to speak to Joe, and Richard said he was sorry, Joe was in a meeting, but could he help me with anything?

"Um, uh, no that's okay."

"Are you sure?"

"Yeah, well, actually, as long as we're talking, I was just wondering if there's anything I can be doing, or if there's something I'm *not* doing, or, um, are my head shots working okay?"

"Your head shots?"

"Yeah, the new ones. I was just checking. I mean, Joe picked that serious one where my hand is on my chin, right?"

"I think so, I have it here somewhere . . . yes, your hand is on your chin, and your head is sort of tilted to the side?"

"Yeah. Is that . . . I wonder if it's sort of *cheesy*? And maybe that's why, uh, no one is calling?"

I didn't intend to complain or bring this up. I must sound rude, like I'm telling them how to do their job. I'm just looking for someone to give me some sort of explanation for why nothing is happening.

"But Franny, Joe loves this shot. I mean, I do, too, but Joe really loves it, which is why he picked it. He's really a master at choosing the picture that best represents you. So, no problem there. Sooo, there's really nothing else for you to do right now but wait. Sorry." There's a pause where I feel as though Richard wants to say something else, but then doesn't.

"So . . . anything else, Franny?"

"Yeah, no, thanks. That's it. Just, uh, checking in."

"Okay, thanks Franny, I'll let Joe know you called . . . to check in."

It was worse when I heard Richard say it back.

I thought my life was going to radically change when I got an agent, but it's exactly the same except that I'm spending more money.

I finally got the check from *Kevin and Kathy*, but I was shocked to see over half of it gone to taxes and commission to the agency.

"That's *it*?" I said to Dan as he looked the check over carefully. I hoped he'd find some error, or maybe realize I'd filled out the tax form incorrectly. But he handed it back and shook his head.

"They're taxing you like you make that kind of money every week," he explained.

"But I don't," I said helplessly, and he shook his head in sympathy.

On top of that, I'm still recovering from the various shifts that Herb docked me for shooting *Kevin and Kathy* that Friday night, plus the cost of the new photos. I had to start picking up some shifts at Best Intentions, the catering place where I briefly worked when I first moved here. At first, watching weddings from the back of the grand ballroom was inspiring. I'd tear up during the toasts, even while clearing glasses. But after a while, the demanding brides wore me out, the grand ballroom felt impersonal and overused, and I became as jaded as the waiters I swore I'd never become, who start eyeing their watches exactly at eleven P.M. and prying half-full glasses out of the drunk attendees' hands.

I find myself wondering whether things would be different if I'd signed with Barney Sparks. I imagine calling him up to "check in," and I don't think I would have felt so awkward. Plus, he has no assistant, so he actually would have had to take my call. But I can't allow myself to picture that—I signed a yearlong contract with Absolute.

Getting an agent was undeniable progress, an actual box I could check and an accomplishment I could point to. But if you have an agent who never calls you for anything, I'm not sure it's any better than not having an agent. In fact, I think it's worse. Before, I wasn't being rejected so much as I was going unnoticed. Now I have someone who noticed me at first, but now seems to have found me lacking.

I called my dad after the sixth week of not receiving any calls from Absolute.

"I think my agent forgot about me."

"I think my daughter forgot about me."

"Dad."

"Who is this?"

"Har-har. It's your daughter, the unemployed actress."

"She lives!"

"I think I need a manager."

"Why do you need a manager? I thought you just got an agent."

"I did, but they aren't getting me any auditions."

"If you have no auditions, what's there to manage?"

"A manager would help me *get* auditions."

"How could a manager do that when the agents can't?"

"Well, managers have fewer people, so they can focus just on you."

"Then why do you have an agent at all? Why not just have a manager?"

"You have to have an agent. They're the only ones allowed to negotiate contracts. Agents are franchised. Managers aren't."

"So, anyone can say they're a manager?"

"Well, sort of, yes."

"Why don't I say I'm your manager and go tell your agent he's doing a crappy job for my favorite client?"

"Thanks, Dad."

A few days later, Jane and I are in the living room sitting cross-legged on either end of the couch and flipping through channels when *Still Nursing* comes on. Dan is working at the dining room table, but he always says he isn't bothered by us sitting and talking in there while he's writing due to his uncanny ability to completely tune us out, and in fact our chatter is so incessant, we're like human white noise. It's a handy thing to have in a roommate.

"I think I don't look right," I say, mesmerized by the actress on the screen.

"Right for what?"

"You know, in general. For show business. I think that's why I'm not getting any calls from the agency."

"What do you think is the *right* way to look?"

"You know, more like these girls on *Still Nursing*." I gesture toward the television, where a buxom blonde in a short skirt and open doctor's coat is struggling to reattach the I.V. of an elderly male patient by straddling his hospital bed, "accidentally" smothering him with her cleavage. The studio audience screams with laughter.

"*Uchh*. Gross." Jane waves a hand dismissively. "This show. It's the absolute end of civilization. One male nurse in a pediatric ward with all female doctors! What a premise! Look at them—none of them are believable as doctors. Half of them got new boobs between seasons one and two. I saw you last season, ladies—am I to believe you suddenly grew those mammaries over the summer? Please. They're too skinny, anyway."

The blond doctor on the television drops her clipboard on the floor and as she leans over to pick it up, the heart monitor of the patient starts beeping rapidly. More laughter.

"Yeah, but maybe that's what people should be saying about me. Like when *The Enquirer* does those covers where they call someone SCARY SKINNY! People don't look at it because they think the people on the cover look bad. They look at the magazine because they wish it was them. They want to be scary skinny, too. I'd be proud if people said, 'She's too skinny.' 'Have you seen that actress, Franny Banks? I'm worried about her. Someone should give her a candy bar, she looks like she might faint.' That's what the people want. That's what makes people look up to you."

"I'm going to order you some of those 'Stop the Insanity' tapes."

"Casey told me about this special pot they have in L.A. that doesn't give you the munchies. That's apparently how those *Still Nursing* girls got so skinny."

Jane shakes her head and speaks to me gently, like you might to a toddler who is sleepwalking. "Casey? Casey, the model who cries in every scene, told you that?"

"Yeah. The pot is really expensive, though, and you have to know somebody who knows somebody in order to get it. Somebody she went to high school with got her some. She could probably get me some, too. Maybe I should start smoking the skinny pot."

Jane clicks the remote and *Still Nursing* fades to black. She turns to face me. "Frances. Truly. This kind of reasoning results in being found dead at three A.M. in a bathtub at the Chelsea Hotel. You're an actor. You used to just worry about being an actor. And anyway, the last time we tried to smoke pot, you fell asleep by eight thirty."

I slump back against the couch with a sigh. "But there has to be some trick. All those people can't just be walking around starving and happening to look great all the time. They must know something that the rest of us don't. Or worse—maybe there *isn't* a trick. Maybe they *are* walking around hungry all the time. Maybe that's the difference between being successful or unsuccessful. Maybe I'm too weak. I'm too concerned with feeling good to be willing to feel as bad as I should to be successful."

"Why would feeling good be bad? People spend their lives trying to feel good. You're not supposed to walk around miserable all the time. You have to eat to stay alive. These are truths you used to know. Who says there's some agreed-upon ideal, anyway? The girls on *Still Nursing* aren't appealing to everyone—just to the dumb people who watch that one show. One dumb show isn't for everybody. Why can't you just be yourself and find the people who like that?"

"I know. You're right. Hey, maybe I should get my hair cut in The Rachel."

"Franny. My ex-stepmother, who moved to the suburbs of Long Island, has The Rachel, as do all of her friends. It's trickled out to the masses already. You missed the Rachel hairdo boat."

"See? That's what I'm talking about. I have follower hair. Successful actresses have forward-thinking, trendsetting, exciting hair that women in the suburbs want to emulate. I should be thinking less about my work and more about my hair."

"Can't you go back to the time when you thought you would magically get an agent if you memorized a Shakespeare sonnet every day? That made about as much sense as this, but at least it was more productive. What about doing important work, like you always said? What about the theater and truth and connecting with humanity, or whatever you used to talk about?"

"I have an agent now. I'm trying to work in the professional world. There seem to be rules. I do still care about humanity and, you know, that other stuff. I'm just trying to be a—a professional. In a professional-looking package."

"I guess. I don't know. I just can't picture Diane Keaton or Meryl Streep obsessing over The Rachel or the dingbats on *Still Nursing*. Isn't it more important that you're a talented actor?"

"I don't know. That's what I'm not sure about, I guess. I used to think that. But now I think I should be talented *and* have better hair. I'm confused. I think it's all important. Maybe I should be a vegan."

"Frances. Seriously. Get a grip. You're not going to ever look like those dumb girls. But if you want to, I don't know, be some sort of superhuman, don't just smoke and throw away the inside of your muffins. Go get a book about nutrition or something."

"I know about nutrition already," I say, waving her away.

Jane looks doubtful. "Is that so? Name three food groups."

"Easy," I say, folding my arms. "Chinese, Mexican, tuna on a bagel." She shakes her head, and I smile at her sweetly. "You know, Jane, I did buy actual vegetables, just last week."

"Yes, I noticed that. This may come as a shock to you, but many studies have shown there's at least a slight nutritional difference between spinach that's rotting in the crisper drawer and spinach that's ingested into the body."

"Details," I scoff.

"I give up," she says, heading for the kitchen. "More coffee?"

I stare down at my bagel, which seems to eye me warily back. Maybe Jane's right. Maybe I need more education. I wonder what Penelope Schlotzky eats on Sunday. Probably not bagels. Maybe bagels are my problem. Although, one bagel doesn't seem like a lot of food. I decide I will finish the bagel but not eat anything the rest of the day. Except maybe a salad for dinner.

Or soup.

No. Soup has hidden stuff in it. Yes, I'm fairly certain, soup is another food that seems innocent but is actually fattening.

Chicken broth. That only has like seven calories. Can I get chicken broth at the deli? Where can I get chicken broth . . .

"You don't need to change anything, Franny. I think you look good."

I swear it takes me a second before I realize it's Dan who is speaking. I had totally forgotten he was in the room. He has never before acknowledged anything we say while he's working. We know for sure he tunes us out completely. We've tested it. Usually it takes three or more tries of us practically yelling at him to get his attention before he'll even look up, blinking like we've startled him out of a dream.

The first thing I wonder is whether Dan has been secretly listening to our living room conversations all along, but Dan is a pretty honest guy and not devious like that. If he were ever distracted, he would have joined in the conversation or kicked us out while he was working.

It's weird, but I'm pretty sure he hasn't been listening all these months, that he hasn't ever heard us before. I'm pretty sure I broke through to him just this once.

"Thanks, Dan," is all I can think of to say.

14

"*What* is *that?*" Jane says, looking alarmed.

I've slumped farther into the abyss. I'm not making enough money. I'm down to one shift at the club, due to Herb's bizarre system, which now includes rewarding the servers who have the most shifts with even more shifts, so those of us who've been penalized for any reason are having a tough time finding our way back in. At least I still have the Friday shift, whose take can almost, but not quite, cover my rent. Even catering has been slow lately.

Russell Blakely's movie is wrapping in a few weeks, and Jane is finally not working nights anymore. She comes down the circular staircase wearing vintage '60s go-go boots, which have different colors of patent leather sewn together in a kind of patchwork pattern, a short blue suede skirt, and a red bomber jacket with a faux fur collar she found at Bolton's on Eighth Street. Bolton's is supposed to be this great discount store, and Jane always finds something there, while I usually just end up with another pair of discounted black tights. Jane already has her signature sunglasses on, which means she's serious about leaving. Nothing would normally slow her exit. That's how I know, for sure, the stuff in the bowl I am holding must look as bad as I thought.

"Wow, look at you! Where'd you get the boots?" Maybe I can distract her by talking about fashion.

"Don't try to distract me by talking about fashion. Seriously, what is that?"

"It's, uh, food?"

"For an astronaut?"

"No, it's this wonderful new diet food? I bought it off the television." I've been trying to keep my spirits up by experimenting with different diets. So far, none of them have worked. But this time is different.

"You paid money for that?"

"Oh yes, Jane, and it's so worth it. It's called TastiLife, and it's not just a quick-fix diet, it's a fabulously tasty new way of life!"

"Okaay," Jane says gingerly.

Why does she look so suspicious? I must make her understand. "Jane. I know it looks weird, but James Franklin was saying in class the other day that everyone on his set did it. In *Hollywood*."

"Really? Hollywood?" Jane squeals in false delight.

"Jane, seriously. Have you seen those commercials? 'Eleven million losers and counting'?"

"Yes, I've seen the people in the commercials who hold their old, giant fat pants away from their tiny new selves. So . . . that guy James told you to do this?"

"Yes, but not—he wasn't telling me I needed it or anything. We were just talking after class—and anyway, I brought it up. I was just making conversation, asking him about his movie, and he was just being helpful by telling me what some of the pros do."

"Mmm-hmm," Jane says doubtfully. "But when did you start doing this? I didn't see any of it in the fridge."

"Yeah, no, that's the best part—you don't have to refrigerate it. It comes in a box. It's freeze-dried in a package and you just take it out and soak it!"

"You *soak it*?"

"It sounds weird, I know, but it's actually very convenient because you can take it anywhere, you know, on the go?"

"Why can't you just eat actual healthy food, the kind that doesn't require soaking?"

"Well, obviously, because I can't be trusted to control myself. This teaches you portion control. Everything you need is in each packet, so it takes the guesswork out of dieting."

"You sound like you've joined a cult. What happens when you have to go back to the real world, the world where you have to think for yourself?"

"Hopefully I'll be so weak and frail that food will have lost its appeal entirely."

"Great plan. And who's on *Leeza* today?"

"I'm pretty sure today's show is 'Women Who Wish Their Best Friends Would Stop Judging Them.' "

"Har-har. I'm going to work now. Do you want me to take the TV cord with me?"

"Jane. Goodbye."

After she leaves, I hover in the living room, eyeing the television warily. I know Jane's just teasing—it's not as though I have a real problem with *Leeza*, though I do happen to know that today's episode is called "Amazing Animals," and it's supposed to include a dog who can actually tie people's shoes. And Jane is sort of right, I guess, that I've fallen into a pattern of watching more television during the day. It started when the residual checks for my Niagara commercial began to slow down, and I wanted to make sure they weren't making a mistake—secretly running the commercial a dozen times a day and just forgetting to pay me or something—so I started scouring the daytime channels to see if I could count how many times it was playing and compare that to what my checks said.

Leeza was on, and she was talking about inspiring yourself, and I felt like I was really bettering myself by listening to her advice. A lot of the shows have weight-loss advice, which is where I got the great cabbage soup diet, which would have worked, I'm sure, if only I didn't hate cabbage. She has celebrities on, too, and people who've overcome daunting odds of various kinds, and I never know when I'll have to play a character who isn't close to me but might remind me of someone I saw on *Leeza*. So really, you could call the time I spend with Leeza almost educational.

But the thing is, *Pinetree Lodge*, the soap opera, is on right after that. When I first started watching, it was just for a few minutes right after *Leeza* and before the first commercial break. I was more fascinated than interested. I would use the show as a kind of acting exercise, challenging myself with the hokey dialogue, saying the lines out loud to myself, just to see if I could make the scenes feel more real than the actors on the show did. I wondered if it was the actors' fault that the whole thing seemed so ridiculous, or if there is truly nothing you can do to make it less phony, given how phony it looks.

But now I've fallen into the habit of watching both shows every day without fail, and sometimes I even leave the TV on longer and watch *Studs* and *Love Connection*, two shows I can't possibly justify as being enriching in any measurable way. I blame Dan partially, who has barely been around. I don't know where he's been doing his writing lately, but it isn't our living room, and if only he were here more I'd probably be too embarrassed to lie on the couch all afternoon.

Because if I'm being really honest with myself, I'm legitimately hooked on *Pinetree Lodge* now, in that I think about the characters during the day as though they're real people and I worry about them over the weekend. "How *will* CoCo Breckenridge hide the facts of her murderous twin's disappearance?" I find myself wondering. Every Friday I resolve to stop watching, but once Monday comes I can't resist seeing how the cliffhanger was resolved.

Sometimes, when I get really frustrated, I fantasize about firing Joe Melville, but I wouldn't want to hurt his feelings, and it seems a little redundant to tell someone to stop calling you who already never calls. Presumably, he's embarrassed to have made a mistake, and perhaps hopes that if he ignores me long enough we can pretend our meeting never happened and can both be saved the shame of confronting our failures. Which puts me back in the place where I'm feeling bad for Joe Melville. I'll admit, it's sort of a sick relationship to have with someone who is hardly in your life.

Leeza doesn't come on until noon, and I'm regularly sleeping until then now, because there's no reason to get up any earlier. Jane is treating it as a big deal, as if there's something really wrong with me. She calls me from work every day just to make sure I get up.

"I'm worried about you. You're depressed."

"I'm fine."

"My roommate, Frances Farmer," Jane says, melodramatically.

"I'm a sensitive, creative type. I'm going through something."

"If I come home to you eating a pint of Häagen-Dazs and watching *When Harry Met Sally*, I'm calling the police."

"What are they going to do, arrest me for being a cliché?"

So when the phone rings at eleven thirty that morning I lunge for it, grabbing it on the second ring. I'll pretend to Jane I'm in good spirits. I'll act peppy, as if I've been up for hours.

"Psychic Friends Network, Dionne Warwick speaking," I trill.

"Uh, hello? This is Richard calling from Absolute Artists. Is Franny there?"

I sit up, as if he might be able to see through the telephone that I was lying down at an undignified hour, still in the shorts and tank top I slept in. I clear my throat and try to make my voice sound more awake.

"It's me. It's her." That doesn't sound right. "It is I."

"Hello, I. Did I wake you up?"

"No. I'm awake. I, um, have a cold."

"Oh, shoot. Is it a really bad one? Joe has an audition for you."

"I've just made an extremely speedy recovery."

"Great!"

"Great!"

"So, it's today . . ."

"Today?"

"In about two hours."

"Today?"

Oh no. I've done nothing for two weeks but sleep late, and drag myself to class and the odd shift at the club. I haven't worked out. I've barely *been* out. I'm unprepared. I'm doughy.

"Sounds great!"

"Sorry it's so last minute. They need to replace someone on *Pinetree Lodge*."

"On *what*?"

"*Pinetree Lodge*, the soap? Excuse me, the daytime drama? Do you know it?"

"You're kidding me."

"Uh, no. Are you a fan?"

My heart is pounding out of my chest. I can't believe it. *Pinetree Lodge*! Am I a fan? I'm more than a fan. I'm a student, a devotee. I could write a thesis on my knowledge of *Pinetree Lodge*. What luck! Maybe this is going to be okay. Maybe I'm not repulsive and mushy after all. I'm a genius who has been in studious self-imposed exile whilst honing my craft, waiting for this day to come, with patience and nobility. It was meant to be!

"Yes! I know it. I know it a little too well, actually."

"Great. Then just get over there as quickly as you can. They're closing the session at two P.M. I'll fax you the sides and the appointment info. Just call us with any questions, and break a leg."

"Thanks."

I've got to hurry. But for a moment I stand there in the middle of my room, still holding the receiver, strangely frozen. I should shower. Should I shower? I should. But my hair. If I wash my hair, then I'll have to dry it. I'll shower but not wash my hair. I'll put a towel on my head to keep my hair dry while I take a shower. Where's my slutty outfit? Most of the girls on *Pinetree Lodge* are slutty, except the older star, Angela Bart, who's slutty but in a classy, older way. Is that shirt clean? I'll wear my Wonderbra. *Where's my Wonderbra?*

I'm in and out of the shower in record time. I use the towel that was on my head to dry off. The moisture from the shower has done something helpful to my hair, for once. I can hear the fax machine whirring, the paper falling onto the floor. I'm curious to see the material. I'll skim it before I get dressed to make sure I'm picking the right thing to wear.

I go to the machine and uncurl the first page.

ABSOLUTE ARTISTS—APPOINTMENT

SUBJECT: Franny Banks/*Pinetree Lodge* reading
WHEN: WEDNESDAY, APRIL 12, 1995
TIME: 2:30 P.M.
WHERE: ABC Studios, 49 West 66th St, 5th floor
WITH: Jeff Ross and Jeff Bernbaum, Casting

CHARACTER BREAKDOWN:

{ARKADIA SLOANE} 23-25 years old. Arkadia is the long-lost daughter of millionaire patriarch ELLIS SLOANE. Arkadia was believed to have been drowned by millionaire playboy Peter Livingston's third wife, millionairess real estate maven ANGELA BART, who hoped to be named sole heir to his fortune, but is discovered to have survived the assassination attempt by making it to shore, although she was only eight months old. Exhibiting the pluck and sass that enabled her to survive as an infant, Arkadia arrives in Pinetree, ready to settle the score and break some hearts. MUST BE COMFORTABLE IN LINGERIE, MUST BE EXCEPTIONALLY BEAUTIFUL/PLEASE SUBMIT ALL ETHNICITIES.

INT. PINETREE LODGE LOBBY—DAY

ANGELA BART gives instructions to a bellhop as other hotel workers assist a few guests. Breathtakingly beautiful ARKADIA SLOANE enters, carrying a suitcase. She stops short in the lobby, spying Angela. One by one the workers and guests notice Arkadia. They stop what they are doing, paralyzed by her awe-inspiring beauty. Finally Angela also looks up.

                    ANGELA
          Yes? Can I help you?

                    ARKADIA
               (Giggles nervously.)

          Yes! (regains composure) No. I'm sorry.
          That's just funny, coming from you.

                    ANGELA
          I'm sorry, I'm Angela Bart. Do we know each
          other?

                    ARKADIA
          I'm sorry to say we do.

                    ANGELA
          If we've met before, I don't remember. I'm
          sorry. You're very beautiful, you know.

(Arkadia begins to sob uncontrollably.)

ARKADIA

Beautiful? Do I know I'm beautiful?
No, I don't know! My name is Arkadia
Sloane, I know that! You tried to drown
me when I was eight months old, I know
that! Am I beautiful? That's the ONLY
thing I don't know, Angela. I DO know
that I was found on the banks of a
stream by a kindly family of
apple-pickers, in southern Vermont, whose
crops were regularly the victim of blight
and vermin, whose children had long since
grown up and moved away, who didn't need
nor want another child, but who took me
in, who——although kindly, as I
said——believed that mirrors were the Dev-
il's handiwork. They believed in being
honest and hardworking, but plain, as
plain as possible! So I grew up without
mirrors, without lipstick, without
brushes or combs, without proper under-
garments! But I made my way to New York
City, and I scraped and I struggled, and
I made a name for myself! In lingerie!
Perhaps you've heard of my lingerie line,
Arkadia's Lament?

(Angela gasps.)

ANGELA

That's YOU?

(Tears stream down Arkadia's cheeks.)

>   ARKADIA
>   Yes Angela, that's me. Now are you "sorry"?
>   Are you "sorry" now?

>   ANGELA
>   Yes. I am. I told you I was, before knowing
>   how truly sorry I was.

(Angela opens her arms wide, welcoming Arkadia.)

>   ANGELA (CONT'D)
>   But you're wrong. You're wrong about me.
>   I'm so happy you're here. Your father will
>   be so happy, too, my darling. Please let me
>   welcome you. Join me, everyone!

*Patrons and hotel workers gather around Arkadia, AND
IN UNISON . . .*

>   EVERYONE
>   Welcome to Pinetree Lodge!

ANGLE on: *Arkadia—surprised, happy, tired, and
maybe even a bit defiant . . .*

I lower the page and blink a few times.

Holy shit. I can't do this.

15

Before I know exactly what I'm doing, I've dialed Richard back at the agency.

"Did the fax come through?" he asks.

"Um. Yes. Um . . ."

"The speech is a little heavy-handed I know, but you'll be great!"

"I'm not sure I can do this."

"Huh?"

"This—with the lingerie—everyone stops, because she's so beautiful, I mean, please—and then at the end, I'm supposed to look both tired *and* defiant, how could anyone possibly—I'm *sobbing*, on top of everything? I don't even understand . . ."

"Franny, you're nervous. You haven't had an audition in a while. Jeff and Jeff are good casting people, though, and they're nice guys, too. They'll know you haven't had a ton of time with the material. They do other projects besides *Pinetree Lodge*. We just want to get you out there, to be seen. Of course, if you really aren't comfortable with the material, I can tell Joe . . ."

"No, no," I say, quickly backpedaling. "I'm just, uh, having a moment of . . . um . . . I'm sure I'm just nervous, like you said. Never mind. I'll be going now."

"Have fun with it, Franny, really. It's just one audition."

I'm on the D train heading over the Manhattan Bridge, going over my lines in my head. At least, I thought I was doing them in my head until I heard myself. "Oh!" I say, too loudly, and a girl across the subway car looks up from her book and stares at me, hungrily, as if she enjoys entertainment of the deranged subway-rider kind and is hoping I might say more.

I read the pages over and over again, trying to make them sound more real. But the script is so awkward. All those "sorrys," and that speech with all the information about the character's past. No one talks that way. I try to think of what Stavros would say: be truthful, say what you mean and mean what you say, don't ignore the given circumstances. I just have to use what I've learned in class and I'll be fine.

The given circumstances: abandoned child turns up to see her father. She's become a success but has stayed away all this time. Why?

Stavros always tells us when we're analyzing a script to ask, "Why is this day different from any other?" Why did she pick today to show up?

I don't know; I don't have enough information. In class we would have had the whole play, not just a single scene, and we'd have studied it for weeks. We would read what other people wrote about it; we would talk about how other directors and actors interpreted the material. How am I supposed to do that with four pages and a twenty-five-minute subway ride?

In a way, I've watched enough of the show in the past few weeks to have accidentally done this research already. I know the character she's speaking to; I know the world they live in. Arkadia is brand-new in town, though. No one on the show has ever spoken about her before. Angela Bart recently had a cancer scare that turned out to be acid reflux, and has also been given a key to the city of Pinetree for all the humanitarian work she did, which she did only because she plans to run for mayor and siphon the campaign funds to pay for the special "youth pills" she gets from an illegal source in Guam. I know a lot about her world, but none of that helps me know how to play Arkadia.

Also, there's the crying. I've never had to cry in an audition before, let alone "sob" like the stage directions say. In class I've been able to eke out a tear or two now and then, but I can't imagine just bursting into tears in an audition room. I'll have to be so otherwise riveting and compelling that the casting directors won't notice. *Make it your own,* Stavros always says. That's right! That's all I have to do. I'll show them who *my* Arkadia is. I will be the Arkadia who's coming home for the first time, who's been hurt and angry and discarded, who for some reason has bravely chosen this day to stand up for herself, and who does it all without crying.

By the time I sign in with the guard in the lobby (name, who I'm seeing, floor, time) and get my name tag (Frances Banks—Visitor, Jeff and Jeff Casting, 34th floor), I'm flying high. I've convinced myself that I know Arkadia Sloane as well as if she's a real person. I have pushed to the back of my mind such annoying issues of reality as how she possibly found out who her real father was while isolated on a farm in Vermont, the likelihood of an eight-month-old infant swimming to safety, and why anyone would buy underwear that has "Lament" in the name. None of that matters now. I *am* Arkadia. I'm feeling pretty confident.

I realize on my way up that I forgot to change out of my lace-up Doc Martens. The elevator is almost full, so I have to scrunch myself into the corner to avoid hitting anyone while I switch into my heels. When I look up, we're already at the thirtieth floor, next stop thirty-four. I jam my left heel onto my foot and stuff my chunky boot into my bag just as the doors open. I spill out of the elevator, almost losing my balance. I should have put my heels on outside and practiced for a block or so to get used to them, but it's too late to worry about that now.

The elevator bank separates the building's two wings: to my left is a large frosted-glass door with a shiny plaque that says "Sunshine

Productions." To my right is another large frosted-glass door with a piece of notebook paper taped to it. An arrow is drawn in thick marker and underneath it says "Casting." That must be the place.

Finally—my first real audition in ages. I'm back on track. Today is the first day of my *actual* career. "I remember the day things turned around for me," I will say to the packed house at the 92nd Street Y. "Ironically, given the amount of theater I've been lucky enough to do over the years, the audition wasn't for a play; it was actually for a *soap opera.*" And the audience will laugh, amused, surprised.

The elevator chimes and the doors open, bringing a new flood of people into the hallway and me back to reality. I can't stand here forever imagining wonderful things that haven't happened yet. I have to go in there and make them happen. My heart is pounding so hard that I feel a little dizzy, and I'm so shaky that it takes all my effort to push open the massive door.

There is a large receptionist's desk, behind which sits a pale young man wearing a tie, his thin face almost buried behind several stacks of scripts and a giant bouquet of flowers. A clipboard faces out on his desk with the words SIGN IN written in bold letters at the top, and I go straight for it, not wanting to look hesitant or inexperienced. My hand jerks as I try to write my name and social security number, but I feel a burst of pride when, for the first time, I can fill in something under the AGENCY column. "Absolute Artists," I write, and I feel a bit steadier.

Maybe it's my imagination, but the pale receptionist seems to be staring, looking at me with something like curiosity, or is it disdain? Is it that obvious I'm still brand-new?

I don't care. I'm not going to let him intimidate me. I look at him with a smile, but with a little challenge, too, and I think of Arkadia at the end of the scene, who has to look defiant yet vulnerable, and I understand that now in a way I didn't only a few hours ago. A lucky sign! I will remember this feeling, I will use it in my work. The receptionist seems about to say something to me but I'm not going to let him steal my confidence, so I turn away from him, like Arkadia would, sure of herself.

Only then do I realize I am the only white person in the room.

There are two couches that form an L-shape around the receptionist's desk, and on them sit about fifteen of the most beautiful black women I have ever seen. Young and thin and striking, dressed in the tiniest tops and the shortest skirts.

I want to run out of the room, back to Brooklyn, back to my curtainless room, and hide. To say I'm not what they're looking for is an understatement. I had no idea this kind of beauty even existed, in New York or the whole world, and I'm obviously not right for this part. I'm not even the right *color*.

But, it's strange . . . how are they going to explain the daughter of Peter Sloane being black? I guess they can do anything on a soap, bring people back from the dead, wake them up from comas. But I thought Arkadia's mother was the now deceased, but thoroughly Caucasian, Mary Marlowe, the heiress to the . . .

"Excuse me?" The pale receptionist pushes his glasses up on the bridge of his nose, eyeing me suspiciously.

"Yes?"

"Are you in the right place?"

I square my shoulders and look down my nose at him. I am not going to let him make me feel bad. I am not.

"Yes, I believe I am," I say firmly. I am strong. I am confident. I'm Arkadia Sloane.

"Are you sure? You're here for Ebony Breeze perfume?"

What?

"Oh. No. I'm, uh, here for *Pinetree Lodge?*"

"I thought so. You're on the wrong floor. *P.L.* is on thirty-four, one more up."

"Oh. Oh! Thank God!" I sputter, "I mean, I didn't, uh, I got out too . . . I was confused because . . . uh . . ." I gesture helplessly to the room behind me.

The receptionist pushes his glasses up his nose once more and waves me closer to him.

"Don't feel bad," he whispers. "They're *models*."

By the time I get to the right floor and sign in on the correct audition sheet, I'm almost too drained to dwell on the girls I'm actually going up against, who at first glance are less exotic but just as intimidating as the models on the thirty-third floor. How does everyone know what to wear? They all seem to have studied the same hair and makeup handbook, which apparently involves long straight ironed–looking hair and a dark red matte lipstick. They're all so individually striking that it makes them almost blend together into one big beautiful blur. The group becomes one: The Beautifuls. I try to block them out, keeping my head down, studying my lines over and over, gripping the pages too tightly, the flimsy fax paper starting to look crumpled.

A stocky man with short curly hair and a tight blue V-neck sweater opens the door to the audition room, leading one of The Beautifuls out. Her face is shiny and a little damp. She's clearly been crying. My stomach lurches.

"Beautiful work, Taylor," he says quietly. "Really excellent."

"Thanks, Jeff." Taylor uses the ring finger of her right hand to dab delicately under her eyes, so as not to disturb the copious amount of eyeliner that seems to have miraculously remained intact. "It was my honor to say her words," she says, and walks away, glowing with pride.

It was her honor? To say *those* words? Is that how I'm supposed to act? Do people really buy that?

Jeff looks at his clipboard. "Frances Banks? You're next."

I take a deep breath and try to float up from the chair gracefully, like Arkadia would. But one of my heels catches on the shag carpet and the shoe pops off my foot.

"Oopsy," Jeff says, holding the door open for me as I jam my shoe back on.

"Got to quit drinking at lunch," I sputter.

"Not me, honey," Jeff says smoothly. "It's the only way."

"I don't really—I didn't mean . . ."

But we're through the door already, and Jeff is taking his seat.

"Jeff, this is Franny Banks," tight-sweater-wearing Jeff says to open-collar-wearing Jeff. "Joe Melville sent her."

"Fancy. No, no, not so far back, sweetie, your mark is right there, where the chair is. That's it."

"Here? So, should I stand? Or sit? In the chair?"

"Whatever you like, Angel—the camera sees everything."

I'd never thought of it that way before. It sounds ominous. For a minute, I stare into the camera, which is set up on a tripod facing the chair. Then I realize that if the camera sees everything, it's seeing me now stare dumbly into it. I've had cameras at auditions before, of course, but for commercials you generally look directly into them, a man-versus-machine staring contest. Today, however, I'm going to be reading with a person while the camera regards me from another angle, and I'm supposed to pretend that doesn't make me feel self-conscious. *The camera is my friend*, I think. But when I catch the cold black lens from out of the corner of my eye, it makes me sit up straighter and hold my head in a way I hope looks natural, as I try to impress the camera while also trying to pretend it isn't there.

"Have we met her before, Jeff? Do we know her?"

"You're thinking of the other Franny."

"There's another Franny? Who's that?"

"Oh, Franny's her name? I'm thinking of Annie."

"Which Annie?"

"Annie O'Donnell? Er, McDonnell? I forget."

"Who?"

"You know. She has red hair. We put her in that Lars Vogel movie?"

"*Another Love Story*?"

"That's the one."

"Annie MacDonald!"

"Yes!"

"Annie and Franny are totally different people, Jeff. You're the worst with names."

"So, we don't know this Franny. Franny—not Annie—we don't know you."

They've been talking to each other for so long, I'm not sure whether this is a question that demands a response from me or just an observation I'm privy to. Before I can decide, shirt Jeff says, "How old is she?"

"You can't ask her that, Jeff."

"Franny, I'm not supposed to know your age, apparently." He rolls his eyes and winks at sweater Jeff.

"Well, I guess I can't tell you, then," I say, attempting a smile, but it feels a little wobbly.

"But why don't we know her? Franny, why don't we know you?"

I pause, not sure if I should tell them they don't know me because this is my first real audition ever, and if I say the wrong thing I'm afraid it could also be my last.

"Well, I guess it's because I've only recently joined the ranks of the knowable," I manage to spit out.

The Jeffs pause, then break into a small giggling fit.

"The Ranks of the Knowable! Ahahahahaha! *That*'s the name of my new band!"

"You're too old to be in a band, sweetheart."

"I'm not too old to *name* one, am I?"

The Jeffs giggle some more then sigh and finally pull themselves together.

"Sorry, we're a little punchy. We've been at this for three days straight. We've had to reshoot some scenes, which just isn't done on a soap."

"Unless someone throws up during a take, we use it. We'd probably use it even with the throwing up. There's just no time."

"What happened to the other actress?" I ask, and the Jeffs give each other a look. "She was found to be in possession of a giant amount of cocai . . ."

"Cocaaaa . . . Cola. Right, Jeff?"

"Oh. Yes. That's what I was going to say."

"She did enjoy her *soda pop—didn't she*, Jeff?"

"Sorry, yes. What a fan she was of the carbonated beverage!"

"So. Back to Franny. She's tall, isn't she, Jeff?"

"Mm-hmm. Tall, and pretty."

"Thank you," I say, beaming.

"Franny, how tall are you?"

"Jeff, you can't ask her that."

"But is she too tall for Angela? You know how she can get."

"And that hair! Franny, what ethnicity are you?"

"You can't ask her that either, Jeff. Behave."

"*Uchh*, please. All these *laws*."

"I don't mind. I'll tell you. I'm Irish."

They nod, and smile expectantly. I feel they're waiting for more.

"My hair won't tell you anything, though. My hair is very sensitive, and known to be somewhat litigious."

The Jeffs start giggling again.

"Ahahahahaha! The hair is from someplace different!"

"The hair is Jewish maybe!"

"She's got loud Italian hair!"

"The hair *sues*!"

"Ahahahahahahahaha!"

By the time we get to the scene, I'm feeling pretty relaxed. Sweater Jeff reads with me, mouthing some of my lines as I say them. It's distracting, but I try my best to focus. I get through the giant speech pretty smoothly. I wasn't perfect, but I think I managed to radiate some of Arkadia's hurt, some of her pride.

"Well, *I* like her. What do you think, Jeff?"

"Mmmhmm, me too. Try it again, just for fun, Franny. Go a little deeper, maybe?"

Shit. He wants me to cry. That's what "go a little deeper" means. He's probably seeing if I'll cry on the second take. I have to find a way for it to make sense that she doesn't.

The second time, the speech comes out softer somehow, and quieter, but I still can't quite get myself to tear up. It's okay though, I think, because I do feel something more the second time. I didn't intend to change the volume, but I felt as if, as Arkadia, I'd been practicing what I wanted to say to Angela Bart on this day for years, and now that I had my chance, I didn't need to shout to be heard. This version of Arkadia wouldn't cry, I thought, because her armor was up. It makes sense that she wouldn't want Angela Bart to see her true feelings. It makes sense to me, anyway, and that's the most important thing. I made Arkadia *my own*.

When I finish the speech, the Jeffs look at each other, both smiling, as if they liked what they saw.

"Great, sweetheart."

"Glad you came in."

"Your reading was excellent."

"The hair wasn't bad, either."

"Shut up, Jeff."

"You shut up, Jeff."

- - - - -

Outside, it feels like it's going to thunderstorm and the wind has picked up. I have to lean forward to make any progress as I make my way up 66th Street. When I realize part of the leaning feeling is due to the fact that I still have my heels on, I stop on the corner to change my shoes. Even if I weren't being whipped by the cold wind, I know my cheeks would still be burning.

"Excellent," they said. The reading went well, they said so. And they were fun to talk to. And they didn't say anything about the not-crying.

I wonder if I'll get the role. I wonder how long it takes them to call once they decide who gets it. I should check the home machine. But it's probably too soon. There were still a few girls in the waiting area. They probably have to see everyone before they decide. Or do they? Maybe they're calling the agency already. "We didn't need to see anyone else after we saw her read," they're saying to Richard or Joe right now. "She's perfect for the part."

Maybe I should call Joe, or Richard at least. No. I should wait. Just sit back and be cool.

But, then again, maybe I should call Richard just to tell him it went well, so when he talks to them he has more information. Maybe he's already left me a message and wants me to call him back. Maybe he's trying to reach me right at this very moment.

I finally stop at a pay phone to check the home machine.

You have three messages.

I can hardly breathe as I punch in my code and wait for the tape to unwind.

BEEEP

Hi, Franny, it's Gina from Brill. Just wondering—can you juggle? Or ice-skate? They need an ice-skating juggler for a beer ad. Also, do you have a problem with beer? Let us know!

BEEEP

Frances, it's me, your father. I figured maybe they got rid of all of the telephones in Manhattan, but it seems they still exist. Please call me, your father, back.

BEEEP

Hi, Franny, it's Clark. Sorry we keep missing each other. I'll try you back later.

BEEEP

I don't want to call my dad and talk about Katie's wedding, or call Clark, or anyone else, until I see if there's good news to tell. I strike a deal with myself that I will not make any other calls until I buy the paper, go to a diner, get a coffee, and complete the entire *New York Times* crossword puzzle. Only then will I allow myself to call Richard or check the home machine again.

On the way to the diner, I stop at a newsstand and buy the paper and some Marlboro Lights. I haven't bought a pack in three days, and I recently vowed again that I wouldn't smoke anymore, but I'm too worked up right now to quit smoking. I'll quit again next week.

I'm almost done with my coffee and grilled cheese sandwich when I realize what the problem is. It's Friday. I should have thought about what day it was before I made the deal with myself where I have to finish the *New York Times* crossword before I can make a call. From my seat in the booth, I can see the pay phone through the window of the diner—it's free, ready and waiting for me to make the call. I can always get through the Wednesday puzzle at least, and sometimes Thursday. But not always on Friday, and today's is an especially hard one. I'm not even close, not even halfway through it. Maybe this doesn't count since I made the deal before I realized what day it was. But I don't want to ruin my chances by breaking the deal. I'm itching to try the machine again. My leg shakes nervously underneath the table, and my hand grips the idle pencil too tightly.

Right after paying the check, I hurry outside to call Richard. I'm waiting on hold in the phone booth, shivering with nerves and the cold air, unfinished crossword puzzle still in my hand. I make a new deal with myself. I'll never break a deal again, I swear, if just this once, breaking a deal didn't jinx anything. Let it be good news just this once, and then never again—

"Franny! Did you get my message?"

"No. I haven't checked them yet."

"Well—I just left it—listen, they loved you at *Pinetree Lodge*."

It worked! Even though I didn't finish the puzzle. *Thank you, thank you.*

"They did?" I'm attempting to sound casual, but my voice is tight.

"Yes! They said you made sense out of a crappy scene—their words—and they thought you seemed smart and full of personality."

"They *did*?"

"They did! Great job for a first read!"

"Thanks!"

"So, I can't wait to keep getting you out there!"

I'm confused. It almost sounds like the conversation is over.

"Wait. That's it?"

"What do you mean?"

"I mean," I say, and a little wobble creeps into my voice. I try to control it by clearing my throat. "I mean, I didn't get the job?"

"The job?" Richard says, confused. "Oh, no, this was just a first read for the casting people. There's a bunch of steps that have to happen after that."

"Oh," I say, relieved there's more to come. "So, what's the next step?"

"Well, they *loved* you, like I said. I mean, you know that no matter how well you did today, Jeff and Jeff don't have the power to just give you the job anyway."

"They don't?"

"No, no. Sorry, I didn't realize Joe never—well, anyway, let me walk you through it. They're the casting guys, the first people you have to get past, and sometimes the hardest. They bring people in to read and then pass the best choices, the best people, on to the producers. That doesn't just mean the best actors—it's the people who best fit the part. Then you have to read for the producers, or sometimes you have to read for the director, or with another actor—you know, to see if there's chemistry . . . I've had people have to go back for callbacks three or four times just for a small part, a few lines in something, and not even in something that good. It's so competitive out there, they can afford to be choosy and get exactly the right person. It's rarely a short process."

I didn't know any of this. It makes sense now that he says it, but it didn't occur to me that there would be more to face after today, even if today had gone better.

"It's just, that first time, when I got the job, it seemed like it was going to be so easy."

"Yeah, I know. That was pretty unusual, though."

"So I didn't even make it to the next cut?"

"Not this time. It's not going any further. *This time.*"

"Okay," I say, making an involuntary sound somewhere between a cough and a hiccup.

"Franny, you did really well. This is positive feedback. You did great for a first reading. You said yourself this part wasn't really your thing, right? You did a great reading for a part you're not totally right for, and now they've met you and they like you and they'll bring you in next time for something you *are* right for."

I feel so stupid. Of course he's right. I could hardly see myself in the part—how could anyone else? It would make no sense if I had gotten it. But still, there was a part of me that thought I would somehow. I have to introduce the part of me that feels like a winner to the part of me convinced I'm a loser, and see if they can't agree to exist somewhere closer to the middle.

"Franny. This is a win. Just getting you in a room like that is something we've been working on for weeks, and now it's happened, and you made a great impression. If it makes you feel any better, and you did *not* hear this from me, they're already close to making a deal with somebody. One of our clients, actually. They had a last-minute session today just in case it doesn't go through. But they basically have their choice already. This was, like, a backup session."

It makes me feel even worse to know this whole thing was never a real possibility.

"Oh. Great. Thanks. That does make me feel better."

"Look at it this way, Franny. You lost a job you never had. It's not like you got fired, right?"

As I stand there clutching the phone, it's as if I can hear some kind of siren or alarm, but far off in the distance. It's a feeling I'm not sure I've had before, one in which I know something bad is about to happen but I don't know what it is yet. The alarm is getting louder, and I'm suddenly nervous, not the audition kind of excited/nervous, but nervous like I've done something wrong, something I regret. What is it? Something Richard said: *"lost a job you never had . . . not like you got fired."*

It hits me all at once, the alarm, right next to my ear now, ringing full blast: the realization of what I've done, and the certainty of what the outcome will be.

It's Friday, well past four thirty—past when my coveted shift at the club starts.

It's Friday past four thirty, and I'm 100 percent certain I've been fired.

16

....

Herb didn't even tell me himself that I didn't have my job at the club anymore. He sent Ricky to the phone to give me the news.

"We're slammed here. Prom group. It's better that you hear it from me anyway, Franny. Neither of the understudies answered their pagers, and Herb is pissed."

"But maybe if I tried to explain it to him myself—"

"He said giving you one more chance was one chance too many. He said your head's just not in the game. You know, all his regular cop-show shit. He said you can pick up your last check anytime after Wednesday. Sorry, Franny. You'll still come to my show though, right?"

"Yeah, of course."

Then the following Tuesday in class, Penelope Schlotzsky showed up with a new haircut and lighter blond highlights. She ran her fingers through her new long layers with indifference: "Oh, this? *They* did it. For work. I had to do it for this *job*." "Job" might as well be "jail" for how unglamorous she made it sound.

"What'd she get?" I asked Casey. "What job?"

"She's like, the new lead on *Pinetree Lodge*," Casey said with a shrug.

"Oh, really?" I said, trying not to sound too surprised. "I read for that."

"You *did*?" Casey, said, impressed. "Wow. All I had last week was a go-see for Ebony Breeze perfume."

"I almost went in on that, too." I said, and Casey gave me a funny look as Stavros dimmed the house lights. "I'll explain later," I whispered into the darkness.

Penelope Schlotzsky, I thought. *Of course.* I would have given it to her over me, too. But it still stings. How can a part I had no chance of ever getting still feel like it belonged to me, even a little?

So when Stavros assigned James Franklin and me to do a scene together, I was less excited than I might normally have been. I need a job like his girlfriend has, not a headache like him.

Still, a few days later, when I hear his voice, or what I think is his voice, talking into the answering machine upstairs, I run so fast that I bang my knee on the circular staircase while lunging for the phone.

"Ow, I mean, hello?" I say, a little short of breath.

"Franny?"

"Yes?"

"It's James. Franklin."

"Oh, hi." I actually have to cover the receiver while I try to catch my breath. I'm audibly gasping for air.

"You okay?"

"Yes. Are you okay?" I shoot back, boldly.

"Am I . . . okay?" he says, sounding confused.

I try to adjust my tone and sound more breezy. "I mean, how are you? Okay?"

"Yeah, uh, I am. I'm actually in the neighborhood. Want to take a walk? I thought we could work on our scene, if you're free."

Am I free? I'm not sure. It would definitely be cooler of me not to be free, but I'd like something to do, since I do happen to be free. And anyway, he isn't asking me out, therefore the never-say-yes-to-being-asked-out-on-the-same-day rule doesn't apply here. It definitely doesn't apply to scene partners from class who are just getting together to work.

But I hesitate. Who's actually ever just in the neighborhood? Brooklyn is huge. I've never even told him my address. He could be in Coney Island inviting me to take a walk on the boardwalk for all I know.

"How can you be sure?" My question sounds mysterious and confident, I think, as if I'm a detective in a British mystery. I'm combing the misty London streets at night with my magnifying glass, finding clues no one else can see.

"How can I be . . . what?" he says, after a moment.

"How would you know where I live?" He must have not only kept my number, but researched me, too. Maybe he looked me up in the phone book, although I think we're only listed under Jane's name. That means he must have really had to work hard to find me. Then it hits me—James is also a client at Absolute. Maybe he called Richard at the agency and told him he needed to reach me, and maybe now there's a rumor going around the office that we're dating. I wonder whether the agency thinking that I'm dating an actor who actually gets auditions and books jobs will make them think more highly of me.

At any rate, he found me, I think to myself proudly. He somehow found me, so it must mean he's at least a little interested.

"We're all in the, uh, on the class contact sheet? I live sort of close by."

Oh. Right. Stavros's class contact sheet. I forgot about that. We all have each other's addresses and phone numbers so we can rehearse together. So I guess he didn't really have to work that hard to find me. But that day on the street he asked for my number. Why would he ask for it if he had it already?

"So then, what was the point of asking for my number that day?"

I close my eyes and cringe. *Shut up*, I tell myself. *You'll be working together for the next three or four weeks. Be cool.*

"I guess, because I wanted to call you?"

"Why not just use the contact sheet, then?"

For some reason I'm trying to ruin everything, even before there's anything to ruin.

He clears his throat. "Because I guess I wanted to call you in the personal way, not the class-contact-sheet way."

I've gone from bumbling idiot to positive genius, even if only in my own estimation. I have been forthright and bold, like a woman with actual confidence would be, and in return for my bravery I have received a direct and pleasing answer. I must always be this daring and spirited. I'm like a woman in a perfume ad. I'm carrying a brief-case, skipping through Manhattan in a flowing yellow pantsuit and impossibly high heels, so you know I'm not only hugely successful and independent, but irresistible, too. I picture James and me strolling hand in hand through the neighborhood in Brooklyn, a place where I've never strolled hand in hand with anyone.

I shake my head in an attempt to clear it. It's ridiculous to be thinking of James as a potential boyfriend. He's just my scene partner. We're in class together. We're working together, that's all. His saying he wanted to call me in the personal way is cute, but he didn't actually call me until today, so it doesn't mean anything. Plus, as far as I know he's still with Penelope, which means he likes someone whose signature contains a smiley face in the "o" of her name. If he likes her, I'm definitely not his type. I have to act more professional around James. He's a real working actor in a world I've only imagined, and I want to be composed enough to potentially learn something from him.

"We're both wearing Doc Martens!" I squeal, as I come down my front stoop. So much for cool professionalism.

But he doesn't seem put off at all. He breaks into an easy grin, as if I've just said the most delightful thing. "Want to get a coffee first?" he asks.

He says his apartment isn't far, but as we walk down toward Fifth

Avenue, I realize I've never been this far south in my own neighbor-hood. Brooklyn as I know it quickly falls away, giant trees replaced by overflowing garbage cans, elegant brownstones giving way to more plain, tightly packed row houses. We stop for coffee at a place I've never been, where the coffee is made behind a protective metal grille and handed to us through a small opening that's locked after we pay. The man behind the grille eyes me in a way that makes me feel as if I'm trespassing.

"I love this place," James says, blowing on his coffee to cool it. "Authentic Cuban coffee. Reminds me of a place near where I grew up in Hoboken."

I take a sip of my coffee and practically gag from how hot and strong and almost gritty it is. "Yum, delicious," I say, managing a smile. "Wait, you're from New Jersey? That's so funny. I thought you were from the South for some reason. My roommate and I imagined you were some sort of cowboy."

I shouldn't have told him I've discussed him. I'm revealing too much too soon. I seem to have momentarily lost the attributes of perfume-ad lady. But this time it's his face that flushes.

"Oh. Yeah. Sorry about that. I was . . ."

He trails off, looking up at the sky. He's got one of those ruddy complexions that reddens easily, I've noticed. I imagine him herding sheep on the moors of Scotland or Ireland, somewhere misty and rugged, wearing a cream-colored wool cable-knit sweater and green Wellies, maybe smoking a pipe.

I wonder what it is about James Franklin that makes me con-stantly imagine him as someone else, somewhere else, especially when he's right here in front of me. Shouldn't that be enough of a fantasy? Not that this is a fantasy exactly. I've wondered about him, it's true, but it's just a work session with a classmate I happen to find attractive, which is less of a fantasy and more of a really good day.

"I was probably just working on something, something for work

I mean, and I guess it, uh, crept into my real life without my noticing it."

I'm impressed. James was working on a character, probably for his Arturo DeNucci film, and he's so dedicated that he unconsciously kept doing the character's dialect even away from the set. I want to ask him more about it, but I think I've done enough fawning already. I've regained perfume-ad-lady composure for the moment, and I don't want her to slip away again.

The scene we've been assigned is from a two-character play that was recently done Off Broadway called *The Blue Cabin*, about a woman who flees her wedding ceremony right before she's supposed to say "I do." She runs, still in her wedding dress, as far as she can, until she finds herself in the middle of nowhere, and knocks on the door of the only shelter she can find, a remote cabin in the woods. She just needs a place to sleep—she wants nothing to do with the gruff loner she finds inside at first, and he doesn't want his privacy invaded either, but eventually they open up to each other and begin to fall in love.

James's apartment is on the ground floor of a tan brick row house. It's dark when we enter, and I can't quite make out the room at first, but I can see through to the garden out back. He says he shares it with the upstairs neighbor, but there's a part that's partitioned off just for him. "The outdoor smoking lounge," he calls it.

He doesn't turn on any lights, but he starts to light a few candles, which I would normally think of as a romantic gesture, except I'm refusing to let any thoughts like that in. Perfume-ad ladies in yellow pantsuits don't allow themselves to be torn away from the work at hand by a few candles that may or may not be intended to woo them.

Once my eyes adjust, I can see that, while it's small, the room is clean and well organized, and even sort of formal. I don't know why that's surprising exactly; I guess most of the guys I know aren't that into their surroundings.

James doesn't have much furniture, but what he does have is the exact right size for its role in the room, and the more I take it all in, the more I can see how old and expensive it is. Everything looks so grand that the room, which is perfectly fine, seems apologetically shabby in contrast. It's as if he's royalty of some kind, who had to hurriedly move from a large mansion to far less desirable accommodations and could take only his favorite pieces.

There's even proper art on the walls: a few oil paintings, one of a man in uniform, one of a bowl of fruit, and a few charcoal drawings that look like they could be hung in a museum. His bed is neatly made and dressed with pillows, and the two small windows that face the garden are hung with dark red velvet curtains.

"Wow."

"Thanks." He pauses for a moment. "I think living in a beautiful space is important, since actors are artists after all, and we're therefore more acutely affected by everything around us. Poorly chosen objects are distractions, obstacles we put in the way when we're afraid of telling the truth." Then he stops and his face flushes. "Sorry. I think I just sounded really pretentious."

I picture my bedroom on Eighth Avenue: unframed posters on the wall, twisted pajamas on the bed, towels draped over the desk chair, and shoes all over the floor. Am I messy because I'm avoiding some "truth"? I always thought I was just plain old messy. But maybe my lack of neatness is trying to tell me something. What would it feel like if I took myself more seriously and referred to myself as an "artist," the way James did? When he said it, it did sound a little self-important. But maybe it sounds that way only to someone who doesn't make her bed.

"It doesn't sound pretentious at all. It's an inspiring concept, actually. It never occurred to me to think of my room as an extension of the, uh, craft, or whatever. I'm always more like, who has time for this, you know?" I laugh, but my laugh sounds wrong to me now; it's too loud and uncontrolled in this beautiful space. It feels as messy as my room.

As if he's reading my mind, James says, "It's interesting, isn't it? That you can find yourself feeling so awkward in unfamiliar surroundings that you become more self-aware and more self-conscious? Maybe that lack of connection to an unfamiliar place can actually give you freedom to open up and see yourself. I thought coming here might help you with Kate. She was stifled before, but because she's with a stranger in a strange place, she's finally free to open up. She can finally breathe."

All of that is interesting, except who the hell is Kate?

James is looking at me expectantly.

"Kate?"

"Your character. From the play?"

Oh, right. Kate. I'd almost forgotten that we're here to work on the play whose characters are named Kate and Jeffrey, but in fact it seems we're working already, since everything James has been talking about relates to the play and the work we're supposed to be doing.

In the play, Jeffrey decided to escape from the world after his wife died and create an isolated haven for himself in a cabin in the woods. Kate has lived a sheltered life, never straying far from her familiar surroundings, until the moment she flees the altar. The cabin is completely foreign to her, just like James's apartment is to me.

Coming here was a genius idea of his. I'm already learning so much from him. He's so smart.

"You're so smart," I say.

"You're so pretty," he says.

It hangs there.

I can almost see the letters that formed the words suspended in the air between us. Part of me wants to bat them away and watch them fall to the ground by making a joke, or saying something deflective, but I also want to leave them floating there, to savor the compliment for just a second more.

He said it so quickly and easily—was he serious? Was the compliment even coming from him, or is this part of our scene study? Maybe he's in character already.

Either way, I don't want to ask.

17

....

It's turned dark and pleasantly hazy in James Franklin's apartment. He's lit some more candles and dimmed the lights further. We've done our scene over and over until it's lost all meaning to me. He wanted to keep going even longer, but I finally convinced him to stop and take a break. We step out to his tiny garden to share a cigarette, the only one left, which we pass back and forth as if it's something we're used to doing together.

"Why are you still in class?" I ask him, then immediately wish I could take it back. My face reddens, but he doesn't seem put off at all. He smiles, looking thoughtful.

"What do you mean?" he says, taking a deep drag off the cigarette, then passing it to me, filter end out, like he's handing me a pair of scissors and doesn't want me to cut myself.

"I mean, you're working. Everyone's in class so they can get better, so they can get a job and not have to be in class anymore. So, why are you still in class?"

"I don't want to stop learning. I'm afraid if I stop taking class I'll get, like, complacent or something. Even Arturo still studies."

"He does?"

"Yeah. He studies privately, but he still drops into Ivanka's class." Ivanka Pavlova is the other big teacher in town, although the mention of her name makes Stavros roll his eyes sometimes. "Try that in

Ivanka's class," he'll say, when someone does something he deems unnecessarily showy.

"What's he like?"

"Arturo?"

"Yeah. What's he—is he—to work with I mean. You don't have to tell me anything personal about him. I'm only interested as an actor, you know? Like, how does he . . . what do you think makes him so great?"

"I guess it's that he's so *authentic*."

"Authentic?"

"Yeah. Like, he doesn't fake anything, you know?"

I nod, as if I know.

"He's always *real*." James pauses, as though he's not sure if he should say more. "Like, the other day, we had a scene, or, we were supposed to have this scene where—we're cops, right?—he's my dad, and they've assigned us to be partners, but he doesn't want to be partners, because he's worried about me, like I'm this hothead from Georgia, you know? And he's supposed to blow up at me in the car, and his line's supposed to be 'Get out of here! Just get out!' or something like that, and he just—he decided the line wasn't real for him, in the moment, so he just—he decided not to say it."

"Wow," I say.

"Yeah," he says.

"But—wait. I'm confused. So—if he didn't say anything, then—how does it end?"

"Who knows? Maybe they'll rewrite it. Or reshoot it. Or maybe it'll be perfect the way it is. Arturo has wonderful instincts."

"But why didn't he just finish the scene?"

"It wasn't authentic for him in the moment."

"But, they pay him all that money."

"Well, he makes all that money because he's so authentic."

"But then, isn't it sort of his job to be authentic whenever they need him to be?"

"He's an *artist*."

"Yes. But it's all pretend. I mean, I agree he's very authentic, like you said, an artist, but also, none of what we do is *actually* authentic."

"What do you mean?"

"I mean, you guys aren't actually cops."

"Uh-huh . . ."

"It's all made up. Right? That's the job of being an actor. To make something made up seem real."

"It's not just a job—it's an art."

"Right," I say. "I see."

But I don't really understand. I feel guilty if I take too long in the shower and use all the hot water. I can't imagine telling a group of people waiting for me to finish a scene that I couldn't complete it because I didn't feel I could make it *authentic* enough. But Arturo DeNucci is an inarguably great actor. Maybe that's what it takes. Maybe I'd be a better actor, too, if I weren't so worried about being polite.

"I mean, I agree there's a range of acceptable behavior," James says. "But Arturo's work merits the process. It's like I said to Penny, back when we were together—I said, that soap, don't do it. It will deaden you, because that process, there's no *freedom* there. There's just tons of pages of bullshit that have to be shot no matter what, and story exposition to wade through, and there's no choice but to get through it. There's no fucking beauty in that."

I'm pretty sure he just told me he's not with Penelope anymore, which would normally be exciting information, but my brain hurts, I'm hungry, and my eyes are dry and itchy. I'm done for the night.

"It's past ten," I say, stretching. "I'm exhausted. I need to eat something."

"Let's do the scene again, please? Just once more," he says. "Let's throw away the blocking we've set, and change everything."

"Why?"

"Just for fun. Let's follow any impulse that comes up, anything at all."

"Like what?"

"It doesn't matter. Laugh in the wrong place. Jump up and down. There are no wrong choices. Surprise me."

The thrill I felt when we started tonight has disappeared completely. The concept of jumping up and down for no reason is irritating. I'm tired and I want to eat something bad for me and get into bed. James seems annoyingly actor-y to me now. I don't want to "throw away" all the work we've put into the last few hours. I thought that's why we put the work in, so we would know what we were doing and how we would do it when we performed for the class. This "throw it all away" idea seems pointless and self-indulgent. James is looking at me with his intense brown eyes, waiting for my answer. But there's a sort of smile on his face, and I realize that he's taunting me a little, he's pushing me, even though he knows I don't feel like being pushed. I don't want to give in so easily.

"Jumping up and down is a dumb idea."

"Which part is dumb: Is it the thought of jumping up and down, or the fact that I suggested you do it?"

"Both."

"What else is dumb?" He's enjoying himself. He's enjoying watching me pout and be resistant. It's all part of his challenge.

"This game. This is a dumb game."

"What else?"

"I want to go home."

"Start the scene."

"What?"

"Go. Start the scene right now. Don't censor yourself. Go."

We've been using James's actual front door as the door in the scene. So I step outside the apartment, preparing to enter like I've done dozens of times tonight, only this time I'm fuming. He's just an actor in class, the same as me, and just because he has a few movies on his résumé doesn't mean he gets to play director, too. Working with him a little has demystified him for me. I'm not as impressed by him as I was when we started. I definitely don't want to do what he says anymore. I don't want to play his stupid games.

I enter. The scene is the same, but different. I'm saying the same lines, but not in the careful way I was. I'm throwing things away that should be given great importance, and I'm exaggerating little words unnecessarily. It doesn't always work or make any sense, but I don't care. I want this to be over. I'm just looking for a way to get through it quickly, to satisfy whatever desire he has to mess with me. I feel reckless. Gone is the feeling I've had since our time together began, the feeling that I'm trying to win James over.

We've been rehearsing in the living space near the kitchenette by moving the small dining table and chairs back against the wall. It's enough space to work in, but we've been limited by the presence of James's bed, which takes up a lot of the room.

The scene we're doing is the last scene from Act One, when Kate has finally exposed a lot of her story and becomes exhausted. She's been running for hours and hasn't slept in two days. "I just need to rest," she says. "Just let me rest." The stage directions say: "Kate lies on the floor and falls asleep."

I've been following the stage directions, I've been saying those lines sleepily. This time, though, when I enter, I'm wide awake. I feel agitated. I can't stop moving. I pace all around the room, looking everywhere but in James/Jeffrey's face. For some reason I don't want to look at his face anymore.

My gaze lands on James's bed—his perfectly made, beautifully dressed bed, covered with a dark blue bedspread that might be silk.

I stop my pacing.

I rip off the blue silk bedspread and throw it in the air, not caring where it lands. There's a soft down quilt underneath, and I pull that off, too, tossing it over my head and letting it pool on the floor. Then I strip back his top sheet, which isn't easy, because it's been tightly tucked underneath the corners of the mattress. The effort it takes is helpful, though, in a way. It's reducing my frustration somehow to do something physical. I want to mess his bed up, I think—I deserve to. I'm tired. He's bossy. He's confusing. And people from Hoboken, New Jersey, should not have Southern accents.

Finally, having wrestled all the corners free, I raise the sheet up high so that the released fabric billows out like a sail above the bed. I shake it out a few more times before finally allowing it to come to a landing, settling softly over the mattress. Then I attack it again, scrunching it together in a ball to make it as wrinkled as possible. I take the crumpled mass and fashion it around myself, bandage-toga style, in an exaggeration of the confusing, messy, twisty way I like to sleep at home, and I collapse, twisted and tangled, right in the center of his bed.

I haven't looked at James once since I started to dismantle his bed. I didn't want to lose the unfamiliar, thrilling feeling that I don't care what he thinks.

"I just need to rest," I say, my face to the ceiling. "Just let me rest."

There's only silence in response, which makes sense because that's the end of the scene, but it feels as though there should be more somehow. I'm not sure whether the scene's over or we're still doing this strange exercise. All I know is that I'm not going to be the one to break the spell. I'll wait all night if I have to. He's not going to be the one in control. I am.

I can feel his weight on the bed. I didn't even hear him move there from across the room, but now he's sitting on the bottom cor- ner; I can tell by how his presence has shifted the mattress. He just sits there, not moving, for what seems like a very long time.

I feel the tips of his fingers as they lightly brush the top of my foot. They rest there, but only barely, like hands hovering above a typewriter, as if waiting for permission to start, but then his whole palm covers the top of my foot. His hand is warm and large enough that it can almost circle my whole foot, which he now grasps warmly and firmly, as if it's a hand he's shaking in greeting.

He's touching my foot. *He's touching my foot.*

I've never had my foot touched like this. I'm frozen in indecision. Maybe next he'll move his hand up my leg, and then . . . oh God, when was the last time I shaved my legs? Is this a come-on of some kind? Some version of a first kiss? And if it is, what do I want to do about it? And if I want to do something about it, what's the proper response when being approached, er, podiatrically? Also, my sheet-wrestling finale was so aggressive that I fear I'm kind of bound in place. I would have to perform some sort of awkward constricted sit-up in order to free my arms and untangle myself and properly see the expression on his face, and without seeing his face it's hard to know how he intends this odd gesture, and therefore hard to know how I feel about it. I guess I could pull my foot away in protest, or wiggle my toes in encouragement, but both responses seem to make too strong a statement.

Before I can decide, James appears above me, straddling me, his arms fully extended on either side of my shoulders, as if he's at the top of a push-up and I'm just the mat underneath. He's not touching me at all, but his face is directly above mine, his hair falling forward. He's smiling and his cheeks are red.

"You have no idea how amazing you are, do you?"

"Thanks," I sputter, trying to move my arm so I can shift my body and turn away from him. But in my attempt to roll over, I realize I can't move my arm, or any of my upper body, because I'm definitely stuck in the sheet. Normally I'd push my way out from under him, avoiding the intensity of the moment, but I can't easily move, and I don't want to ruin my apparently impressive performance with an awkward transition out of the bed. I'll just lie here for a beat more and let him think I'm naturally this composed.

But he seems to be reading something into my stillness. He's searching my face for something. I don't know what.

"You have no idea how amazing you are, do you?" he says again.

I didn't know what to say the first time he said that, and I still have no idea how to respond. My face is burning. I wish I could move my arms. My legs have room to squirm a little, but it's no compensation. I want to move off the bed but I'm tangled in the sheet, and it seems I'm powerless to tell him to let me get up. It's as though my body is tied to my voice, and if they can't agree to move together, I'm stuck.

"Uh . . . listen . . ."

But before I can say more, he kisses me, lightly, just once. There's something so careful about his kiss. It's almost chaste, as if he doesn't want me to take his kissing too seriously. And something about the combination of feeling claustrophobic and being so close to him and having not been kissed in a long time and being kissed by him, but not really, makes my perfume-ad-lady bravery come forward in full force, and without planning it I hear myself say:

"Why don't you kiss me for real?"

A look of surprise crosses James's face, as if what I just said makes no sense at all.

Perfume-ad lady evaporates.

I've shocked him. I've made a mistake. But how could I have misread his signs? He touched my foot. He positively *grasped* it. And he kissed me. He's *still* straddling me, for God's sake.

But wait—the surprised look has evaporated. Maybe it was never there at all. James is gazing at me now with something more like— well, he's sort of smoldering now, his cheeks so red he might be blushing. He lowers himself slowly onto one side of me, leaning his head on one hand, and traces the outline of my lips with his other hand, making me shiver.

And then, just like I asked, he kisses me for real.

- - - - -

Hours later I stagger to my feet. I hardly know what's happened. At some point we got up and had some wine before falling back into bed, but I still haven't eaten anything and the combination of fatigue, hunger, and kissing have made me delirious. I'm in a dream. I must be. I can't have spent the last two hours making out with James Franklin. Thanks, Perfume Lady!

"I'm going to walk you home," he says at the door, his palm cupping the back of my neck, pulling me closer. If I don't leave soon, I'm in danger of not leaving at all.

"I told you, I'm fine. It's not that far."

"This street isn't great at night."

"That's why I have this," I say, showing him the canister of mace that hangs from my key chain. "I'm a real New Yohkah."

"Tell me about it. I'm learning how tough you are." He brushes a strand of hair out of my face and whispers in my ear, "After all, I was practically jumped by you tonight."

I pull away from him, too abruptly, but I need to read the expression on his face. Is he kidding? I don't like the sound of that.

"You weren't . . . I wouldn't say I *jumped* you exactly. You were plenty, uh . . . uh . . . jumpy, too, you know . . ." I sputter. I can't get my words straight.

"Relax, Franny, I'm just teasing. I've wanted this to happen since that day on the street. I was just trying to keep it professional tonight, you know, just a little of Act Two to keep things interesting, but keeping the boundaries. But you. You really went there." He pulls me close to him, pressing himself against me. "I'm glad you did. Really glad."

He closes the door behind me after one last kiss, a kiss I'm only partially present for because my mind is racing. I practically run the whole way home, both because the neighborhood is creepily quiet and dark and because of the nagging feeling that I've done something I'm going to regret. How could he, in a million years, say I jumped him, even jokingly? And what was he talking about, "Act

Two"? Our scene is from the end of Act One. He got it wrong, I'm pretty sure. I'll have to look at the play again when I get home.

As I get closer to my neighborhood, I slow my pace. There's nothing to worry about. The night is beautiful, cool, and still, and I've done enough jogging to slow down and feel warm. I want to savor the evening on my own before it fades. Tonight was amazing. The work was so exciting, and then what came after . . . I felt strong and smart and pretty with James—at least I did most of the time.

I pause at the steps of our building, and from the street I can see the glow of our living room light. Someone is home and awake.

I hope it's Jane, home late from work with stories of Russell Blakely, and what it's like to watch a movie star work on an actual movie set. It's funny how close she is to it and yet how far away, working long hours for seventy-five dollars a day. Or maybe it's Dan who's up, writing at the dining room table, dreaming of his script making it into a science-fiction festival. We're all working hard, but so far away from what we actually want to be doing. We're all peering in at the window of a party we aren't invited to yet, a party we wouldn't know how to dress for, or what kind of conversation to make, even if we came as someone's guest.

I bet it's Dan who's up, finished writing for the day and watching TV, his second beer resting precariously between his legs. He spills at least one beer a week on the hardwood floor because he doesn't want to put the bottles on our "nice" coffee table, a table that Jane and I found and hauled up from the street corner on a trash day a few years back.

I don't know why I'm thinking about Dan and that coffee table. I've stood outside long enough now that I'm starting to feel a chill. I should go to sleep before I can start worrying about what tonight means, if it means anything at all. I should go to bed for maximum beauty rest. I should get up early tomorrow and run. I vow to enter the house and greet whichever roommate is there and then go directly to my room, pausing only to look out the window and to see what Frank is watching on television, before moving directly to studying my scenes from *The Blue Cabin*, to ensure maximum retention of tonight's work. Arturo DeNucci probably stays up and studies his lines, even after a long rehearsal. I'm sure James does, too. I'm tired, but tonight I feel like a real actor. A serious actor, on her way to becoming an authentic artist.

THE BLUE CABIN

ACT TWO, SCENE ONE

The curtain rises to reveal KATE as we left her at the end of ACT ONE, sleeping on the sheepskin rug near the fireplace. JEFFREY sits next to her. KATE stirs, throws off her covers. JEFFREY attempts to pull the blanket over her without disturbing her. She wakes just as he is covering her. He hovers over her, awkwardly.

JEFFREY.   You have no idea how amazing you are, do you?

KATE.   I should never have told you that story.

JEFFREY.   *(mocking her)* You don't, do you? You have no idea how amazing you are.

KATE.   *(pushing him away)* It's not funny anymore. Stop. I told you, I don't need anyone's help.

Shit. Oh shit.

1 Monday

GREAT PERFORMANCES CATERING 212·727·2424
    - NOT HIRING, CHECK BACK IN 1 MONTH

BEST INTENTIONS CATERING 212·555·0149
    - MAY HAVE SOME LUNCHES - CHECK IN DAILY

APPLE ONE TEMPS - 212·697·6770
    - WILL CALL BACK
        WINDOWS 95 ?? MUST LEARN

JAMES

2 Tuesday

TOAST
RAMEN
CAN REFRIED BEANS
VANILLA WAFERS
CHICKEN PLATE FROM GROSS PLACE

THE SANDS CONF #
    GK288

FRANNY

3 Wednesday

TWO MONTHS
UNTIL JULY 3

MAIL
RENT CHECK

F3

GOODBYE NY

DINNER w JAMES

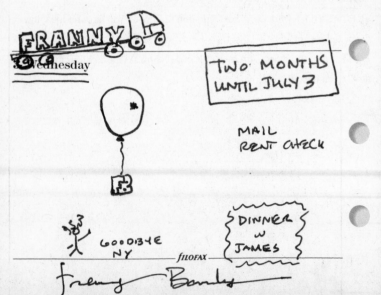

FILOFAX

Franny Banks

SHE RUNS THE GAMUT OF
EMOTIONS FROM A TO B

— DOROTHY PARKER

WHAT
I ATE:
TODAY GRANOLA BAR
     PEANUT BUTTER CRACKERS
     RAMEN
     VANILLA WAFERS
     FRIES AT DINER
       W/ GRAVY

THE CAB IN
MEMORIZED

STAVROS CLASS

WENT HOME AFTER CLASS
          W J.F.

Friday **5**

Franny

RENT DUE
(CALL DAD?)

DONT CALL DAD FOR MONEY

J.F.

Saturday **6**

SANTA FE GRILL W/ JANE   9PM.

Sunday **7**

— FIND DRESS FOR KATIE'S WEDDING

Franny Banks Franny Banks Franny Banks

18

....

It's just as I always thought.

By mistakenly acting like someone with confidence, I found the real personality I always hoped was buried beneath the other one, the one I used to have, full of doubt and unattractively low self-esteem. By accidentally acting like the me I wanted to be, I've convinced someone I'm actually that person, and I've even nearly convinced myself. James and I have seen each other almost every night since the night we rehearsed our scene for the first time, and the thrill of it almost takes away the gnawing in my stomach that's been a constant since the day I got fired from the club. *Money. Where's the money going to come from?*

"So, you're pretending to be someone else?" Jane asks, shaking her head in confusion. We're having frozen margaritas at the Mexican place on Seventh Avenue the way we've done a hundred times before. But it's one of the first nights I've been anywhere but James's apartment and it feels strange here now, as if I'm visiting my old high school after having been away at college.

"No, it's not like that," I say, crushing a chunk of ice with my plastic straw. "I mean, yes, initially, I didn't realize James was doing a line from the play we were working on, so I was bold by accident, but I actually feel like I found my real self in the process. I'm more me than ever before. I feel like I'm finally becoming the person I was always supposed to be."

"So you *are* pretending to be someone else."

"Jane. Seriously. I think this could be the beginning of something."

"So what happened to the girlfriend?"

"Penelope? They broke up," I say, waving a tortilla chip dismissively. "She got that soap and changed her name. Can you believe it?"

Jane nods solemnly, but fixes her gaze just over my head and furrows her brow.

"Jane. Are you listening?"

"I'm just wondering. If, for some reason, you—the *new* you, that is—changed *your* name, would that somehow reverse the process you've recently undergone, making you *less* of the you you were always supposed to become, or would that make you somehow even *more* you?"

"Jane."

"It's very confusing."

"Get this. She's changed her name to *Penny De Palma.*"

"As in Brian De Palma?"

"See? That's exactly what you're supposed to think. She changed her name, which, fine, but she changed it so you associate her with a famous director. Isn't that insane?"

"It's either insane or really smart, I guess. Who knows? Maybe she's actually related to Brian De Palma."

"Why are you defending her?"

"I'm not defending her. I just said, who knows? And who cares? I don't get why she bothers you so much."

"It's not that she—I'm not bothered. She's just so fake, and it's—she bugs me, that's all."

"So you're not at all bothered. You're just bugged."

"That's right."

"You're bugged more than bothered."

"Yes."

Jane nods gravely. "Well, she got your part, but you seem to have gotten her boyfriend. Seems like an even exchange."

I can feel my whole body flush in a mixture of shame over my petty remarks about Penny and flashes from last night with James. Over the past few weeks, we've hardly been anywhere but his one-room apartment, but that seems to be the only room we need, at least for now. I try to stifle a giggle, but one rises to the surface and idiotically slips out.

"Oh, Good Lord," Jane says. "Can we order, please? It's making me queasy just looking at you." But she smiles as she picks up her menu, and I know she's happy for me, too.

"Jane," I say, leaning in and lowering my voice. "Seriously. I know it's new, but honestly, I've never felt this way before."

She leans in, too, and studies my face. "Really? You've *never* felt this way before? Not ever? Not even with *Velcro Man?*"

I smile and roll my eyes, remembering the guy I dated for a month or so, a comic I met at the club who admittedly had an impressive array of Velcro items: shoes, wallet, his nylon book bag, the red hat with the black racing stripe, the light blue jacket with the tab collar he always wore.

"How I miss the familiar *phwisht* of his arrival!" Jane says sadly.

"Yes, Jane, it's very different from Velcro Man."

"I really thought you guys were going to *stick.*"

"Jane."

"And so," Jane says. "You like this hunky actor dude even better than *Purpolo?*"

Phil was an actor from class who took me out a few times, but Jane insisted she couldn't be expected to learn the name of someone who always wore the same purple polo shirt.

"He must've forgotten he wore it the last time he came to pick me up," I'd tried to explain. "Anyway, I'm pretty sure he owns more than one. He told me purple is his favorite color."

"You're going out with a guy whose favorite color is *purple*?"

"Yes."

"And that's *okay with you*?"

I smile at the memory of those minor players and give Jane a nod. "Yes, Jane, I'm fairly certain I like James better than Purpolo. He has a wider variety of shirts."

Jane lays her menu down and looks at me more seriously now. "Franny, do you think he's—well, what about Clark?"

Of course it's occurred to me that James is the first person I've met in the last couple of years who might be in a different category than the likes of Velcro Man or Purpolo. And of course I've wondered what to do in the event that our relationship gets really serious. "Clark, I've met someone," I try to imagine saying to him over the phone in a grave tone, eliminating any joyful note from my voice as a gesture of respect. We never really made plans about how to handle things in the event either of us met someone else. I'm not sure what the right thing to do would be, and I'm not sure I want to think about it yet. Anyway, it's too early to tell if there's something I need to tell him.

"We'll see, I guess."

"Okay," Jane says with an understanding nod, picking up her menu again. "So, Fran, you know I'm honestly the last person to care about this, and may I say again, you look great already, but what, uh, what exactly are you eating these days, if I might ask? Are we splitting that cheesy thing, or are you ordering a bowl of ice cubes for dinner, or what?"

"I don't know. I'm too hungry to think straight. I haven't eaten anything at all today."

"*What?* It's nine o'clock at night. How are you still standing?"

"No, it's—I'm fine. I have a new thing I'm doing."

"Uh-huh."

"I've figured out a new way to view eating—it's like, if you think about it, calories are like money, you know?"

"Umm. Nooo."

"I mean, you get, or, I get, I'm allowed, let's say, a certain number of calories a day, right? So, let's say it's a hundred—obviously it's not, but what if you think of it as cash, and in cash, for the sake of this explanation, it's a hundred dollars. Let's say I'm rich, okay, and I'm in France or somewhere, and someone's given me a hundred dollars a day to spend."

"I'm so confused . . ."

"Stick with me. Let's say I'm in France and I get one hundred dollars a day to spend on anything I want. Well, at first I might think the best thing to do is use it in little amounts throughout the day, a coffee here, a pack of gum there . . ."

"Why'd you go to France for *gum*?"

"But then, I figure out that if I save my money, I'll have it all left over at the end of each day, and then instead of a hundred packs of gum, I can use it all at once for something bigger and better, like on a really cute hat or something. Doesn't that make more sense?"

"But, then," Jane says, shaking her head. "What do you eat in France all day? Your hat?"

"Anyway, if I was in France, I would've saved up all my packs of gum today." I fold my hands and rest them on the table in triumph.

"So we *are* getting the cheesy thing."

"Exactly."

Jane exhales in relief and lays the menu on the corner of the table, and our usual, terminally deadpan waitress comes by and takes our order.

"She seems happier today," says Jane. "Don't you think?"

"Positively buoyant."

Jane looks around the room, full of young couples and families with small babies in tow. "I feel like everyone in this neighborhood agreed to start having babies at the same time."

"Remember when we first moved here?"

"It was just scholarly lesbians in sensible shoes," Jane sighs. "And the elderly."

"You don't think it'll ever get *hip*, do you?"

"You mean turn into a neighborhood with actual *good* restaurants?"

"Or places that sell jewelry that *isn't* handmade?"

"God, I hope not. I can't imagine. Have you and James come here yet?"

"No . . . not yet."

"Upstairs Chinese place?"

"Nope."

"Where do you guys like to go?"

It occurs to me we haven't actually been anywhere, not for dinner, anyway. We mostly go to the Cuban coffee place with the gritty espresso, and the diner near his corner that smells like old grease. And to bed.

"We mostly order food in. Sushi," I add, as though he should get points for that. "He's going to be my date for Katie's wedding, though."

"He is? That's great!"

I'm only slightly exaggerating the exchange I had with James after I asked him to be my date for Katie Finnegan's wedding:

JAMES.   *(studying script, distracted)* Aww, that's so sweet.

FRANNY.   *(hopeful)* So . . . yes?

JAMES.   Well, I'll try. I'll check the schedule.

FRANNY.   These are my favorite cousins. We're really close. And they're really fun.

JAMES.   Oh yeah?

FRANNY.   Yeah, they're just—crazy—and—heh, heh *(laughing as if remembering something really fun),* really fun. There was this one time . . . well . . . nothing's coming to me . . . it's hard to describe. But take my word for it.

JAMES.   Well, like I said *(gets up, pats her on head),* if it works with the schedule.

FRANNY.   So, maybe then?

JAMES.   *(wandering off, perhaps to smoke cigarette)* You got it, babe.

"He's coming—probably—yes. If he isn't working."

"He's coming, or he's probably coming?" Jane says, narrowing her eyes.

"Jane. He's a working actor."

"They don't go to weddings?"

"Working actors work."

"Well, I'll go with you if something comes up for old Scarfy. I always have a blast at those Finnegan things."

"Jane, no, please. He doesn't always wear a scarf."

"Yes he does. I saw him."

"Once. You only saw him that one time we rehearsed at the apartment."

"It's a gut feeling."

"You can't nickname him. He's a real person, not a joke person."

"You don't have to tell me. Only a *real* person would try to shake hands with my best friend's foot."

"Jane, you're not explaining it right. It was very romantic, and—"

Thankfully, our steaming bowl of bright yellow melted cheese with flecks of green chiles arrives.

"Listen," she says, dipping a chip into the creamy depths. "You're the one with the brand-new personality. I'm still the same old Jane."

"Here's to that," I say. And our salt-rimmed margarita glasses meet in the middle with a clink.

19

You have three messages.

BEEEP

Frances, it's your father. I renewed your subscription to The New Yorker. *Also, I don't mean to nag, but I'm just reminding you to call me about the wedding. Will you be taking the train? We're starting* Crime and Punishment *this week, one of my favorites, as you know. Reread it if you need a reminder that things could be worse. You're not in prison, only in show business.*

BEEEP

Hello, this message is for Frances Banks. I'm calling from Girl Friday Temps. We've reviewed your résumé, and we're sorry, but we aren't able to place you at this time. You don't seem to have any office skills whatsoever, and we aren't hiring receptionists right now. Feel free to check back with us in a few months or if you're able to add office experience, Windows 95, or typing to your résumé.

BEEEP

Hey, baby. Wow, what a night! I'm just sitting here thinking about you... Damn, girl. So (cigarette exhale), *catch you later, okay?*

BEEEP

I have to smile, since I learned very quickly that "Catch you later, okay?" means there's almost a 100 percent chance we'll be seeing each other later. Ninety percent at least. It's James's way of making plans.

The only thing is, while I've been spending all these intense, giddy, sexy evenings with him, staying up late and sleeping past noon, it seems as though all the regular waitressing jobs in Manhattan have disappeared. The temporary gigs I've always done in the past to fill in the cracks haven't been steady enough, I've had a few commercial auditions but no callbacks, and I'm pretty sure Niagara has stopped airing entirely. I desperately need a job. There have been no weddings to cater, either, so I've turned to picking up lunches, but lunches pay the least because no one tips, and the hourly wage stinks because the shifts are so short.

It's better than nothing, though, so I wash my regular uniform—a white button-down shirt and polyester black pants—every night and I call in every morning, both hoping I'll get a shift and hoping I won't, because the shifts—mostly held in soulless, musty corporate conference rooms—are so miserable. They keep promising me things will pick up when wedding season starts in June, but I need a break *now*.

I haven't had to call my father for money yet. But it's getting close to that time.

I literally cross my fingers as I wait on hold while they check what's available for today, hoping for I'm not sure what. Just not the worst-case scenario.

"Franny?"

"Yes?"

"So, all we have is a buffet lunch at United Electric—it's in Midtown. Two servers. Just setup, breakdown, and beverage. Want it?"

This is almost the worst, but not quite. It's one step up from busboy. You set up giant chafing dishes full of brown slop that the office workers help themselves to, buffet-style, and take their drink orders, then stand in the back of the room until they finish and it's time to clear the dishes. It's hardly even waitressing. Only one thing could make it worse.

"Black and white?"

"No, sorry, their uniform."

This *is* the worst, the absolute worst, the most humiliating level of all. I can picture the polyester dress, worn by hundreds before me, in a drab color and shapeless no-size-fits-anyone. But then I picture the number in my bank account.

"Okay, I'll take it."

"Also, it says bring pantyhose and a hairnet." She must be able to hear me take a deep, sad breath.

"Better luck tomorrow," she says.

I thought I left the apartment in plenty of time, but the train stopped between two stations for the usual unexplained reason, and all my nylons had holes in them so I had to stop at a drugstore on the way, and the only color they had was a burnt orange not found in actual human flesh. I arrive late, and the only other server with me is clearly one of the regular career lunch ladies who looks like she's worked there for a thousand years. She doesn't introduce herself or bother to ask my name.

"Hurry up, hurry up," she says to me brusquely. "These trays don't lift themselves."

I change as fast as I can into the bulky brown uniform, made of some fabric that doesn't breathe, and by the time I'm lighting the butane warmers, I'm already in a sweat. At least there's no one here to see me, or to care what I look like.

"Franny? Franny, is that you?"

I turn and see an attractive woman in a dark tailored suit. The voice is familiar, but I don't recognize the face at first.

"I'm sorry, do I know—"

And then it hits me. It's Genevieve. Genevieve Parker, who lived on my dorm floor when she was a senior and I was a junior. Genevieve, who was always in her room working, but would leave the door open and offer you coffee if you stuck your head in. Sweet, smart Genevieve. She was that category of friend from college who was a happy constant in my daily life, but for some reason we never kept in touch. I didn't recognize her at first because it's been a few years, and because she appears to have lost about thirty pounds.

"Oh my God! Genevieve!" I put down the metal tray I'm holding and give her a hug. Her nails look recently manicured, and her hair smells like expensive shampoo from a salon. "You look great! What are you doing here?"

"I was just hired as a junior associate. I work here now."

"Well, how about that? I work here, too!" I smile and gesture grandly around the shabby room, as if I'm proud to own the place. *"Voilà!"* I add lamely. I put my hand up to wipe a bead of sweat that has started trickling down my forehead, and my fingertips graze the elastic of the hairnet. I had forgotten for a moment what I must look like. I look down at my uniform and my face starts to burn. I see Genevieve's eyes take it all in, and I'm overwhelmed by embarrassment. "I mean, this isn't my regular . . . I'm just temping. I do work here, but just for today."

"Sure, yeah, of course!" Genevieve says brightly. "I mean, I practically just got out of law school myself, and only recently . . . well!"

She trails off, struggling to compare our situations, to find a way to show they're similar, but I can see the gap between us as if we were standing on either side of a massive canyon. I've been on my own timeline, but now I'm looking at the results of a regular person's life plan, and the reality is a little shocking. Regular people go to law school and graduate and get a job and get a promotion and get a better job. In the years since college, Genevieve became a junior associate who gets waited on in conference rooms, while I played Snow White in elementary school auditoriums, and somehow became the person who waits on people with real jobs.

"So," she says, her smile undiminished. "You're still doing the acting thing?"

"Yep. Yeppers," I say, and put my hands on my hips like I'm a brown-polyester-uniformed superhero.

"And it's . . . it's going well?" Genevieve says, a little tentatively.

"Yes, it's going—" and, out of nowhere, I start to laugh. "It's *so* good—I'm *so successful* that—" I try to speak, but I can't even finish my sentence. Suddenly, the situation is totally hilarious. Suddenly, I'm thrilled to be standing in my grungy costume that's in such stark contrast to Genevieve's elegantly besuited one, because nothing could be funnier than being dressed in a hideous hairnet and burnt orange nylons, being asked sweetly by an old friend how my career is going. I'm covering my mouth with the back of my hand, cracking up but trying to control myself so that I don't attract the attention of my surly co-worker, who fortunately has disappeared for the moment, but then Genevieve starts giggling, too, and we're instantly transformed back into college girls living on the same floor who've turned punchy from too much studying and lack of sleep. Finally, we pull ourselves together.

"It's really good to see you, Gen," I say, dabbing under my eyes. "It's not as bad as it looks, I swear."

"Honestly, Franny, I know you're fine. All the stuff you did in school—you're so talented—there's no way you won't make it."

"Aw, thanks." I can see my lumbering cohort down at the far end of the hall pushing a tray of glassware toward us. "Shoot, I should go."

"Catch me up—just quickly," Genevieve says. "Do you see any-body? Anyone from school?"

"I see a lot of Jane—we're roommates in Brooklyn."

"Oh, great! Tell her I said hello."

"Yeah, and, uh, let's see, we were seeing Elisa and Bridget a fair amount, but Elisa's on a kibbutz, and Bridget had kind of a—"

"Yes, I heard," Genevieve says, with a conspiratorial frown.

"But she's okay now. She teaches Jazzercise."

Genevieve smiles. "I heard that, too."

"And, well, I'm sure you know that Clark ended up in Chicago. Even though we're still in touch."

Something passes across her face. "Are you?" she says, nodding delicately. "So you've—you've spoken with him recently?"

"Well, I guess it's been a few weeks, or gosh, maybe longer. I owe him a call, in fact. We're each other's 'backup plans,' as dumb as that sounds, and he called—"

"Franny," Genevieve says with a strange sharpness in her voice. "Oh. I thought you'd—you know, Clark and I, we actually overlapped at the University of Chicago. Just by one year, but . . ."

Something small and cold grips my heart. Something I can't quite name.

"Oh, right!" I say, too happily, smiling a little too hard. "Of course—you went there, too. I forgot!"

In my head, I'm struggling to do the math. It's suddenly very important that I figure out the timeline of when Clark and Gene-vieve were in school together. Genevieve was going straight to law school right out of college, I remember that now. But she graduated one year before us, and Clark took a year off, which is why it makes sense, as she said, that they only overlapped there for one year. The first half of the year out of school he traveled, teaching English in South America. Then he had that internship, but I forget what the firm was called. He was a proofreader, I remember that, and he had terrible hours. What was the name of the firm? I make a deal in my head that if I can remember the name of the place where Clark worked before Genevieve speaks, then whatever she's about to tell me won't be as bad as I think it's going to be. *Please don't tell me you're dating Clark, Genevieve, please. It would make sense, I know. You're so sweet and pretty and successful, but please don't say it.* Where did he work? If I can only remember the name of the place—

"I hope this is the right thing to do, but since you obviously don't know, I'd feel wrong if I didn't tell you that Clark just got engaged to my sister."

While my brain accepts this simple arrangement of words, and their literal meaning, my body seems to be on some sort of delay. For a moment, while I understand what's just been said, I mercifully don't have any physical reaction whatsoever. Then, it hits me so hard, my knees almost buckle.

"Oh!" I say, brightly, trying to hide the feeling that I'm being dragged underwater. "How great!"

"It was pretty sudden. I'm sure he was going to tell you himself."

"That's okay," I say. "Really. Guess I should've returned that last phone call, huh?" My frozen smile is stretched too tight. If it were a rubber band, it would have already snapped.

"Franny . . ." She places a hand gently on my arm, but now I'm self-conscious about the uniform, and how scratchy it must feel to her manicured hand, and I pull back slightly. "I'm okay." I say weakly. But she seems unconvinced, so I put my hand over hers, so now they both rest awkwardly on the stiff brown fabric. "Really. I'm okay."

The best performance I've ever given was in that conference room for the rest of lunch. I smiled and said congratulations to Genevieve, and I wished her sister the best. I took her drink order and remained calm throughout, even when the room filled up all at once with older men in blue suits and brown loafers demanding seltzers and coffees and the occasional cocktail. I cleared the trays of half-eaten mushy tan casseroles onto a cart with wheels, and rolled the cart into the freight elevator and back down to the main cafeteria. I said thank you to the other server, who grumbled something unintelligible back to me. I hung up my borrowed uniform in my temporary locker, and I went into the bathroom to wash my hands.

Only when I go to splash my face with water at the sink, and catch a piece of my reflection in the bathroom mirror, do I come close to cracking just the tiniest bit.

Everyone has moved on.

And it's not that I don't want Clark to be happy. There's even a part of me that's genuinely pleased for him. If Genevieve's sister is anything like her, she's someone nice, at least. It's what he always wanted—to settle down and start a family. I guess I tried to pretend that's what I wanted, too, when I knew it wasn't really. Of course I must have known he wouldn't wait forever, must have realized somewhere deep down that backup plans aren't what adults rely on. They're what adolescents make when they're not ready to grow up. It's obvious to me now that people who might still end up together don't go for weeks without talking. Suddenly it's clear that making our "agreement" was just the only way we knew how to end things. But it's a shock to have learned so much and grown up so quickly today, to realize the Clark who said "call me when you change your mind" isn't my person anymore; now he's someone else's Clark.

Somehow I find myself on the D train headed back to Brooklyn. I hardly remember walking to the station or putting my token in the slot. It's just past three, but already the train is filling up with shoppers and commuters leaving work early, and there's no place to sit. I grasp onto the nearby silver pole, steadying myself as the train lurches along, my hand slipping on the smooth surface, vying for a safe position along with half a dozen other hands. Today, everything about New York leaves me feeling like I'm competing for space, and just barely hanging on.

20

········------------

I'll call James the minute I get in, I think, as I drag myself up the stairs to the apartment, fumbling for my keys. Tonight I won't wait for his "catch you later, okay." There's no rule that says I can't call him and ask to make plans. We'll drink some wine and he'll help me forget the awful day I've had. But when I reach the top of the stairs, keys in hand, the door is already a few inches ajar, and Dan is lying on the sofa with what looks to be an open beer bottle wrapped in a brown paper bag sitting beside him on the floor. I don't think I've ever seen Dan lying down fully, his legs so long that his feet dangle off the arm of the sofa. I'm so used to finding him in his regular spot, writing at the dining room table, that it's shocking to see him anywhere else, especially flat on his back with his eyes closed.

"Dan?" I whisper. I can't tell whether he's sleeping or not.

"Hmm?" he says, eyes still closed.

"Are you asleep?"

"No."

"Are you sick?"

"No."

But he doesn't move. I place my bag down carefully, quietly, as if despite what he's said, he's potentially both asleep and sick. I take my shoes off and tiptoe across the living room, up the circular metal staircase, and into my bedroom.

I decide I'll call James after I shower, secretly hoping that he'll call me first. I'll wait until I'm completely ready to go out before I'll allow myself to even glance at the machine. If I don't cheat, if I'm strong, it will work. I bet he'll have called me by the time I finish getting ready.

I shower and use the diffuser to dry my hair. I can't hear a thing with the water running and the blow dryer on, so I can't tell if the phone already rang. I won't allow myself to check—not just yet. I put on some makeup and then I decide I'll borrow those dangly earrings from Jane, requiring me to cross the landing from my room to hers. It's a challenge, but I look straight ahead, and don't give in, even though I'm desperate to sneak just the tiniest glance at the machine. I run back to my room across the landing, eyes up, and pull on jeans, then trade the jeans for a short black sweater dress and black tights. By the time I allow myself to peek, at least thirty minutes have gone by, and there it is! A single number "1" blinking happily in the little LED window of the answering machine.

You have one message.

BEEEP

Hey there. Hi, Fran, it's uh, it's me, it's Clark. Listen, I'm so sorry, I uh, I guess you ran into Genevieve today? I kept wanting to talk, but, well … I want to explain, will you call me? I feel just ter —

I hit the stop button on the machine and the tape dies off with a pitiful *beeep.* Briefly, it crosses my mind to call him back, but what would be the point? I can imagine everything he's going to say already. I'll call him back tomorrow, next week, never.

When I come back downstairs, Dan is still in the same odd position on the sofa.

"Franny?" he says, without stirring.

"Yeah?"

"Can we do something?"

"What do you mean?"

Dan is silent for a moment. "Did you just come from the city?" he finally asks, his voice strangely measured.

"Yeah."

"Can we go back there?"

I'm torn. I don't want to admit it, but I'm still half hoping to hear from James. But then I'm struck by how bad it would feel to wait for him on the night I just learned that no one's waiting for me anymore, and that "catch you later, okay" isn't a plan, not a real one anyway. Maybe it wouldn't be such a bad thing if James called and got no answer.

"Uh . . . okay. For what?"

He sits up, swinging his long legs down to the floor, then rubs his eyes and squints at me, as if he's not sure whether he's awake or dreaming.

"Well," he says. "I've had the worst day."

"What a coincidence! I've had the worst day, too."

"I'm sorry to hear that, Fran. Maybe you'll know, then—I mean, can you help me with—I'm not sure what to do about it."

"What to—*do*?"

"Yes. It might sound crazy, but I don't have a lot of experience with this—with how I'm feeling."

"Okay . . ."

"I'm not from a terribly emotional family, if you understand what I mean."

"Yes."

"And frankly, I don't have too much experience with, ah, failure, or the, ah, concept of failure."

I want to ask him what's happened, but suddenly I catch a glimpse of what Dan might have looked like at fourteen or fifteen, with his shaggy hair and serious face and the pressure to do his best. Somehow it seems better to wait for him to tell me in his own time.

"You've come to the right place. It just so happens that I've had quite a bit of experience with both the concept and the reality of failure," I tell him.

"Great. I mean, not great exactly, but thank you. Let's do something, then."

"Like what?"

"Let's go see something. Let's go to the theater or something."

"I can't afford it."

"I'll take you."

"Dan, *you* can't afford it. It's too expensive for everyone. Let's just go get a beer in the neighborhood."

"A beer won't fix this. Let's do something reckless. Let me take you to see a show. We'll go to TKTS and see what's on the board."

The look Dan gives me now is frankly a little unnerving; he looks so different today, so lost, so vulnerable. "Okay," I say, because I can't possibly say no to this strange new version of Dan who needs my help.

On the train back into Manhattan, and then later, as we wait in line for half-price theater tickets, I try to keep him entertained. I retell the story of my day, but I give him the version where waiting on someone I went to college with was a kooky misadventure, a wacky scene from an old episode of *I Love Lucy*. It's a relief to make light of it, to make fun of myself and my ridiculous polyester uniform. Telling Dan about the most hilarious part of my day makes the worst part of it fade. But even so, I leave out the news about Clark for some reason. I'm not ready to laugh about that yet—it's too new and too raw. I can still feel where it sits in my stomach like a punch.

Before I know it, we're in front of the TKTS board, where we can see what's available at half-price. The long list of shows makes my heart flutter like it's Christmas morning, but the prices are staggering to me, even at a discount.

"What should we see?" Dan asks, squinting up at the board.

I want to make the right pick—I want something that will help him feel better, that will lift us both up. I want something that will take the sting of the bad day away from both of us. Then, I see it.

"Phantom of the Opera!"

"You're kidding," he says, looking at me amused.

"Have you seen it already?"

"No, but I would've pegged you for something more avant-garde, more serious."

"Today, I think something big and fun and fluffy's what we need. Plus, it's been running for six or seven years already. Who knows how much longer we'll have the chance to see it? Let's be like tourists in the city, just for one night."

Dan looks down at me, his hair falling over his eyes, and for the first time since I found him on the sofa, his face brightens and his spirits seem to lift.

"Okay," he agrees.

"Okay?"

"Yes, we'll be like tourists," he says, almost happily.

"Yes!"

"What else do tourists do?" His eyes light up. "I know! We'll go to Sardi's after."

"And see how many caricatures we can name!"

"No way," he says, actually looking a little concerned. "I don't stand a chance against you."

Even though Dan and I turn to each other in the darkened theater and roll our eyes after the chandelier falls at the end of the first act, dipping eerily close to our heads, my heart still jumps, and I have to admit it's sort of a thrill. When the audience bursts into thunderous applause, I'm swept along for a moment against my will, if by nothing else but the feeling of being part of something, whatever that something is.

Out on the street after the show, the night is clear and the blinking lights from the various theater marquees are dazzlingly relentless, demanding our attention. People spill from the sidewalk onto the street and the taxis compete for space, their horns complaining loudly. Dan looks at me and smiles. "Quick," he says. "What do you remember most about the show?"

I want to say the actors, and their powerful voices and the catchy songs; I want to talk about how beautiful the costumes were, or even marvel at how they got the boat to cross the stage in what looked like actual water, but I can't.

"The chandelier," we say, in unison, and burst out laughing.

"That's so embarrassing! We're only supposed to be *acting* like tourists," I say, after finally catching my breath. "What'll we do next, complain about how dirty the city is?"

"It's so *crowded*."

"Everyone's so *rude*."

"How can anyone stand all that *noise*?"

"And the *crime*."

"Let's just go to the top of the Empire State Building and get out of here."

The dining room of Sardi's is beautiful, with burgundy walls and little yellow shaded lamps on all the tables, but the menu is too extravagantly expensive and the dinner crowd is too intimidating, so we find two stools at the smoky bar. The bartender—dressed in a tuxedo shirt and bow tie and a dark red jacket that matches the walls—comes over right away and waits solemnly for our order. I'm oddly shy and tongue-tied in his presence.

"I—um—let's see now . . ." I'm overwhelmed by the jewel box

of dimly lit liquor bottles, arranged like colorful soldiers awaiting their orders behind the bar, and my mind goes completely blank.

"Um, uh . . ."

"May I?" Dan finally asks, placing a hand gently on my arm.

"Please," I say, relieved.

He clears his throat. "The lady will have a sidecar, and I would like a gin martini, dirty, shaken but not stirred, please." The bartender nods respectfully, then glides away, and I clap my hands in appreciation.

"Well done!" I say. "Sorry—I panicked. Maybe it was the bow tie. He seemed impressed by our choices, though, don't you think?"

"I think we may have won him over, yes," Dan says with a grin.

"I have no idea what you ordered, but I'm irrationally comforted to have the waiter on our side. Thank you."

"You're very welcome, Fran." I'm glad to see Dan smile, but it gives me a pang, too, to have Dan order for me in his gentlemanly fashion, as if we're on a date. *Call me when you change your mind.* I shake my head, pushing the thought away.

"Did you see the old wooden phone booths on the way in?" I ask, and he nods.

"With the ashtrays and the built-in leather seats?" he adds.

"And the folding glass door, for privacy?"

"That's how they all should be. A place to have a long, comfortable conversation."

"Or a long, horrible conversation with drinks and cigarettes to help," I agree cheerfully.

"The phone booths still had doors that closed when I first visited New York with my family," he tells me. "In the ones in London, there's a ton of room to sit down inside."

"Those are so beautiful. That gorgeous red."

"You've been?"

"No. I've only seen pictures."

"You'd love it."

"I bet."

"We should go."

I blink at him. "We should . . . ?"

"What? Uh, *you* should go, I mean. You should go someday," Dan says, his face reddening. "To see the phone booths," he adds, somewhat lamely. "Sorry. Force of habit. I've only recently stopped being a 'we.' Everett broke up with me."

"Oh, Dan, I'm so sorry," I begin, but our drinks arrive, and Dan waves me away with his hand.

"There's time enough to tell you all about it. Let's enjoy these first." He picks up his glass and gestures for me to do the same. He seems at a loss for the appropriate toast, then his face lights up. "To the theater!"

"To the theater!" I agree, clinking his glass lightly with mine. I want to ask Dan questions about Everett and what's happened, but the sidecar he ordered for me is sweet and strong, and my questions are swept away by its golden thick flavor. It slides down easily, and after a while we order another round, although this time Dan gets a scotch on the rocks.

"Try this," he says, sliding the glass over when his scotch arrives. "It's meant to be sipped slowly." I tilt the glass back gingerly and try to take just the tiniest sip, but even that burns the back of my throat, and I can't help coughing.

"How can you drink that?" I say, sticking out my tongue and pounding my chest dramatically.

"My father started us young," Dan says, somewhat ominously. Then he lets out a long breath and frowns, shaking the ice in his glass.

"So," he says, after a moment. "My script got rejected by that festival."

"You're kidding—how can that be?" I say, truly shocked. All those nights he spent poring over his pages at the dining room table, all that effort. To me, it seems impossible that Dan could fail at anything.

"Everett said that me not getting into the festival had nothing to do with her decision, but I think it was her last hope."

"Hope of what?" I say gingerly.

"You know, that I'd be *legitimized* somehow. Otherwise, to her, what I'm doing has all been some sort of folly. A waste of time." Dan drains the rest of his scotch in one gulp and puts his glass down with a thud. "The most frightening thing?"

"Yes?"

"This all happened yesterday, and I came home and decided I'd start over, keep working on the script, submit it somewhere else. I'll just work harder, I thought. But nothing came. I couldn't write. That's never happened to me before. I've never not been able to write."

I remember the night I sat with Everett, when she compared Dan's work to some juvenile rite of passage, "like backpacking through Europe," and that it was she who mentioned seeing *The Phantom of the Opera*, and being dazzled by the effects that Dan and I were just mocking. But I don't think Dan needs to hear my thoughts on why he and Everett weren't right for each other at the moment, or my theory about how people can be divided into groups based on whether their reaction to the chandelier in *The Phantom of the Opera* is sincere or ironic. With a start, I realize my hand is on his arm, and I've been absentmindedly stroking his tan corduroy jacket this whole time, in an attempt to soothe myself, I think, as much as him. I pull it away quickly and sit up straighter on my bar stool.

But then we order a third round, and Dan a fourth, and the crowd in the dining room thins and the lights seem to dim, the bottles behind the bar transforming into a colorful blur like an abstract watercolor. As he pays the bill I try to remember when the last time was that I had three drinks in a row without any food to go with them except for a few free crackers that we spread with soft cheese from the little pots they offered at the bar. When I try to stand up, I almost lose my balance and I have to grip the back of my bar stool to steady myself. Then it comes to me: I'm pretty sure the last time I had three large drinks in quick succession on an almost-empty stomach was never.

"Izzat Lisbeth Taylor?" I hear myself slur, as I weave unsteadily toward one of the framed caricatures on the wall, bringing my face almost close enough to kiss the glass. I squint my eyes and blink a few times, but I still can't seem to make sense of the blurry signature beneath the drawing.

"Nah. Nutter," Dan says, coming up behind me to take a look. "Ishhhhtockard Shhanning, I think."

"Whahh?"

"Not her, I mean. Ishhhtock—'scuse me." Dan clears his throat, takes a deep breath and steadies himself by leaning one hand on the wall. "It. Is. Sssstockard Channing, I think."

"Ohhhhhh yeah! It *is* her! I *love* her, don't you?" I say, turning to face Dan and clapping my hands. "She looks *so good*, don't you think? She's *so* talented! I saw her in—"

Dan leans his other arm against the wall, so now I'm enclosed on either side in a sort of Dan-tent, and then he leans his whole body against me and kisses me, deeply and softly, in a way that makes the whole world go silent. There's no sound, no past or present, nothing at all except me and Dan kissing while Stockard Channing gazes down at us, her pastel-pencil red lips smiling in approval.

In the distance, the silence is broken by the faint sound of silverware clinking, and even that is soothing, a sound like little bells swaying in a soft breeze.

I've never kissed anyone in a public place. Not like this. Clark wasn't one for reckless displays of affection. He'd hold my hand, but that's about it. I've never cheated on anyone, either, although I try to tell myself that just one drunken kiss isn't so bad. Even so, I know I'll feel embarrassed and guilty in the morning. I can tell even now, through my drunken haze. But for tonight, I feel too good to feel bad. For tonight, it all seems oddly inevitable. If only I hadn't run into Genevieve, if only Dan hadn't been lying on the sofa, if only James had called, if only the lights at the bar weren't so pleasantly dim, if only I didn't stop to examine a portrait of Stockard Channing. It almost seems as if it couldn't be helped, as if this was supposed to happen.

"It's okay," Jane will tell me in the morning. "You needed to feel good. You're just friends who got confused. Just steer clear of each other for a while."

And without even having to discuss it, that's exactly what Dan and I will do.

Starting tomorrow, I'll draw a line in my mind between myself and Dan, as if we're two kids traveling in the backseat of a car who need an imaginary wall to give us the illusion of having our own space.

I'll be more careful from now on, I promise myself.

After all, I know better than anyone what can happen when you accidentally go the wrong way down a one-way street.

21

....

You have one message.

BEEEP

*Franny. It's Richard calling from Absolute Artists. Call me as soon
as you get this. I have an offer for you.*

BEEEP

These are the words I've been waiting for months to hear, and
there they are, recorded ninety-five minutes ago according to the
digital voice on the tape of my answering machine, but for some
reason I haven't called Richard back yet. I catered a lunch shift at a
giant investment firm in the financial district earlier today, and it's
been almost fifteen minutes since I got home from the corner deli,
where I bought a slightly bruised apple, a blueberry yogurt, and two
fruit-punch-flavored wine coolers (they were on sale). I'm winded, as
if I've come in from a run and not just a trip to the store, but I feel
calm and focused, too, as if I'm about to take a final exam for a subject I've prepared for thoroughly.

I place the wine coolers, yogurt, and apple in the refrigerator.
Then I change my mind and take the apple out and set it on the

counter. I look at it for a while, as though it might open up its mouth and say something, then I take a knife out of the drawer and cut a piece that is slightly less than half, avoiding the core and the seeds. I take a bite and decide it tastes better than it looks. I finish the almost-half and run my hands, which have now become slightly sticky, under the tap, rinsing them, shaking off the excess water, then drying them methodically on a dish towel. From the center of the kitchen, I could almost reach out and touch a wall in any direction, but even in this small space I feel lost. I might as well be bobbing in the middle of the ocean. I'm so excited that I've gone completely numb. I'm in shock—that must be it.

I got a job, I got a job. After all this time, I finally got a job!

But which one?

I auditioned for a revival of *Brigadoon* at a regional theater in Poughkeepsie. I auditioned to play the quirky assistant in that new sitcom, *Legs!*, that takes place in a modeling agency and stars a formerly famous model from the '70s. I auditioned to play someone whose purse has been stolen on that cop show where one of the policemen is alive but his partner is a ghost. I auditioned for two parts on two different soaps, one to play a college student who says, "Does anyone have the homework assignment?" I auditioned to be the co-host of a Saturday morning children's show. I auditioned to represent a line of blenders on a home shopping channel, and I auditioned to say one line in an Eve Randall film: "Can I take your order?"

Maybe that's the job I booked: "Can I take your order?" The casting person seemed to like me that day. Or was that the casting person who seemed to not like me? What day was it? What was I wearing? I could look it up in my Filofax, but I'd rather remember it myself. The job I booked has to have stood out in some way, some special way that separates it from the others.

"Can I take your order?" I say out loud in our tiny kitchen, to an imaginary Eve Randall sitting at a booth in the imaginary diner in my head. "The soup of the day is chicken noodle," I tell Eve with a smile. Only the first line was scripted, but I had thought of more I could say for the audition just in case there was room to improvise, in case I had the chance to show something more than that one line, to prove I had thought about the waitress not just as a generic waitress, but as a person who was in the middle of a specific day, who got up late maybe, because she had a fight with her boyfriend the night before, who read the specials off the board that morning and wrote them down on her order pad, or maybe was the type who knew them by heart.

"It all started with one line in an Eve Randall film," I will say to the audience assembled for *An Evening with Frances Banks* at the 92nd Street Y. "Can I take your order?" I'll say, just like I did in the film, my very first, and the audience will laugh in recognition.

Finally I get up the courage to call the agency. "Oh, hi, hello there, it's uh, Franny Banks, for Richard?" I say to the receptionist.

"Hold on a minute, Franny. Joe will be right with you."

Joe will be right with me? Joe Melville is actually going to take my call? Now I'm nervous, since he and I haven't spoken in so long. It makes sense, I guess, that he would talk to me only when there's actually a job to discuss. Of course! This must be their system, that Joe calls only when it's really necessary. I wished I'd figured that out earlier, and not spent so much time worrying about why he never called.

The classical hold music is finally interrupted after what seems like a very long time but was probably under a minute.

"Hello, Franny, congratulations, you've booked your first real job." Joe sounds confident and familiar, as though we talk all the time.

I don't want to correct him, but he must remember that I booked *Kevin and Kathy*, the very first audition he sent me on. *Don't be difficult*, I think. *Just be positive.*

"Oh, thanks! Besides *Kevin and Kathy*." Thankfully, Joe doesn't say anything, so I blaze forward. "I'm excited. I mean, I think I'll be excited when I find out which job it is."

Joe covers the receiver for a minute and I can't hear what he's saying.

"Sorry about that," he says, talking to me again. "I thought you'd been told. You got the female lead opposite Michael Eastman in the feature film *Zombie Pond*."

The female lead in *Zombie Pond*! Wait. *Zombie Pond, Zombie Pond*. Of course I remember going in for a movie called *Zombie Pond*, but I'm struggling to remember the material exactly, and can't recall going in for the female lead of anything. Surely I'd remember that.

It's coming back to me, sort of. There were barely any lines in the scene. *That's* the female lead? I don't remember it going that well. There wasn't a lot of dialogue—she screams more than she speaks. She's described as quivering and whimpering quite a bit, and she gets tied up by zombies and left in the basement wearing nothing but her underwear.

That's the job I got?

"Wait. Sorry. The girlfriend who gets locked in the basement?"

"Well, of course!" Joe says confidently. "They loved you!"

I am playing the female lead opposite Michael Eastman, in a story of a girl who's being tortured by zombies while in her underwear? But I have no credits. Why would they give me the lead in a movie? I've never even said one line in a movie. I don't look good enough in underwear. I must stop eating immediately, and possibly forever.

On the other hand, I allow myself a tiny flush of pride. I'm good enough to be in a movie opposite Michael Eastman. I saw him the other night on *Entertainment! Entertainment!* wearing a tank top and walking on the beach with some actress he's dating. I'm going to be in a movie with him? James will be impressed. Well, maybe not impressed exactly, but not horrified. Michael Eastman's work is at least considered not horrifying.

I try to imagine myself as the actress he held hands with on the beach. I can almost picture myself with him, although it isn't exactly me. It's more like my head on the actress's slight body, wearing her tiny pink bikini. Just me and Michael Eastman, walking on the beach together, admiring each other's abs.

Joe covers the phone again and mumbles something, then comes back. "No, uh, sorry, not *the* girlfriend, not the lead. It isn't the part you read for, apparently. It's for the part of Sheila, the girlfriend he met in high school, the one we see in the flashbacks?"

Oh. My walk on the beach comes to an abrupt end. Sheila. I wasn't given the whole script, so I have no idea whether Sheila is a good part or not. Of course I'm not the lead. But my sudden demotion is a disappointment nonetheless. Joe doesn't seem to really have all the details straight. Now I'm suspicious. What if I didn't really get that part, either?

"But so, you're sure? I really got it? I don't have to read again, or meet the producers or anything?"

"No, the part of Sheila is all yours. Film is different from television that way. The director has much more control. Plus, the character, while important to the plot, doesn't have a heavy amount of dialogue, so he saw what he needed to see on your audition tape for the other character."

"Okay," I say, still unsure.

Joe covers the receiver and there's a shuffling of papers and the muffled sound of Joe barking orders to someone.

"Uh, let's see, here it is, I'm reading from the breakdowns here—it says: Sheila is killed by zombies while they're seniors in college. Sheila's death inspires Sutton to seek revenge, his anger propelling him into studying science and creating a poisonous serum in the lab, which transforms the zombies from the undead to the actual dead, enabling them to be extinguished blah blah blah . . ." More whispering from Joe's assistant, then, "Oh sorry, I didn't realize they didn't give you the whole script. They try to keep these big horror movies confidential. Anyway, we're faxing the pages to you now. It's only two scenes, but she's a very memorable character, like I said. Congratulations. The director found you very wholesome, exactly the sort of all-American girl next door whose death would inspire a man to kill. His words. So give it a look and then we can proceed with the clause and make sure we keep you protected. All right?"

I understood everything up to the last part of what he said, something about "the clause" and being "protected." That must be agent jargon, something to do with the union or the contract or something. I'll find out eventually. For now, I just want to get off the phone and look at the material. I just want to see what this "memorable character" gets to do and say. From the sound of it, even if it's small, it's something more than "Can I take your order?"

I can hear the light but quick creaking of someone jogging up the stairs, which tells me it's Jane coming home. Dan coming up the stairs sounds heavy and deliberate. Dan is rarely in a hurry.

This is thrilling. Jane can be with me while I read the script for my first-ever actual acting job. The fax starts to ring, but I know it will take forever to answer and print, so I whip down the metal circular staircase to tell Jane the news.

"Jane. I got a job!"

She turns away from the counter where she's unloading groceries and claps her hands, her face all lit up.

"*Oh my God!* That's fantastic! What is it?"

"It's a scary movie. A sort of thriller. They wouldn't let me read the whole thing. It's with Michael Eastman, who I know isn't the greatest, but . . ."

"Franny, don't do that. Don't put it down. I don't care if the movie stars Bozo the clown. This is amazing."

"Bozo the clown actually read for it. Ultimately they thought he was *too* frightening, and they decided to stick with zombies. It's called *Zombie Pond.*"

"You're going to be in a movie with Michael Eastman, *and* a bunch of zombies? This can't get any better! What's the character like?"

"I play his girlfriend who gets murdered, inspiring him to go on a zombie killing spree! That's all I know. I'm told it's very memorable. It's coming through the fax right now."

There's a key in the lock, and Dan appears with ruddy cheeks and a twisted paper bag that's no doubt covering his single evening beer. I realize I can't remember the last time I've seen him—he hasn't been sitting at his usual place at the dining room table, hasn't been in front of our television with a beer in ages, and we haven't had a real conversation since our drinks at Sardi's. It's been long enough now that our kiss has faded into something I can almost convince myself never happened. Still, it's good to see him.

"Dan! I got a job in a zombie movie!"

"A zombie movie?"

"Don't get too excited, Dan. She's playing one of the humans," says Jane, giving him a wink.

"Very funny, Jane," Dan says. Then he turns to me. "That's great, Franny!" And he adds, in a strange sinister voice: "They're coming to get you, Barbara."

"What?"

"They're coming to . . . Oh, never mind. That's the famous line from *Night of the Living Dead*. Forget it. Zombie history lesson later. For now, I have forty ounces of malt liquor in my hand to toast you with. Who do you play?"

"It's coming through upstairs. I'll go get it and we can all read it."

"*I* know," says Jane. "Why don't you and Dan read it out loud, together? He can play Michael Eastman's part!"

"Uh, no thanks," says Dan with a frown. "That's a bad idea. I'm a terrible actor."

"Aww, would you Dan, please?" I say, grinning. "I haven't read it yet. I'd love to do it out loud for the first time. It will be like a cold reading."

"A cold, dead, zombie reading!" Jane exclaims. "Come on, Dan, this is a big occasion. Do it for Franny. I promise to be a kind critic."

"There's no such thing," Dan says, but then he shrugs in surrender. "Okay, Franny, I'll read it with you."

I take the metal stairs two at a time. I'm flying.

"Who is Michael Eastman?" I hear Dan ask Jane from down below.

There they are on the floor of the landing, the pages that contain my first real job, my first real character with an actual name. "Sheila," I say out loud, trying on the suit of my first real character whose name doesn't include a number or the word "the."

I decide I won't even skim the pages before reading them with Dan. This is like an exercise we do in class sometimes where Stavros gives us pages from something we've never seen, and we cold read them out loud, piecing the character and situation together as we go. It's an exercise I love. I'm better the first read sometimes than I am after I've rehearsed, after I've had time to doubt my choices.

I pick up the pages, all five of them, and take care not to uncurl them yet. I glance at the page numbers in the upper right-hand corner to put them in order but resist the urge to look any farther, and head back downstairs. Dan has put his glasses on, as he does when he's working intensely on something. He looks a little nervous, as if he's about to give his campaign speech for class president. Jane is playing director and fussing with the dining room chairs, pushing the table out of the way.

"I need to know where this takes place. I need to properly dress the set," she says, gravely regarding her furniture placement. "Here, let me see those. Two scenes, right?"

She separates the pages into the first and second scenes, picks up the first scene, and reads.

```
INT. LAB—DAY


SUTTON is hunched over his microscope. The lab is
hot. Stifling. A trickle of sweat rolls off his
forehead and onto the microscope slide. He sighs.
He will have to start again. He removes his shirt,
trying to cool off. Sutton's girlfriend, SHEILA
(20s, fresh-faced), enters.
```

Jane cracks up, lowering the pages. "Hahahahaha! Remove your shirt, Dan!" She collapses onto the sofa in laughter.

"Jane, please," I say. "Get a grip. Don't crumple those. Can we take this seriously? Dan, you may remain clothed for the purposes of this rehearsal. Now, Jane. Who has the first line?"

"You do. Excuse me, Sheila does. Here." Jane hands the script to me, then dutifully sits upright on the sofa.

"Ready?" I say to Dan.

"Okay," he says, even though he looks unsure.

"We'll just pass the pages back and forth okay? No looking ahead?"

"Okay," he agrees.

"And . . . action!" says Jane.

```
                    SHEILA

(enters quietly, watches Sutton unseen for a moment,
then)

        Knock, knock. Hello, Professor. Am I inter-
        rupting you?


                    SUTTON
        I'm not a professor yet. And no, not at all.
        I was actually just thinking about you.
```

                    SHEILA
Well, I hope so, dressed like that.

                    SUTTON

              (laughs)

Well, it *is* about a hundred degrees out.
And I figured, no one around but me and
some lab rats.

                    SHEILA

              (laughs)

Well, I'll let you get back to work. I just
wanted you to have this, for tonight.

Sheila opens her bag and hands Sutton a thin wrapped
package the size of a manila envelope.

                    SUTTON

              (taking the envelope)

Thanks. What is it?

                    SHEILA

              (smiling, eyes shining)

It's a secret. It's for tonight. No peeking
until then. Promise?

                    SUTTON
I promise.

```
                    SHEILA
          Well, tonight, then?


                    SUTTON
          Tonight, then.

HOLD on Sutton as Sheila exits. He looks down at the
package, then back to where she has just exited. His
eyes fill with love; he is overwhelmed by her. A
single tear falls, and he smiles.


                 SUTTON (CONT'D)
          Tonight.
```

There is silence in the apartment. Jane looks at each of us in turn, then leaps to her feet, applauding loudly.

"Yayyyyy! I loved it! I felt it! The heat! Also the temperature! The lab experiments! The nearby rats! I felt it all! I laughed! I cried! It was better than *Cats*!"

"Jane, shush, the neighbors," I say, but I'm laughing, too.

"But seriously," Jane says, with a grin. "That's a pretty long scene!"

"I can do something with it, don't you think?" I say proudly.

"Definitely," says Jane. "You're like, the ingénue. You're Michael Eastman's babe!"

Dan is still holding the sides up close to his face, the pages practically touching his glasses, so I can't exactly see his reaction.

"Dan?" I say. "What do you think? I mean the script isn't too terrible, right?"

"I was distracted by having to read it out loud," Dan says, a bit grumpy.

"But you're not the actor we're paying attention to in this scene, Dan," Jane tells him. Then, trying to help, she says, "Come on, be a pal. Say something nice to Franny about her new job."

Dan thinks for a second, then says, "The dialogue isn't bad, although too many sentences start with 'Well.' " He pauses, then as if he can't help himself, he adds, "And the single tear at the end is unrealistic."

Jane and I just stare at him. Then we look at each other. That's his reaction to my first-ever reading of my first real acting job?

"The movie is called *Zombie Pond*, Dan," I tell him. "I'm not sure realism was at the top of their list."

"*Well*," Jane says, sarcastically. "*Well* then, let's read the second scene, shall we? *Well*?"

"Sorry, you guys," says Dan. "I suck. I don't know how actors do it. I want to help. Can I just read this next scene to myself first before we do it out loud?"

"Of course," I say to him generously, then I turn to Jane and roll my eyes. "These method actors!"

"Here you go, Mr. James Dean, sir," says Jane, handing him a single sheet of paper. "It's just the one page. What a drama queen he is! Don't quit your day job, Danny."

Dan pores over the single sheet, holding it tightly on either side. He's taking forever, reading so slowly, and I'm feeling a little impatient. I want to know what happens, and what I say.

"How many 'wells' in this scene, Dan?" I joke, trying to hurry him along. But he doesn't answer.

"Dan, you look like you're reading your own obituary," says Jane. "Chop-chop."

Finally he looks up, regarding each of us with a serious expression. "This is wrong," he says.

"What's wrong? What do you mean, wrong? What do I say?"

"Nothing. You don't have dialogue in this scene. But this is wrong. They can't do this."

"Dan, what are you talking about? Let me see." I take the paper from him, my heart pounding.

INT. SUTTON'S HOUSE—NIGHT

Sounds of lovemaking. A Motown singer croons
soft and low from the stereo. The camera PANS
across the floor. Sutton's sneaker. Sheila's bra.
We see a velvet ring box on the nightstand,
opened but empty. We see remnants of the wrapping
from Sheila's gift, and as the camera moves
closer to the bed we see it's a framed collage,
homemade, simple but beautiful, the word "yes"
repeated a hundred times in different sizes and
shapes and colors. She knew tonight was theirs.
The ring on her finger says the proposal went
well.

   CLOSE-UP on Sheila's face. She is on top of
Sutton, riding him, moaning softly, when—her
eyes POP open. She GASPS for air, a stifled gurgle
of a SCREAM as BLOOD pours out of her mouth,
blocking her throat, she can't breathe! PAN DOWN
to reveal: a ZOMBIE emerging—CLAWING its way out
from INSIDE Sheila's body, rupturing Sheila's
chest as it struggles to be free, screeching with
the effort. But it isn't a ZOMBIE we've seen
before, it's a SMALLER ZOMBIE with the eerie face
of a child, at once sinister and innocent, it,
too, gasping for air, the undead born anew!
SUTTON SCREAMS, tries to stop the flow of blood,
but he knows it is too late, they have possessed
her, they have killed her. And with that
realization comes the next, as the truth of what
has happened dawns and a look of horror crosses
his face . . .

```
                        SUTTON

                     (whispering)

            They're hatching . . .
```

The screen fades to black

"See what I mean?" Dan says, waving his hands. "It's outrageous."

"Sheila's *bra*?" I say.

"What's with the collage?" says Jane, reading over my shoulder.

"They can't go changing the existing rules," Dan says. "Everyone knows Zombies can't 'hatch'; that's just ridiculous."

I'm still staring at the page. "A zombie emerges—wait—from *where*?" I say.

"Ohhh, I get it," Jane says. "Sheila knew Sutton was going to propose to her that night, so she made him a collage of the word 'yes.' "

" 'Riding him'?" I say to myself. " 'Moaning softly'?"

"I hate these movies where they blatantly defy a well-established trope," Dan continues indignantly. "Zombies are, and have always been, the walking dead. How could the walking dead procreate? They have emerged from the grave, from the *dead*—"

"Oh shit, I didn't even think of that," says Jane, looking up at me.

"Well, no, I mean you wouldn't," says Dan. "But I've seen *every* one of these . . . and I can tell you—"

"You're topless," says Jane, reality dawning. "Shit."

"They have to follow a sort of code—and—wait. What? You're topless?" says Dan, his face going pale. "Oh. Oh, Franny. Shit."

"I'm topless," I say.

Shit.

I don't know what I want to do about the movie, so I've been taking a poll.

JAMES FRANKLIN:
There's nothing to be embarrassed about. Our bodies are our instruments.

JOE MELVILLE:
Let me see what we can do with the nudity clause. Perhaps there's a way to minimize your, er, expo-sure.

RICHARD:
Joe is the best one to advise you on this.

JANE:
I'm not sure. What does your gut tell you?

DAD:
I don't know, honey. We're starting Dorothy Parker this week, your favorite.

CASEY:

Oh my God, Michael Eastman is such a fox!

DAN:

I, uh . . . I'm going to the store, do you want anything?

According to Joe Melville, the director is "someone special" and only doing *Zombie Pond* as a favor to the studio, because they agreed to make two other movies with him after that: smaller, more interest-ing, character-driven pieces. Joe said if we connect on this film, it could be the beginning of a longer relationship. "This business is all about relationships," he told me.

"It isn't just about talent?"

Joe laughed, then paused. "You're kidding, right?"

"I got a part in a scary movie," I say to Dave, a waiter I've catered a few lunches with. We're outside the entrance to the General Electric building, grabbing a last smoke before our shift starts in one of the colorless lunchrooms we're sure to soon find ourselves in. Dave is a scruffy stand-up comic with crazy hair who looks about thirty but could be much younger. I learned back when I worked at The Very Funny that stand-up comedy tends to age people prematurely, so it's risky to ever guess out loud.

"That's great," he says, taking a drag off his cigarette. "Good for you."

"I'm not sure if I'm going to do it, though. I have to be topless in one of the scenes."

"So?" Dave says. "What's wrong, you got funny-looking tits or something?"

"Um, no, Dave. I don't think I have funny-looking tits."

"So, who gives a shit? What are you, swimming in job offers or something?"

"I'm standing here with a piece-of-shit canvas book bag whose contents include a corkscrew, an order pad, and a festive assortment of pens. Obviously, I'm not swimming in job offers, Dave."

"**D**on't do it," Deena says, shaking the ice in her almost drained vodka as we sit at the bar at Joe Allen after class. I agreed to have a drink with her after checking the home machine from the pay phone outside the theater. No message from James. And he wasn't in class tonight, which isn't that unusual, but it still gives me an unsettled feeling.

"They said you would only see me, uh, like *that*, for a few seconds. Then the zombie breaks free from my, uh, clavicle area, and I fall down dead. It's all right here in the nudity clause. It's very specific about what you see and for how long." I realize I'm hugging the manila envelope with my two-page nudity clause to my chest while talking about my chest. "They had their lawyer guy write it up."

Deena shakes her head.

"I need the money," I say in a small voice.

"You don't need it that bad."

"Yes I do. I got fired from the club, remember? I don't have insurance. I need four fillings."

"You can't do a job just for the money. What about doing work you believe in, like the actresses you look up to? You think Diane Keaton would take her shirt off in a zombie movie?"

"Who knows? Maybe they've yet to uncover the lost zombie films of Diane Keaton. Maybe they'll put out a whole anthology on VHS."

"You're funny."

"I'm not forgetting my goals. The director is apparently someone really special. It's just my body—everyone has one. My body is my instrument. And I'm on a deadline, to prove to myself this is what I'm supposed to be doing. Here I have an actual speaking part in an actual feature film. It's a sign that I'm headed in the right direction. I need that sign."

"You don't need this job."

"This is the only job I have."

"Currently. This is the only job you have, currently."

"But what if this is the only job I ever get? What if doing this job would lead to other jobs and therefore a career, happiness, worldwide acclaim, love, better hair—but *not* doing this job leads to nothing, and I never get another job, and I end up spending the rest of my days in obscurity serving chicken fingers, and this is the one story I tell over and over, the zombie-movie-I-turned-down story, and I end up with fat ankles from being on my feet all day?"

Deena drains the last of her drink. Then she takes my hand and looks at me seriously.

"Frances. Listen to me. You know you're talented, right? And beautiful?"

"Talented, maybe. I believe I can be good, yes. The other—beautiful—I don't know."

"You're kidding, right? It's part of your thing. You're saying that as a joke. But deep down, you know it's true, right?"

"Maybe. Sometimes."

"Well, *I'm* telling you, then. You have to believe me. Today is the day you have to start believing in yourself. No one can do it for you anymore. I'm telling you, if you turn this down, I can one hundred percent guarantee you will, someday, get at least *one* other job worth doing. Perhaps you will even get two worthwhile jobs in your lifetime, just perhaps. Right now, this is a fun idea to you. But I know how it will feel to shoot it. You're lying there shivering with a towel thrown over you, while a bunch of crew guys adjust lights and run cable. Imagine, there you are, straddling Michael Eastman, or Michael Eastman's stand-in more likely, cause that guy sure as shit doesn't work harder than he has to, while the special-effects guy pours red goo all over your naked body and adjusts the plastic zombie head that's glued on between your boobs, just to get a better angle for the cameraman. The director comes over, tries to make you comfortable, looks you in the eye so you don't think he's a creep, talks about the sofa he just got for his new house in the Hamptons, or whatever. You feel like shit. You go home and cry. That's the sort of day I'm picturing."

I'm sure Deena is exaggerating. I can't imagine it would be that bad. Of course, I can't actually picture any of it. "But it's just a few days. Even if it's awkward. It's just a few uncomfortable days in which I will make half the amount of money I made last year. In the *entire year*. Not to mention residuals. And I have a nudity clause that protects me. You should read it. It's a long, detailed essay. The more you read it, the more the concept loses all meaning. It becomes sort of hilarious."

"It's not hilarious. It's not meaningless. It's your body. On film forever. Naked, with a first-time director, in a monster movie. It isn't worthy of you."

"Well, the worthy-of-me jobs don't seem to be appearing," I say, squirming away from her slightly on my bar stool. "I can't be better than the job I have if I have no other, better jobs. So maybe this is just exactly as worthy as I am. It's as good as I deserve right now."

"That's what you think, but you're wrong. Something better could come along tomorrow. You only start out once. If you compromise now, at the very beginning, before you've really given yourself a chance, where do you go from there?"

"Um, up, I guess?"

"Look. I have a friend—he wanted to be in movies. He went to Los Angeles. He was the best actor in my class at drama school. Hands down. He goes out to L.A., he can't get a job. He tries everything. He has a wife, a little girl. Finally he interviews at a theme park. He hears they pay well. He's a big guy, strong. They tell him they could use him to be Fred Flintstone in one of the live shows they do for kids. The money's great. The beginning of the show he's supposed to enter on this giant water slide, right, so it looks like he's Fred sliding down the rock wall in the beginning of the cartoon?"

"Um, you mean, 'yabba-dabba-doo'?"

"That. Classically trained actor, this guy. And he's hired to say 'yabba-dabba-doo.' But he's okay with that. Someday, he thinks, he'll be in movies. Today, he's going to be the best Fred ever. He takes it seriously, right?"

"Okaaaay," I say, shaking my head, confused.

"So he does the training to play Fred, and he's doing well. He's training with a bunch of other guys, and they're teaching them all to do everything the same way. All the shows have to be the same—it's a rule of the park, so that no one sees a better or worse show than anyone else. During the training, they all learn to go down the water slide with their hands up in the air, 'yabba-dabba-doo,' right? Like on TV? Then they hire this one guy—maybe he's someone's friend or someone's kid or something—and he doesn't have good balance. He can't slide with his arms up in the air. So they retrain all the guys so the shows will match. My friend is pissed, because the way Fred enters in the cartoon on TV is arms up, the way everyone else learned it was arms up, it's the *right way*. So in his shows, when he plays Fred, he keeps doing it the original way—arms up. He gets in trouble; they want him to change it. He refuses." Deena brings her face just inches from mine. "So they fire him," she says, then leans back on her stool and slides the empty drink away from her. "Can I get another, Patrick?" she says to the bartender. "You want something? You want to split the omelette or something?"

I stare at Deena, then look over my shoulder as if maybe I missed something that just whizzed past me, something I was supposed to notice but didn't catch.

"Wait—that's it?"

"That's it."

"So, the moral of the story is—stand up for what you believe, even if it's a silly technicality that means losing a job?"

"The moral is: there's always someone who'll tell you it's just as good with your arms down, when you know it isn't. There's always someone who says the talking cat is cutting edge. The only thing you have that isn't in the hands of a dozen other people is your sense of what's right for you. You don't have to do a job that makes you feel bad. This is a business where it's real easy to think you like something you don't really like because you're flattered to be chosen at all. The moral is: Every actress, from Meryl Streep to Dr. Quinn, Medicine Woman, has boobs. Not every actress has 'no.' 'No' is the only power we really have."

I agree to split the omelette and I excuse myself to use the bathroom, when all I really want to do is use the pay phone in the narrow hallway. I check the home machine, to find that James has called and invited me to come to his place "if it's not too late for you," and my heart leaps a little. I can see my smile reflected in the glass of *Evita*, one of the framed show posters that line the wall. When I come back, there are two fresh drinks waiting at the bar.

"I, ahhh . . ."

"Cancel the omelette?"

"Is it that obvious?"

"You're lit up like a Christmas tree," Deena says, and gives my arm a little squeeze. "Can we eighty-six the omelette, Patrick?" she calls down the bar, and Patrick nods.

"Thanks. Sorry," I say, putting on my jacket quickly. I feel like I'm late for an appointment suddenly, that I'm rudely keeping someone waiting, even though it's nearly 10:00 and I just got his call.

"What does *he* say about it?"

"He thinks I should do it. Nudity doesn't bother him. And he's heard good things about the director's next film."

"Well then, I give up. He's probably right—he's got the eye."

"What do you mean?"

Deena pauses, as though she's said the wrong thing and now needs to choose her words more carefully. "Nothing."

"What? Tell me."

"Nothing—just. I've been in class with the guy for years, you know, since when he was just starting, before any of the—" She trails off, still looking stuck.

"Say it."

"Historically? He tends to pick the girls who are the most talented—who seem to be the most potentially successful—to be with."

I've been holding my breath, waiting for Deena to continue, to say something that reflects her solemn face, but I see that she's finished and allow myself to exhale. "I thought you were going to say something *bad* about him. That may be what he used to do, but he's obviously not doing that with me. He's broken his streak—"

"Franny. You have to stop this." Deena's voice is sharper than normal.

"What?"

"You don't get it."

"I don't—"

"Do you know how many other people in class got signed from the Showcase?"

"No."

"Two. And they were both guys."

"I thought Molly had—"

"A meeting. Molly had a meeting at a small agency that told her they had too many of 'her type.' You and Fritz and Billy were the only people. You passed this major hurdle, you had this huge accomplishment, but you barely noticed. You don't see how well you're doing. You don't see how I see you, or how James sees you."

"I'm grateful he sees me at all," I say in an attempt at humor, but Deena doesn't crack a smile.

"I want the best for you. You're twice as talented as I ever was, but I've learned a few things along the way. I want you to do everything you can to avoid making the kinds of mistakes I made. I just don't want you ending up on a show about a talking cat from France, you know?"

23

·················

"Don't read it out loud! Please, James, I'm begging you."

I want him to stop, but I'm laughing, too, lying on the bed in his apartment the next morning while James stands over me at the foot of it, holding the pages of my nudity rider in his hands solemnly, the way a messenger in a Shakespeare play comes to deliver a decree from the king.

He clears his throat.

"Ladies and gentlemen, for one night only, I bring you: Nudity Rider."

"What night? It's eleven A.M.! Boo, hiss! I wanted to see *Starlight Express*!"

He shuffles the pages dramatically, bows slightly to the imaginary audience. "In which reference is made to the agreement between blah, and blah blah, 'Producers,' and Frances Banks, 'Artist' . . ."

"Who's that?! Never heard of her!" I heckle.

"In conjunction with the motion picture currently entitled *Zombie Pond*, which will heretofore be known as 'The Picture.' "

"Stop! No more! Don't read all the . . ."

"I'm sorry, there seems to be a disturbance in the house." James lowers the papers. "Yes, madam?"

"Seriously, please don't read all the—the details or whatever. It's embarrassing."

"Madam, silence, if you please. Ahem. As I was saying, 'Producer' will shoot an overhead of Sutton and Sheila in bed, Sutton without a shirt, Sheila in a silk front-opening pajama top—"

"No! Stop! Why not a flannel nightgown? Footie pajamas, please!" I say, but I can't stop laughing.

"Artist agrees to perform what will heretofore be referred to as the 'foreplay sex scene,' in which: Sutton will unbutton Sheila's top, slowly, kissing her chest, between her breasts, with the top on . . ."

"Help! Somebody help me!" I squeal, hiding my face in a pillow.

"At this point a creature (herein known as 'creature') will emerge from between Sheila's breasts, and a brief, two-to-five second shot of Sheila's mangled chest and the screaming Zombie baby ('creature') will be shown, after which point Sheila slumps to the floor, dead, and no further nudity shall be required. Producer assures the set shall be closed to all persons, except those essential members of the cast and crew, and there shall be no still photographers allowed during filming. Except as specifically set forth herein, blah blah blah, agreement shall remain as such on this day, blah blah blah, the end. Ladies and gentlemen, thus concludes this evening's performance. Refunds will not be given. Tip your servers, thank you, and good night."

I'm clapping and bouncing up and down on the bed. "Brilliant! What a performance! I can't wait for the sequel!"

"Nudity Rider 2—Bottoms Up!"

"Bottoms Off!"

"Barely There!"

"Back to Backless!"

"Slutty in Seattle!"

James and I collapse together on the bed, face-to-face, out of breath from laughing.

"Seriously, James, that was torture. To hear it described so specifically, so clinically. I can't imagine I'll be the person they're talking about. How do they know already what the costume and the shots, or whatever, will be?"

"They're trying to be specific so you aren't surprised. That's what a good agent does. He's trying to get the parameters from them ahead of time so they don't pressure you on the set into something you aren't comfortable with."

"I guess," I say. I'm still hedging, but it's reassuring to hear James speak so knowledgeably.

"So does it?" he asks. "Make you feel more comfortable?"

"Yes. No. I don't know. Hearing you read it makes it sound fun. Talk about the phone book. You can make anything compelling."

He smiles. "So then . . . what aren't you sure about?"

"I know it's a silly movie. But I like the other scene, and it's kind of an important part, and I can't believe I'd be in an actual movie that would play in an actual theater. But I'm still not sure if being topless would feel horrible or embarrassing or whatever."

"Why embarrassing?"

"Well, duh, it's my body, you know?"

"So?"

"Well, I'm not sure . . ."

"Not sure how it will feel, or how it will look?"

"Both, I guess."

"But you're beautiful."

"Says you."

"Do you doubt that?"

"Of course."

"You shouldn't."

He brushes a hair from my face, then gently runs his finger along my cheek. "I get that it's hard to have confidence. But like I've said before, as actors, our bodies are our instruments. We have to have a sense of objectivity about the body, the face, so that we don't get in our own way of telling the story, any story. I'd gain fifty pounds or shave my head if it meant getting a part right, wouldn't you?"

"Yeah," I say, although I'm not totally sure. James pauses, looking deep into my eyes. I think he's about to kiss me, but instead he comes closer to me and whispers, "You know, if you want, I'll help you."

"Thanks. You've helped already, reading the scenes aloud, not to mention your recent perform—"

"No, I mean, I'm starting to make some real money. They're really paying me on this new film with Hugh, you know."

"Oh. That's great," I say, although I'm not sure why he's reminding me the Hugh McOliver film is paying him well.

"And, not that it helps you on this job, but if you wanted to, you know, in the future . . ."

James trails off, but a grin starts to spread on his face, as though he's having trouble keeping a really juicy secret from me.

I'm totally confused. "In the future . . . what?"

"If you wanted to jump on the bandwagon."

"Sorry, I'm lost. What band? What wagon?"

"C'mon, Franny, it must be on your mind, even a little. The whole time you've been agonizing over this decision, you're telling me it hasn't occurred to you?"

"What?"

"Don't get me wrong. I think you're beautiful the way you are, like I said, but if you wanted to get them done, just so you felt more confident, more competitive, you know, so you didn't have to agonize over this kind of stuff anymore. It won't be the last time it comes up, you know? So why not take the anxiety away? So many of the girls in L.A. are doing it, and they can make them look really natural . . ."

I feel as if someone just jabbed me hard in the ribs. My mouth falls open.

"You're talking about . . . you're suggesting . . . you want to buy me a *boob job*?"

The smile slips from his face. "Franny, no, I'm sorry, please, calm down. I mean, yes, that's what I was saying, but only because I thought that's what you were struggling with. I was just trying to help. I'd never—I thought we were talking about the same thing, feeling more sure of yourself."

"I'm not sure *what* we were talking about," I say, my throat closing up and something like a sob threatening to slip out. "I'm going." I slide out from under him on the bed and grab the one boot I can see.

"Don't go."

"I have to go. Where's my other shoe?"

"Wait. Don't go like this. You're taking this totally the wrong way. You're mad."

"See, that's where you're wrong. I'm not mad at all. It's just, now I feel like the penis pump I got you for your birthday isn't that original."

"See? That's funny. You made a joke. We're laughing about this."

"We are *not* laughing about this. I'm saying sarcastic things as I walk out the door. I'm exiting. I'm making a spunky exit."

"Frances, this is a total misunderstanding. Please don't go."

I whip around and try to look as intimidating as I can while wearing only one shoe. "Why, because you want to pitch me your 'face-lift before thirty' concept?"

He takes a deep breath, and the look on his face is as soft and sweet as any I've ever seen. "No," he says quietly. "I don't want you to go, because I love you."

I have to admit, this is probably the one and only thing James could say that would stop me in my tracks, the one and only thing I wasn't expecting to hear from him, certainly not today, and I'm not sure I've ever allowed myself to think it could happen at all. But my brain is a jumble of conflicting feelings, so I find myself in an awkward suspended moment somewhere between lacing up the rest of my one boot and collapsing back onto the bed in relief. I'm stuck, one shoe on, one shoe off.

"What?"

"I mean it. I love you. I really do. I've been wanting to say it to you for a while."

"Okay . . ."

"And I didn't even get to talk to you about the premiere."

Now I'm really confused.

"The what?"

"The premiere, for the movie I did with Arturo. It's coming up in three weeks. I wanted to ask you to be my date."

James said he loves me, which is frankly only slightly more shocking than the fact that he's asking me out to a public event where we'll actually be out of this apartment and among not just regular people, but also very public people.

I'm equally confused by both things that just happened. I don't even know which thing to think about first.

"But I thought you weren't—you said you couldn't go to my cousin's wedding because of the shooting schedule."

"Yes, but I meant to tell you they changed the schedule to let me go to the premiere." It flashes through my mind for a brief moment that if they changed the schedule for him for the premiere, maybe they could have changed it for the wedding this weekend, but of course a premiere is work, and my family wedding isn't as important, I guess.

James picks up my sweater from the floor, revealing my missing shoe, and takes a step closer to hand them both to me. His face still looks so open and wounded, I'm afraid I've hurt his feelings. "Look, I'm going to L.A. tomorrow and the weekend is wide open. Why don't you come with me? I can probably get production to . . ."

"My cousin's wedding is this weekend." My face gets hot again and my stomach tightens. He could have come if he wanted to, I think to myself. He just didn't want to.

"Oh, yes, right. Look, when I say the weekend is open, I mean I have a lot to do to get ready for the scenes with Hugh in the desert on

Tuesday, so I left myself time to work, you know. But if you were there, we could grab a bite and, you know, be together." James starts to come closer, but I pull back, not yet ready to be appeased.

His work is important. I know that. That's a perfectly reasonable explanation for not going to the wedding. It doesn't exactly sound right somehow, but then I don't know what it's like to be in a big movie with big movie stars.

"So—you can't come because you're working on Tuesday? You're not working on Monday?"

"Well, I'm not scheduled right now, but I'm rain cover."

"I understand," I say, though I can't help but consider how likely a day of rain in the desert might be.

"Look, we'll be shooting in the middle of the desert like I told you, but we'll talk soon—I just don't know when exactly. I hate that I won't see you until then, but please come to the premiere with me. And after that, I hope we can put this behind us. You're really, really special to me."

I go through the motions of an affectionate goodbye, but my heart isn't really in it. I feel detached, as if I'm watching myself from a few feet away. Out on the street, under the bright sunlight, my head starts to clear a bit and a wave of embarrassment hits. But maybe he was just trying to give me what he thought I wanted. I'm muddled and disoriented, as though I just woke up in a strange house and, for a minute, can't remember where I am.

But there's one thing I'm suddenly sure of.

I need a pay phone, but one that's not on James's street. I want to get farther away from here first. I half-jog the two long blocks to the corner of Seventh Avenue and Union Street. I'm only a few blocks from home, and though I could just use the phone there and not have to compete with traffic sounds, I don't want to wait another minute.

"Franny Banks for Joe Melville, please."

The receptionist said "one moment please," but it seems to be taking forever for Joe to pick up. The hold music is that same classical station but today there's some strange static interference, so the music keeps fading in and out, which hurts my ears, and I want to pull the receiver farther away, but I'm afraid I'll miss Joe picking up. To distract myself, I fix my eyes on the door of The Muffin Café, a ramshackle little storefront directly across the street. One person enters, then a second, then a third. When the first person exits, now with coffee and what looks like a bagel wrapped in white paper, I realize I've been on hold long enough for a bagel to be toasted and spread with cream cheese and wrapped, and for pleasantries and money to have changed hands, which has just become my new definition of forever.

"Franny?"

It's Richard instead of Joe, which is disappointing, but I'm also relieved not to have to explain what I'm about to say into the calm, silent abyss that can sometimes be Joe Melville on the phone.

"Richard. Hi. Listen, I feel bad, I'm sorry, but I can't do the movie."

"The movie?"

"The movie. I can't do *Zombie Pond*. I'm really sorry. I've thought a lot about it and I've realized that I'm just not the nudity type. Not that that's a bad type to be, necessarily. And it's not because of the zombie thing, either—it's no offense to zombies or monsters or man-eating sharks. In fact, I wouldn't even do this if it were *Jaws*, which is one of my top ten favorites. Although, actually, I take that back, since if Steven Spielberg—no—you know what, even if Steven Spielberg were calling, I'd have to say no. To being naked, I mean. And I'm sorry. I know that's not *artistic* of me or whatever, and I know this is my first real job and I hope Joe won't be mad—or maybe it's something he'd want to discuss, right? So, sorry, anyway, I'll just call back when he's back, which is when?"

"When . . . ?"

"Sorry, when's Joe back? So I can call him back. When he's back."

There's a long pause, and then Richard clears his throat.

"I'm sorry to have to tell you this, Franny, but Joe's not here."

"No? Oh, yeah, look at the time. He's probably at lunch, right? That's okay, I'll just call back tomor—"

"No, Franny, I mean Joe's not here at all. And listen, this has nothing to do with—even if you'd decided to do the movie it wouldn't have changed anything. You should know that."

"What wouldn't have changed anything? Sorry, I'm confused . . ."

"He was supposed to—I'm sure he'll call you to explain. As of yesterday, Joe Melville doesn't work here anymore."

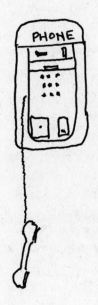

AAAND THIS WEEK ....

29 Monday

YOU HAVE NO AGENT!

ABSOLUTE
ARTISTS
ABSOLUTELY
DUMPED
YOU

J.F ♡

30 Tuesday

DROP OFF RESUMES
O'NEALS BALLOON
CAFE DES ARTISTES
COMEDY CELLAR ? (ASK FOR MARTY)

J.F. ♡

31 Wednesday

AIR HOLLYWOOD ★★★★ ~ JAMES ON LOCATION UNTIL ♡ JUNE 11

♡= DORK

Thursday **1**

WILL
NEVER ~~MUST~~
ATTAIN
STICK
FIGURE
BODY
TYPE

STAVROS CLASS

DRESS FOR WEDDING
(SORT OF)

Friday **2**

SEND
RENT
CHECK.

PICK UP RENTAL CAR 8 AM
7TH AVE

Saturday **3**

KATIE'S WEDDING
4 PM

CHECK-IN TIME 3 PM.

Sunday **4**

ONE MONTH LEFT*

* TIME TO PANIC

24

....

You have three messages.

BEEEP

Frances, it's your father. I hope you'll still recognize me when we see each other at the Finnegans'. You're still coming, right? With Jane? Call me back, please. I'd like to—there's something—call me, please. Also, one of my students says there's a show called E.R.? I think that's the name of it. About doctors, I suppose? Anyway, that's supposed to be a good one you should apply to.

BEEEP

Frances, Joe Melville calling. I'm sorry to leave you a message, but I'm not going to be reachable for a few days, during the, uh, transition. I want you to know that I've thoroughly enjoyed working with you, but I'm moving on to a more exclusive, er, a smaller agency, and I'm only able to take a very few of my clients, who are the, uh, top—well, only bigger names, you understand, are making this transition with me. I want to thank you, and wish you luck in all of your endeavors.

BEEEP

Franny, it's Richard, from Joe's office. I wanted to tell you how much I enjoyed working with you. I really tried to convince one of the other agents to take you on, but everyone's freaked out about Joe leaving, and no one's taking new clients right now. I'll still just be the assistant at the new office, or I'd represent you myself. Take care and keep in touch, okay? I wish I could be more helpful. Maybe someday in the future? Anyway, good luck.

"Pinkeye?" I keep repeating the phrase as if that will somehow make it disappear from Jane's face. "Pinkeye? You have pinkeye? How can you be sure?"

"Well, by looking in the mirror, for one thing."

"But maybe you just have something in your eye? Or allergies?"

"Sorry, Franny. I've had it before. This is what it looks like. It's really contagious. There's no way I can go."

Jane was going to be my date for Katie's wedding. Jane had arranged the rental car in her name. Jane has pinkeye.

"If you can't go, I can't go. Metro-North is on strike, so I can't take the train. I have no wallet, no driver's license. I can't pick up the rental car."

Two nights ago on the way home from James's, I arrived at our front door just as our downstairs neighbor was leaving, and Dan and Jane were home with the door to our place already open, so it wasn't until I went to get bagels the next morning that I realized in my rush to leave, I forgot my purse at James's apartment. I left him a message, but he must have already taken off for Los Angeles.

"Shit. I forgot about the license thing," Jane says, her good eye widening in sympathy. "I know. Maybe I can give you my I.D. and you can pretend to be me?"

"Good thinking. Where can I get colored contacts, an olive complexion, and darker, straighter hair in about an hour?"

"I'm just brainstorming here."

"It's fine. Forget it. I just won't go."

But it feels terrible to even speak that possibility out loud. I've never missed a Finnegan wedding. I haven't seen my dad in months, haven't even really spoken to him. His messages have had a strange sound to them lately. I think he's lonely.

"I can rent the car. I can take you."

I look over to see Dan hovering in the doorway of the kitchen, and I blush at the thought of him escorting me to the wedding. "Oh, thanks. Really. But this is a very crazy, giant wedding. It would be awful for you. This family is insane. And there's no time to get you a tux."

"All families are insane. And I have a tuxedo. In my closet."

I've only ever seen Dan in a T-shirt and jeans. He has no coat or blazer that I know of. In the winter he wears this sort of windbreaker-type blue jacket that can't possibly be warm enough, but if you ever ask him if he's cold, he says no, he's fine. He has one white-collared shirt and one blue-collared shirt that he used to alternate when he went out to dinner with Everett. I've never seen him wear a belt or a tie or socks that aren't white tube socks. Yet, Dan owns a formal tuxedo?

"But there's only one, ah, room, you know, in the motel," I stammer. "Just the one. So . . ."

I can't imagine bringing him into this party. The thought of it makes me unaccountably nervous. Our lives have gone back to normal: back to simply co-existing here in this apartment, the three of us going out occasionally to the upstairs Chinese place, or sitting on the couch and guessing who the killer is on *Law and Order.* The daily routine of being roommates has almost eclipsed what happened that one night out after the theater. I don't want to go outside these familiar surroundings, don't want to leave Brooklyn let alone spend a night with him in a motel—even one with two beds. But the thought of missing Katie's wedding, and not seeing my dad, makes my heart ache.

"This is silly," Jane pipes in. "We already got a double room for the two of us. So, what's the big deal? It's not like you two aren't already used to sleeping under the same roof. Make a wall out of throw pillows or something. It's Katie Finnegan's wedding, for Chrissakes! You're going! Yay, Dan!"

Jane smiles at me, as if it's all been decided.

"But how will I explain it to James?"

"Just tell him the truth."

"But don't you think leaving my purse, plus a Metro-North strike, plus pinkeye, plus Dan happening to have a tuxedo seems, I don't know, fishy?"

"No. I think, 'I'm shooting in the desert and I don't know when we'll talk' sounds fishy. He could've been your date if he'd wanted to."

"Jane. He's *working*," I say, but she rolls her eyes.

"Okay, Dan, listen." I turn and reach up to put my hands on Dan's shoulders, looking him in the eye like a football coach giving a pep talk to a player who is on the verge of winning the big game. "Really. I'm fine if I don't go. Are you sure you want to do this? You're sure this is how you want to spend your Saturday night? With a bunch of crazy drunken Irish strangers?"

My coach move was meant to be mock-serious, to lighten the mood and make it easy for Dan to laugh and say no, sorry, on second thought I really don't want to go. But with my hands on his shoulders, which are stronger than they seem under his slouchy T-shirt, my face tilted up to his, way up, because he's so tall, making me feel almost dainty by comparison, his big brown eyes free of bangs for once, gazing steadily into mine, that night at Sardi's comes tumbling back, and all this time I've spent convincing myself I never kissed Dan is wasted because I remember it all as if it happened five minutes ago.

I'm going to tell him he shouldn't come with me to Katie's wedding. I'm going to call my dad and say I'm sorry, that I'll make it up to him another weekend. I'm going to take my hands off Dan's shoulders and never, ever put them there again.

"Yes," he says without blinking. "Let's go."

25

....

I'm telling you. We went to high school together. We did. I'm sure of it. Are you sure you didn't go to Carver High? That's so weird. You look so familiar. Well, then, where do I know you from? You're a what? Really? You don't look like an actress. No offense, I mean you're pretty, but I thought they all had to be like anorexic or something. What show? You're in a what? A commercial? Oh no, God no. It can't be that. I don't watch television. I mean, once in a while I flip through the channels, but, no. Especially not commercials. No offense. But seriously, where do I know you from? Maybe we went to the same summer camp?

Congratulations, Franny! How exciting! Remember at the last wedding when you said you were trying to be an actress? And I said 'How are the tips?' Remember that? Hahahahaha! Because people who say they're actors are usually just waiters? Get it?

But your father said you wanted to be a real actress. In the theater. What happened to that? He says you got an agent, right? So that's something at least. What's that? You had an agent but you don't have one anymore? Oh, how terrible!

See Len, I told you she didn't get her nose done. It just looks that funny way on the TV. Sort of squashed or something? Whatever it was, it made you look so much older. I told him, Franny. I said, 'Len, Franny would never get her nose done. And even if she did, why would she give herself a little, short, squashy nose that added years to her face? It's the TV,' I said. You've heard that thing about the camera adding twenty pounds. It must do something to the face, too. What? It's just ten pounds the camera adds? Hmm, well, it looks more like twenty. Maybe it's our television. We have a new one. Everything looks so much larger than life. Those lovely girls from Still Nursing *look fine, though, those delicate figures! Maybe it's just when commercials play...*

Aunt Elaine is continuing on and on, hardly stopping for a breath, and, finally, I reach over and squeeze Dan's forearm in an attempt to say "save me."

"Will you excuse us?" he says to her politely, guiding me away with his hand on the small of my back. "Franny and I—we need to—we have to call the sitter."

I'm afraid Aunt Elaine can hear the giggle I try to suppress, but she hardly seems to notice, not skipping a beat, turning her monologue seamlessly onto the next victim.

"Sorry, I wasn't sure how to help you," Dan says sheepishly. "That's what my mother always used."

"It's okay," I say, smiling, happy to have Dan by my side, like a giant tuxedoed security guard. "I hope we left enough food out for the baby."

All the Finnegan weddings take place in a tent in the backyard of my aunt and uncle's huge old house right on the shore in Madison, Connecticut. As a kid, I could never get over the excitement of their house being right on the beach. I thought they were so lucky to live like they were on vacation all year long. The house itself would be beautiful, if anyone ever painted over the peeling dove-gray paint, or repaired the formerly white shutters near the front door that hang crazily at opposing angles, or mowed the backyard more than twice a year. But as much as my father's sister, Mary Ellen, tries to keep her house in some kind of order, with eight kids, there was always just "too much goddam fun to be had." You were lucky if you could find a bed with an actual blanket on it, but I always went to sleep happy, even if I had to use my rolled-up sweatshirt as a pillow. At the Finnegans', it wasn't neat but it was comfortable, and there was always someone to play with and always something to do.

When we'd visit, my mom and Aunt Mary Ellen would usually stay up after us kids had gone to bed. They'd sit on beach chairs on the front lawn talking, and I'd fall asleep to the sound of their laughter and the Joni Mitchell albums playing through the open windows of the porch. I can't help thinking about that now, as we stand gazing out over the water, and I look around for my dad, wondering if he's remembering her too, but can't find him in the crowd.

Even though the guests are encouraged to wear tuxedos and long dresses, it's just for fun—the rest of the event is down-home casual. The "cocktail hour" (which mainly consists of a couple of coolers full of ice and some cans of beer) is held on the sand right in front of the house. There's a crowd on the beach now, but Katie pushes through, squealing when she sees me. "You're so *skinny*," she says as she hugs me. "Well, hello," she says to Dan, and gives me a wink. Then she peels off her shoes and veil, tosses them on the sand, and dives headfirst into the ocean, her fully clothed new husband by her side. "It's a family tradition," I explain to a visibly shocked Dan. "They have a special dress they all use for the ocean. She'll put her real dress back on for the reception."

Beers on the beach is usually my favorite part of a Finnegan wedding, but after tonight's assault, I'm relieved to finally enter the tent and find our table. My dad has taken his seat already and has an expectant look that tugs at my heart. *He's missed me,* I think to myself. He's wearing the tuxedo I've seen him in a dozen times. The cut still fits him as it did when he was younger, but the lapels are shiny now from wear. He's recently had a haircut, and something about him looks unexpectedly youthful. I give him a big hug.

"You look beautiful!" he says, still holding on tightly.

"Doesn't she?" Dan agrees, and I blush and smile at him from over my father's shoulder.

A ragged band of local musicians, regulars at all the Finnegan events, play an almost recognizable version of "Strangers in the Night" at varying tempos. The chair next to my dad is empty, and my cousin Tom and his wife, Beth, are seated across from us, struggling to keep their toddler from eating the centerpiece. Dan goes to find us another couple of beers and a scotch for my dad, who leans toward me once he's gone.

"He seems like a smart fellow," Dad says. "Very polite."

"Yeah, he is. But he's not my boyfriend."

"You mentioned that."

"Len and Elaine asked me if I got my nose done."

"They don't know what to say. They're excited for you. People aren't used to seeing someone from their television in person," he says, giving my arm a little squeeze.

"I'm barely even on TV. I've done two dumb commercials in two and a half years, and now I'm getting stuck in these bizarre conversations with total strangers. I've hardly seen any of the cousins tonight. I've hardly seen *you*."

"We've got the rest of the night. You know these things never end early. Now listen, I wish you'd called me back, because—"

"Dad, I call you. I call you lots. You just don't know it because I can't leave you a message because you don't have an answering machine."

"I don't *want* an answering machine. A taped message is redundant information at best. I need so-and-so just letting me know that they called when I wasn't home? Or I'm supposed to tell them on a recording that I'm not at home, or that I'm too busy to talk right now? I already know I'm not home, due to the fact that I'm the person who's not home."

"But me leaving a message is a way of letting you know I called."

"If you call and I don't answer, you already know I was busy and couldn't have a conversation. I get the same information when I get your machine—it lets me know you're absent or too busy to have a conversation. If we both had machines this could go on forever, this never actually speaking. I'm saving you a step by not having a machine. If the phone rings—"

I'm distracted by the presence of a strange woman who has appeared just over my father's right shoulder. She's wearing a soft blue dress, and she's swaying slightly, as though she's deciding whether to sit down in the empty chair beside him. Or maybe she's just had a few too many. She must be another drunken Finnegan, but it's odd because I don't recognize her from any of the other weddings. Is she my aunt's cousin Maureen from Ithaca? She puts her hand on my father's shoulder, obviously confusing him for someone else, since if I don't know this random Finnegan, he certainly doesn't either. I should warn him that he's being approached from behind by a drunken woman who thinks he's someone else, and who—eerily—looks like she might be about to kiss him.

"Dad, um—"

"Eddie?"

She says his name, so I guess she isn't a stranger, not to him at least. In fact, the look on my father's face as he turns and then springs to his feet to greet her tells me she isn't a stranger to him at all.

"Franny," my father says to me, beaming. "I'd like you to meet someone."

Her name is Dr. Mary Compton, and she's some sort of eye surgeon my father met when he had "that thing with his cornea," which he apparently told me about but I don't remember. She's divorced and has a daughter "about your age," which immediately makes me fatigued as I imagine a future where Mary Compton's daughter and

I are forced to go shopping and have lunch and pretend to enjoy our-selves because our parents are dating. "I've always wanted a sister!" I imagine Mary's daughter saying to me, as we lunch in a brightly lit department store café.

My father and Mary don't seem to notice the cloud that settles over me while they chat away together easily. "Dr. Mary had to per-form an emergency surgery tonight," Dad says, beaming at her. "We're so lucky she could make it at all."

I nod in what I hope is convincing agreement.

When Dan returns to the table with our drinks, I slump down in my chair and take too many gulps of my beer all at once. As Dad in-troduces him to Mary, I watch as if from a great distance, unsure why I feel so strange. I truly want to be excited to meet this new person my father likes. I want to ask her questions and make her laugh and show her how well he raised me. But instead, I'm strangely quiet, inexplicably unable to think of a single thing to say.

Thankfully, Dan takes over, engaging her easily, learning about her recent promotion, and the fact that she lived in London for ten years, and hearing stories of her daughter's time at Oxford, and how she met my dad. I try to nod and smile in the right places, but I'm finding it hard to focus.

Numbly, I watch my father behave in a way I've seldom seen. I'm riveted by how unfamiliar he seems to me and I can't look away, even though his loopy expression makes me feel a little queasy. He's grin-ning so wide, he looks positively goofy. He calls her "Dr. Mary," as in "Dr. Mary and I both loved the New Haven Symphony's season," and in response she laughs and rolls her eyes.

"It's so embarrassing when he calls me that, isn't it, Frances?" she says, winking at me conspiratorially from across the candlelit table. "Like I'm one of those radio call-in hosts who isn't really a doc-tor?"

"Actually, it's just Franny," I say, and my voice sounds strangely cold.

"Of course! So sorry. I knew that. I guess I'm a little nervous to finally meet you," she admits shyly, and my father gazes at her, delighted.

Dinner arrives, and I finally manage to sputter out a few sentences as I pick at my burger. The Finnegans always have a barbecue instead of a caterer, and usually I love how homey and informal and comforting the food is, but tonight I've lost my appetite.

"Would you like to dance with me?" Dan asks, once the dinner plates are cleared and the cake has been served, and though normally I wouldn't want to dance, at least not to this slow song, I'm relieved to have an excuse to get up from the table.

"Yes, please," I say, and Dan takes my hand, guiding me smoothly to the dance floor.

From the start, it's obvious he can dance—that he can *really* dance. His lead is gentle but confident, and it almost makes me look like I know what I'm doing, too.

"Cotillion," he says, before I can ask. And then, "You okay, Franny?"

"I'm fine," I say. "I don't know why I'm acting so weird. It's just—Dr. Mary? It's so *cute*. Cute is the one thing I never thought my father would suffer from."

"He seems happy, though."

"I know. He does. And of course I want him to be. He's just never brought someone to a family thing before."

"I understand," Dan says, pulling me a little closer so I can hear him over the music.

It's the perfect thing to say, and I lean my head on his shoulder, grateful not to have to explain myself further.

My cousin Katie makes her way across the dance floor, hand in hand with her new husband. She's still in her wedding gown, but has traded her heels for high-top sneakers more comfortable for dancing. She hugs everyone as she passes, and her groom shakes hands, and sometimes they join in to dance with some of the couples on the floor. When she spots me, she leaves his side for a moment, reaching out to grab my hand and putting her arm around Dan.

"Your boyfriend's so cute!" she squeals. "I didn't get a good look at him before."

"He's my roommate, Katie," I say emphatically, not looking at Dan. "I told you, my boyfriend had to work. You looked beautiful today, by the way."

"Yes," Dan says. "Beautiful ceremony, too."

"Thanks, Fran. Thanks, Roommate." Katie raises her eyebrows at Dan and looks him up and down. "You're a good dancer," she says, a gleam in her eye.

"Thank you," he says, with a funny little bow.

"But this Sinatra stuff they're playing now, this is just the warm-up, you know."

"I've been informed about the upcoming mandatory dance party, yes," he says formally, but grinning a little.

"Good, 'cause the DJ takes over after dinner, and this place is gonna get *ugly*," Katie says. "After the old people leave, there'll be *real* music. And by real, I mean old music, and new music, and horrible, shitty music. We don't care, as long as you can dance to it. We're gonna *Macarena* this thing if we have to, to keep this party going. The Macarena—that's how low we're gonna go. You're not too good for that, are you, Roommate, with your fancy dance moves?"

"Certainly not," says Dan, with pride.

"I like him," Katie says to me. "You're sure he's not your boyfriend?"

"Ha, ha," I say, and even though I'm sure, I'm glad she approves of the first-ever person I've brought home since Clark.

After she leaves, Dan and I continue to dance, swaying back and forth without saying anything. It's strangely comfortable, this not talking. In my heels, his shoulders are the perfect height to rest my arms on. I can just see over him to where the light has faded outside, and the little fairy lights inside the tent are beginning to glow, making everything feel magical and warm.

"So, why *do* you have a tuxedo?" it occurs to me to ask, tipping my head back to look up at him.

"Well, ah, we had to have one. For my college a cappella group."

"No!" I say, taking a step back, trying to picture what Dan would look like in a line of tuxedoed college boys, bobbing merrily in unison.

"Yes," he says proudly.

"*Really?* You sang in one of those groups?"

"Yes. Is that so hard to picture?"

"It's—surprising, I guess. I've never even heard you *hum*. And don't you have to, like, do backup singer–type choreography and sing all that barbershop stuff?"

"We weren't a typical group like that. We made unusual selections, musically speaking. We did some parodies, which were well received. We actually got the chance to . . ."

"What?"

"Well, we got the chance to appear on *The Tonight Show*."

"What! *The Tonight Show?* Why haven't you ever told me that before?"

"Oh, I don't know," Dan says, hanging his head a bit. "I didn't want to brag, I guess."

I want to tease him for not telling me, for keeping a secret like this, but there's something about how humble he is in this moment—his looking embarrassed to have drawn attention to himself—that makes my heart swell.

"I hope I can see it someday," I say, and I can see him blush.

"The thing is, it turned into a bit of a sore spot. Within the family."

"How is that possible?"

"Well, my father's side has been going to Princeton for three generations, and there have been certain, well, expectations. I'm the first to defy some of them."

"They considered appearing on *The Tonight Show* a form of *defiance*?"

"It was considered a distraction from my studies, artistic nonsense, you know," he says bitterly. "Later, when I announced I wanted to write, my father blamed it on the group somewhat, as if one creative endeavor had somehow opened a floodgate to them all. But studying to be a doctor, as the generations before me did, well, that wasn't for me. Right before we appeared on the show, I announced to my father I was dropping out of pre-med to be a screenwriter. The idea of writing movies for a living—never mind the subjects that I've chosen to write about—well, that's been a little bit difficult for them, for the family. I'm actually somewhat of a disappointment to them, it seems. My father cut me out of my trust fund and never saw the show."

"But how do you . . ."

"How do I live?"

"Well, yes."

"I have a small inheritance from a great-uncle who always wanted to be a painter. When it runs out, I'll get a regular job, I guess. Or go crawling back to my father, which would probably mean going back to school to be a doctor."

"So, you're on a deadline, too!"

He smiles. "I suppose we have that in common, yes."

I picture Dan at the dining room table back in Brooklyn, poring over his notebooks and computer every day, eating the same cheap chicken plate from the same horrible place, nursing one beer each night that he's afraid to put on the coffee table, and the thought of him being made to feel that anyone is disappointed in him shifts something inside of me. I can almost hear it, a sound both sharp and soft, like a piece of heavy paper being ripped out of a notepad, and all of a sudden I feel overwhelming respect for Dan. I care about him, but it's more than that—I'm proud of him, too.

It's a relief to recognize that these feelings are nothing at all like my feelings for James. With James there's heat—it's exciting to be with him. My feelings for Dan are more like a warm glow, like the lights in the tent, and similarly contained. *He's a good person*, I think. That's all.

Later, somewhere between "Whoomp There It Is" and "I Saw the Sign," my father and Dr. Mary come over to say goodbye. They're gleaming with sweat, and with the low lights and his flushed cheeks, my father looks like he could be thirty again. Suddenly, I'm terribly sorry for how I've behaved, and I wish I could go back and replay the whole evening, getting to know her better, and in general inserting a better version of myself into the picture.

"No, don't go!" I say to them both, clasping Dr. Mary's hand in mine.

"We have to," my dad says, somewhat out of breath.

"It was so nice to finally meet you," Dr. Mary says, bringing her face closer to mine. "I hope we can see you again, very soon."

"Me, too," I say. And I realize that I mean it.

The next two hours fly by as Dan and I dance to every silly song the DJ plays. Somewhere around the B-52s' "Rock Lobster," I can feel my legs have turned to jelly.

"I don't think I have anything left," I say to Dan, a little breathlessly.

"Thank God," he says. "I'm soaked."

"We'll have to sneak out," I yell to him over the blaring music. "If Katie sees us, we're toast."

"Okay," he says with a grin, up for the challenge. "You break right, I'll duck left, and I'll meet you outside."

We get lucky when "This Is How We Do It" comes on and the dance floor floods with the remaining guests. At our empty table, still littered with cake crumbs, I grab the vintage clutch I borrowed from Jane, then slip out the front door of the tent, trying to assume the nonchalant look of someone who isn't leaving, only going out for a breath of air. Outside the tent, the night is impossibly dark and I blink a few times, disoriented, trying to get my eyes to adjust.

"Pssst," Dan says from behind a tree on the lawn. I catch the moon's reflection on the ocean, lighting the way to the beach.

"Run!" I whisper, and I take off, suddenly giddy and giggling uncontrollably.

I reach the sand well before Dan, and I kick off my shoes and catch my breath, lulled by the sound of the waves softly kissing the shore. The motel where we're staying is just half a mile down the beach, close enough to see from here. I hardly paid attention to the room when we checked in—we only had time to dump our things on the beds and change quickly before the wedding. But now I see the motel's softly glowing neon sign and the images come to me: the small room, the two beds that seemed uncomfortably close together, the bathroom we'll share, the decisions we'll have to make about brushing our teeth and who showers first.

"Franny?" Dan has somehow crept up behind me without my noticing. It's too dark to see him exactly, but I can tell he's close and my heart beats faster. My dress is damp from the dancing, and now there's a breeze from the sea that sends a chill through my body. I have a feeling that he's about to kiss me, and I start to shiver. I can't let that happen, no matter what. It would mislead him—I have feelings for him only as a friend. But I'm paralyzed in this spot on the beach for some reason, powerless to move away from him.

I can't see Dan well enough to read his expression, and I can't summon the words to explain to him how I'm feeling, and now there he is, a step closer, close enough for me to smell the beer on his breath. He takes my hand in his and holds it to his chest so I can feel his heart beat, and then he steps even closer, so close he towers above me, just inches away, his body sheltering me from the breeze. But I can't let it happen; I don't want anything to happen to change things between us, although in a way I do.

"Don't," I say too sharply, and Dan freezes.

"Don't," I say again, unnecessarily, since neither of us has moved.

And so we simply stand there, for I don't know how long, completely still, with only the sound of the ocean and the beating of Dan's heart against my hand.

26

···················

That night in the hotel I lay awake staring at the ceiling, irrationally irritated by the sound of Dan's snoring, as if his ability to sleep when I can't is intentional, his snoring a deliberate intrusion, keeping me awake another boundary he's recklessly disregarding.

The next morning is even worse. Dan insists on paying for the room, a gesture that annoys me for some reason, and while I wait for him to check out, I grab a local paper from the stack on the worn coffee table in the motel lobby for protection. *I'll read this in the car to avoid having to talk*, I think to myself. But once we're on the road I realize it's one of those free papers that have a single two-paragraph story about a high school teacher's retirement, and about thirty-two pages of ads and classifieds. Still, it's the only armor I have against holding an actual conversation, so I pretend it's the most compelling read ever, almost convincing even myself. I'm so engrossed in surveying the details of the Angelo's Pizza two-for-one coupon for the tenth time that I practically jump when I hear Dan's voice.

"The traffic's so bad, it looks like Russia, don't you think?" he says, glancing over at me.

What am I supposed to say to that? I already told him I've never even been to London. Why would he think I've been to Russia, of all places? He's just showing off his fancy education, and his tuxedo and the dumb a cappella group he mistakenly thinks is cool.

"You would know better than I," I say, stiffly.

"Huh?" he says, sounding genuinely confused.

"I've never been."

"You've never been where?"

"I've never been to Russia," I say too loudly. "So I wouldn't know what the traffic is like."

He tries to hide his smile, but fails miserably. " 'It looks like rush hour,' I said."

"Oh," I reply in a small voice, and return to pretending to read.

James eventually called from L.A. and got his super to open his apartment and I retrieved my purse, Jane started work on a new movie starring Julia Hampton, and Dan and I spent the days wandering our respective floors of the apartment, separately restless. I could hear his footsteps pacing on the creaky floor below, could hear him open the refrigerator, could imagine him hovering in front of it, staring absently into its emptiness as if some new contents might suddenly have appeared since the last time he looked.

I come down the narrow staircase softly, not wanting to disturb him. I'm planning to take a walk, to leave another application at another restaurant, to go somewhere, anywhere.

"I'm blocked and unable to write," he calls, from his usual place at the dining room table, hardly looking up from the computer screen.

"I'm agentless and unable to find employment," I say from the bottom stair.

"Want to go to the movies?"

"Sure," I say, and he closes his laptop with a *thwack*.

We leave the house without looking in the paper or calling ahead. The sun is shining and the tops of the trees in Prospect Park have turned bright green. We walk down toward Atlantic Avenue, our sneakers making no sound on the pavement. The bustling street in front of the theater is another world away from our sleepy neighborhood—full of commuters coming from the buses and subways, and shoppers flooding the discount stores. Only one movie fits our timing—a romantic comedy starring Cordelia Biscayne as a popular wedding photographer unlucky in love.

"*Capturing Kate?*" I say doubtfully.

"I hear she can capture love on film, but in real life she's underdeveloped," he says drily, reading from the advertising poster by the ticket booth.

I usually like these kinds of light Cordelia Biscayne movies—better than the ones where she's bravely defending a wrongly accused criminal, or bravely fighting a losing battle with an obscure disease—but nothing about *Capturing Kate* rings true for me today. In the story, Kate is torn between two men: a handsome, slick, wealthy Manhattan art dealer who wants to make her famous and take her to parties, and an even more handsome but much more kind and unassuming photographer who works in the darkroom, who wants her to travel to third-world countries with him and be a photojournalist. After it's over and she picks the guy you knew she would pick all along, the movie finishes with a cute photomontage of the pictures they take of each other in exotic places. I sigh in the dark theater.

On the walk back home, I'm feeling off. My head hurts from the giant diet soda I chugged and my eyes haven't yet adjusted to being back in the sunlight. Dan seems unburdened, happy, and says he actually enjoyed the film.

"I can't believe you liked it," I say, hugging my arms around myself even though it isn't cold out.

"Why, because I'm a guy?"

"No, because it was so dumb. It wasn't even well written."

"I thought some of the dialogue was pretty sharp, actually. A real-sounding romantic relationship is the hardest thing to write." He lumbers along, face turned up to feel the sun, hands stuffed in his pockets.

"But the relationships *didn't* sound real. That love triangle. So unrealistic! She's choosing between a rich jerk and a good guy who seems to be poor, but eventually turns out to be rich, too. *That* took two hours to figure out? I mean, the whole 'love triangle' *thing* bothers me. Who even thought of that? I've never been in a love triangle. Especially one where the girl is torn between the obviously right guy played by the more famous actor and the obviously hideously wrong guy played by the slightly less famous actor. And also, why does the heroine always have a sassy best friend? And why is she always a brunette?"

"Um, Franny, you have a sassy best friend who's a brunette."

"Wrong. I'm *her* sassy best friend who's a brunette."

"Well, I suppose you have a point there. It's a toss-up between you two for the part. Look, the romance in these movies, it's not supposed to be some sort of dark mystery. It's a conceit, a way to show different sides of the main character, what she's struggling with. It's a way to make an internal struggle dramatic. People see themselves in that struggle. They keep using that structure because it's familiar to most people and makes sense to them."

"Well, it isn't familiar to me. Anyway, why is it always a triangle? Why isn't it a square or an octagon? That seems more realistic."

"You've been in a love *octagon*?"

"No, but, you know, if you aren't with one person you really love, it's more complicated than a stupid triangle. The problem isn't because of *one* other person you wish you were with. In life, there's a million people you might have feelings for, depending. There's either one person you love and you're happy or there's a bunch of people who could be right, if only the timing was better, or they didn't still have feelings for an old girlfriend, or whatever. It's mostly timing. I'm in a good relationship, but I pass three people a day I could imagine going on a date with."

"You pass three people a day you could imagine going out with? That's being in a good relationship?" Dan is smiling, which frustrates me even more.

"You're twisting my words. I don't mean I'm in love with the random people, but I think about the random people and wonder about them, whether it's the guy on the subway or, you know . . ." Dan looks at me expectantly, but I trail off, suddenly worried that we're not just talking about the movie anymore. I press on, determined not to let go of my point. "And then there's work, too—I mean I have a very strong attachment there, too, you know, so maybe that gets mixed in . . . and, anyway, you see how quickly one could get to a love octagon." I stop abruptly in the middle of the sidewalk, causing an old lady pushing a little trolley with her groceries on it to nearly crash into me. "Excuse me," I say to her, suddenly flustered. "Anyway, I'm not talking about us."

Dan's eyebrows raise a little, and he stops on the sidewalk, too. "I didn't say you were talking about us."

"No. Right. I know. I'm not. I'm just trying to illustrate how ridiculous the love triangle concept is."

"I understand," he says.

"By saying there are potentially other shapes."

"Mmm-hmm," he says, nodding sincerely.

"Other unique shapes. Other shapes that feelings take. Other feeling shapes," I say idiotically, as if randomly rearranging the order of the words helps strengthen my point.

"But you've never been in a love triangle?"

"Definitely not."

"You've never had feelings for two people at the same time that were confusing?"

"No," I say, but I can't look him in the eye.

"Can we talk about the wedding?" Dan says gently, after a pause.

"No. What? Why? What is there to talk about?"

"I held your hand, and it seems to have upset you."

"Oh God, I haven't even thought about that."

"No? You haven't thought about the night at Sardi's either?"

"No—hardly—not at all, really. I just had that weird anxiety thing at the wedding for some reason."

"I know. You started sweating."

"Did I?"

"And shaking."

"Oh, well—"

"Because I took your hand . . . ?"

"Yes—well, no. Because of what it meant, I suppose."

"There's something here, don't you think?"

"I don't know . . ." I say, involuntarily walking backward away from him on the sidewalk.

"Well, *I* feel something. I do. And, I've thought about it since . . . watch the mailbox—"

"Can we not talk about this?" I say, and turn, sidestepping just in time, narrowly avoiding the big blue mailbox on the corner, and start walking fast, head down, wanting to put distance between us.

"I don't know either," Dan calls after me. "That's all I wanted to say. I don't know what it means either."

I'm stopped on the sidewalk by the sound of Dan's voice, but by something else, too—something more specific that's caused me to come to an abrupt halt. With a start, I realize that what stopped me in my tracks was disappointment. I realize I'm disappointed to learn that Dan isn't any clearer than I am about what happened, or what didn't happen. I expected he was for some reason. I pivot on my heels and start to walk slowly back to him.

"I mean," Dan says, looking sheepishly at his feet, "I haven't really recovered from the fact that I was engaged not that long ago. And I'm still not able to work, not really, and so I feel like I'm all over the—"

"Dan," I say, planting my feet, noticing a strange hint of sarcasm in my voice. "Puh-lease. You don't owe me an explanation. After all, I have a *boyfriend*."

Dan's face reddens a bit, maybe in response to my tone. "Is that what he is? A guy I've never met even though I live with you, who calls you to come over late at night? That's your boyfriend?"

And even though James hasn't ever used the word to describe himself, and I've never called him that to his face, I don't like Dan's insinuation. "Yes," I say with as much certainty as I can summon.

"Franny, if this was the movie of your life, and you happened, in the movie, to be in a love triangle, which I know is impossible given your very valid shape theories, can you say *he's* the guy our heroine ends up with? Can you honestly say he's the obviously right guy in the movie?"

"Why are we making a movie of my life at all?"

"For the sake of argument."

"Who would go? Nothing happens in it. What would we call it? *Counting Tips? Unemployed Actress? Losing Joe Melville?*"

"Maybe I'm wrong. I'm just wondering if perhaps what's bothering you about the movie we just saw is that you recognize something of yourself in what you claim is an unrealistic cliché."

Dan isn't trying to be mean, he never is, but his words sting as if he meant them to. The worst part of having this discussion is that it can't be over, not really, because now we both have to walk home to the same place. I wish I could just go home and tell my roommate about this strange afternoon I spent with a guy I know, and how he insulted me with his preposterous theories about me, but I can't, because they're the same person. We walk the rest of the way in silence.

What a mess. *Maybe I should move out*, I think to myself. I'm amazed it hasn't occurred to me before. I guess because generally I'm so happy to come back to the apartment and sit on the sofa and watch something on TV with Dan while he balances a beer between his legs. What if I moved out? Jane and I would still see each other all the time, I'm certain of that. It would be hard to find a new place, especially one as big and relatively inexpensive, but maybe it's time.

Things have become too complicated. What would it feel like if I didn't live in our apartment? I wonder.

I would miss the place itself. I would miss the way the light floods my room in the morning, would miss the view of the rooftops of other apartment buildings, would miss watching our neighbor Frank predictably have the same day over and over, would miss the beautiful creaky wood floors that broadcast whoever is coming up the stairs by creaking in direct proportion to their weight and mood.

And I'll admit, I would miss Dan in some ways. I like watching *Law and Order* with him, even when he ruins the ending by guessing who the killer is before I do. I'll miss his overly elaborate explanations of why the director is moving the camera in a certain way. I'll miss his comments on a piece of dialogue he finds particularly poetic. I've learned a lot from seeing those kinds of things through his eyes. But the feelings I have for him are confusing, and having to see him all the time makes figuring them out impossibly complicated.

Whether or not my deadline runs out, and whether or not I stay in New York, I have to face the fact that living with Dan has become an uncomfortable proposition.

I think I should move.

27

·················

You have three messages.

BEEEP

Dude, it's Deena. I just got a call that I'm finally going in for fucking Law and Order *this week. Wish me luck! See you in class, kid.*

BEEEP

Hello, I'm calling from Dave O'Brien's office, over at Kevin and Kathy? *We're just calling to let you know the show's coming back next Tuesday at eight thirty, and your episode will be airing then. We tried calling your agency, but, er—anyway, just calling to let you know.*

BEEEP

Hey, babe. Can't wait to see you tonight. A messenger's going to drop off the clothes and the passes, and I'm sending the car for you at six thirty, okay? Screening's at seven, don't be late.

BEEEP

The minute James got back into town, any doubts I might have had about us evaporated. He was tanned from the sun, proof of his days spent shooting in the desert, and the sight of him made me melt.

I'm confused by his message, though. We'd discussed going to the premiere of his movie together.

"You're sending a car?" I say when he picks up. "Like, a rental car?"

"No, like a car with a driver. To pick you up."

"Like a *limousine*?"

"Well, no. It'll probably just be a town car. A sedan. Is that okay?"

"Of course! I mean, I've never even . . . But where are you going to be?"

"The cast has to be there early. I'll meet you at the end of the red carpet."

I'm curious, but I'm not going to ask how one knows where the beginning or end of a carpet is, red or otherwise. I imagine the beginning to look something like the swirl where Dorothy sets out with Toto to follow the yellow brick road. I picture a welcoming committee of munchkins, and Glinda the Good Witch, who will help me find my way.

"Okay, great," I tell him, managing to sound more confident than I actually feel.

That afternoon, a messenger arrives with a garment bag I have to sign for. In it are two beautiful cocktail dresses, both with the tags still attached.

"He bought these for you?" Jane asks, impressed.

"Well, I'm only keeping one, but yes."

"These are like *real* designers," she says, running her fingers over the shiny satin.

"Which one's better, do you think?"

"Well, I'd have to see them on, of course," she says, tilting her head to one side, as if trying to picture me in them. "At first glance, the black is safer, but the green makes more of a statement."

After trying each one on a dozen times in front of the bathroom mirror, I decide to wear the green dress with the plunging neckline. I put on my highest heels, beautiful to look at but nearly impossible to walk in, and I enter Jane's room and pose with my hand on my hip and one foot angled in front of the other, model-style.

"I've decided to become a statement person from now on."

"I'm so proud of you!" Jane squeals.

I put on much more makeup than I normally do, and Jane helps me put my hair up using about a thousand bobby pins. I check my reflection in the mirror from every angle. *James will be impressed*, I think with pride.

I make a grand entrance, gliding daintily down the circular staircase where Jane and Dan wait, beaming up at me with pride, like I'm going off to prom.

Dan's face goes red as I get closer and he lets out a long slow whistle. "Wow," he says in a husky voice, as I reach the bottom stair.

Jane nods her head with the pleased air of an expert. "Gorgeous."

But then my hair starts to fall in the back, and Jane takes me back into our upstairs bathroom to put another thousand bobby pins in it. I can hear the driver ring our intercom and my heart leaps as I race downstairs, but then I can't find my lipstick, so I take off my shoes and run back up, where I discover it under the bathroom sink. I tear back down the stairs and hover in the kitchen for a moment, putting my shoes back on and trying to catch my breath.

"Do you have any cash?" Dan asks. "You should tip the driver."

"Shit! I forgot," I say, already feeling that I'm slightly miscast in the role of premiere-attending actress. He takes a ten and a twenty out of his wallet and tucks them into my evening bag. There's something so sweet about seeing his giant hands fumble with the clasp on the small satin bag, the same vintage loan from Jane that I brought to Katie's wedding, and for a moment I wish I were staying home to watch something with him on the couch instead of going off into the unknown of whatever a "premiere" might be.

I have to make about three more trips up and down the stairs to retrieve my forgotten powder, change the bra whose strap is showing ("switch it for the black one," Jane says), and do one last hair-and-makeup check in the mirror. Finally, I say goodbye with a "ta-daa" at the door, and Dan and Jane give me a little applause as a send-off. I walk gingerly down the carpeted stairwell, slightly unsteady in my heels, gripping the banister for support, and find the impressively shiny black town car in front of our building, with a driver standing beside an open door that's waiting just for me. I pause on our stoop, looking east and west, hoping a neighbor might see, but there's only an older man walking a small dog way off down the block, and I enter the car without an audience.

The driver's name is Benny, and he asks what radio station I'd like to hear.

"Anything's okay. Whatever you like."

He turns to a station playing an old Carpenters song, and for about ten minutes I just stare out the window, enjoying the music and the quiet and the cool feel of the soft black leather seats. I'm going to my first premiere. I feel pretty and confident, as if I'm Diane Keaton or Meryl Streep, attending the opening of one of their own films, surrounded by friends and well-wishers. Someday, maybe . . .

The car glides along gently, so different from the rattle of the back of a cab. After a while, I notice an ashtray in the armrest of my seat, and a box of Kleenex, and some individually wrapped red and white peppermints in the middle console.

"Is it okay if I smoke, Benny?"

"Of course, madam."

It's then that I realize the evening bag I've been gripping tightly in my lap isn't my evening bag at all, but my brown leather Filofax. I must have grabbed it instead of my purse.

"Oh!"

I must have put the evening bag down on the table by the front door as I was saying my goodbyes, and in my rush to leave, picked up the Filofax instead.

"If you're out of cigarettes, madam, I can offer you one."

"Yes, please, I—I forgot them," I say, trying to swallow the panic that is trying to rise in the back of my throat.

Benny hands me a menthol cigarette from a crumpled pack he produces from his inside jacket pocket, and expertly holds a lighter for me over his shoulder without taking his eyes off the road. I crack the window and exhale deeply.

I don't have my powder.

I don't have my lipstick.

I don't have my house keys.

I don't have any money.

I don't have the passes that say I'm invited to the screening.

It also occurs to me that I'm not sure how I'm getting home. I suppose James and I will go back to his place, but what if I can't find him at the theater? Suddenly our plan seems so flimsy, and without my purse I feel totally unarmed to face the night.

"Benny, do you . . . are you taking me home as well?"

"No, Madam, I'll only be taking you to the event."

"Oh," I say, my voice very small.

It's too late to turn back now. We've already crossed over the Brooklyn Bridge, and James said not to be late. I'll just have to find him when I get there. I press my lips together lightly. It feels like there's plenty of lipstick still on them, but I'll have to be careful not to accidentally wipe it off. I try to hold my lips apart a bit, which makes them feel dry. My head is pounding now, from nerves and the menthol cigarette and all the bobby pins.

The premiere is at the Ziegfeld on 54th Street, where I've been once before with Jane to see a re-release of *Funny Girl*. But as we turn onto 54th Street from Sixth Avenue, I hardly recognize it. Even though it's nighttime, the face of the movie theater is so bright it looks like the sun is beating down on it, but it's hard to tell where all the light is coming from. There's a crowd spilling off the sidewalk in front of the theater and a line of people across the street waving and taking pictures. A police car and two news vans are blocking traffic, and a policeman with a whistle is waving cars toward the next block.

"This is as far as I can go, I'm afraid, madam. You'll be all right from here?"

"Yes—I'm—I'll be fine." But my voice sounds tinny and faraway.

Benny pulls the car to the curb and steps outside, and for a moment I'm confused and a little hopeful—maybe he's going to park the car and walk me in? But then I see he's just coming around to open my door for me. I wobble unsteadily to my feet.

"Thank you so much, Benny. I forgot my—I don't have any . . ."

But Benny waves my apology away with a smile and a nod.

"Please, madam, enjoy your evening."

I totter to the sidewalk as the town car glides away. I've gone only a few feet, but already Benny and the dark comfort of the car seem part of an evening long ago that's now been swallowed up into the night. I try to walk as gracefully as I can, although my shoes make me feel like I'm walking on tiptoe. I keep my head down and I aim for what I hope is the entrance.

Thankfully, there does seem to be a "front" of the red carpet, in the form of a velvet rope and a girl wearing a black cocktail dress and a tight ponytail, holding a clipboard in one hand and a walkie-talkie in the other. I look around, hoping to see James, but I can't spot him anywhere. I hang back for a moment and watch the girl as she waves a few people in without checking their names. Maybe she won't check mine either. I decide I'll try to walk past her as if I don't see her. I try to look confident and in a rush, but my attempt at walking briskly backfires as my left heel snags on the carpet, and I trip and practically fall into her clipboard.

"Oooph," she says, pushing me back upright.

"Excuse me," I say, smoothing the front of my dress and trying to look nonchalant.

"Can I help you?"

"Sorry. Yes. I'm, uh, a guest here? Tonight?"

"Okaaaay," she says, looking me up and down. "Can I see your credentials?"

"I don't have—that is—I had them, but I forgot them at home." She sighs, as if that's exactly what she expected me to say.

"Well, who are you with?"

"James Franklin?" I say, hopefully.

"James Franklin, *the actor?*" she says, narrowing her eyes doubtfully.

"I'm—yes."

"Like, as, *his date?*" she says, frowning, looking me up and down.

"Yes, I'm with him—yes."

"But he's in there already," she says.

"I know. He told me—I'm meeting him."

"You're meeting him?"

I'm tired of everything I say to this girl being repeated incredulously, but even to me my story sounds weak. Why didn't we go together? Why am I here by myself, feeling like I'm trying to crash a party to which I wasn't invited?

"Yes, I'm supposed to be meeting him."

She's still eyeing me skeptically. "We-elll, what's your name?" she says.

"Franny, uh, Frances Banks."

As she searches her clipboard, I'm jostled by a couple I can't fully see, but even out of the corner of my eye can tell are shiny and happy, and look like they belong.

"Hi, Taylor!" cries the happy voice of the shiny girl.

Taylor with the ponytail looks up from her clipboard, and her face goes from cloudy to bright, as though she just found out she was picked for the cheerleading squad. "Hiyeee! Ohmahgosh!" she gushes. "Hi, Penny! You look *so* beautiful."

I know it's her before I even turn my head, but there's a small hope in my heart that I'm wrong, that it isn't Penelope Schlotzsky—now Penny De Palma—who's sparkling behind me, who's looking *so* beautiful, that it isn't Penny who's going to see that I'm not being allowed into the party she's breezing into, but as I turn, it isn't Penny I recognize first, it's her dress.

Penny De Palma and I are wearing the same dress.

Her jaw drops and she blinks quickly, as though she's trying to get a piece of dust out of her eye. But then, a beat later, her face re-arranges itself into a smile, and she holds her head high and straight.

"Franny!" she says warmly. "We're twins! You look wonderful!"

I realize my mouth is still hanging open, and I snap it shut and attempt a recovery of my own. "Thanks! Uh, so do you."

And she really does. The dress fits her better, and her long, straight blond hair shines in glowing contrast to the bright green silk. My hand goes to the back of my head, where I can feel the lumps of bobby pins, and I can only hope that none of them are sticking out at the moment.

"You guys know each other?" Taylor says, baffled.

"Hello, Frances, lovely to see you again," says Joe Melville, who seems to emerge out of nowhere.

I hadn't even focused on who Penny's escort was, since he turned for a moment to talk to someone else, and now I'm sure I've flushed beet red, because my whole body feels hot. It couldn't possibly be any worse. I'll be turned away at the door, not just in front of Penny De Palma, but in front of my former agent, too.

"Oh, hello, Joe." I sound like I'm reading a children's book out loud. *Is the crow slow in the snow?* I'm tempted to continue, but Joe has seen someone else he knows and has already turned his back to me.

"Who are you here with?" Penny asks, looking around for my invisible date.

"I'm—well—James was supposed to meet me and I forgot my

passes because I grabbed my Filofax instead of my purse, and I'm sorry I'm wearing the same thing as you, and I'm thinking I might just go home."

I'm expecting a look of pity, an embarrassed smile, a polite brush-off. But Penny De Palma grabs my hand in hers and looks me straight in the eye.

"Nonsense," she says. "You're with me."

She takes my Filofax from under my arm and thrusts it against Joe Melville's chest.

"Hold this," she says to him, and she pulls me past Joe and Taylor and several others who are hovering nearby, hoping for a glimpse of someone they recognize.

There's a line of photographers on the curb facing the theater. Some must be standing on some sort of risers or bleachers, because they're impossibly tall and staggered like a stadium audience. I hang back, letting Penny strike a pose in front of them. Flashbulbs start to go off like huge white fireworks exploding in the sky.

"Penny! Penny! Penny! Penny! Penny! Penny!"

They yell as if she's miles away, shouting her name over and over, frantic and demanding. To me they seem almost angry, as if her pose is not what they came to see, isn't meeting their high expectations. But Penny just smiles and giggles and waves as if they're all old friends and they're blowing her kisses instead of screaming hysterically. She looks back at me and waves for me to join her, and when I shake my head, she reaches out and grabs my hand.

"C'mon!"

"Penny, no, wait—I don't know how to—"

"Angle your body so you aren't flat to the cameras," she says, cupping her hand around my ear so I can hear her over the crowd. "Put one foot slightly in front of the other. Follow me! Matching dresses might land us on Page 6!"

And she pulls me beside her into an empty space opposite the wall of popping flashbulbs, where a giant poster for the movie is set up on an easel. She puts her hand on her hip and gestures for me to do the same, so we're like dancers in a chorus line.

"Look, you guys," she calls out, tossing her hair over one shoulder. "My friend and I decided to wear the same dress tonight! Aren't we just *mad*?"

I try not to squint against all the flashbulbs, and I'm trying my best to keep smiling, but my mouth is starting to shake and my knees are wobbling. Penelope pulls me along tirelessly, past the photographers and down the line of interviewers, happily telling each one the story of why we're wearing the same dress, even expanding it as she explains how we cooked up this wacky prank and how much fun we had getting dressed together.

"My friend here, Franny, and I, we're just crazy!" she tells the reporter from *Entertainment! Entertainment!* "We love daring each other to do crazy things!"

"Are you having fun?" she asks, as she shepherds me through the crowd to another interview.

"I'm—I guess so." I'm thankful to be helped by her, but the truth is I don't think I am having fun. "I had no idea you—you're really famous now."

"Oh, that?" she dismisses my comment with a breezy wave. "They yell like that for everyone. Some publicity person tells them my name. They have no idea who I am or if I'm anybody at all. They yell like that and take everyone's picture, in case."

Penny doesn't seem to care, but I'm embarrassed to have misinterpreted yet another element of this baffling world.

The volume of the crowd increases, and behind me I can hear the photographers screaming, "Arturo, Arturo, Arturo!" I turn around, and there he is, Arturo DeNucci, two feet in front of us. Without any hesitation, Penelope pushes through the crowd surrounding him and sticks out her hand.

"Arturo, I wanted to introduce myself. I'm Penny De Palma. I'm a huge fan of your work."

Arturo DeNucci seems amused by this, and looks her up and down while still holding on to her hand.

"Penny . . . ?"

"De Palma," she says. "Like the director."

"You're Italian?" he asks, looking skeptical.

"No, sir," she says, proudly. "I'm from Tampa!"

Later, as Penny talks to another reporter, I'm bumped by an aggressive-looking man in a suit.

"I'm sorry," he says, exasperated, looking over my shoulder at Penny. "Maybe you can—I have Annelise Carson here, and she's supposed to be next to talk to *E!E!*, but Brad Jacobsen's people keep jumping in front of us."

"I'm sorry," I say, though I'm not sure if this has something to do with me.

"Well, can you—is Penny almost done, or . . . ?"

"Uh, yes, I think so."

"Well, but, so—wait—you're with her, right? I mean, I saw you walking her down the line."

"Um, I'm with her, I guess, yes."

"Sorry, I'm sure we've met before, but I'm blanking—you're her—publicist, right? Or, no, wait—manager?" He's smiling at me, tensely, and I know his smile will fade when he realizes I can't help him, that I don't know any of the people whose names he just said, that I'm the last person who has any power here.

"No, I'm sorry," I say. "I'm no one."

28

Penelope and I get separated as the man in the suit pushes his client in front of me so she can be interviewed next. I wave to Penelope, to gesture that I'll see her inside, but she doesn't see me, and I'm swallowed back into the crowd and carried along for a moment by the sea of people. They're all trying so hard to shove their way forward, wanting to get past me, to get past everyone, to get to the front of something, *to get there first,* that I hardly have to make any effort at all to move.

Up ahead, I think I see him. I know it's him, in fact, from the back of his head, by the way his hair curls slightly over the collar of his blue shirt. And I'm flooded with relief to see even a part of him. I struggle to free myself from the current of people, and I finally emerge and make my way to an open pocket in the crowd, directly behind James. But when I tap him on the shoulder, he doesn't turn around. I tap him again, a little harder this time.

"—as I said to Arturo, it's our work, as artists—" he's speaking to an interviewer, and he glances back and catches my eye.

"Just a second," he says to me, roughly, then turns back to the reporter. "Like I was saying, it's all in the connection to the story, to the world of the story and the message—"

He had to have seen me, even though there was nothing in his eyes I recognized from the way he usually looks at me. But he didn't give the slightest smile or wink, nothing to let me know he's even secretly glad to see me.

I don't want to try and get his attention again, but I'm afraid I'll never find him if I go into the theater alone. So I wait awkwardly off to the side, feeling completely out of place. I don't know what to do with my hands, or where to look, so I keep my focus on the back of his head, as if that's what I've come here to do, as if he's some new animal at the zoo I've been assigned to study. I'm jostled by the crowd, but I hold my ground. I'm a rock in their ocean, the only thing not moving forward. I'm nothing much to look at, not one of the beautiful fish that continue to stream past me, only something to pass over swiftly. I'm just taking up space.

James finally finishes his interview and turns around.

"Inside," he says stiffly, not making eye contact.

The crowd has thickened even more, and it's even harder to make our way through it than it was a moment ago. I can see the entrance just ahead, but we're progressing toward it so slowly, moving only inches at a time, that it feels as though we'll never reach it. James and I almost get separated by the crowd at one point, and as I'm getting swept away from him, without thinking, I reach for his hand, feeling for his fingertips to hold onto, because I don't want to lose him again. Our hands brush, but before I can get a grip he swats mine away like it's a bee that might sting him, then forges ahead, hands firmly at his sides, not once looking back.

The crowd spills into the cool, relative quiet of the theater. Finally the traffic thins and we're deposited into the lobby like something coughed up by the ocean, and I glance around, dazed.

My eyes take a moment to adjust to the darkness of the lobby, and I can't find James, can't see anyone or anything familiar.

"Franny?" comes a voice from the darkness on my left. "Over here."

I'm surprised to feel James grab my hand, and I almost fall out of my shoes once again. He pulls me around the corner, behind a bank of pay phones, where he kisses me deeply, pressing his whole body against me. I surrender for a minute, then push him away. For a moment I can't breathe properly. "Why—you," I'm sputtering. "What the fuck?"

"What?"

"What? *What?* What was that? You totally ignored me. You slapped my hand away."

"Oh, well, yeah."

"Yeah?"

"Franny, we're in public."

"I know, but you invited me here."

"Yes. To see the work. To see the movie."

"But—I thought you invited me here as your date."

"Yes. And here we are. On that date. You look very pretty, by the way."

"Penny DePalma is wearing the same dress. Did you buy one for her, too?"

"Really?" he says, looking more bemused than concerned. "That's funny. I didn't even pick it—one of the PAs picked them out."

"Oh," I say, deflated, and for some reason that information makes everything worse. "So, what? I can be with you here, in the dark of a theater, but you can't—I can't be seen with you, or something?"

"Well, no, I mean, it's probably not a good idea," he says, as though it's something that should be obvious.

"Why not?"

"Franny, it's no big deal," he says, flashing me a smile. "There's just a ton of press here, that's all. The movie's getting a lot of coverage."

"And?"

"And, I don't want them crawling all over my private life."

"Is that why you wanted me to meet you here?"

"Sort of, maybe. Arturo wanted me to have a drink with him first."

"I thought you said there was a cast thing."

"There was. Me and Arturo having a drink."

"And you couldn't bring me to that?"

"It's—well, no. Arturo's very—private."

"I don't understand all this sudden need for privacy. Why would you care? What happens if he knows—or *anyone* knows—you have a, a . . . you told me you loved me."

"And I do. But that's for us, that's our space."

I swallow hard, trying to calm down, feeling dangerously close to tears. "But you brought me to this space. To this public event. You invited me."

"Right. I came here to promote the movie. Which is part of my job. As an actor."

"But aren't you also a person when you do that? An actor who also has the personal life of—of a person?"

"No, not—well, okay, I suppose at some point, if you're part of an established—look, you're upset over nothing. You're being unreasonable. Honestly, I feel like you want me to meet you halfway on this thing."

"Isn't halfway where two people usually meet?"

"Well, in general, maybe, but tonight—this is sort of a big deal for me. It's my night. I'm not sure you—"

"You think I don't get it?"

"Well, no—I mean, how could you?"

I'm having trouble making sense of this conversation. James is speaking with authority, but there's something wrong, something feels so wrong somehow. I don't care about waving and smiling and having my picture taken with him, it's not that, but somehow I'm getting the feeling I'm an embarrassment to him, as if he's not sure

I'm good enough. And suddenly I need to get away and think, even just for a second.

"Excuse me. I have to go to the bathroom."

"Franny, wait."

"I'll be right back. Can I—will you be here, or should I meet you somewhere?"

"Yes, of course—I can wait here for you," he says, then hesitates. "Although, I mean, it's starting in about five minutes. Maybe I should give you your ticket, and I'll just see you in there?"

"Sure. Okay. I don't want you to miss any of it."

"Oh, I've seen it already."

"You have?"

"Oh yeah, a bunch of times. They screen it for Arturo whenever he asks."

"Oh." I don't know why this information hurts my feelings. Maybe it's just that the world of things James doesn't share with me keeps growing.

He shrugs. "I just want to see, I want to see how the audience likes it."

"Oh."

"But, you know what? I'll wait. I'll be here," he says. "Unless—do you need more than a couple of minutes?"

"No, that's fine. I'll be right back. I just need to—to wash my hands, I think."

"Okay," he says, taking a deep breath, and I can see he's trying not to look impatient, trying not to *be* impatient, while he indulges my sudden urgent need for cleanliness.

As I tiptoe awkwardly across the carpeted lobby, I feel a wave of shame. What's the big deal? I understand why he wouldn't bring me with him to have drinks with Arturo DeNucci. I probably would have been so shy and overwhelmed to be sitting in public with Arturo De-Nucci that I would have made them both uncomfortable. I wouldn't have known how to act in front of them any more than I know how to act in this situation. I'm just a person making a big deal out of nothing, and leaving James to wait by some pay phones so I can wash my hands, when he'd rather be settling in to watch his movie. I'll just take a minute and pull myself together, I decide, and when I emerge from the bathroom I'll be a completely different person: I'll morph into someone who bounces back easily from forgetting her purse and wearing the same dress as someone else. It'll be like Clark Kent turning into Superman, only he had a phone booth to change in, and I have a stall in the ladies' restroom of the Ziegfeld Theater. Oh, well. We all have to start somewhere.

Where did I hear that? People say it all the time, of course—*we all have to start somewhere*—but now it jogs something in my memory, a specific picture of hearing the phrase, even though the focus is blurred. Then, all at once, it comes to me—Barney Sparks! That day in his office, where he kept quoting his father—all those clichés, but told with such pride and reverence that, somehow, they all sounded profound. Why didn't I sign with him that day? Or wait to make a decision at least, even when I got the job on *Kevin and Kathy*? I was so desperate the day I met Joe Melville at Absolute Artists, so unsure of myself and anxious to be liked. Now, I can hardly picture the girl who would choose unsmiling, pink-faced Joe Melville over Barney Sparks. I'm not that person today. Today, I would pick the person who made me feel warm, rather than the one who left me cold.

A wave of perfume crashes over me as I open the door to the ladies' room. I step into an old-fashioned lounge area with pink carpet and a long mirror against one whole wall, where three leggy girls in short tight dresses are applying lipstick.

"You guys, like, hurry," one of the girls says to the other two. But, hypnotized by their own reflections, none of them moves.

In the second room, where the sinks and bathroom stalls are, I wash my hands, proving I came to do what I said I was going to, as if James will be able to tell. I examine my face in the mirror. My lipstick has almost completely worn off, except for a strange red line staining the outside of my mouth. My eyeliner has smudged, leaving two black rings beneath my eyes, and the whole effect gives me a dirty, unfamiliar look, as if my face had been colored with crayons by a messy toddler who couldn't stay within the lines. I take the damp paper towel I used to dry my hands and sweep it across my lips, then dab underneath my eyes, trying to restore myself to something I recognize.

"Thank goodness! There you are!" Penelope's voice emerges from the very last stall in the row, and her heels clack on the tile as she moves to the sink next to mine, where she gives herself a quick glance in the mirror. "*Uchh,*" she says, as if it's all a terrible disaster, and rummages in her small pink satin bag, producing powder and lipstick, even though it looks to me like both were very recently applied.

"I was hoping I'd find you! Here," she says, handing me my Filofax.

"Oh, thanks," I say, running a hand lightly over the worn brown cover.

"Did you find him?" she asks. "Did you find James?"

"I did, yeah. He's—waiting for me. Shouldn't you be in there, too?"

"Who, me? Naah. I'm not going to the movie."

"You're not?"

"No. I hardly ever do. I usually just walk the line and move on to the next thing."

"Walk the line?"

"The press line. I just come for the photos and interviews."

"Oh," I say, baffled. It wouldn't even occur to me to come to a movie to do something other than watch the movie.

"Plus, and I don't mean to make you uncomfortable *at all,* 'cause I'm totally happy for you, but it's still a little awkward between James and me. I just felt *insulted* by him, no offense."

"Because of the soap, you mean?"

"The soap?"

"I, uh, I guess he said it would deaden you, or some—"

"Oh *God* no," she says, rolling her eyes at her own reflection. "Isn't he funny? So *serious* about everything. Like I need him to tell me those things are a grind. I was never going to sign for years—I was just doing it for some quick cash. I'm moving to L.A. anyway, to do *Diamonds Are for Heather*?"

"Oh? That's a—?"

"Just this feature. I'm, like, playing Cordelia Biscayne's little sister. You know me, always the sassy sidekick!" She laughs then shakes her head. "No, insulted because he offered to pay for me to get my boobs done."

I can feel my face redden, but Penny continues without noticing, cheerily powdering her nonexistent imperfections.

"But you—you're perfect," I stammer.

"What?" she says, turning away from the mirror, flashing me a dazzling smile. "*Hardly*, but you're sweet to say so. I mean, I know girls are doing it like it's the new *Rachel* or something, and as a concept it doesn't even bother me, but I make my own money—more than he does—and if I'm going to do something like that, I can effing well pay for it myself!"

It occurs to me that in all the Stavros classes in the world, I'd never learn the things about acting I've learned in one evening with Penelope Schlotsky: Angle your body to the camera, Page Six is a *good* thing, some jobs are just for the money, and tiny perfect blond people can be cast as sassy sidekicks, too. I wonder what else she could teach me, besides the fact that James Franklin's concept of *authenticity* involves an idea of perfection that's completely fake.

Penelope flips her silky hair so it pools over one shoulder. "Never mind me!" she says, closing her compact with a *snap*. "I totally get it—he's an awesome, hot guy. I don't mean to be a Polly Party Pooper!"

"That's okay, I'm not sure it's working out with us anyway," I say boldly, even though it's a realization I had only seconds ago. Saying it out loud makes me feel strong, takes some of the sting out of tonight. "I wanted it to be right between us, but I think somewhere deep down I always knew it couldn't work, if that makes any sense?"

"I know *just* what you mean," she says, knitting her brow in sympathy. "Like when Julia Roberts married Lyle Lovett."

"Yes," I say. "Something like that."

29

·················

As I pass the three girls again, still primping in the mirror of the lounge area, it occurs to me how young they are. It's odd, because when I entered the ladies' room, I didn't notice any difference between us, but I feel older now, and wiser somehow. I know more now than I did just moments ago, before entering the bathroom. I know, for instance, that James won't be in the lobby by the pay phones waiting for me. I know he left almost immediately after I went to wash my hands. I know he didn't wait one minute, let alone five, before heading to his seat, and just a glance in the direction of where we were standing earlier tells me I'm right.

I also know I won't be staying for the movie and that I won't even try to find James to tell him I'm leaving.

I haven't yet informed the driver of the taxi making its way slowly through the traffic on the Brooklyn Bridge that I don't have a penny in my wallet—that I don't, in fact, have a wallet at all. Before I hailed the cab, it had occurred to me to jump the turnstiles at the 47th and Sixth Avenue station in order to get home, but even if I could manage to get over the lawlessness of that plan, I couldn't picture how I'd pull it off in such a tight dress.

For some reason, the thing I'm worried about the most isn't

James's reaction when he realizes I'm not coming back to sit beside him, but how I can pay him back for the dress he bought me. For now, I push the thought away. I can't think about the dress, or talking to him, or seeing him in class. I can't think about anything except getting home.

As the taxi glides over the Brooklyn Bridge, I look up at the lights, a series of white globes strung together like pearls, and I silently count them as they pass: *one, two, three* . . . until my eyes start to tear from not blinking. When I tilt my head back down again, my vision is still blurred so that the taillights in front of us melt into a series of shimmering red balloons. But then I see there *is* a balloon, a single red balloon floating in front of the taxi, its white string just brushing the windshield, before the wind pulls it past us and it drifts up, up, up, and out of sight.

"You see that?" The cab driver says to my reflection in his rear-view mirror.

"Yeah."

"How'd it get this far and not go *pop*?"

"I don't know," I say, still craning my neck to see if I can catch it one more time.

Eight days from now, I think, as I absentmindedly run my fingers over the worn leather cover of my Filofax, noticing that the stitching around the edges has started to unravel. I haven't said it out loud even to myself, but I know my deadline is just eight days away, and all I have to show is a calendar full of doodles and lists of what I ate that day, movies I saw, two days crossed off except for the word "shoot," Katie Finnegan's wedding where I leaned my head on Dan's shoulder and was happy, but felt his hand in mine and panicked.

My deadline is here, and it isn't even a tough call to say whether or not I've achieved what I came for: no agent, no job, and as of tonight, no boyfriend—or whatever it is a person who says he loves you but ignores you in public should be called. *How'd it get this far and not go pop?*

As the cab pulls up to our building, I pretend to the driver that I've only just realized I'm a little short on cash. "I'll be right back," I try to reassure him, but he doesn't seem convinced.

"*This* is why I hate coming to Brooklyn," he sighs, hitting the steering wheel emphatically with the palms of his hands.

I fly up the creaky stairs, barefoot, carrying my shoes by their heels, my Filofax tucked under my arm. The door is open a few inches, and there, at the dining room table, his bangs completely covering his eyes, is Dan, sitting in front of his computer. I don't think I've ever seen anything so comforting.

"You're writing!"

He looks up at me, startled. "Oh—hello—yes. Something came to me after you left."

"I'm glad you found my absence inspirational."

"I don't mean it like that," he says, his face solemn. "In fact, just the opposite. I actually think it's—"

"What?"

"Don't take this the wrong way. I don't want to scare you. But I think it's something I'm writing for you."

"How many heads do I have?"

"Very funny. Actually, I'm trying something new. No creatures this time, just people."

"Why would that scare me?"

"I have a history of freaking you out."

"Only when you're nice to me."

"Or affectionate."

"Well, naturally. Who wants kindness or affection?"

"Exactly," he says with a nod. "So I hope you'll take this— whatever it turns out to be—as merely a gesture of cold-hearted professional respect. Nothing more."

"*That* I can handle. I'm definitely more comfortable with your feelings for me as an actress."

"Good. We're agreed, then. I appreciate you solely as a professional. As a person, I have no thoughts regarding you whatsoever."

"I'm so relieved," I say, grinning like an idiot.

I hear the sound of angry honking and remember I've left the cab running outside. I grab my purse—my actual purse this time—and I fly down the stairs barefoot. I pay the driver and tip more than I normally would, both because I'm feeling guilty for forgetting about him and because I'm inexplicably giddy to be home. He drives away but I stay there for a moment on our stoop, listening to the trees rustle up and down Eighth Avenue, feeling the spring air across my face and letting the cement cool my bare feet.

My brain has been shrouded in a cloud since I left the movie—everything happened so fast. But the cloud is dissolving now, and the reality of the evening is beginning to show through, sharp and cold. My stomach flips as I think again about the empty theater seat beside James, the dress I can't afford, and my looming deadline.

My momentary relief at being home has faded, and my footsteps are heavy and slow this time on the way back up the stairs, and while the sight of Dan in his regular spot is still comforting, it can't take away the pain that's begun to gnaw at my stomach.

No job. No prospects. No relationship.

I drop my purse on the table by the door with an unintentionally violent thud, and Dan glances over and cocks his head.

"So?" he asks after a moment, leaning back in his seat, his long arms raised in a stretch.

"What?"

"How was it?"

"Fine."

"Then why are you home so early?"

I sigh, then flop down on the couch, shifting my head around on the pillow until I find a relatively comfortable spot where I'm not being stabbed by all the bobby pins stuck in my hair.

"Well, a funny thing happened to me on the way to the bathroom." I tilt my face up to the ceiling, because I don't want Dan to see that my expression doesn't match my lighthearted comment. There's something calming about looking up into the sea of white and not making eye contact. I'll just face this ceiling forever, I think. It will be so much easier than talking to people.

"You didn't faint, did you?"

"What? No, I didn't faint. Why would you think I fainted?"

"I'm sort of kidding. You just made me think of—that's what happens to the Franny in the J. D. Salinger story. Do you know it? She has a bad time on a date and then feels sick and faints on her way to the bathroom."

I have to wrench my gaze from the ceiling I pledged never to abandon. I have to swing my feet to the floor and sit straight up to look Dan in the face, because I can't believe he's bringing this up.

"That's me."

"What's you?"

"I'm *that* Franny. I mean, I'm not her exactly, but that's the character my mother named me after. Did I never tell you that before?"

He shakes his head. "No."

"Are you sure?"

"I'd remember. He's one of my favorites. I've read those stories a hundred times."

"I only read it once, right after my mother died. I didn't understand it. I didn't get why she'd name me after a character who wants to make some shallow guy like her, and then gets herself so worked up that she smokes too much and doesn't eat and faints on the way to the bathroom. Never mind that it's only a *short story*. She couldn't even name me after somebody in a full-length book?"

I realize that as I've been talking, I've been absentmindedly removing the bobby pins from my hair, so that sections fall in front of my face as they're released from captivity. I must look terrible, but I don't care because the pins are hurting my head and I want them gone.

"You were eleven, right, when she——?"

I nod, but the combination of the night I've had already and Dan now bringing up the story of my namesake makes tears well up in my eyes. I don't want them to fall, so I become very focused on lining up all the bobby pins on the coffee table just so, like regiments preparing for inspection.

"Well, I think it would speak to you more now. Franny, the character, is trying to be real in a world full of people who constantly *talk* about how real they are, but seem to her to be a bunch of phonies." Dan's head is tilted back a little, and I can see his eyes are shining the way they do when he's talking about a filmmaker he loves. "Sort of like Franny the person, don't you think?"

I think about how often James Franklin used the word "authentic" to describe everything from Arturo holding up the work on set to the Cuban coffee place I didn't like very much. My chest feels tight and my breathing is shallow. I know exactly what Dan means. I nod a little but keep my head down, still perfecting my line of bobby-pin troops.

"She wants to be an actress, too—do you remember that?"

I shake my head, miserable. I'm remembering how painful it was when I read the story that first and last time, poring over it for clues, trying to find some message from my mother, something she'd left to me, some piece of her tucked into its pages. But I couldn't find anything at all.

I steal a quick glance at Dan and he smiles back, but in a distracted way. He seems simultaneously very focused on me and entirely lost in his own world, as if it's very important that he piece the story together properly.

"She's in a play, remember? But then she quits. She quits acting altogether, almost because she loves it too much. It's too important to her and she doesn't want to do it for the wrong reasons, for anything resembling *ego*. She's ashamed of herself for even wanting to compete, for 'not having the courage to be an absolute nobody.' I always loved that line."

I nod again, but I'm sniffling now and my eyes are so full I can't hold back anymore, and a few tears spill over. I think of how many times I've wanted to quit because I didn't think I was worthy, and how guilty I felt that I wasn't satisfied by the idea of a simple, normal life with Clark, and how many clues there are in this story my mother left to me, and how I'm only just starting to understand what they mean.

"Also, there's the book she carries." He nods, looking very serious. "*The Way of the Pilgrim*. Remember that? That's actually the most beautiful part."

"Yes, sort of. It's that—the book is about chanting or something, right? I don't get it."

"Well, yes, but the mystic who's supposed to be the author of the book that Franny is reading isn't advocating any particular belief. He's counseling that the repetition of a simple phrase—just the act of repetition itself—will bring enlightenment. That's the thing that always stuck out to me—the idea that quantity *becomes* quality. I always took it to mean if you do anything enough, if you keep putting effort in, eventually something will happen, with or without you. You don't have to have faith when you start out, you just have to dedicate yourself to practice *as if* you have it. She carries the book to remind her what she's after." Dan pauses for a moment, his eyes resting on my brown leather Filofax on the coffee table. "You have a book like that," he says, nodding toward it.

"*This?*" I say, picking it up, trying to imagine my worn leather Filofax as some kind of mystical book. "No. This is totally different. This just shows I haven't accomplished anything. This, in fact, *proves* it."

"Maybe you haven't accomplished what you want *yet*," Dan says. "But what that book shows is how you've kept filling up the pages. Quantity becomes quality by itself, like the story says. You don't even have to believe in your success. Just keep at it, like the fictional Franny, keep filling up the pages, and something's bound to happen."

I'm slightly cheered by Dan's theory, and the thought that all my days have not been wasted, but that's not the reason for the small but unfamiliar glow rising in my chest, a happy fragment of some memory from long ago. I can almost, but not quite, feel the presence of my mother in the room. I try to pin it down, to make it last a little longer, but it's like waking up from a dream that slips away when daylight comes. Still, I'm glad to have been warmed by it, even a little.

I'm a complete mess now; my nose is running and my head is swimming, and I realize I should probably pull myself together and survey the damage in the bathroom mirror. I attempt to stagger to my feet, but my dress is so tight that the lumpy sofa sucks me back in, and I sort of fall back onto it in defeat. This starts a new wave of tears.

"Do you need a Kleenex, Franny?" Dan asks softly, and I nod and hiccup as he gets up from the table. He's back a moment later with a wadded-up ball of toilet paper that looks big enough to sop up an entire ocean, and a cold beer from the fridge. He stands above me patiently while I dry my eyes and blow my nose and take a sip of beer.

"Can I show you something?" he says, after my breathing has calmed down a little.

"Okay," I say, and Dan takes my hand and helps steady me as I get up from the sofa.

He doesn't drop my hand as he leads me across the living room floor and into our tiny kitchen, and he hesitates only briefly before continuing through the door that leads from the kitchen to his bedroom. I have to suppress a flash of annoyance as it occurs to me that

Dan is trying to seduce me again, and at the worst possible time, when nothing at all makes sense and I'm upset and vulnerable. I pull my hand away.

"Look, Dan, this really isn't the—"

"Franny, it's all right, I'm not—just look."

"I can't—I want to go back to—"

"Just look," Dan insists gently, pointing toward the window above his bed, which looks directly into our neighbor Frank's apartment—Frank the mysterious loner, whose regimented days we sometimes use to tell the time. At first, everything looks like it always does. It must be around nine o'clock, and as usual there's the familiar sight of the back of Frank's head silhouetted by the glow of the television light.

"I don't under—oh!" I inhale sharply as I see her, a woman in Frank's apartment. She walks into the room holding two glasses of wine, which she must have poured in the kitchen we can't see but know exists. She hands a glass to Frank and sits down next to him on the couch, so now the backs of two heads glow from the light of the television, a sight I haven't seen once in three years.

Dan and I watch them quietly for a moment, even though they do nothing more exciting than sip from their glasses and watch TV.

"See, Franny?" Dan says with a little catch in his throat. "There's always hope."

June 1995

26 Monday

- JUST
- KEEP
- FILLING
- UP
- THE
- PAGES

27 Tuesday

RAN 3 MILES

28 Wednesday

RAN 3 MILES

CALL BARNEY SPARKS?

RAN 3 MILES

DRINKS AT
JOE ALLEN AFTER
w DEENA
STAVROS CLASS   AND PENNY (!)

CALL BARNEY SPARKS ????
(TOO AFRAID)

MAIL RENT CHECK

BEST INTENTIONS 3ʳᵈ SOUTH ST. SEAPORT
CATERING WEDDING BLACK/WHITE · BOW TIE

CALL DAD

JAMES CALLED
DON'T CALL BACK FOR
EAT CHEESE PUFFS INSTEAD · WAY BETTER' YOU

July 1995

DEADLINE!

(3) Monday

R.I.P.
F. B.
CAREER

---

4 Tuesday

CALLED BARNEY SPARKS
(NO ANSWER)

4TH OF JULY + DUH

PARTY ON ROOF
W JANE + DAN
CAN'T SEE FIREWORKS
BUT LIT A FEW
SPARKLERS

---

(5) Wednesday

RAN 3 MILES

RENT DUE

$ 111.48
LEFT IN BANK ACCOUNT

CALLED BARNEY SPARKS !!)!)!)
GOOD JOB

filofax

Thursday 6

BABY WELL DIAPERS 11AM
DONNA DESETTA CASTING
584 B'WAY #1001

STAVROS CLASS

Friday 7

RAN 3 MILES

L. 4PM
APPT. W/ BARNEY SPARKS

DON'T TALK
TOO MUCH
AT MTG.

SO
THAT'S
SOMETHING

Saturday 8

STEP AEROBICS CLASS W PENNY

10 AM

OWWWWWWWWCH

BLACK/WHTE
B&W 712

Sunday 9

BEST INTENTIONS

WEDDING 11 AM.

FULTON MARKET BUILDING

filofax

EXTRA $50 TIP YAY
FROM SOME DRUNK DUDE
WHO SAID CALL ME DR. JOE EWW

30

....

Although it's been almost six months, it feels as though time has stood still in the office of Barney Sparks. He's wearing the same blue sport coat he had on the first time, and when he pounds his chest to help a cough escape, dust explodes like tiny fireworks in the rays of the late afternoon sun, just as it did on the day we met.

I've been seated for about twenty minutes now in the familiar giant chair that makes it impossible to sit up straight, and over a cup of the extremely weak coffee he poured for us both ("I'm not supposed to be having this—Mrs. Sparks would have my hide."), I've managed to explain much of what's happened since the day I first climbed the creaky stairs to his office. It all tumbled out in a rush: how I booked my first audition and signed with Joe Melville, how I got fired from the club and had to go back to catering, the movie I turned down and being dropped by the agency. I even told him about going to my first premiere and how exciting I thought it would be, but how disappointing it ultimately was—although I didn't tell him all the reasons why that night was so painful.

"Horrible way to see a movie. All that glad-handing. I avoid them like the PLAGUE," he agreed, shakily raising his chipped white mug to his lips for another sip.

And with that, we arrived at the day I called him—just last

week—when I stammered and struggled to get out even the most basic information—my name and why I was calling.

"Franny BANKS. My favorite KLUTZ," he'd bellowed cheerfully into the phone that day, and then asked if I'd like to come by on Friday around four.

So here we are, Friday a little after four, and I'm comfortably sunken into the ancient chair, wondering, but afraid to ask yet, if Barney Sparks still might want to be my agent.

"My episode of *Kevin and Kathy* is supposed to air next week," I tell him, trying not to sound too naively optimistic. "Could that be a—do you think that could mean anything, or uh, do anything for me?"

Barney tips precariously back in his chair, the hinges creaking in protest. "GOOD NEWS," he yells to the ceiling. "It's the first episode back on the air and there'll be lots of press. BAD NEWS—the show is in its ninth year and has lost some juice—but HEY, you never know."

"It's just that, well, I set a sort of deadline for myself, and it just passed actually, and I swore I wouldn't be one of those people who stays too long, and I'm wondering if I'm fooling myself into thinking that I'm—"

I stop, unable to even say the words.

"GOOD enough?" Barney barks the words in a matter-of-fact tone, as if I've just said the most obvious thing in the world.

"Well, yes."

"My dear," he sighs, leaning forward on his desk and clasping his hands. "My father, the great theater director Irving Sparks, often asked his actors: 'How do you get to Carnegie Hall?' "

I stare at him, not sure if he's joking. "Um. Hold on. Are you telling me that 'practice, practice, practice' was *your father's saying*?"

"Well, he never got the CREDIT for it, but do you think Jack Benny came up with that line himself? HA! A talented comic, yes, but a wordsmith like my father he was NOT."

"Wow."

"YES. And it seems to me perhaps you've not yet had enough practice. That comes with time. And AGE."

Barney seems positively cheerful about my age, as if approaching twenty-seven years old isn't a time to panic. He's talking to me as though I'm young. Doesn't he know Diane Keaton was twenty-four when she understudied the lead in *Hair* on Broadway, and Meryl Streep won an Academy Award before she turned thirty? But for some reason, he doesn't seem to think I'm behind at all.

"But even with all the auditions I've had, and being in acting class—I just can't shake the feeling that there's something I'm doing wrong, or something I'm not doing right—either way, there's a trick I haven't learned, a secret that other people know but I don't. It's like these nightmares I get sometimes: I'm onstage and I don't know what play I'm doing, or there's a song or a speech I'm supposed to perform but I open my mouth and nothing comes out. And I'm not sure if I have that feeling because I don't have enough experience, or practice, like you said, or if it's that I don't know the secret . . . the secret language . . ."

I've lost the point I was trying to make and I'm out of breath, as if I've just climbed Barney's four flights of stairs a second time.

I look up from the threadbare spot on the worn Persian carpet where my gaze has been fixed, to see that Barney's hands are folded neatly on his desk, and his blue eyes are bright and focused, as if he's very interested in what I've been saying and has all the time in the world in case I'd like to continue. He raises his eyebrows and smiles encouragingly, but I realize that, for once, I've actually said everything I can think of—at least for now.

"My dear," he says, taking a shallow breath that sounds like two pieces of sandpaper being rubbed together. "It's sad but TRUE. Even

IF you're talented, this business is NOT for everyone. Think of dear Marilyn. She was just TOO sensitive."

"Like me?"

Barney frowns for a moment as if I've confused him. But then his frown lifts a little and his eyes light up, and his shoulders start to shake up and down. He allows a thin whistle-like wheezing sound to escape from his chest, signaling that either his respiratory system has shut down completely or he's laughing—I can't tell which. For a precarious moment, I'm truly unsure whether I should smile at him or call for emergency help.

"On the contrary. You may be sensitive INSIDE, but what I see on the outside is a SOLDIER. You fell down on that stage that night and stood right back UP, better and more focused than before. You didn't CRY, or forget your place, or ask to start again. ALL of which I HAVE seen. You think there's a trick, something the successful people out there know that you don't know. I understand the feeling, but I'm here to tell you there is NOT."

Barney stretches his hands over his head, which causes his office chair to lurch back so far that I'm certain he's going to flip backward and land on his head. But it stops at an impossible angle, almost parallel to the floor, and he somehow avoids tipping over.

"My DEAR. Did I ever tell you what my father, the great Broadway director Irving Sparks, always said?"

"Well, uh, yes, you *have* mentioned a few . . ."

"To his actors, I mean. Before each run-through? The best advice for actors I can think of."

I try my best to lean forward from the sunken seat of my chair. My throat feels dry. My heart is beating fast. I don't want to miss a word.

Barney looks into the distance with a dreamy expression from his almost prone position, and then turns to me and speaks so softly I have to strain even farther forward to hear him.

"He said: 'Remember, kids. Faster, funnier, louder.' "

I'm trying my best to stay forward but the chair finally wins and sucks me back into its depths, the cushions deflating with a sigh. I'm sucked backward but I'm still gripping the arms of the chair tightly, waiting for him to continue, but he's turned his face away now and seems lost in a happy memory.

"Wait, I'm sorry. That's it? That's the best advice he ever gave?"

He returns his chair with a lurch to its regular upright position and wheels himself back to his desk, clasping his hands again and returning his light blue gaze to me. "Yes, dear. That's the advice. Why? You've heard that before?"

"Well, yes. I mean, of course. It's a famous expression. *Every-one's* heard that."

"Have they, dear?" he says, his eyes crinkling at the corners. "How wonderful!"

"But, I guess," I begin, fumbling for the word. "I guess I always thought it was sort of a, a joke?"

Barney looks confused.

"I mean, not a joke exactly, but, well, it makes it all sound so simple, I guess. *Too* simple."

He gives me a long look, then draws in a breath so deep it whistles. "FASTER—don't talk down to the audience, take us for a spin, don't spell everything out for us, we're as smart as you—assume we can keep up; FUNNIER—entertain us, help us see how ridiculous and beautiful life can be, give us a reason to feel better about our flaws; LOUDER—deliver the story in the appropriate size, DON'T be indulgent or keep it to yourself, be generous—you're there to reach US." Barney takes a few gulps of air and beats his fist just once on his chest. "There you go, my dear. It might SOUND simple, but if I know you, you'll spend your life dedicated to getting it right. And that's it, my dear. THAT'S the whole banana."

July 1995

(10) Monday

6 MONTHS UNTIL (NEW)

DEADLINE*

LET'S TRY THIS AGAIN

11 Tuesday

GOT RESIDUAL
CHECK

89.21
- 20.00 CHECK-
            CASHING
= 69.21   FEE

BLART
AARF
BLECK

12 Wednesday

* ONE TIME EXTENSION DUE TO EXCITING NEW
DEVELOPMENT - AN AGENT I LIKE
                            ACTUALLY!

REMIND
DAD

8:30 pm.

KEVIN & KATHY AIRS

BUY CHIPS
SELTZER
WINE
DIP
BLANK VHS TAPES
— LEARN HOW TO WORK
VCR

RAN 4 MILES
WHOA

31

You have nine messages.

BEEEP

Yes, hello, this call is for Frances Bakes? Or, sorry, Frances Backs? I'm calling from the office of Dr. Leslie Miles, nutritionist. I have an appointment for you tomorrow, Thursday, at nine A.M. If we don't hear back from you in the next hour, or if for any reason you have to reschedule, you'll unfortunately be placed back on the wait list. The wait list is currently fifty-two months long. Thank you.

BEEEP

Hi, Franny, it's Gina from the Brill Agency. Wondering if—do you have any problems with feminine hygiene? As a product, I mean. And also—can you ride a horse? They need someone who can ride a horse on the beach. Or on a mountain or something. Anyway, let me know!

BEEEP

Franny! It's Katie. We're all here (Hi, Franny!). Shush, you guys. You're so awesome on the show! That laugh! We're just at the first commercial break, but wow. Great job. This is so exciting!

BEEEP

Franny, it's Casey. I'm watching you! And leaving you a message! At the same time! You're so funny. And seriously, those jeans make you look tiny, are you like a twenty-seven now? Are you still doing that TastiLife thing?

BEEEP

Dude, it's Deena. You stole the show. They're fucking nuts if they don't bring you back. The last time that show was this funny was the late eighties. Although I'm not sure how they can keep pretending Kathy is in her thirties. Also, I'm working on Law and Order *next week. Can you believe it? Drinks on me.*

BEEEP

Hello, hon, it's your father. Mary and I watched the show tonight, at her apartment as requested, so that I was able to view you in this new invention they've come up with called color. Amazing how unnecessarily big these television screens are becoming. At any rate, I thought you seemed a very interesting character, although I wish they'd given you more lines, as you're certainly deserving of some. Mary says I should also tell you that you looked very pretty, although I believe that goes without saying. At any rate, I'm— we're both—very proud.

BEEEP

Hello, uh (clears throat), *this is Dan, uh, from downstairs? I just wanted to say that as funny as you were on the show last night, that still doesn't justify you hogging most of my beer. I'm calling to invite you to dinner, perhaps at the upstairs Chinese place whose actual name no one can ever remember, to discuss the script I'm writing, which may or may not have been inspired by you. This is a formal business invitation only, with no strings attached, unless you should find at some point in the future that I belong in any of the odd geometric shapes your feelings sometimes take. Okay, see you soon. When you get home. To our apartment. Our apartment. That sounds kind of nice, don't you think?*

BEEEP

Hello, Ms. Banks (labored breath), *this is Barney Sparks, your AGENT. The ratings were much better than expected AND I got a lovely call this morning from an old friend of mine on the COAST who's producing a half-hour pilot* (coughs). *He saw you last night and would like to put you on tape to audition for his show. It's a series for a new CABLE channel and there's NO money, BUT, if they like you they'll fly you to Los ANGELES next week for a test. Are you available, dear?* (cough, cough)

BEEEP

Franny. It's me again. James. Please call me. I'm sorry.

BEEEP

I'm shivering, either from the air-conditioning in the hair-and-makeup trailer, which is blowing full blast on the back of my neck, or from nerves, or possibly both. I've been in Los Angeles for only a few hours, but I've already noticed there seem to be only two temperatures: too hot and too cold. There's an empty ache in my stomach, and I know I should have eaten more on the plane from New York this morning than the coffee and half a bagel I managed to choke down, but every time I went to take another bite, my stomach would sort of flip and my heart would start to thump unevenly in an odd mix of excitement and dread.

I could hardly even enjoy being in first class, something I'd never experienced before. The seats were so roomy and comfortable that for the first hour I didn't even notice the buttons by the armrest that make the back recline. It was perfectly comfortable the way it was. There was a bottle of lotion near the sink in the tiny bathroom and the headphones for the movie were free. But I kept thinking how much more fun it would be if I were traveling with Jane or Dan, pretending to be important executives, accepting a mimosa from the flight attendant's outstretched tray or building our own sundaes from the ingredients on the dessert cart. I was simultaneously too nervous and too sleepy to really appreciate the experience. Instead, I spent the first two hours of the flight studying my lines and the last three accidentally falling asleep, which I regret now that I've met the other two girls I'm auditioning with today: a lanky brunette with milky skin and bright blue eyes, and a gorgeous tall blonde with a pixie haircut and dimples that flash adorably whenever she smiles, which seems to be most of the time. They both live here in Los Angeles and have tested for things before, I gather from the chirpy snippets of their conversation I'm trying my best not to overhear.

"Have you lost, like, a ton of weight since we tested for *Cubicles*?" the brunette asks.

"I know, I like, totally got the 'rex somehow," the blonde replies, rolling her eyes.

"Lucky," the brunette says, narrowing her eyes in envy.

I duck my head down, focusing on the script I've already been over a hundred times. This is *my* job, I allow myself to think, and picturing it makes me smile. *Positive thoughts.*

- - - - -

Jeff and Jeff turned out to be the New York casting directors for *Mr. Montague*, the cable pilot about a decadent millionaire playboy. They had me do my scenes as Belinda the dog-walker over and over, laughing appreciatively every time.

"A little more of that ditzy voice, I think," Jeff said encouragingly. "That feels like her."

"Yeah, try it again all breathy like that," the other Jeff agreed.

A few days later, the call came from Los Angeles, and the director flew out to meet a few of us, and I had to do the scenes all over again for him. "She's our favorite," tight-sweater Jeff whispered to him loudly over the back of his hand, giving me a wink. The second call came soon after—that of all the people they saw in New York, I was the only one they were flying to L.A. for a test.

"SUCCESS!" Barney wheezed into the phone.

The director will be here in Los Angeles today, along with a few producers and The Network and The Studio, who I picture as an assortment of people who wear suits and nod in unison, just like The Client was on my commercial. Everything happened so fast that the last few days have been a blur. Travel plans were made and my deal had to be negotiated quickly. I missed my appointment with Dr. Leslie Miles, and I didn't have time to have that dinner with Dan, or to consider how—or even if—I wanted to respond to the message from James Franklin. If I get the job, I'll make seven thousand five hundred dollars every episode we film, which is just a little over half of what I made all of last year, so I'm doing my best to stay focused.

I'm keeping my eyes on my own paper.

My father wanted to meet me in the city the day before I left. "Let's go to the Oak Bar at The Plaza," he said, with unusual flourish.

"Really? Dad, I don't know—I have so much to do for the trip."

"This is a special accomplishment. And I want to see you before you go."

"Well, okay then. Would you like to . . . should we invite . . . ?" I stammered.

"I think just us, don't you?"

"That sounds nice," I said, relieved.

At the subway token booth, I splurged and used one of the crisp twenty-dollar bills fresh from the cash machine I'd just visited in preparation for my trip. "I'll take five, please," I said, recklessly spending the $6.25, even though it made no sense since I'd be leaving the next day. The token clerk hardly flinched, but in the almost imperceptible widening of her eyes—something I suppose I could have imagined but assured myself I didn't—it kind of seemed like she was giving me the New York City token-booth clerk version of a thumbs-up.

M y father was tucked in a leather chair in a corner of the bar, under a massive mural of a snowy horse-and-carriage scene. With his crumpled newspaper and brown cable-knit cardigan, he looked comfortable and warm in contrast.

"There she is!" he smiled when he saw me, putting down his half-finished crossword, and my heart swelled at the sight of him. We'd been here twice before: after my college graduation, and then for his fiftieth birthday, and I was proud my trip to Los Angeles ranked among those other reasons to celebrate.

He was, as usual, full of questions about the part, and the cable station that he'd never heard of before. "But how can they charge people to watch television? Television is free," he said awhile later, nursing a gin and tonic.

"*Regular* television is free. But cable is, in some ways, better than regular television."

"Then why don't they air the cable shows on regular television and make better free television?"

"Well, because, they do things on cable that you can't do on regular TV."

"Like what?"

"Well, there's—you can curse on cable, and show nudity."

"I'd pay more just to hear proper English and have everyone keep their clothes on," he said with a mocking frown. "And you said the salary is less on cable than it would be on a network?"

"Yes. That's what Barney told me."

"But if they're charging me and the rest of the audience to watch, shouldn't you get paid *more* than what you'd get acting on the free channels?"

"I think it has something to do with the ads on network TV."

"So you're telling me if I sit through the ads for those strange air-freshener capsules, my daughter's salary somehow gets higher?"

"I guess. Something like that."

He threw his hands up in surrender. "It makes no sense to me," he said, squinting happily. "But I hope you get it. I've never been to Los Angeles."

Until that moment, I hadn't really thought about the fact that getting the job would mean I'd have to move, away from my father and my friends. And Dan. I shut my eyes and squeezed them tightly. I couldn't think about that yet. "I love you, Dad."

"Me too, hon."

Afterward, there was a wait for a cab, and so we stood side by side on the carpeted stairway outside the hotel, watching as the doorman in the gold braid–trimmed cap expertly signaled to the passing taxis, waving them into the entrance, then gesturing grandly to the next passenger in line.

"You know, Franny, she would've been so proud," my father said, his voice a little raspy. I was taken aback at his mention of my mother—we seemed to talk about her less these days. My eyes filled up instantly at the thought of her, and what she might think of me today, and tears stung my eyelids. But I kept looking straight ahead, willing myself not to cry, not here.

"I worry that you expect the worst sometimes, because of what happened," he continued softly, and I managed just a small nod. "Imagine the best for yourself now and then, won't you, hon?"

My vision was blurry from the tears I'd held back, but when I wiped my eyes and looked up again, I suddenly recognized what had been right in front of me this whole time, the dramatic, almost theatrical backdrop that loomed large, setting the stage behind the doorman hailing a cab, and a strange, throaty laugh escaped me.

Dad gave me an odd look. "What is it?"

As I admired the water cascading down the tiers of the fountain across from the hotel, I remembered the conversation I had with Dan all those months ago, when we hardly knew each other, and when everything I wanted had seemed so far out of reach. And I thought how wonderful it was to see her tonight, the glorious bronze goddess statue shining at the very top.

I looked over at my dad, smiling. "It's—Abundance," I told him.

"There you go," Linda, the hairstylist, says, and I look up from the script in my lap to see that while I've been daydreaming, my hair has been ironed stick straight. It's completely smooth and shiny-looking, an effect I've attempted unsuccessfully a thousand times in the past. But now I look more like a stock broker than a goofy dog-walker. All my other auditions for this part were with my other hair, my real hair, and although it strikes me as somewhat funny that I'm suddenly protective of the aspect of my appearance that drives me the most crazy, I also have a wave of panic that the people I've been auditioning for won't even recognize me.

"Oh—wow—it looks great. But, um, it's a little different than . . ."

"The producers asked that all the girls have their hair blown out today," she says, flashing a smile that tells me that's the end of our discussion. "Now, down two chairs to Makeup!"

"Oh. Great. Thanks." I'll have to resign myself once again to accepting all the decisions made about me that don't seem to factor me into the equation. I shuffle down to where the dimply blond is just finishing up with a tiny, pale makeup artist wearing a beret and a worried expression.

"It's just, I'm not really a red lipstick *person*?" the blond says from the chair to her own reflection and then stands to examine her face more closely, bringing it just inches from the mirror and narrowing her eyes. She shakes her head and takes a tissue from a nearby box, then wipes off her perfectly applied shiny cherry gloss. The tissue makes a messy smudge around her mouth, leaving her lips looking stained and dry. She steps back from the mirror, pleased with her work. "Like that," she says to the makeup artist. "I like it blotted."

The makeup artist nods and smiles weakly, and the blonde struts down to Hair as I slide into her recently vacated chair.

"Sally," the makeup artist says nervously from beneath her beret, and I shake her hand, which feels cold and a little damp.

Sally methodically goes about cleaning her station, snapping shut the open compacts and putting the used brushes aside. She peers at my face closely for a moment, then lightly brushes her thumb over my cheek. "You feel a little dry," she says, though not unkindly.

"I just flew in from New York this morning," I say apologetically. She nods, as if she knows exactly what to do in that case, and begins to assemble a new group of brushes and glossy plastic containers in an assortment of sizes and shapes, lining them up around the perimeter of her workspace.

"Do you have any preferences or allergies I should know about?"

she asks, and I hesitate for a second before shaking my head no. It's silly, but I'm reminded of the first time I was ever asked that, on the Niagara detergent shoot, and I have to force down the feeling of disappointment that even after all I've been through, I still don't have an answer to such a simple question.

As she continues to set up her station, I think I see her hands trembling. Or is that my imagination? Maybe she's cold from the air-conditioning, too.

"Is that blowing on you?" I say, pointing to the vent on the ceiling. "Because I'm freezing."

She steals a glance at me from beneath her beret and says under her breath, "Sorry, no. I mean yes, but it's not that." She ducks her head shyly. "It's just that it's my first day—my hands are shaking because I'm new."

"Oh," is all I can think of to say, and then I smile in what I hope is an encouraging way.

Sally smoothes a cotton ball over my face, then begins to apply a thin layer of foundation with a silky brush.

I don't know why I'm so surprised that someone else is new. I guess it's sort of a shock to realize anyone could be more of a novice than I am. In the last three years I've become used to always being the one in the room with the least experience, and it never occurred to me that someday that wouldn't be the case, that someday it would be someone else's first day.

Sally starts to bring a now familiar object close to my face, something that was completely foreign to me only a few months ago, and though it's small, something about it reminds me of how many things I've learned since the day I set my deadline three years ago, things both profound and trivial. Not just these smallest of signs, but larger ones, too, that tell me I've changed: being able to recognize the meaning in the story my mother named me after, the warmth in Barney Sparks's voice, and the sincerity in Dan's brown eyes—all of them telling me that maybe, little by little, I'm heading in the right direction.

Now just inches away, Sally is looking at me expectantly. "Shall I . . ."

I take the eyelash curler from her outstretched hand.

"Thanks," I say with confidence. "I can do it."

3²

RING   RING   RING

CLICK

I can't come to the phone right now, so please leave me a message.

BEEEP

"Hi, Dan, it's Franny. I'm calling you from my hotel room, in Los Angeles. Crazy, right? How are you? Umm... so... yeah, I think it went well today. Really well, actually. We're supposed to find out tomorrow—hopefully I'll know something before I get on the plane. Hey, did you watch Law and Order tonight? The teacher did it! I didn't see that coming, did you? You probably did, knowing you. Anyway, it's strange, but, I wish you could see what I'm looking at right now. The hotel is right next to the studio where we had the test—it's this giant high-rise building that overlooks this massive freeway, which sounds really awful I know, but my room is so high up, and the cars are so far away, that the lights below are actually pretty, can you imagine that? It sort of puts everything in perspec-

tive. It reminds me of when I cross the bridge on the D train—oh, I'll just tell you at our dinner, it's hard to explain. Anyway, I've been standing here for a while, just watching them, and—shoot—you know what? I just realized—oh—I forgot about the time change, I think it's really late there. I'll hang up now. I just wanted to tell you, well, that I was thinking about—"

There's a click and a rustling sound, and for a moment I think the phone's gone dead, but then Dan's sleepy voice comes on the line. "Franny? Is that you?" he says.

"Yeah, hi, it's me," I whisper. "Sorry—did I wake you up?"

"Yes, but, no . . . I mean, it's good, though. Let me just turn off the machine . . . the tape is still recording—"

"Dan, you're half-asleep. Is it too late?"

"Not at all . . . I'm happy, I mean, I just . . . I've almost got it. I can almost reach the . . . aha! There. Now then, Franny, tell me every—"

BEEEP

Acknowledgments

I could not have done this, or gotten anywhere close, without my genius editor, Jennifer Smith. Jen, I was so fortunate to have you as my mentor in this process. Thank you for believing in me, challenging me, and accepting my loose interpretation of "deadline."

Esther Newburg is the ideal literary agent: smart, honest, funny, tough, and as dismissive of my early doubts as she is toward anyone who doesn't love the Boston Red Sox. Thank you, Esther, for sending out this manuscript way before I was ready for anyone to read it.

My sister, Shade Grant, was a tireless champion, cheerleader, and best friend throughout and contributed immeasurably to this book. Shade, your ambition, intelligence, kindness, and excellent fashion sense would have made our mother so proud.

Thank you, Diane Keaton, for responding to some long boring story I was probably telling with "You should write a book," instead of "You should really save this for your therapist." Your inspiration meant the world to me.

My early readers were invaluable. Thank you to Hannah Elnan and Ratna Kamath for your helpful notes, and to Allison Castillo, Ellie Hannibal, and Mae Whitman, for your thoughtful feedback, and for being some of my very favorite people.

Thank you, Kathy Ebel, for being friends with me even back when I wore that jumpsuit, and for your generous writerly support and encouragement.

I am blessed to have a team who represent me in my actor life with the perfect mix of humor, vision, love, and cold-blooded aggression. Thank you to John Carrabino, Adam Kaller, Caryn Leeds, Gary Mantoosh, Leslie Sloane, and Eddy Yablans.

Thanks also to Sam Pancake, Oliver Platt, Gary Riotto, Jen and Pete, and everyone at *Parenthood*. None of you had anything to do with this book, but I couldn't pass up an opportunity to say how important you've been to me.

Thanks, Mom, for living with creativity, originality, and bravery. You paved the way for me to imagine the possibilities. Your beauty, wisdom, and sparkling laugh are missed.

Thank you, Dad, for always letting me buy as many books as I could carry, and for reading to me every night until I thought I was too cool. This book, not to mention my acting career, is a direct result of all the funny voices you probably got tired of doing.

Thank you to Karen, Chris, Maggie, the Grahams (Cousinhood!), Mama and all the Grants, Roman and the Krauses, and all their loved ones. I'm lucky to have a colorful family, filled with interesting stories and excellent storytellers.

Thank you, Peter, for carrying my dresser up the stairs all those years ago, for keeping me company in the office when inspiration eluded me, and for the thousands of other gestures of your strength and kindness. I love you so.

Someday, Someday, Maybe

Lauren Graham

A Reader's Guide

A Conversation between Lauren Graham and Mae Whitman

MAE WHITMAN *is a child-turned-actor who hails from and currently resides in East Los Angeles with some dogs, a turtle, a cat, and a super cool roommate. You can find her acting on the shows* Parenthood *and* Arrested Development *or hear her speaking as the voices of Tinkerbell and April O'Neill. She enjoys reading comic books, eating kale, sitting down outside and showing people her scars from when she fell down the stairs at the premiere of the movie* Twilight.

MAE WHITMAN: So, I was extremely happy to be one of your earliest readers . . .

LAUREN GRAHAM: I was extremely nervous! I'd hardly showed it to anyone at that point, and while I hope it appeals to a broad audience, it was especially important to me that it appealed to someone your age, in the field, never mind you in particular as my friend. Plus, work would have become incredibly awkward if you hated it.

MW: But I loved it. I think I texted you on page three, asking if Dan was based on a real person and when I could meet him.

LG: I love that Dan appeals to readers. I think there aren't enough nerd heroes out there.

MW: I also loved the Filofax so I just wanted to know how you got there.

LG: Before people were really using computers and smart phones, you had pen and paper—a physical representation of what was going on in your life. Back when you had to write things down, you got a real sense of the times that were busier and times where nothing was happening. So much of being an actor is waiting for the phone to ring, and I can remember the worried feeling I'd get when I looked ahead to an empty week in my datebook. I thought it would be a fun aspect of the book to show those pages, since time is such a major issue—how much time should Franny give this before she has to accept that it's not going to happen? How many empty weeks can she handle?

MW: As a reader I thought it was great because it's another way you really get to feel like you know her. And it also makes her so relatable. I know I get really stressed sometimes when I look at my planner and think *Oh, I have so much stuff coming up!* Or worse, nothing at all.

LG: It used to be that everyone had a datebook. I'd keep them for years, lining them up in my closet when the year was over, and it was such a great way to look back and measure your accomplishments. I'd save notes people wrote me, I'd doodle, and then I'd have this diary of small moments that would jog a memory of place and time. Nowadays, all that communication and expression has been replaced by information you store in your phone and probably never print out. Back then, we had no computer, only a fax machine, and you'd have to go physically pick up scripts from your agent's office. So you'd spend entire days getting on trains and buses and walking from place to place.

MW: And that affects your whole day, your whole life, really. All that extra travel time . . . how does that change the way you think?

LG: Well, you have much more time for reflection. You might be listening to your Walkman or CD player, but you weren't playing a game, you weren't texting, googling things, etc. You were staring out the window or reading. When I first started writing the book, it was surprising to me to think of that way of spending time as something I'd grown nostalgic for. It doesn't seem like that long ago, but these changes have happened so quickly. I also liked the idea of setting the story in a time when you had to work a little harder to make a plan with somebody. You could arrange to meet, but no one really had a cell phone yet, so if something went wrong, you'd be left standing on a street corner wondering what happened. You'd have to find a pay phone and they didn't always work. I remember going block to block sometimes looking for a working pay phone.

And anyway, no one expected you to get back to them right away. Wow, I sound like an old person: *We used to walk to school barefoot in the snow . . .*

MW: *Uphill both ways . . .*

LG: Exactly! But it *was* different.

MW: Another thing that comes up in the book is the idea of a deadline. There's such a strange disconnect between having a dream and then trying to put a deadline to it . . .

LG: In most careers there are signs that you're doing well, signs that you should continue. In acting, and in writing as well, you have to make those for yourself. No one is going to tell you "Your time's up, go home now." And no one is going to tell you, "We really need more actors, so please stay!"

When I started out, I didn't exactly give myself a deadline, but I did have an internal ticking clock. When I was in college I knew I wanted to be an actor, but I also thought, *Should I get a teaching certificate, just in case?* At one point in the story, Franny runs into a friend whose accomplishments are a lot more measurable than hers, and it serves as a wake-up call. We set these goals in our careers and in life, and sometimes you get what you want and sometimes you don't, and only you can say when it makes sense to keep going or when it's time to throw in the towel.

MW: I'm relating to this so much more than you can understand. I related to the whole book, obviously, but this point specifically—it's such a difficult thing. For me, you know, I've been acting since I was young. But still, if anything, it's only gotten more unclear how to gauge this sort of progress.

LG: Which is insane, since you've worked steadily since you were five years old! But I think that's good insight into the mind of an actor. I don't know who you have to be to have a sense of security. Does Meryl Streep still worry where her next job is coming from?

MW: Which leads me to my next question, which is about Clark, who is Franny's ex-boyfriend, and sort of her backup plan. What does he represent for her?

LG: One element of Franny's journey is going from being an uncertain person to having a little more confidence. And reflecting on that made me think of those agreements you make before you know better—the kind of deals that no one over thirty ever seems to make—which is the joking yet semi-serious *Hey, if we don't meet anybody else by the time we're thirty . . .*

MW: The Thirty Pact.

LG: Starring Jason Segel and Kate Hudson.

MW: Brilliant. I gotta go make a call!

LG: It's that idea that if your dream scenario doesn't come through, you have a Plan B that extends not just to a career realm but also a personal one. So much of life just happens to you, but there are also times when you make these more overt decisions. You think: I could choose to be this person or that one. I could be an actress living in New York, or I could live in the suburbs and marry this guy and live another kind of life. Clark was this wonderful relationship she had, but their career paths sort of went in different directions and he got into school in another city and she wanted to pursue her dream. But there's a sense of safety in Clark as her back-up plan. And to me, that seemed like part of coming of age, and of coming into yourself is letting go of those security blankets and accepting that there are no guarantees.

MW: I was in a relationship all of my early twenties, and I remember it being full of so many possibilities, but also thinking, *Yeah, but if I was out of this relationship, it might be you or you or you . . .*

LG: You're still trying things on for size to see what fits—jobs, people. It's a process of getting to know yourself, like being in a dressing room and trying on jeans.

MW: *This one doesn't fit!*

LG: It's terrible! But even once you find a pair that fits, there are still problems . . .

MW: And you'll grow out of them eventually and need a new pair. But that's the thing, it does get easier. You do sort of realize that wherever you are, that's where you are. For me it's happening a lot more, being able to let go. You realize that you know you won't fit in the same jeans that you've kept for years and that's okay.

LG: It's rare when you see those people—I'm just really loving this jeans metaphor, by the way—who buy a pair of jeans in high school, and they're still wearing them thirty years later. It can be a good or a bad thing.

MW: Or they have them in a drawer and they're thinking *I'm aimin' to fit back into these bad boys someday*. It's like, just acknowledge the nice new capris that you have!

LG: It's a funny thing too in terms of being a young woman and having a real career drive. There's still no easy answer as to how to balance that. There's no way that having immense ambition isn't going to impact your personal life. And this career in particular can be all-consuming. It has these odd aspects to it, where you're endlessly meeting new people and having to connect and pretend they're your husband, for example. It can be treacherous personally because it invites new opportunity all the time, which can invite insecurity. Maybe you have to go film in Toronto, maybe you have to go do a play in Poughkeepsie. There's no predictable routine. Clark represents Franny's path not taken, someone who, if she weren't pursuing this acting career, she might have followed into a different kind of life.

MW: That unpredictability and variety is the reason why I'm an actor, and the reason that sometimes I wish I wasn't. I love everything so much; I wake up and go *I don't know what I want to put on—safari clothes? Do I want to dress like a hip-hop artist?* I get to go be a drug dealer without having to get arrested. I get to be all these things in one life. Then I come home and I'm like, what's *my* thing?

LG: I tried to show that in the book too—the impact of all that time spent imagining what you would do *if*. And how, even though you're trying to bring your own light to everything, you also spend your day trying to please other people, hoping that you're their vision of what they wrote, or what they saw in a part, and it can take a toll on your own sense of—

MW: Your life!

LG: Yeah. It's a really odd profession in that way. Plus, in the nineties, there were maybe two tabloids—not ten, like there are today. There was no *American Idol* . . . .

MW: Hardly any reality TV at all.

LG: Right, so there wasn't this sense of what to emulate, the idea of *Anyone can do this,* which I think exists slightly more now. There were the performances you'd see in the movies and onstage but there wasn't as much exposure to actors' personal lives. There wasn't that *celebrity* thing that there is now. I went to grad school with a bunch of aspiring actors and I don't think anyone ever once said "I want to be famous." That was not the point. The point was to work at a great regional theater somewhere. The point was just to be an actor at all.

MW: One other thing I was thinking about is Franny feeling like she has to squeeze into a character that is so not her. How does that affect whether she's true to herself?

LG: Right. So, Franny gets offered a part that requires her to be topless. Another odd thing about this acting journey is that you're confronted with these sorts of questions along the way. You didn't write the material, but you're the one playing the part, and it affects and reflects on you personally. So this was just another way that I was trying to depict these *Who am I?* situations, which never end.

MW: You get confronted with that every day, with every choice, with every new project . . . .

LG: It's one of the quirks of the job. You're probably not going to be asked to be topless in your law firm, unless things have taken a really unusual turn. But as an actor, it's different.

I remember a friend once saying that the only thing you have as an actor is "no." And that's on a good day, when things are coming to you, and you have the ability to pick and choose, since normally this is a career where there's not enough work going around. It's so interesting that it attracts as many people as it does given how draining it can be.

MW: It's interesting that you say that, because I was thinking about morals and such, and that scene with Barney Sparks, where she clicks with him at first, but then sort of gets suckered into this situation with another agent that's so not her. . . .

LG: At one time or another, most people fall prey to trying to belong to the club that wants them the least. For Franny, on the one hand there's this agency that feels very slick and fancy, and on the other hand there's a man who seems to really understand her. And that also goes on with the two boys she's interested in: James Franklin and Dan. I think it's rare that difficult choices are all that clear. You're never choosing between the right job and the wrong job, the right guy and the wrong guy. So I liked the idea of a character like Barney Sparks, who isn't obviously the right choice, whose language is a little bit cliché, who's older and maybe past his prime. There's that element of time again—it isn't a business that treasures aging. But the wisdom he has for Franny is really simple, but true. The acting process, as a business and a craft, is really about finding yourself. I just liked the idea of this older guy who's seen the journey a thousand times. It's sort of a Dorothy and Oz thing. It was always Kansas. She just has to realize it.

MW: That's something I understand so deeply, but it's also a constant battle. You do need people who want the best for you but ultimately it comes down to your own heart's song. What feels like the most honest, pure thing for you.

LG: Well, you're relying on yourself. And that's a theme too, and will be even more so in the next book. It's a calling, it's a craft, it's an art, but it's also a job. How much of your life do you give to your job? And what does it cost you? How do you cope with a job where you've spent the day crying because Amber was in a car accident or whatever?

MW: If I think of the number of scenes where I've gone back to my neighborhood and to a bar afterward, and stared blankly at a wall with a beer, just trying to come back again . . .

LG: When I started out, it didn't get to me like that. It does now. But at first, I mainly did comedy and I was like, it's fine, nobody's going to need me to cry in anything; I'm a comedian. So it's been surprising to me to do as much drama, because I never saw myself that way. Another example of how this business tells you where, or if, it wants you. There are so many things that aren't in your control. It's a slippery shifting thing.

It's never a job where you go home and think, "I've really licked this whole acting thing; boy, do I know what I'm doing!"

MW: Never! So, given that you're already in a baffling and challenging field, what made you want to write a book?

LG: I was an avid reader as a kid—I came to acting through reading.

As a young reader I always pretended I was all the characters, anyway, so it was an easy transition to becoming an actor pretending that the lines I was given were just coming to me off the top of my head. So, while the process itself wasn't easy at all, the practice of imagining what these characters might say or do was familiar in a way, and very gratifying. And I could do it all myself, without waiting for the phone to ring.

Questions and Topics for Discussion

1. Why do you think the author chose to tell parts of the story through pages of Franny's Filofax planner? What elements does it add to the novel?

2. Is setting a deadline on your dream a good idea? Or is it unrealistic? Do you think it ultimately helped or hindered Franny's career?

3. Although he only appears as a recorded voice on the answering machine, Clark plays an important role in the story. What does his and Franny's back-up plan represent? What does his engagement force Franny to do?

4. For parts of the novel, Franny adapts to a situation by playing a character she is not. When is she being true to herself? When is she most happy?

5. Why didn't Franny sign with Barney Sparks? What would you have done in her position?

6. Franny appreciates the bridge on the D train because it helps her put things in perspective. Do you have a D train bridge in your life? What is it?

7. Do you agree with Franny's interpretation of love triangles on page 281?

8. Penelope and Franny have an interesting relationship throughout the novel. In what ways does it change? What does Penelope help Franny understand?

9. On page 307, the taxi driver remarks, "How'd it get this far and not go *pop*?" Why does this resonate with Franny? What could it represent in her life?

10. What does everyone else see in Franny that she doesn't see for herself?

11. On page 335, Franny's father tells her, "Imagine the best for yourself now and then, won't you, hon?" Discuss the importance of having a positive attitude, and how this changes for Franny.

12. The characters throughout the novel have their own individual takes on authenticity. What does it mean to James? How is that different from what it means to Dan, Franny, or Penny? Which definition do you agree with? Is it possible to be authentic in an industry that is in itself an artificial craft?

13. How has Franny changed by the end of the novel? What were her most transforming moments? Who most strongly influenced her?

14. Of all the themes in the novel—dreams, hope, friendship, believing in yourself, etc.—which did you find the most compelling? What do you think is the takeaway lesson of the book?

About the Author

Lauren Graham is an actress best known for her roles on the critically acclaimed series *Gilmore Girls* and *Parenthood*. She has performed on Broadway and appeared in such films as *Bad Santa*, *Evan Almighty*, and *Because I Said So*. She holds a B.A. in English from Barnard College and an M.F.A. in acting from Southern Methodist University. She lives in New York and Los Angeles.